LET'S GET Physical

ELLE FIORE

OMNIFIC PUBLISHING
LOS ANGELES

Omnific Publishing
1901 Avenue of the Stars, 2nd floor
Los Angeles, CA 90067
www.omnificpublishing.com

First Omnific eBook edition, November 2014
First Omnific trade paperback edition, November 2014

The characters and events in this book are fictitious.
Any similarity to real persons, living or dead,
is coincidental and not intended by the author.

Library of Congress Cataloguing-in-Publication Data

Fiore, Elle.
  Let's Get Physical / Elle Fiore – 1st ed.
  ISBN: 978-1-623420-82-6
  1. Contemporary Romance — Fiction. 2. Rubenesque — Fiction.
  3. Divorce — Fiction. 4. Weight Loss — Fiction. I. Title

10 9 8 7 6 5 4 3 2 1

Cover Design by Micha Stone and Amy Brokaw
Interior Book Design by Coreen Montagna

Printed in the United States of America

*This novel is dedicated to my cousin, Alessia.
Had it not been for you,
I wouldn't have begun to write.
You unknowingly sent me on the path
to finding my passion,
and I will forever be grateful.*

1
The Ugly Truth

Linda watched from the bedroom door as her high school sweetheart, the man she had known for twenty years and been married to for fifteen, threw his clothes in assorted bags. She wrung her hands in misery, not quite believing this wasn't some strange nightmare. She'd had ones like this before over the years, and she silently willed herself to wake up. It wasn't working.

Finally, he was done. He yanked on the strap of one bag viciously, pulling it over his shoulder and grabbing the handles of the second.

"Graham," Linda croaked, "why are you doing this?"

He stopped in front of her, looked her up and down, and sneered. It was part laughter and part disgust, and she recoiled from the look on his face.

"Have you looked at yourself lately?" he said with contempt. "Linda, when we first got together, you looked amazing—"

"I was *fifteen*," she said, cutting him off unceremoniously.

"Now look at you," he continued, overriding her. "I barely recognize you anymore! You know, I tried to be a good husband. I tried to be supportive as I watched you turn into the Goodyear Blimp, but I can't do it anymore. Just thinking about laying a hand on you makes me sick. I'm done."

Linda stood there, stunned. She grabbed at her shirt and pulled it away from her body, feeling as if it hugged every pound she had gained over the last seven years. "Why are you doing this?" she whispered in distress as she fought to keep the tears pooling in her eyes from running down her face. "Why are you being so cruel?"

"It's not cruel, Linda. It's honesty. Being cruel is letting you continue to get fat without telling you how gross it is."

Linda lost the fight. The tears started to fall unbridled, and Graham pushed past her into the hall and started down the stairs.

"Wait!" she called after him desperately. "I can lose it! I can get back into shape!"

Graham halted on the steps and looked up at her as she leaned over the balustrade. "It's too late." He turned away from her and headed down the stairs again.

"Graham!" she yelled out after him, hating the panicky breathlessness of her voice. "Come back!" She ran around the landing, trying to catch him. He was already out the door and had shut it behind him.

Never the most graceful person, Linda's ankle twisted halfway down the staircase as she tried to go after him. With a scream, she stumbled, managing just barely to catch herself before she fell headlong down the stairs. She took the rest slowly, having heard Graham start up his car. There was no way she could catch him now.

Slumping down on the bottom step, Linda tried to catch her breath. After the emotional outburst, the running, and the adrenaline pumping through her system after the near fall, she just couldn't. She tried to draw air into her lungs in desperate gasps, but it wasn't working. She felt as if she would never get enough oxygen, which added another layer of panic, making things all the more difficult.

Tears were still running down her face, her lungs were screaming in her chest, and her ankle and wrist throbbed from being wrenched. She still had enough presence of mind to bend over and stick her head between her knees so she could try to get a hold of herself and stop hyperventilating. Her midsection hit her thighs a lot sooner than they used to, and everything Graham had said up in the bedroom came back to her in shattering blows.

It was true that over the last six or seven years, she had let herself go. Between aging, her decelerating metabolism, and finding solace in food whenever she and Graham fought, well, it was no wonder she had packed on a good seventy pounds. It had been gradual enough. Every year, her waistline increased by a size or two, and suddenly she could hardly recognize herself anymore. She felt as if she had been swallowed whole by this fat version of herself.

Linda's breathing finally slowed back to normal. Her heart stopped beating quite so fast, and even her wrist and ankle had numbed a little, but she couldn't stop the tears. They still came, filling up and overflowing in a torrent that spilled onto the carpet at the foot of the stairs. She remained bent over, her arms trapped under her upper body and her hands fisted in self-loathing. Her mouth opened, and she began to keen. It was a sharp and desolate sound that couldn't even be classified as a cry. It was more primal and like nothing she had heard before. In some far-off way, she was mesmerized by the sound.

Linda reared up and screamed. She let one after another rip out of her throat as she pounded her fists against her thighs. Somehow she stumbled to her feet, but her leg buckled as she put weight on the twisted ankle. Throwing a hand up, she supported herself using the wall and limped toward her kitchen.

The tears had stopped, but the screaming continued in intermittent bursts of anger. Her ankle was a flare of white-hot pain. Surely it was sprained, if not broken, but still she kept going. Linda threw open her cupboards and started sweeping out all of the junk food that had been piled in there. Bags of chips, boxes of cupcakes, all manner of candy and other unhealthy food rained onto the floor. Her fridge was next as she yanked out Jell-O treats, fattening dips, and cartons of take-out food chock-full of calories. Her freezer was no better, and frozen pizzas, French fries, waffles, and pancakes got dumped to the ground at her feet.

Linda's screaming had subsided into grunts and pants as she grabbed and threw, grabbed and threw, all of the junk food piling around her. Kicking boxes out of her way, she went over to her kitchen drawers and yanked out a few garbage bags. She didn't care that her wrist was killing her or that her ankle couldn't handle much weight. The pain galvanized her, and she fought past it as the garbage bags made loud, thunderous noises when she snapped them open. They were systematically filled with all the food she had been living on over the last few years.

The purging took quite a while, but it was worth it. Linda dragged two garbage bags of food out to her front porch and then limped back inside. She made her way into the living room and called her friend Tony. As she listened to the ring of the phone, her face was dry of tears, and she didn't feel like screaming anymore. She was eerily calm in her now empty house.

"Yo, Lin!" Tony answered in his usual enthusiastic way, and she smiled for the first time in what felt like eons.

"I need a ride to the hospital," she said without preamble.

"Jesus, what did you do to yourself *now?*" he asked in loving exasperation. "And why isn't Graham bringing you?"

"Can you meet me outside in fifteen?" Linda said and hung up the phone.

Tony was at her door in ten minutes, helping her into his car. She tried not to grimace too much, but the pain had finally caught up and was punishing her for the antics in the kitchen. Lips set in a line and teeth ground together, she waited for Tony to get into the driver's seat.

"Hey, Lin?" he asked quietly. "Did you know you have two bags' worth of food sitting out on your porch?"

"Take whatever you like," Linda replied, looking out the windshield. "I don't need it anymore."

As she sat on the ER gurney, Linda studiously tried to avoid the penetrating gaze of her best friend of thirty years. It wasn't working very well. There were only so many places you could look in such a small space while trying to avoid a hulking mass like Tony Cross. Finally, she just dropped her gaze to her lap and watched her fingers twist in the fabric of her gray T-shirt.

"You're going to have to tell me eventually, you know," Tony said to her in a stern voice.

Flipping her eyes back to his face, she answered him in a monotone. "Graham left me because I'm *fat.*"

"Fuck off," Tony said in a dismissive way. It wasn't until he really looked at Linda that he realized she wasn't joking. "You serious?"

Linda simply nodded once and smiled tightly. She watched as Tony's heavy brows drew inward and down and his lips pulled back from his teeth in a feral snarl. That look was never good. Tony was generally mild-mannered and genial, but he could be quite fierce when angered.

"Are you serious?" he asked again, rage making his voice deeper and somewhat dangerous sounding.

"He's right, Tony," Linda said softly. "I mean, look at me. I'm gross."

"Linda, you're being ridiculous!"

"No, I'm not," she insisted. "You're really going to sit there and tell me I look great? That Graham is blind? That I'm just *curvy?* Come on, Tony! Really?"

"Fine," he spat out. "You've gained weight. Yeah. But that's an okay reason to dump someone you've been with for twenty years? You're telling me if it was the other way around, you'd have left Graham if he gained weight?"

"Well…no," she conceded. "But it's different!"

"Why is it different?" Tony demanded, crossing his arms over his chest.

"It just is," Linda insisted. "Women are wired differently. We aren't as visual as men. We can look past stuff easier."

"That's a crock of shit."

"It is not! It's scientifically proven." She pointed a finger at him. "So, no, I probably wouldn't have left him for gaining weight." She paused for a moment and then grinned slightly. "But I *should* have left him for having a small dick."

Linda was awoken with a start when someone started banging on her door. She hadn't wanted to manage the stairs with her ankle, so she had taken a pill, lain down on the couch, and passed out. She thought she was going to cry some more but hadn't. The dissolution of her marriage had been a long time coming. She had just been too scared and ashamed to admit it.

Truth be told, she had been miserable over the last few years. Instead of doing the right thing and leaving Graham, she had turned to food for comfort, swallowing empty calories much like she swallowed his verbal abuse, possible infidelity, and stony silences. She had been too afraid to just kick the no-good bastard out because he was all she knew. All she had ever known. And now he was gone.

Like Tony had said, good riddance.

Now she had the kick in the pants she needed to move on with her life.

The knocking started up again, and Linda scrubbed her eyes and sat up. "Just a minute!" she yelled toward the door as she reached down for her crutches. Her ankle was feeling somewhat better, but she figured she'd better not take a chance. As she thumped over to the door, she swore a blue streak under her breath. This had better be good.

"El?" she said, looking out and seeing her BFF standing on the porch with her hands behind her back.

"Tony called me. Is it true? Is he gone?"

"Yeah," Linda answered. "He's gone."

"Woo hoo!" Eliza yelled out, pulling two bottles of wine—one white and one red—from behind her back. "Let's celebrate!"

Linda stared at her friend in disbelief as she stumbled backward against the hallway wall. Eliza bounced past her with wine in tow and headed to the kitchen. Getting her wits about her, Linda closed the front door and thumped after her friend, who was busy hunting for the wine bottle opener. Two glasses were already set on the table, waiting.

"My husband leaves me...and you want to *celebrate?*"

"Hell yes!" Eliza answered, her back to Linda as she uncorked both bottles of wine. "I've been praying for this day for years! Except I was really hoping you would be the one to kick his sorry ass out. It really sucks he hurt you, but Tony's going to make him pay for that shit. Roy and John will be trolling for him tonight. He better have left town, that's all *I* have to say." She turned to Linda, a bottle in each hand. "Red? Or white?"

Unable to keep up with the crazy, Linda sank down into one of her kitchen chairs and just stared at Eliza, stupefied. "I'm on Vicodin," she finally managed to stammer out.

"When was your last pill?" Eliza asked, frowning slightly.

"About six hours ago?"

"Oh, you're fine!" she exclaimed happily. "So, no more Vicodin for you tonight. Just ibuprofen and the nectar of the gods! You'll be feeling no pain soon enough."

"Fine." Linda sighed. "White."

"*Yes!*" Eliza tipped the bottle over Linda's glass and filled it to the brim.

Just over an hour later, much like Eliza had said, Linda *was* feeling no pain. In fact, she was limping around the living room, where they had moved to be more comfortable, drinking wine straight from the bottle.

"And you know what he says to me?" Linda asked, turning to face Eliza and throwing her hand out to catch herself on a chair. "He says I'm *fat!* And that he can't even stand to look at me, much less touch me. Fucker! Well, how the hell did he think I got fat? It was his goddamn fault! Whenever he was an asshole to me—which was a *lot*—I ran to food and ate myself into oblivion!"

Eliza merely sat there, nodding through the tirade, owl-eyed and swaying slightly.

"So, now?" Linda continued to rant, "Now, I'm *old* and I'm *fat!* I gave that piece of shit the best years of my life, and then he up and leaves me. *Fucker!*"

"You're not old," Eliza replied, wagging her head, her straight brown hair whipping to and fro. "And you can lose weight!"

"That's right! I can lose weight!" Linda crowed. "And I'm gonna be hot!"

"Yeah, hot!" Eliza agreed loudly.

Linda went over and flopped down on the couch. "Why didn't you tell me, El?" she asked in a small voice. "Why didn't you tell me before that you all hated him?"

"He was your husband, Linda." Eliza sighed. "What were we supposed to do besides support you?"

Linda burst into tears again. Not because Graham was gone—he could rot in hell for all she cared—but because of her lost youth, spent on a man who was undeserving. And her lost self-esteem, which he had hammered at until it was virtually non-existent. She cried because she felt that most of her life had passed her by and she had spent the last fifth of it in misery.

Eliza reached out and hugged her. Linda was rocked back and forth, her hair was stroked, and soon her tears had subsided. She remained where she was and fought off a wave of fatigue that came out of nowhere. Her jaw unhinged in an almighty yawn.

"Time to go to bed, Linda," Eliza said as she pushed Linda back, grabbed her arm, and hauled her off the couch.

Linda didn't remember much after that, except them stumbling up the stairs and her being led to her bed. She remembered rolling over during the night, careful not to jostle Graham. When she realized he wasn't there and never would be again, loneliness crept up and tried to suffocate her. But then she remembered what he had said to her before he left, and she swore to herself she'd rather live the rest of her life alone than one more day with him.

After that, Linda slept the peaceful dreams of one who had resolved to change.

2
What Do You Mean He?

A few weeks after her drinkfest with Eliza, Linda found herself outside *Self-sational Fitness Club*. The front of the club was a window wall, with fitness equipment set up in rows on both sides of the entrance. Spandex-clad, tight-bodied women jogged, cycled, and used the elliptical machines in plain view of everyone walking by on the street.

Linda looked at her reflection in the window. It completely engulfed the woman who was running on the treadmill in front of her. Glancing down at herself in her loose-fitting clothing, she swallowed hard. She thought about turning around, getting back in her car, and going home so she could burrow under her duvet and just go to sleep. Taking a step in the direction of the parking lot, she hesitated. This was something she wanted to do.

She had already gotten rid of every bit of junk food in the kitchen, leaving it painfully bare in the wake of Hurricane Linda. That had been step number one. Luckily, Tony had offered to drop it all off at the local food bank, and she felt much better when the bags of food had been taken from her sight.

While eating well would help her avoid gaining weight and also shed some pounds, she knew that ultimately, she'd have to give her metabolism a boost, and the only way she could do that was through exercise. And she knew she couldn't do it without help.

"Graham has probably already replaced you with some pretty young thing," she grumbled to herself. "Show him what he'll be missing."

With that, she walked up to the glass door, yanked it open, and strode into the fitness club like she owned the place. That lasted about five steps, and by the time she got to the counter, she was intimidated again. The girl who worked the reception area was wearing a sports bra and barely-there boy shorts. Every square inch of her toned skin was a toasty brown, as if she lived near a sunny beach in Florida instead of in the town of Arnold, Maryland.

"Hi!" the girl said enthusiastically. "Can I help you?"

"Umm…yes. I'm looking for Amanda Reese."

"Oh, Amanda! Yeah, sure. Let me grab her for you. I think she's between sessions."

And just like that, Malibu Barbie sauntered off with a bounce in her step and a swing to her hips that made half the men working out in the weights section of the gym stop what they were doing so they could stare. Linda wanted to bolt again, and the only thing that stopped her was seeing Malibu Barbie talking to Bombshell Barbie and pointing toward her.

Now both women came across the gym, and *all* the men stopped what they were doing to stare. Linda sighed, a mix of contempt for the men, envy of the women, and resignation that she would probably never look like that. Malibu Barbie went back behind the reception desk, and Bombshell Barbie, who Linda assumed must be Ms. Reese, headed her way.

"Hi, I'm Amanda," Barbie said, putting her hand out and smiling brightly. "Can I help you?"

"I hope so," Linda replied, shaking the other woman's hand. "I'm Linda Tanner. My doctor gave me your card. I was hoping I could hire you as a personal trainer."

"Oh, jeez," Amanda said, biting her lip and looking somewhat torn. "Did you know when you wanted to get started?"

"As soon as possible," Linda stated, figuring if she put it off any longer, she'd never do it.

"That's what I thought you'd say," Amanda replied with a cringe. "I'm sorry. I'm completely booked for at least three months."

"Shit," Linda mumbled to herself. "Well, can I leave my number in case of a cancellation?"

"You don't have to do that," Amanda said, shaking her head enthusiastically, her platinum-blond curls bouncing around her face. "We have another trainer. My housemate."

"Oh, you do?"

"Yeah, and I know he just had a cancellation recently, so he has some free time."

"Wait," Linda said, slightly mortified. "*He?*"

"Yeah! Jack. Here, let me call him over." Raising her hand, she waved it over her head. "Hey! Jack!"

"No," Linda hissed, clamping a hand around Amanda's arm. "Don't do that!"

It was too late. The other personal trainer looked up from whatever he was doing and, after a few seconds, started to jog over to them from the back of the facility.

"Fuck," Linda muttered under her breath as the most perfect male specimen she had ever seen walked over and smiled at her.

Jack had one eye firmly set on the clock above the workout area and the other on the woman who was lying on the weight bench, trying to bench press thirty pounds. He kept having to step back away from her head because she was more concerned with trying to look up his shorts than benching the weights he had placed on the bar.

"You're doing great, Mrs. Bellham," he said, smiling at her even though he was ready to blindfold the hornbag. *One more time, lady,* he thought. *Look up my shorts just* one *more time!* Then again, she'd probably like that. This one looked like she got off on the kinky shit.

How in the hell had he ever let Amanda talk him into moving to this tiny little town? He had been happy in Hawaii. And yet, here they were.

But this place was a whole new kettle of fish. The women were man-hungry. He couldn't go through one whole day without being propositioned at least once. And what made it more appalling was that half the come-ons came from married women. This was a whole new dynamic for him, and he wasn't quite sure how to handle it.

Jack heard his name being called from across the club.

Speak of the devil. Amanda was waving her arm in the air to get his attention and standing beside what looked like yet another horny housewife that she wanted to pawn off on him. He was going to kill her. Just pull up her Spandex bra and strangle her with the damned thing. It would be so easy. *Sooo* fucking easy.

"I'll be right back, Mrs. Bellham," he said as he helped her ease the bar back on its struts.

"Jack, how many times do I have to tell you to call me Candy?" She simpered up at him.

"Yeah, right," he said with a nod. "Don't do anything while I'm gone. Okay?"

She bobbled her head up and down, batting her stubby lashes at him.

"Last thing I need is a fucking lawsuit," he grumbled under his breath before plastering on the fakest smile in his repertoire and jogging over to the bane of his existence and his newest client.

When he got to the women, he was actually perplexed by what he saw. His newest potential client had a death grip on Amanda's arm and looked absolutely horrified. Her face was beet red, and she was pulling her baggy shirt away from her body in nervous plucks and tugs. She looked…*scared*. Completely unlike all the other vapid bimbos who preened and puckered their lips at him.

This woman looked at him as if he was going to attack her.

What the hell? He took in her huge, worried gray eyes and compressed lips.

"Jack," Amanda said, shaking the lady's hand off her arm and continuing as if she were completely blind to the whole situation. "This is Linda Tanner. She needs a personal trainer right away, and I'm booked solid. Do you think you can slip her in?"

"Yeah…that's fine," Jack replied casually and bent slightly to catch the poor woman's eyes. "If you want?"

To his utter dismay, the lady turned an even deeper shade of red and grabbed fistfuls of her shirt, pulling desperately, as if she were trying to hide herself from him. He couldn't understand what he had said or done to cause her such distress, but something in the way she was avoiding his eyes made him want to find out.

"Hey, Mandy," he said, looking at his best friend. "Think you can give me and Ms. Tanner a minute here?"

"Yeah, sure!"

The woman turned large eyes up to Amanda and looked as if she wanted to beg her to stay. In normal Amanda fashion, she simply smiled and wandered off. Jack loved her to death, but her head was so far up in the clouds sometimes. He often wondered how she hadn't strolled off a cliff by now.

He shook his head at Amanda's back before turning to face the woman again. She was eying the door as if it was her salvation and refused to make eye contact with him.

"Hey," he said softly, as if he were talking to a wounded animal in search of escape. "Are you okay?"

She finally looked up at him, and he saw the sheen of tears in her eyes. "I can't do this," she said in a soft voice. "I came here expecting to hire a woman."

"Look, you don't need to hire me if it makes you uncomfortable." He could kill Amanda for this. Why hadn't she checked to make sure this woman would be okay with a man being her personal trainer? This chick was a mess, Jack thought. Maybe she had been hurt or abused. Maybe she didn't like or trust men. And now she was being forced to endure the intimate attentions of one—'cause the truth of the matter was physical training could get pretty hands-on and intense. "You can just wait until Amanda is free," he suggested. "Or maybe I can talk her into taking an extra client."

"You'd do that?"

"Sure. We're pretty close. I know she can swing it." He was positive Amanda would swing it, because if she didn't, he'd kill her for real. She *owed* him one. Especially after this. "Why don't you leave your contact info with the front desk, and I'll have her call you. Okay?"

"Okay," she answered, smiling at him slightly.

Somewhere throughout their conversation, she had stopped fidgeting. Now that her face had cleared and she no longer seemed terrified, she was actually kind of pretty. If you liked that sort of thing. Her hair was a burnished auburn, long with a slight wave, and her large gray eyes were light in contrast. She was a quite a bit more full-figured than Jack preferred, but at least she was trying to do something about it, which made him respect her.

"All right." He ran a hand through his hair. "Maybe I'll see you around sometime."

"Yeah, probably," she said, a wry lilt in her voice. Then she ducked her head and scuttled toward the reception desk.

Jack watched the woman leave, still somewhat confused by the whole encounter. He groaned when he remembered he still had about half an hour of his session with Candace Bellham to get through. Damn it. He should have worn some bike shorts under his normal workout gear. He'd have to remember for next time. He trudged toward the back of the club.

Amanda was with her next client, so Jack couldn't grab her by the back of the head and drag her into the employees' lounge for a verbal tongue-lashing like he wanted to. He would just have to remember to tell her she was taking on Linda Tanner whether she wanted to or not, and if that meant booking extra hours, too damned bad.

Linda practically ran to her car. When she got there, she locked herself inside and relived her absolute humiliation. It had been bad enough when Amanda Reese revealed that their second personal trainer was a man, but seeing the man in person made things worse.

He was absolutely stunning. Linda had never seen such a good-looking man up close and personal before. He had looks that should be on the big screen: curly, sandy-brown hair, big blue eyes, and a jaw that looked chiseled out of marble, except for the light scruff on his chin.

And that was just his face. From what she could see, his body looked fantastic. His form-fitting T-shirt outlined wide shoulders, a nice set of pecs, and a flat stomach. He had lean hips and long, defined legs, and his arms were corded with muscle but not to the extreme. It was just enough to make a girl want to swoon so he'd catch her. And Linda had been ready to do just that.

Then she remembered that she was fat and would likely crush him under her immense weight, no matter how muscular those arms looked.

And she was old.

He looked like a baby, probably not even thirty, and she felt mildly perverted for even thinking of him in *that* way. But damn if he didn't look fine standing there in his workout clothes. Of course, that's when things got critical. Graham's words echoed in her brain, and Linda's shirt felt way too tight across her midsection. She'd pulled it away from her body relentlessly as the introductions had been made, but all she could think of was how disgusting she must look and how someone like him wouldn't want to be subjected to touching her.

She had just wanted the floor to open up and swallow her whole when he sent the other girl away and tried to calm her down. And he had been so *nice* to her. She had almost been hoping that he would be a conceited, egotistical dickwad. But he had been sweet and concerned, and he'd tried to make her feel better about being an inept moron.

Jesus, what had happened to her? Before Graham had left, she knew she was overweight. It wasn't like it was some big revelation or anything. But for some reason, she'd never felt this horrible about herself. Maybe it was because she was married and figured she'd always have a husband, so what did it matter how she looked?

But now all that had changed. Linda was single, and how she looked mattered a hell of a lot more. How others saw her would be different. She no longer had the security of her marriage—even if it had been a sham. She was on her own and would always be alone if she didn't do something about her weight, because as long as she felt this way, she'd never see herself as worthy of love.

The mind was a powerful weapon, especially when turned on oneself.

Linda sat in the car a little longer, replaying everything that had happened, and then she made a decision. She wasn't going to be bound by her weight. She had come here to get a personal trainer, and damned if she wasn't going to get one. Perhaps Amanda *could* fit her in, but now she didn't want Amanda. She wanted Jack. She didn't stop to examine the many ways she wanted him. For now, personal trainer would suffice.

Making up her mind, Linda exited her car and ran back to the front door of the fitness club. She didn't stop to think about what she was doing; she just marched through those doors, head held high and shoulders thrown back. She even shook her ass a little. Sure, none of the guys in the weights section stopped what they were doing to watch her strut her stuff, but she didn't care. If her plan worked, it wouldn't be very long before they *did* pay attention, and that was why she had come here in the first place.

She found Jack quickly enough. He was standing over a woman on a weight bench and rubbing his eyes as if he were in pain. For some reason, that made her smile and gave her a little extra strength.

"Jack?" she said in a breathless voice.

"Yeah?" he replied tiredly before dropping his hand to register who was speaking to him.

"I changed my mind," Linda said more confidently. "I want you to be my personal trainer."

The next day, Jack was experiencing a mild case of déjà vu as he stood over Candy Bellham while she tried to peek up his shorts. The only difference was this time, he'd remembered to throw on a pair of bike shorts under his workout gear, and the disgruntled look on Mrs. Bellham's face was worth having to deal with sweaty balls later. He tried to keep the grin to himself, but it wasn't working very well. Unfortunately, Mrs. Bellham took it the wrong way and smiled at him coquettishly.

Luckily, the longest hour in the history of the world finally came to an end, and he was bidding adieu to Mrs. Bellham. Jack smiled his best smile and didn't particularly care that it didn't touch his eyes. A shallow woman like her wouldn't notice anyway. When she finally walked out, his mouth drew down in a scowl as he looked at the clock. He had about fifteen minutes to grab a drink and de-stress. And get the hell out of those restricting bike shorts. Jack was going to give Ms. Tanner the benefit of the doubt. He had the impression she wasn't the kind to look up his shorts, even if given the chance. He wasn't even certain she had enough nerve to look in his eyes, much less at his crotch.

It wasn't long before he was paged to meet with Linda Tanner for their first official session.

"Hi, Ms. Tanner. Nice to meet you again," he said politely. "The change rooms are in the back if you want to get into your workout clothes."

"Uhh…this is what I'm wearing," she said in a quiet voice.

Jack eyed her heavy hoodie and matching sweat pants. They were huge on her, as if she were trying to hide herself from the public. "But you'll get too hot in that," he pointed out reasonably.

"I'll be fine."

Jack frowned but said nothing more. She would have to learn the hard way. He hoped she had brought water with her, because she was going to need it.

After that awkward exchange where she mostly avoided his eyes—surprise, surprise—Jack decided to show her the club and see what type of experience she had with the equipment. As they walked around, he became more and more dismayed when Linda shook her head every time he pointed at a machine.

"You've never worked out? Ever?" he asked, trying to conceal his shock. "No running? Bike riding? Nothing?"

"Umm…no," Linda replied, now a painful shade of red. "I'm kind of clumsy." Finally, she looked up at him, and the shame in her eyes made Jack feel cruel and insensitive. He didn't like the feeling. Not at all.

"So, what made you decide to do it *now?*" he blurted out.

"This!" she said emphatically, grabbing fistfuls of her plump thighs. Now they looked like a matching set of tomatoes.

Jack turned away slightly, rubbing the back of his neck in embarrassment. First he'd made her feel shitty for not knowing about exercise equipment, and then he'd forced her to publicly admit she was overweight. This was quickly becoming even more mortifying than the first time they had met.

A pale forearm shot into his view, and he jumped slightly.

"This is what happened the first time my dad took the training wheels off my bike," she said in a soft voice. His eyes followed a slim finger as it traced up a long, winding scar that went from halfway up her forearm to almost the crook of her elbow. It had a faint silvery sheen, and you could tell it had happened a long time ago. "The ER doctor said it was a good thing it was over to the left a little, or I probably would have bled out. My dad was horrified. He sold my bike to a neighbor the next day."

Jack glanced up at the woman by his side, but she wasn't looking at him. She bent over, pulled one of her pant legs up, and pointed to a healed gash over the top of her knee. "This happened when they added mandatory cross-country in my high school gym class," she continued in a wry tone. "I managed to step in a pothole, twisted my ankle, and fell on a broken bottle someone had left in the gutter beside the road. I had to get a note to be excused from that class."

He stared at the scar and the smooth knee underneath.

She let her pant leg fall back down and stood up. "Anyway, I've never been much into sports, so exercise was never really high on my list of priorities."

Looking at her, he noticed Linda had a small grin on her face. It was catchy, and he found himself grinning in return. She really did have pretty eyes…and then it struck him that she was actually looking at him. Really looking at him. Not the furtive glances of before. Showing off her battle scars had enabled them to bond, and instead of making her more awkward and uncomfortable, it had made her a little bolder than usual. He realized something else. It was her concern for *him* and how he had been feeling that had given her the courage to distract him from this odd situation.

She had sacrificed a little bit of herself in order to make him feel better.

Jack stared at Linda in confusion until she coughed and gestured to the exercise equipment in front of her. "So…umm…are we going to get started?"

"Yeah," he replied quickly, burying his strange feelings. "Yeah, let's get started. You're going to want to warm up first before we do anything."

And so it began. A trainer and his client. So, why did Jack feel different this time? He supposed he'd never know.

3
I Never Agreed to Jiggling

Jack McAllister was evil.

Of this Linda was convinced. Far from taking it easy on her, he pushed her like a slave driver. Maybe he got off on it? Every single time she heard him say, "Ten more, Linda! You can do it!" she wanted to punch him in his incredibly straight, perfect nose.

He was a sadist. And Linda must have been a masochist, because every time he did say ten more, instead of punching him and walking out, she did ten more.

He also took every opportunity he could to berate her for wearing a ridiculous fleece-lined sweat suit. It was a sweat suit, for goodness sake. *Isn't the whole purpose to sweat in the damned thing?* she thought irately. After the first fifteen minutes of the workout, she became acutely aware as to why less is more when it came to working out.

In truth, Linda had worn the damned thing because there was no way she was getting caught in anything remotely Spandex-like while being surrounded by hard and toned bodies. It was not happening. She would die first. Maybe after she lost the first fifty pounds, she would consider it, but absolutely no way right now.

So she sweated. And she tried not to pass out from sheer exhaustion and dehydration. And when Jack passed her a bottle of cold water, she drank it so fast a shot of pain sliced through her head, as if she had been poleaxed.

Brain freeze.

Following the end of the first session, and after Linda had gotten her things from the back, she saw Jack waiting for her at the front counter. He smiled and waved her over, and she tried her best to not look like she was in too much pain as she shuffled her way to him, her bag bumping into her back with every lurch.

"How are you feeling?" he asked solicitously, looking her over carefully.

"Just peachy...*Master*," she shot back acerbically.

"Master?"

"Isn't that the proper terminology for a slave driver? Sorry, I'm not up on my BDSM lingo."

Jack leaned back against the counter and laughed whole-heartedly. The sound of his rich baritone made her smile and forget that every joint in her body was in full revolt. After their rocky start, the banter throughout the session had gone similar to this, which had made the experience at least a little bit enjoyable.

"Oh, come on. I wasn't that bad."

"Hmph," Linda snorted, giving him the evil eye.

"Look, you're going to want to stretch when you get home and maybe tomorrow when you wake up," Jack advised. "Take a long, hot bath tonight to soothe your muscles, or else you'll be pretty stiff."

"Yes, Master." She nodded, trying to look serious even as his lips curled up in a half-smile.

Then he placed a card in her hand. "And I want you to go here and pick up some actual workout gear," he said, plucking at the string of her hoodie and making a face. "I'm surprised you didn't collapse while wearing this."

"Listen, mister—"

"Don't you mean Master?" he chided with a grin.

"Listen, you," she continued, scowling fiercely. "There is no way I'm squeezing into anything Spandex. Not around here anyway." Her voice had lowered, and she was glancing around surreptitiously at the scantily-clad women wandering around.

"You don't need to buy anything tight." Jack sighed in exasperation. "Just something lighter. Like yoga pants and a T-shirt."

"Yoga pants?"

"Yeah. You'll love them, I swear." He smiled reassuringly. "Ask for Cici. She'll take care of you."

And that's how, after going home to do some cool-down exercises and take a shower, Linda had found herself in the middle of a small shop catering to everything female while a short, mocha-skinned, cropped-haired fashion freak on acid whipped around her like a teeny whirlwind, shoving all types of clothing in Linda's open arms. She felt like the world's biggest clotheshorse.

"Umm…" Linda mumbled, trying to get the girl's attention.

"And you'll need this. And one of these. And you *definitely* have to try on this…" And so it went until the tornado dissipated, leaving Cici standing in front of her, breathing heavily and staring at a human-shaped mound of clothes. Or at least that's what Linda imagined the diminutive girl was now seeing.

"Umm…" Linda tried again. "Help?"

Cici laughed in delight and started to de-clothe Linda. Together they walked to the nearest change room so she could start trying everything on. She had to hand it to Cici. The items picked were light, with some give, but weren't overly clingy. Linda had been dreading this part of the process, having to stand in front of a mirror while wearing form-fitting clothing, but it wasn't as bad as she had anticipated. The yoga pants were thin but had wide legs and were even kind of flattering. They had a placket built in that sucked in tummy fat but were still comfortable. The tank tops had a similar effect and built-in bras so she could wear them under a loose T-shirt and still feel comfortable.

An hour later, Linda headed to her car, shopping-bag laden and having spent much more money than she had bargained for. A new kind of determination took hold of her. Nothing was going to deter her from this plan.

That resolution lasted all of about another couple of hours until her muscles started to seize up, and Linda felt as if she was going to die. She ended up retiring early that evening after a very hot and relaxing bath, and she hoped she'd be okay in the morning.

Much to Linda's chagrin, she was not okay the next day. She groaned as she stretched, and it felt as if someone had taken a baseball bat to her body in the middle of the night. It took her almost five minutes to make it down the stairs, and she was practically sobbing by the time she arrived at the bottom step.

Holy hell. How was she going to be able to keep this up when it hurt so badly? Linda was relieved that she didn't have to work out today because she knew there was no way she could manage it. Jack had started her off every Monday, Wednesday, and Friday, with the weekends off. Today was Thursday, so tomorrow she had her next session. She figured by then that she should be good to go.

Hopefully.

On Friday, Linda picked up the phone and called the gym, asking for Jack.

"Hey, Linda!" he said cheerfully.

"Hi, Jack," she replied and was shocked to feel herself blush. *Oh, brother!* she thought in annoyance. "I don't think I can make it in today."

"Too sore?"

"Yeah."

"I figured that's why you were calling."

"Oh, good." She sagged with relief. "So, we can reschedule?"

"Nope."

"Oh…umm…you're not free?"

"No, I'm free. But I'm not letting you reschedule," he said in a firm tone. "You're coming to the club today for your regular session."

"'Scuse me?" Linda squeaked. That was definitely not the answer she had been hoping for.

"The first session is always the hardest," Jack continued. "If I let you cancel now, it sets a bad precedent. Then you'll think you can do this every time the sessions get tough."

"I just need one more day—"

"No."

"But—"

"No," he repeated sternly. "Tell me, Linda, are you serious about losing weight? About this commitment?"

"Well, of course I am!" she sputtered indignantly.

"Good. Then I expect to see you at the club at our specified time, or I'm calling it quits."

"What?" Linda asked, her jaw dropping. "Wait a second! *I'm* the one hiring *you!*"

"Yep," he answered. "But that doesn't mean I have to accept. And it's not like you have many choices, do you?"

"This is blackmail!"

"I like to think of it as a persuasion tactic," he said, chuckling darkly. "Just trust me, okay? We'll take it easy for this session and get you nice and worked out. Sound good?"

"Are you this persistent with all of your clients?" she asked, still somewhat piqued at his "persuasion" methods.

"Oddly enough, no," he answered, sounding slightly surprised. "But you came to me for help, and that's what I'd like to do. So, you're coming?"

"Yes, Master," she sighed in resignation.

"Excellent," he said with a laugh. "You know, I could get used to this Master business."

"Don't push your luck," Linda groused, making him laugh some more.

They said their good-byes, and Linda stared at the phone in her hand, wondering how she had gotten roped into making it for her workout session today. She huffed out an annoyed breath and then looked at her staircase. Nothing had ever looked so daunting in her life. And to think she had to make her way up, get dressed, and try to get back down in only an hour? She realized she better get started *now.*

On the other side of town, Jack was looking at the phone in his hand and wondering why he had made such a fuss about Linda canceling her session today. Had it been any of his other clients, he wouldn't have cared. In some cases, he would have even encouraged the cancellation. He thought of Candy Bellham and shuddered. Yes, some of his clients would be welcome to cancel any time they pleased.

But Linda was kind of different. He actually had fun with her. She reminded him why he used to enjoy this job, even if it wasn't what he wanted to do for the rest of his life. Her self-deprecating humor made him laugh, and she also had a sharp wit that kept him on his toes. Jack really wouldn't have suspected any of that had he based it on their first meeting. But once the awkwardness fell away and they became more comfortable with one another, her true personality began to come forth.

So, on a day when he had one pervy, disgusting client after another, could anyone blame him for wanting a slice of normalcy and maybe a little bit of fun in the middle of it all?

Jack tried not to chuckle as he watched Linda hobble past the huge glass window wall to enter the club. He was happy to see she'd ditched her horrible sweat suit and had replaced it with some normal exercise clothes. While closer to the skin, it was much more flattering to her size. At least this way, he'd be able to tell if the workout sessions were helping her.

Linda scowled at him as she made her way over. "Okay, I'm here."

"Still sore?"

"Fuck yes," she ground out through a clenched jaw, and Jack pressed his lips together to keep from laughing.

"Good. That means I'm doing my job right." Linda's scowl deepened, and this time he couldn't help but smile a little. He hoped it was reassuring. "Come on, let's go."

"Yes, Master," Linda sighed as she trudged along behind him.

Jack led her into one of the aerobic rooms. It was currently unoccupied, and he knew the next class wouldn't start for a while, so he didn't have to worry about anyone disturbing them. He flipped the light switches and went over to the corner where the exercise mats were stacked. Grabbing a quartet of them, he made a large cushioned area in the middle of the floor. When he glanced up, Linda was still standing by the door, watching him with a quizzical expression on her face. He made a gesture for her to join him, so she pushed off the wall and walked over to the edge of the mats.

"Jeez, I didn't realize I'd embarrassed you so much last time that you need to do my session in private," she said wryly.

Jack chuckled. "Take your shoes off and lie down, Linda." She did as she was told, and then he kneeled down next to her. "Okay, now spread your legs."

"Come again?" she squeaked.

"Just trust me," Jack said patiently. "We're going to do some loosening exercises, and they can look a little odd. That's why I brought you in here."

"Umm…okay…"

Linda spread her legs, and Jack knelt between her calves. He noticed that there was a creeping and persistent flush that was rising up her neck and was about to engulf her face any second. "Relax," he told her soothingly before gripping her ankles and lifting them so that they were braced on the outside of his hips. "Okay, I'm going to stand up now."

"*What?*" Linda's eyes flew to his as he began to stand, keeping her ankles held in his hands. "You know, Jack," she said in a dry tone, "if you wanted to seduce me, you could have just *asked.*"

Jack started laughing again, more at the way she said them than at the words themselves. He knew this would probably be a somewhat uncomfortable position to be in with a virtual stranger, which is why he wanted them to be in a more private area. Linda was still looking at him like he was off his rocker, so he decided to explain.

"I need to get you loosened up, so this session is going to be mostly stretching and some resistance training."

"Okay, so, what does that have to do with you getting into position number forty-three of the Kama Sutra?"

"We're going to jiggle you loose."

"Jiggle?" Linda practically shrieked while simultaneously trying to yank her legs out of his grip. "I never agreed to any jiggling. Jiggling is a hard limit," she babbled. "Just say *no* to jiggling."

"Linda, calm down!" Jack said, gripping her ankles tighter. "It will feel good. I promise."

"Jesus Christ," she huffed. "*Jiggling!*" Then she threw an arm over her eyes. "Fine! But if Arnold has an earthquake for the first time in history, I'm telling everyone to blame you."

Once she had relaxed a bit, Jack rose on the balls of his feet and then back down to his heels. He started off slowly so she would become accustomed to the sensation and then began to pick up speed.

"Ow, ow, ow…I thought you said this was supposed to feel good."

"It will," Jack told her. "But you have to stop flexing."

"You really don't know what you're asking!"

"Just do it."

Jack felt the tension go out of her legs, and the grimace of pain Linda had on her face gradually dissipated. She let out a little moan as her muscles loosened.

"Feel better?"

"Yes," she said, stretching out the word until it was almost a hiss.

"Okay, good," Jack said before coming to a stop. He stepped back, still holding onto her ankles, and knelt down. "Bend your knees," he instructed, and then he placed her feet in the middle of his chest and began to lean forward, applying pressure. "Now push."

Linda stared at the Adonis perched against her feet, and her mind was slightly scrambled. He continued to lean forward, and it took all her willpower to push against his chest instead of parting her legs and letting him fall between them. This scene right here would be going into the "to be fantasized about later" file.

True to his word, Jack had somehow gotten the large muscles in her legs to loosen up and stop being so painful. It was an incredibly embarrassing way to do it, but after a while, she stopped caring. Anything to get rid of the tension, and she was all for it. It helped that Jack wasn't paying attention to her thighs as they wiggled in a successful Jell-O impression. If she'd had to see a look of disgust on his face as she jiggled around, she thought she would die. As it stood, he was a complete professional and just stared forward with a look of concentration. Occasionally, he'd glance down at her face to see if she was okay, which made her fall just a little bit in love with him.

He really was incredibly sweet.

Even bringing her here so they could work out in private had been a sweet gesture. He seemed to genuinely care that this experience be as painless as possible and an easy transition, despite the muscle spasms. All in all, Linda was happy he had forced her to come in for this session.

They did more resistance training on her legs, with Jack using himself as her weights. Then he moved on to her arms and did the jiggle thing to them as well, only this time he knelt by her side, grasped one of her hands in both of his, and shook her arm back and forth vigorously. Once again, she felt the embarrassment creep up as her upper arm wiggled like crazy under the sleeve of her T-shirt, but Jack didn't seem to care. Well, why would he? She was just his client, after all.

LET'S GET PHYSICAL

Once both arms had been loosened up, they did a few upper-arm exercises for strength. Nothing too strenuous but enough so that Linda could feel the pull of the muscles as they got a good workout. When that was over, Jack had her sit up, and then he went to kneel behind her, keeping one foot on the ground, knee bent. He placed that knee in the middle of her back, grabbed her shoulders, and pulled back so that her chest popped out. Linda groaned aloud as the muscles across the front of her chest stretched almost to the point of pain and several of her vertebrae cracked back into place.

"Fuck!" she muttered under her breath, and Jack slackened his hold.

"Too much?"

"Jesus, who knew you had so many damned muscles in your chest?"

Linda shivered as warm breath washed over the nape of her neck when Jack began to chuckle. He was now fully kneeling behind her, and his thumbs were circling against the muscles beside her neck, easing out the tension. Linda dropped her head forward and groaned again, this time in pure bliss as his hands worked out kinks she wasn't even aware she had.

"You're a masseuse, too?"

"No," he replied, amusement tingeing his voice.

"Too bad. I was about to say, 'You're hired!'"

"I just want to make sure you'll be all right over the weekend. I don't want any cancellations come Monday."

Linda laughed and then almost moaned as his hands moved lower down her back. For an instant, she imagined it was because Jack wanted to touch her and not because it was part of his job. Either way, she'd take it. Pathetic as it was, it had been so long since she had been caressed in any way, shape, or form, she craved it as intensely as she would air or water. At that moment, she couldn't care less that she was paying this man money. She could just fantasize that he cared about her.

"How's that?" Jack asked, patting her shoulders and snapping her out of her reverie.

"That was great. I'm glad I came today," she replied, honestly meaning it.

"Me, too. Session's up. So, I'll see you on Monday?" he asked, leaning over her shoulder so she could see his face.

"Mm-hmm."

He stood in one fluid movement that made Linda sigh internally and feel a pang of envy as she struggled to get her legs under her. A broad hand waved in front of her face, and she smiled as she took it. Jack yanked her up effortlessly, and she helped him put the mats away. Once they were done, she headed to the door while he followed.

Neither of them noticed a pair of beady eyes following their progress out of the secluded room.

4
The First Ten and the New Hire

The next few weeks flew by quickly for Jack. His favorite days were the ones when Linda came in to work out. Between her outlandish remarks that he was out to kill her, her insistence on calling him Master, and her putting him in his place if he got too mouthy, he found himself laughing more than he had since moving here.

Of course, that didn't stop him from being the slave driver Linda accused him of being.

Amidst the fun, he also put her through her paces, alternating between one hard session and one that was less strenuous so that her body had a chance to recuperate in time for the next difficult workout. As always, they would hole themselves up in one of the unoccupied aerobic rooms to shake Linda loose before continuing with the resistance training. She didn't even bother complaining any longer, merely got on the mats and assumed the position. However, her face always held that look of martyred resignation, which never failed to amuse him.

To be honest, he preferred these private sessions, because Linda always seemed less self-conscious when it was just the two of them. She wasn't always glancing around to see who was watching as she navigated her way through the exercises while trying to maintain her balance. They also didn't have to worry about being too rowdy and attracting undue attention when they bickered over exercise choices or laughed over something silly. Things felt more natural and easy.

Today was one of their slow days, so Jack led Linda into the back room. She seemed giddier than usual, which made him smile. As soon as he flipped on the lights, she shut the door and beamed at him.

"Guess what?" she asked excitedly.

"What?"

"I've already lost *ten* pounds!"

"That's excellent, Linda," Jack replied genuinely.

"Thank you!" she said and then threw her arms around his waist and squeezed tight.

Jack was taken by surprise. He stared down at the top of Linda's head for a moment before gingerly putting his arms around her, patting her lightly on the back. Usually he didn't encourage unsolicited touching from any of his clients, but Linda's actions weren't pervy in the least. All he felt was intense gratitude emanating from her. Jack would have expected to be somewhat put off. The fact that he wasn't confused him.

Linda was a nice woman and all, but not really his type physically. The thing was, she was his type in other ways. In a sudden burst of clarity, he wondered if she *could* be once she lost the weight. As soon as the thought arrived, he felt disgusted for being such a shallow asshole. A woman like Linda deserved to be loved for who she was, not what her body looked like, and he was ashamed of himself for not being able to see past her physical appearance.

As quickly as Linda had hugged him, she let go, forcing him to drop that line of thought. Stepping back shyly, she said jokingly, "Ten pounds down, five hundred to go!"

"Linda," he scolded, frowning at her.

She waved a hand at him in dismissal and walked over to the mats, calling over her shoulder. "Yeah, yeah."

"How much do you want to lose, anyway?" he asked curiously. "I don't think you've ever told me."

She thought it over, a pensive look on her face as Jack helped her wrestle the mats into place. Whenever they had talked about her weight loss goal in the past, she had avoided the question, and he figured it was due to the embarrassment of having to admit how much she had to lose. He had hoped that eventually she'd get over it so he could help her formulate a better plan to reach her objective.

Linda sat down cross-legged in the middle of the now padded area, and Jack knelt in front of her. He sat back on his heels and fought the urge to prompt her, hoping she was on the brink of opening up just a little bit more. Finally, she looked up at him, a small pucker between her brows.

"Seventy pounds total," she admitted and then winced slightly, awaiting his reaction.

"That's doable," he answered slowly, keeping his face impassive. "But I don't particularly think you need to lose all that much."

"That's how much I want to lose."

"Okay." Jack tried not to frown. He didn't want to discourage her, but he did think the number was slightly excessive. "So, sixty more to go?"

"Yeah."

"And when you reach your goal, what's your prize?"

"My prize?"

"You know, like a reward for losing the weight," he explained. "There always has to be a prize. It gives you incentive to keep going."

"You mean besides a big, fat, greasy pizza?" Linda snickered at him, and he smiled, shaking his head.

"You can get pizza anytime. It has to be something good. Something you've never had before but you've always wanted."

Linda looked at him and frowned again. "I don't know," she replied. "I guess I'd have to think about it."

"Good!" he said, rising to his knees once more before saying in a stern tone, "Time's wasting. Assume the position."

After a groan, she flopped onto her back and put her legs on either side of his. "Yes, Master."

Usually, Linda threw her arms over her face as he worked on her legs while he just looked straight ahead, not wanting to cause her additional discomfort. This time, Jack watched Linda's body covertly. Once again, he was surprised that the way it moved as he loosened the muscles of her legs didn't bother him as much as he expected.

There was no real sexual heat as he examined her form, but he wasn't turned off either.

"Is something wrong?"

Jack's gaze snapped up, and he saw that Linda had been watching him from underneath her arm while he was watching her. He fought the flush that was rising to his cheeks at getting busted, but it was no use. "Nothing's wrong," he said quickly. "Why?"

"You're frowning," she replied in a subdued voice. "I thought maybe I was flexing again."

Her words made sense, but the look on her face told another story. It felt like she expected him to react in a certain way, and that bothered him. Like she was waiting for him to say something less than flattering at her expense. For a moment, he wondered why.

The rest of the session passed in relative silence. Linda seemed to have withdrawn and wasn't her usual animated self. Something had been lost, and he felt himself becoming more agitated as the end of the session drew near. When their time was up, instead of helping Linda off the mats like he normally would, Jack sat down beside her. He could see Linda in his peripheral vision as she turned a surprised face to him.

"So…I, uh…wanted to thank you for hiring me," he said in a quiet and deliberate voice.

Linda snorted. "Why? Was there no one else on whom you could unleash your sadistic tendencies?"

This made Jack smile. It was more like her usual attitude, and he was happy that she wasn't mad at him for some reason.

"No," he replied, shaking his head, "but you do make me want to kill fewer people."

"Excuse me?"

When he glanced over at her, Linda looked somewhat alarmed. Her eyebrows had risen as high as they could go. Jack began to laugh in earnest at her expression.

"I mean, I know I call you a sadist and all," she said, "but I wasn't being serious!"

"Not like that." He chuckled and shrugged one shoulder, trying to figure out how to explain. "When I first moved here, everything and everyone drove me crazy. I hated it here. All of my clients were the equivalent of barracudas. But things are different with you. You make me laugh and have fun. You make me less homesick. So…thanks."

"Oh…Well, you're welcome," she replied softly. He noticed that the small pucker between her brows didn't really go away, however, and she just stared at her lap and plucked at the hem of her pants.

"Is everything okay?"

"Yeah," she answered, nodding her head and offering a little smile. "Anyway, I really have to get out of these clothes." Linda winced and huffed out a breath at what she'd said, and then she turned red. "What I *mean* is, I need to go."

"Okay." Jack would have liked to talk for a little bit longer, but he didn't really want to force her to stay. He rose to his feet in a quick move and offered his hand to Linda, who took it after a moment's hesitation.

They followed their regular routine; however, Jack noticed that Linda had lapsed into silence once again. Instead of walking out together, she bade him a half-hearted good-bye and hurriedly left for the women's change room. At that moment, he decided he'd wait in the reception area to make sure she was okay. He had a feeling she probably wouldn't tell him what was really wrong, but he was willing to take the chance anyway.

Linda walked into the change room in a fit of depression. The day had started off so well when she'd gotten on the scale and realized she was down ten pounds. Unfortunately, it had gone downhill from there. She'd caught Jack staring at her body as it was in the middle of the jiggling, and the look on his face was disgusted. How else would he feel? And then afterward had come his little chat that completely reinforced what a great *friend* Linda was.

Linda had admitted to herself early on that she had a huge school-girl-like crush on her personal trainer. And while she knew that at the age of thirty-five, she was a little too old for a crush, that was the best way to describe it. He made her grin like a fangirl and blush with his proximity, and since he had to help her with many of the exercises, he was physically close to her a lot. She almost thanked God she was fat, because then at least she could blame her permanently red cheeks on the workout and not because Jack was close enough that she could feel the heat of his body through the thin shirts he wore.

It wasn't only how he looked. Underneath the movie star good looks, he was simply a wonderful person. He always seemed to have her comfort and wellbeing uppermost in his mind. Also, they were simpatico in so many ways, sharing similar feelings about world events, finding the same things amusing. Even when they bickered, it was never serious. Then one of them would crack a joke, and the tension would dissipate right away. They shared the same tastes in music, literature, TV, and movies, which had surprised her, given their age difference. Jack came across much more mature than his years. He'd made mention that the solitude in Hawaii had given him a lot of time to concentrate on a wide variety of things. Linda had been blown away by his unassuming intelligence and quick humor, which had only served to make her like him even more.

Every so often, Linda had to remind herself that her feelings were one-sided and always would be, but damn, she hated to do that. Sometimes the way he smiled at her made her almost feel like that wasn't the case, but it wasn't like she knew much about men. Graham had been her only frame of reference.

Of course, the thought of her ex was always like a bucket of ice water dumped over her head. And just like that, all Linda could think of was what Graham had said to her the day he left, which firmly reminded her that Jack was miles out of her league. If Graham didn't want her, what made her think this young, funny, sweet, caring man did? Or would? Like she'd told Eliza, even if she lost all the weight, he probably still wouldn't have wanted her.

In the shower, she crossed her arms over her chest — the only thing that *hadn't* expanded like the rest of her — and cried. It wasn't the wrenching sobs of before but just an overflow of salty liquid that washed away with the shower water. After a few minutes, she picked up the soap and cleaned herself off.

When Linda stepped out of the shower stall, she was relieved to see that she was blessedly alone. After she threw on her clothes and fixed her hair, she examined herself in the mirror, happy to see that her eyes weren't red-rimmed and her nose wasn't pink like she had expected. She looked a little flushed, but that could be attributed to the heat of the shower.

Taking a deep breath, she left the ladies' change room and headed for home.

While he waited, Jack noticed Amanda standing by the doors peering out the window. As she scanned the streets, she looked at her watch impatiently a few times, and he wondered what the hell she was doing. More time passed, and then he saw her smile and wave as a petite blonde headed up the walk. When she walked in, the two girls squealed and embraced, jumping up and down slightly, much to the excitement of most of the male population in the club.

Jack shook his head and turned in time to see Linda coming out from the back. She was looking down at the floor as she came toward him. When she finally glanced up, Jack smiled at her and noticed that her cheeks had a pretty pink blush to them, most likely from the hot shower she had just taken. With her hair up in a high ponytail and her large eyes framed with thick lashes, she looked sort of cute and much younger than when they had first met. He gestured for her to come over, and she rolled her eyes and gave him a little smirk.

"Yes, Master?" she asked when she was close enough for no one else to hear.

"I just wanted to make sure you were okay," he said, reaching out and giving her ponytail a tug. Her hair felt silky against his fingers. "You seemed more quiet than usual."

Linda frowned again and looked at the floor, as if she were contemplating something. It was driving him a little bit nuts, and he wished he knew what the hell was bothering her. Finally, she just shook her head and looked back up to him.

"It's nothing, really...Just feeling a bit out of it. That's all."

Just as he was about to tell her he didn't really believe her, he heard Amanda call his name. Frustrated, he turned to see her heading his way with the blonde.

"Jack," Amanda said excitedly, "this is Vicky. She just got hired here. Vicky, this is my housemate, Jack."

"Yeah, nice to meet you," he said quickly before turning back to Linda. He noticed she had gone quite pale as she looked at the new hire. When he looked back to Vicky, she was also looking at Linda in an incredulous manner.

"Mrs. Hunter?" the blonde said to Linda in a high falsetto. "What are you doing here?"

Mrs. Hunter? Jack thought, wondering if the girl had a case of mistaken identity.

"Hello, Vicky," Linda said in a resigned voice before adding wryly, "I'm here working out, pretty much like everyone else in the place. What are *you* doing here?"

"I'll be working here for the summer," Vicky replied somewhat smugly.

"Wonderful." Linda smiled tightly.

Jack was still reeling over the Mrs. Hunter part of the conversation as he watched the two women talk to one another. There was an obvious undercurrent of dislike that would have been more distracting if not for the fact that he just found out Linda had been using what must have been her maiden name this whole time and had never once mentioned a husband. Had he been wrong about her? Maybe her cougar skills were more sophisticated than his other clients.

"How is Mr. Hunter, anyway?" Vicky simpered.

Jack's ears perked up. *Yes, how is Mr. Hunter, Linda?*

"I'm sure Graham is fine, as usual," Linda returned, the tight smile making another appearance.

"Can you tell him I said hi?" Vicky asked sweetly.

"Sure thing. Well, as much as it's been fun catching up, I really have to go." Linda turned to Jack briefly. "See you in a couple days?"

"Wait, Linda—" he tried once more as she put up a hand to stop him.

"I really have to go."

Jack barely had a chance to say good-bye before she tore off for the front door. He followed her with his eyes until she was out of sight. He considered grabbing the little blonde and shaking till he got the story out of her, but he figured that wouldn't go over well.

"So, you're Jack," Vicky said, appraising him openly. "Amanda's told me a lot about you."

"Funny," he deadpanned, "she hasn't said a thing about you."

And with that, he walked to the employees' lounge, second-guessing his plan to permanently give up his designs as a serial killer.

Linda sat in her car behind the club and took some deep, cleansing breaths. Her forehead was pressed against the steering wheel, and she could feel the ridge of it digging into her skull. What a screwed-up day.

Vicky.

Even now, sitting in the car, Linda felt her hackles rising. The little twat. She had been a major bone of contention between Linda and Graham. The young girl had interned at Graham's company as his assistant. She had been invited into Linda's home and treated like family, only for Linda to become convinced later on that Graham had been fucking the girl behind her back. Of course, there had never been any proof. Her husband had always been too slick and sure of himself. He had also been very careful, but that hadn't quelled her suspicions. Linda would have bet an appendage that he had been shoving his teeny tiny dick into that girl, and Vicky had most likely pretended to like it.

To think that poisonous little viper had now weaseled her way into working at the same fitness club as Jack. And to make things worse, she seemed to be fast friends with his friend Amanda. Wonderful. She was just the kind of girl Jack would like. Or so Linda imagined. Blond, petite, frail, *skinny,* with big doe eyes and a porcelain complexion. She was young as well. About five years younger than Jack, which would put her at about twelve years younger than Linda.

She lifted her head and began banging it on the steering wheel. What a fucking mess. She was barely holding on to her sanity and wanted nothing more than to march back into the club to make sure that little witch wasn't casting some sort of voodoo spell on Jack.

But what right did she have to do that? Absolutely none. All she could do was hope that Jack had sense enough not to fall for Vicky's devious charms. With a sigh, Linda lifted her head from the steering wheel, started her car, and headed home.

That night, Jack stopped at the local diner to pick up food for himself and Amanda. He was still in a foul mood from the events of the afternoon and didn't feel like doing anything that required him to be social. He just wanted to go to his room and eat his burger in peace. Then he wanted to take out his frustrations on his unsuspecting guitar.

Jack also wanted a chance to figure out what the hell had happened this afternoon when he found out Linda was married. Between her odd behavior and the confrontation with the new hire, Vicky, he was a miserable bastard.

Something didn't really make sense. For starters, Linda had never used her married name, going by Tanner the whole time. But despite his flicker of doubt, he knew she hadn't done that because she was hot to trot for her new personal trainer. That had just been his paranoia talking. The woman hadn't even been able to look him in the eye when they had first met and was a weepy mess at the mere thought of having him as her trainer. It definitely hadn't been some crazy scheme to get to know him better.

So then what the hell was going on?

The way Linda looked when Vicky asked about her husband had been very odd. So had her answer. *I'm sure Graham is fine as usual.* What did the "I'm sure" part of that sentence mean? You didn't say something like that about a person you saw or spoke to daily. Perhaps they were separated? That would have made sense. But then why had Linda promised to send along Vicky's hello to her husband if they were no longer together?

Jack decimated his burger and fries as he tried to figure it all out. He didn't stop to wonder why the fact that Linda *Hunter* née Tanner being married even bothered him so much. All he knew was that it did indeed bother him, and he thought he'd combust if he didn't get some answers soon. But none would be coming because he wouldn't see Linda for another two fucking days. How he was going to make it that long he'd didn't know.

Balling up the greasy bag his food had come in, he tossed it in the trash can. He leaned over the side of the bed and picked up his guitar. After plucking at the strings, he tuned it a little before giving it a few test strums. Everything sounded good, and he launched into playing "Black" by Pearl Jam. It was a song he liked to play when he was in a bad mood. Maybe he should have asked himself why his mood was so dour, but he didn't.

After playing a few more songs, there was a gentle knock on his door.

"Yeah?" Jack kept playing, his head bent over the guitar.

"Hi," a timid voice said from the doorway.

His head jerked up, and he was surprised to see Vicky. He took a second to look over the small blond girl standing mostly in the hall. She had a pitiful look on her face, but that wasn't quite enough to make Jack feel sociable.

"What are you doing here?" he asked, frowning.

"Umm...Amanda invited me over to hang out."

"Okay. So, why are you knocking on *my* door?" He realized he was being rude, but he really preferred to be alone at the moment.

"Well...Jimmy came over, and..." Vicky glanced over her shoulder and turned back to him, shrugging slightly.

"Let me guess," Jack said in a flat tone. "They went upstairs to fuck and left you alone."

"Yeah," Vicky replied, her relief evident. "Anyway, I was looking for the bathroom and heard you singing..."

She trailed off suggestively, and Jack groaned internally. He really wasn't in the mood to entertain anyone tonight. Feeling a bit like a dick, he said, "Bathroom's up the hall to the left."

"Oh, okay," she answered, her shoulders slumping. She turned away from the door and started to close it behind her.

Jack muttered curses under his breath before finally calling, "Vicky!"

"Yeah?" she answered, sticking her head back into the room and looking at him with big, sad, puppy dog eyes.

"Come back when you're done," he said in resignation.

Vicky's face lit up, and Jack hoped he had made the right decision. She turned and bounced away down the hall. He took a deep breath and ran a hand through his hair in agitation. And then a thought came to him that maybe he could find out what the deal was between her and Linda. Suddenly, Vicky hanging around didn't seem like such a bad idea.

She returned quickly and stood just inside his room, looking around. Jack realized there wasn't anywhere else to sit except his bed. For a moment, he considered going with her out into the living room but figured it should be safe enough. The only curves he'd have his hands on tonight belonged to his guitar.

"You can sit down here, if you like," he mumbled and then re-thought that decision when Vicky flitted over to him with obvious excitement. *Here we go,* he thought with a sigh.

"You're a really good singer," Vicky gushed. "And you play awesome, too."

"Umm…thanks," Jack replied, speculating on just how long she had been listening outside his room before she knocked.

"So, how long have you been playing?"

"Long."

"Oh. Who taught you how to play?"

"No one you know."

"Oh."

Vicky shut up, and Jack continued to play. He had stopped singing, however, not wanting her to get the impression she was being serenaded. He was still in a bad mood, which had now just been compounded by Amanda's defection to have another sexual escapade with Jimmy, leaving him with this girl sitting on his bed.

Oh well, maybe she'd be good for something tonight after all.

"Hey, so, how do you know Linda Ta—uh, Hunter?"

"I used to intern as her husband's assistant," Vicky said offhandedly.

"How long ago was that?"

"Few months, I guess," Vicky answered, frowning. "Why?"

"No reason," he replied coolly. "Just asking."

"How do you know her?"

"She's my client."

"Oh, really? Yeah, I was surprised to see her there," Vicky said in a scornful tone. "I'm amazed she had the energy to drag her lazy ass to a gym of all places."

Now it was Jack's turn to frown. "What's that supposed to mean?"

"Well, you've seen her!" Vicky snickered. "She's a fat slob, and she treated her husband like shit. You should have heard the stories he told me."

Jack was torn between being pissed off at the girl for insulting Linda and curiosity about this husband of hers. Pissed off won. "Look, Linda's my client. I'd appreciate it if you didn't say things like that about her. She's working really hard to lose weight, which is more than I can say about a lot of people. And, plus, she seems really nice to me."

"That's 'cause you're not married to her, Jack." Vicky snorted, and Jack decided he hated the sound of his name coming from her lips.

"What am I saying? Like a guy who looks like you would ever go for a chick like *that.*"

"You know…" He put aside his guitar. "I think it's time for you to go."

"What did I say?" Vicky asked, turning innocent eyes on him. He wasn't fooled.

"I don't appreciate you cutting down my client," he replied. Getting off the bed, he went to the door and opened it all the way. "Good-bye."

"But, Jack…"

"Please go."

"All right," she said in a whisper, throwing her legs off of his bed and coming toward him. "Sorry."

Jack nodded but said no more.

When Vicky left, Jack closed the door behind her. This time, he made sure it was shut all the way.

5

Sunshine, a Scuffle, and a Song

Linda was daydreaming about Jack and congratulating herself on being down another five pounds as she walked through the parking lot in Baltimore, heading toward her office building. She usually made it into the city a few times a week to pick up her assignments and meet with her editors. Today was a Saturday, but there was still a buzz of activity as she entered the building. She made her rounds, talking to various coworkers before checking her e-mail. Generally, most of her work was done remotely, so there wasn't anything too pressing to attend to. She went over some article ideas with her team and then prepared to leave.

When Linda got outside, the sun was shining brightly, so she stood still for a moment, turning her face up into the rays. She had her eyes closed and a small smile on her face as she basked in the glow. Today was a good day, she thought. The only thing that would make it better was...

"Linda?"

She heard the smooth velvet voice and thought for sure she was daydreaming.

"Earth to Linda," he sang, laughing softly under his breath.

Slowly, she opened one eye, and then the other flew open. Jack was indeed standing right in front of her; she hadn't been dreaming after all.

"Hi," she said in surprise.

"Hi," he answered, still smiling largely, as if he was happy to see her. "What are you doing here?"

Linda pointed behind herself at the sign advertising the Baltimore Daily News.

"Oh, right! You told me you worked for the paper."

"Yeah," she answered, grinning like an idiot. Sunshine and Jack all in the same day. Linda was feeling lucky. "But what are you doing here?"

"I had a few errands to run, and then I…uh…have a gig to set up for."

"Gig?" Linda wracked her brains to remember if he had ever mentioned anything like this before. Not coming up with anything, she asked, "Gig for what?"

"Music," he replied, knuckling his forehead shyly. "I play guitar. There's a bar down the street that has an open mic night."

Before Linda could be suitably impressed and give Jack hell for not mentioning this before, something caught her eye. Turning the corner, there was Graham with his arm around a tall, raven-haired woman. He was whispering in her ear as she giggled at whatever he was saying. Because of this, he hadn't spied Linda yet.

"Shit!" she hissed, clamping down on Jack's arm and looking around frantically for somewhere to hide.

"Linda, what's—"

"Shh!" she said desperately. "My ex! He's coming this way."

Jack looked over his shoulder, and then in one smooth move he wrapped an arm around Linda's waist and spun her around so that she was pressed against the brick wall of the building. Before she could ask what he was doing, he took her arms and placed them around his neck, leaning into her closely. He bent his head so he could whisper in her ear, effectively blocking her face from the couple walking toward them.

"I don't think he saw you," Jack said softly, his breath tickling her ear.

She just shook her head, not trusting her voice not to squeak. She also didn't want Graham to hear her and potentially recognize it. Not that she would care so much, considering who was pinning her against the wall. It may have done that asshole some good to see a man as gorgeous as Jack all over her. Even if it was a farce.

Jack had one hand on her hip and the other braced against the wall, offering additional camouflage. His long, lean body wasn't fully pressed against her, but he was close enough that whenever she inhaled, her chest brushed lightly against his. And because he smelled so damned good, she was inhaling even deeper than usual. Here, out in the fresh air, there was nothing to mar his natural scent. Not like at the club, where there was always that miasma of perfumes, deodorants, and the faint odor of sweat. Right now, all she could breathe was Jack.

Linda's automatic reaction was to slide her hands up into the hair at the nape of his neck. She imagined it would be soft; it looked soft, and she so wanted to *touch*. The only thing that stopped her was the fear that Jack would think she was taking this too far and pull away before Graham and his little ho-bag had a chance to pass them fully.

As the other couple walked by, Jack moved his head so that he could switch sides. That way if Graham looked back, he still wouldn't recognize Linda. He kept his face close to hers, and their noses brushed softly, making her close her eyes for a fraction of a second. God, how she wished it was his mouth brushing hers instead. Her lips parted in anticipation of something she knew wasn't going to come, but her body reacted on instinct just the same.

"Almost safe," Jack said into her ear. He had brought his other arm up, and now she was trapped between them — not that she minded. This change made him shift his body so that it was even closer than before. His hips brushed against hers in a maddening way, if only because they were off limits.

"Get a room," she heard her ex mutter at them. She had to press her lips together to stifle a giggle.

Linda couldn't see Graham and the girl since Jack had his cheek almost pressed to hers, but she could hear them moving down the sidewalk. She almost wished they would stop right where they were and chat for a few hours, just so that she could enjoy the feel of Jack's body against her own for longer. Unfortunately, they kept walking, and after a couple of minutes, Jack pulled back slightly and grinned down at her. It didn't escape her notice that he left her hands around his neck and hadn't stepped away from her. Of course, she figured, he was just playing it safe.

"Thank you," she said in complete gratitude. "That could have been...ugly."

"Anytime." Jack brushed her hair back from her shoulder and looked conflicted. His eyes flickered down to her mouth for a moment before looking back into hers. She noticed they were a little darker than usual.

He reached up and took hold of her hands, reminding her that the act was over. She sighed internally as he eventually moved away from her body, but she was happy to see he didn't let go of her hands.

"So that was your ex, Graham?"

Graham? Graham who? she thought foggily. It took her a second or so to get her mental faculties in working order. Once that was accomplished, she nodded, still feeling a bit giddy. She probably should have been more upset about her husband and his mistress, but Jack and the way he made her feel eclipsed everything else.

"He sounds like an asshole," Jack said, and then, in an eerily accurate impression, he mimicked, "'Get a room!'"

Linda started to laugh at the look on Jack's face. He began to snicker, making it even more hilarious. Soon Jack joined her, and they stood laughing freely, without inhibitions, in the sunshine. It felt very nice, and Linda wasn't sure of the last time she had felt so happy and lighthearted.

"I guess I should get going," Linda said when their laughter died down. She was loath to let go of Jack's hands but did anyway.

"Oh," he said, frowning a little. "I thought maybe...Well, that's okay if you have to go."

"You thought maybe what?"

"Since you're here, would you—do you want to hear me play?"

Linda was surprised and touched that he would invite her to hear him sing.

"Yeah, I'd love to. What time is the show?"

"I have the eight o'clock slot," he told her, grinning happily.

"That's almost four hours from now," Linda mused. "I think I could go home and make it back in time."

"You don't have to go home."

"Well, I guess I could just go back to the office and work a little."

"Linda," Jack said, sounding slightly exasperated. "You don't have to go at all. We could, you know, hang out till then. I have to run into that store across the street, and there's a sound check in half an hour, but then maybe we can grab a bite to eat?"

She blinked at him stupidly, relatively sure her mouth was hanging open as well. In a few minutes, she'd start attracting flies. It sounded almost as if Jack was asking her out on a date.

"If you want," he was quick to add. "I know I 'work' for you, but we can hang out, right? Friends do that, don't they?"

"Yeah," Linda replied, perhaps a little woodenly. "Friends do that. Of course." She rolled her eyes and laughed a little for his sake, but she was kicking herself in the ass for ever thinking this was more than just a friendly overture.

"Great!"

"What store do you have to go to?"

"The music shop over there." Jack turned a little and pointed to a storefront where guitars were displayed. "I need a new guitar pick. Shouldn't take long."

"Okay." Linda peered at the store. "Why don't you go, and I'll meet you there? I just have to run this stuff to my car."

"Do you want me to come with you?"

"No, I'm just right over there," she said, gesturing to the parking lot beside the building. "We'll probably be done at the same time."

Jack nodded his assent, and they went their separate ways. Linda had needed these next few minutes to come to grips with the disappointment and remind herself that a man like Jack McAllister wouldn't be interested in a woman who looked like her. With a deep sigh, she tossed the knapsack holding her assignments into the backseat of her car. After a few more seconds, she started back toward the music store. Oh well, she supposed she should just enjoy tonight. Even if it wasn't a real date, she could always pretend.

Linda was so preoccupied with that idea that she didn't notice anyone else walking in her direction. Not even her soon-to-be ex-husband.

Jack was in a very good mood as he rifled through the jar of guitar picks. It was a superstition of his that he buy a new pick every time he played a gig, to bring him luck. Maybe one day he would find the pick that would set off his career. Maybe today was the day; he was feeling a little lucky.

Nothing was catching his eye as he fingered through the container. Finally, he just dug his hand straight to the bottom and grabbed a handful. He opened his fist and sifted through the ones he'd grabbed.

There it was, he thought suddenly, picking one out of the bunch. It had been lying in the center of his palm. It was a muted gray color with flecks of navy and swirls of silver that caught the light when he moved it. This was his choice. In some remote part of his brain, he recognized that he chose this specific guitar pick because it reminded him of Linda's eyes.

When he was at the counter paying, he looked at his watch and wondered why Linda hadn't joined him yet. Was she outside enjoying the sunny day?

Jack smiled when he thought of how he had found her, standing stock still, face raised to the sky with a peaceful, happy look. He'd watched her for a few seconds, examining how the sun shone on her hair, bringing out dark-gold highlights he'd never noticed before. He also had a chance to observe that her neck was long and slender. It was brought out in sharp relief since she'd had her head tipped back.

He hadn't wanted to disturb her but felt a little odd about watching her like that when she was unaware of his presence. Jack had decided to say hello and was happy he had, since that led to him inviting her to open mic night. For some reason, having a close friend come to see him play meant a lot to him. At least now he was guaranteed one friendly face in the audience.

He pocketed the guitar pick and walked out the door. What he saw there stopped him dead in his tracks. Linda was standing on the sidewalk with a hurt and haunted look on her face. Her ex was standing in front of her, sneering and spitting out words too low for Jack to hear. But what was worse was that he had Linda's upper arm in a grip so tight his hand looked like a bloodless claw digging into her flesh.

Unbidden, Jack had one singular thought that roared in his brain as he took everything in.

Mine.

He didn't stop to wonder where that had come from, or why, as a feeling of the murderous variety took him over. He stepped out onto the sidewalk. "Excuse me," he said in a deceptively calm voice. "Do you mind getting your hand off the lady's arm?"

Both heads swung toward him, Linda's showing nothing but relief while Graham just sneered. "Mind your own business, kid."

"I said," Jack continued, balling his fists at his sides, "get your hand off the lady."

"This *lady* happens to be my wife. That makes her my possession. Hasn't anyone told you that possession is nine-tenths of the law?"

"Wrong answer," Jack growled a fraction of a second before clamping his hand on Graham's wrist and squeezing it as hard as possible.

Not expecting such fierce retaliation from a stranger, Graham screamed and let go of Linda, which was Jack's desired effect. It took only a moment to wrench the man's arm behind his back and shove him up against the storefront.

Jack heard Linda inhale sharply, making a small noise as he pinned her ex with a forearm to the back of the neck. He leaned forward until his mouth was near the man's ear. "Didn't your mother teach you never to hurt a woman?" he said in a deadly voice as he punctuated the sentence with a shove of his forearm.

"Jack," Linda said in an undertone from behind him.

"You know this clown?" Graham hollered at her, and she whimpered a little.

"Do *not* talk to her," Jack seethed. "Shut your fucking mouth, right now."

When Graham snapped his mouth shut, Jack called over his shoulder, "Linda? Why don't you go wait in your car? I'll be there in a minute."

"What are you going to do?"

"Nothing. Graham and I are just going to have a little chat," he said in a conversational tone. From where Linda stood, he knew she couldn't see him press his arm against Graham's neck just a little bit harder. The man groaned slightly but wisely kept his mouth shut.

She didn't say anymore, merely turned on her heel and walked to where her car was parked. Jack watched until she was out of sight.

"Fucking useless *bitch,*" Graham spat, and for that, Jack wrenched his arm even higher at an almost impossible angle, making Graham squeal.

"I want you to listen to me closely," Jack hissed. "From now on, you do not talk to her, you do not see her, you do not *touch* her. If I hear you've come anywhere near her, I will find you."

"And do what?" Graham wheezed out belligerently.

"You don't want to find out. Trust me," Jack warned, all feint of civility dropped, his voice as sharp as a honed blade. "So go back to your little whore and leave Linda alone."

Graham inhaled sharply, and Jack could almost hear the clicks as the pieces fell into place. He recognized Jack as the guy from earlier. And he also figured out it was his wife who'd been pushed up against the wall. Jack couldn't give two shits that he'd recognized them. All he cared about was getting this guy away from Linda.

"Now," Jack said, back to his conversational tone. "I'm going to let you go, and you're going to walk away. Understood?"

Without waiting for a reply, he shoved Graham into the wall one more time before letting go of his arm and stepping away. He kept his stance loose and casual, but he was still tensed for action, just in case Linda's ex tried anything stupid. The man just pushed away from the wall angrily and adjusted his clothes. He was a pussy, just like Jack figured.

"You're lucky I don't call the cops on you," Graham said irately with dark, narrowed eyes and balled, impotent fists.

"Go ahead," Jack challenged. "I'm sure they would be very interested in the bruises on Linda's arm — the ones shaped like your fingers."

Graham's face paled, and Jack felt like punching him. If not for his promise to Linda that he was only going to talk, he would have. He did, however, plan to make good on his threat if he ever found out Linda's ex had come anywhere near her again. Baltimore wasn't that big of a city.

"Get the hell out of here before I change my mind," Jack sneered, stepping forward in a menacing manner, which caused the smaller man to flinch back. Turning on his heel, Jack headed toward Linda's car, keeping an ear out for an attack from behind. He wouldn't put it past the guy to pull a stunt like that. Jack actually wished he would so he'd have a reason to beat the ever-living fuck out of the loser for hurting Linda.

Nothing happened.

When he got to the parking lot, Linda scrambled out of her car. She looked him over. Her eyes were darting to and fro, checking perhaps for damage or maybe just signs of a struggle. "Are you okay?" she asked nervously when he was close enough to ask.

"Me?" he replied, hand on chest. "I'm fine. How are *you?*"

"I'm fine." She lifted one shoulder, trying to shrug it off, but she was a horrible liar. Jack could tell she was far from fine.

In a gentle voice, he asked, "What was he saying to you, Linda?"

"Nothing much." She shrugged again and looked down, shaking her head.

Jack slid a finger under her chin and lifted her face so he could see it. She avoided his steady gaze.

"Linda…tell me."

With a sigh, she looked into his eyes, and the hurt and pain he saw made him want to lock her in her car and go running back after that asshole. He kicked himself for wasting time in the music store and not going to find her sooner.

"Well…" She laughed uncomfortably. "He noticed I lost some weight. Then he told me that if I'd made this kind of effort when we were married, he might not have left my fat ass."

Jack hissed in anger, once again fighting the urge to find Graham and beat him to a bloody pulp. It was tempting, and Linda must have read the desire clearly on his face because she grabbed at his hand and held it tight. He closed his eyes and grimaced.

"Then I told him to fuck off, and he didn't like that very much."

Jack's chest rumbled as he came close to growling.

"It's fine," she said quickly. "He used to say stuff like that all time. Well, not exactly that…Just…stuff like that. Other…stuff…" She trailed off, her eyes clouding over and going somewhere distant.

"It's not fine," Jack ground out between clenched teeth. "Shit like that is not fine. I should have punched him while I had the chance."

She laughed thickly, and he noticed that her eyes had taken on the sheen of tears. "Maybe next time," she whispered in a choked voice.

"Linda," he sighed, and then he reached out to pull her to his chest.

She came willingly, if a little stiffly at first. It didn't take her long to exhale deeply and relax as her hands crept around his waist, stopping just above his hips.

Jack caressed her hair. He'd always loved how soft it was whenever he'd touched it before. Usually it was up in a ponytail, but now it was down against her back, the thick strands silky against his palms and fingers. This was the second time today he had been this close to her, and even though the first time had been as a favor to her, this time was not.

He could have just given her a quick hug and let go. That had been his original plan—to offer some comfort and then step back—but he found he didn't want to step back. Or let go. Her body was a soft weight against his, so very different from other women he had been with but not at all unpleasant. And nothing like he'd imagined it would be.

Jack thought about how he had felt when he saw Graham with his hand on Linda. That possessive, territorial, *confusing* urge that had come over him. It had been like nothing he'd felt before, and he didn't understand his feelings for this woman who had become much more than just his client.

But was she only just a friend? Or was this more?

Before he could give it more thought, Linda pulled away from him gently. She stepped back and patted a hand on his chest, keeping her eyes trained there. After a deep, cleansing breath, she whispered, "Thank you for being a good friend."

"Anytime," he replied in a low voice while giving her a small smile.

She returned it shakily. "Maybe I should just go home," she said, turning toward her car.

"What?" Jack said, suddenly losing his warm and fuzzy feeling. "No way. I'm not letting you out of my sight tonight."

"Exactly what do you think is going to happen to me, Jack?" She laughed breathily.

"I don't know," he said in a slightly panicked voice. "What if he comes to find you back in Arnold?"

"I doubt that's going to happen."

"Are you sure about that? Can you guarantee one hundred percent that he will not come after you tonight?"

"Well…no."

"Then you're staying with me," he said definitively. If he had to steal her keys, he would.

"Jack, you can't protect me forever, you know," she said, rolling her eyes and shaking her head at him.

"Why not?" He frowned down at her. "I want to know if that guy comes anywhere near you again."

"Jack," Linda said with a laugh, "I wouldn't even know how to get in touch with you if that happened."

"Give me your phone," he demanded, putting out his hand.

"What?"

"Your phone. Give it to me."

As Linda grumbled and fished around in her pocket for her phone, Jack realized he was being slightly irrational. Did he care? Not in the least. With a raised eyebrow, she stuck the small device in the palm of his hand, and it took him less than ten seconds to get his number entered and stored into it.

"There," he said with satisfaction. "Now you have no excuse not to call if he makes an appearance at your door."

"And you're going to drop everything and come running, right?" Linda snickered at him good-naturedly.

"Yes."

"All right," she drawled in an I'll-believe-it-when-I-see-it voice.

"So, tonight? You'll stay?" There was a hopeful note to his voice, and he tried to look as pathetic as possible so she would feel pity for him and be forced to stay.

A small smile was playing at the corners of her mouth. Finally, she nodded.

"Okay! Let's go!" Jack made his way around to the passenger side of Linda's car and waited patiently.

"What are you doing? The bar is just a few blocks up the street. We can walk."

"I want you to park over there," he told her and watched as she looked at him like he was being paranoid. "My car is there, and it'll be dark when you leave. I want to make sure you get in your car safely."

"Now you're just being silly," she huffed, putting her hands on her hips.

"Linda." Jack used the same tone he did at the gym. The commanding one. The one that told her he wasn't going to put up with any bull. It was a power play, and even though she pressed her lips together and glared at him, he knew she was going to do whatever he asked, despite her defiant appearance. He cocked an eyebrow to seal the deal.

"Yes, Master," she said, exhaling sharply and stomping to the driver's side door.

When the automatic locks sprang up, he grinned and got into the car.

"Linda?" a high voice said from behind her. She spun around at the sound of her name. *Everyone was coming out of the woodwork in Baltimore today,* she thought as she saw Cici from the clothing store.

"Hey, Cici!" Linda smiled at the girl. "What are you doing here?"

"My boyfriend Rob plays in a band," Cici said, smiling widely and pointing at the men currently on stage doing a sound check. "He does the open mic nights most weeks. I'm the one who told Jack about them."

"How exactly do you know Jack?" Linda asked curiously. It seemed like such a strange friendship.

"He came in the store looking for his friend—you know, Amanda?"

Linda nodded.

"She was still trying on clothes, so we got to talking. I gave him a ton of my business cards to pass out to clients." At this, Cici cut her eyes toward Linda and grinned slightly before continuing. "It was a match made in heaven."

"I guess so," Linda said, laughing slightly.

"Yeah, so I ran into him at the grocery store and mentioned coming here to hear Rob play, and the rest is history! What are you doing here?"

"Umm...I ran into Jack, and he asked me if I'd come see him play. So, here I am."

Linda figured it was easier just to tell Cici the short version of the story. No point in getting into all the gory details. It wasn't like it was a lie, since that had been what actually happened before the confrontation with Graham. She shuddered as she thought about it. Running into him had been brutal, and he'd started to say the most horrible things to her until Jack had walked out and seen them. Linda had never been so happy to see anyone in her life and had been somewhat stupefied at the force of Jack's reaction to what was happening.

Stupefied and a little turned on.

To have someone champion for her and defend her from the man who had tormented her so much had been a blessed relief. To, for once, not feel *alone* in all of this made her want to sag to the pavement and bawl her eyes out like a little kid. It certainly helped that her hero was also a man she had come to care for very much. Watching him manhandle her ex had to be one of the single most incredible sights ever.

"Lindaaaa…" Cici waved a hand in her face, bringing her back to the present.

"Oh, sorry! What were you saying?"

"I was saying that you and Jack should come out with me and Rob for dinner," the girl said excitedly. "Say you will?"

"Umm…I'll have to check with Jack, but I think that'd be okay."

"Yay!" Cici crowed, bouncing on her toes and clapping her hands together. Linda secretly wondered if the girl should be taking Ritalin. She was like a puppy on speed.

The din on stage had died down as Rob and his band stopped playing. They seemed satisfied with the way things sounded in the small bar. When they had all ambled off the stage, Jack walked on with a chair in one hand and a guitar in another. The guitar was a beautiful, wide acoustic number, the wood varnished to a shiny golden hue. She could tell by the way he carried it with care that it was a precious instrument to him.

Jack placed the chair in front of a lone microphone in the middle of the stage, threw the strap of the guitar over his head, and then sat down. With both hands, he expertly handled the mic and lowered it so that it was in front of his face. With the adjustments done, he turned back to the guitar resting against his leg and ran his hands up the neck and along the front of it. He positioned his fingers and began strumming out a few bars of a song.

How had she never noticed how magnificent his hands were?

The world stopped when he leaned forward a little and began to sing. Linda was mesmerized. She hadn't quite known what to expect, but this resonant tenor was not it. The sound of it seemed to pierce straight through to her soul. He sang a song she didn't recognize, and she wondered if perhaps he had written it himself. Even if he hadn't, the man was talented; this much she knew for a fact. She wondered why in hell he was wasting that talent on being a personal trainer.

Jack stopped singing and moved on to a faster song, his hands moving fluidly, as if with no conscious thought. He didn't sing this time around, and Linda mourned the loss of that angelic voice. She couldn't wait to hear him sing tonight. He would be performing three to four songs, and she hoped they all had lyrics. After a few more minutes, he stopped and nodded toward the back of the bar, indicating he was done, and then left the stage.

"He's really good," Cici said after a few seconds.

"Yeah," Linda breathed. As if she needed *another* thing to make Jack more attractive to her.

Cici's boyfriend came over to them, and introductions were made. Jack joined them shortly afterward, and she tried not to moon at him like a lovesick groupie. When Cici brought up the idea of everyone going out for dinner, Jack looked at Linda and raised a shoulder in a silent question. She nodded and smiled at him, and they all headed out of the bar to a diner down the street.

"You're really good," Linda said to him quietly. They had fallen behind chattering Cici and her more laid-back counterpart.

"Thanks," he replied, squinting and running a knuckle down the bridge of his nose. It was something she noticed he did when he seemed nervous or embarrassed. Linda wondered if he was second-guessing his invitation to her.

"Do you regret asking me to come?"

"What?" he asked in surprise, turning his face to her. "No! I'm glad you're here. I wanted you to come…but it can still be a little…I don't know…"

As they walked in silence for a bit, she could feel that he was trying to figure out a way to express himself better.

"Soul baring," he continued softly. "It makes you feel vulnerable. Like laying yourself all out there."

"I make you feel vulnerable?" Linda asked in an astounded voice.

"Yeah, a little bit."

"But you sing in front of strangers."

"But I don't care what *they* think of me."

Jack looked at her askance as Linda absorbed what he'd said. In a way, she understood how he felt. Was it any different than their sessions? She seemed to be so much more embarrassed by Jack seeing her in unflattering positions than she did about anyone else in the gym. But that was because she cared for him...

Linda glanced back up at Jack slowly. Could it be possible he felt something for her? Before her mind ran wild, she reined it in fiercely. Thinking like that was liable to cause her a ton of grief. Jack had said she was his friend. That was all.

"Well," she said slowly, "I think you're incredible." Jack beamed at her, and she felt her heart thump just a little bit harder in her chest. He didn't know that she meant all of him, not just his music.

Dinner was a lot of fun. Rob was quite the entertaining storyteller, and something about his presence calmed Cici down so that she wasn't quite so manic. You could tell they loved each other very much, and it was sweet and sickening to be with them. Linda smiled fondly at the young couple even as she wished that she and Jack could be like that. She sighed internally and glanced over at him often during dinner.

They almost didn't make it back in time for Jack's set, but luck was with them, and he slipped backstage as Cici and Linda found a table close to the front. They clapped wildly when he came onto the stage, making him blush as he prepared the mic. She held her breath when he started to play and then let it out in a slow exhale as he began to sing. It was even better the second time around, and she couldn't take her eyes off him. She knew that in a way she was being rude by ignoring Cici so completely, but the girl didn't seem to mind. She glanced back and forth between Linda and Jack with a speculative look on her face. Linda knew she wasn't doing that great of a job hiding her adoration, but there was simply no way to mask what she was feeling.

After the third song, Jack spoke into the microphone. "This will be my last song of the night." He smiled sweetly as quite a few patrons of the bar began to boo. It didn't escape Linda's notice that most of them were women. Jack looked directly at her before starting to speak again. "I'd like to dedicate this song to a very special friend. It's called 'Such a Lonely One' by Prairie Oyster."

He began strumming his guitar, and then his voice filled the bar once more. Linda listened to the words of the song, and it was almost as if it had been written with her in mind. He kept eye contact with her when he reached the chorus, and she felt tears prickle.

Jack's tenor carried beautifully as he sang. There was resounding applause when he stood and made a small bow to the audience.

Linda was busy collecting herself. She got it all under control by the time Jack joined them at the small table. When he sat beside her, he reached for her hand and gave it a small squeeze. She smiled at him appreciatively and mouthed, "Thank you."

They stayed until Rob's band played, and Linda was surprised at how much fun she'd had. Jack, true to his word, walked her to her car like an absolute gentleman. He thanked her for staying and then bent and brushed his lips across her cheek in farewell. The spot tingled the whole way home, and she could have sworn he was with her the entire way.

6
You're Moving In Where?

Jack burst into Amanda's room without bothering to knock. He didn't particularly care that Jimmy was humping her like a bunny at the time.

"Jack!" she hollered when she saw him, making a frantic grab for a blanket to cover them with.

"The name's *Jimmy*," their boss growled at her.

"Not you!" she yelled, smacking at his shoulder. "Him!"

"How could you tell Vicky she could move in without asking me first?" Jack bellowed at her.

Jimmy jerked at the sound of his voice, and then he joined Amanda in the mad grab for covers. "Dude! What the fuck?"

"You, shut the hell up," Jack yelled, directing his fury momentarily on his perhaps soon-to-be ex-boss before turning back to his buck-ass naked roommate. "Well?"

"She needed a place to stay!" Amanda yelled back, finally pushing Jimmy away and facing off with Jack. "She told us at dinner that she'd been trying to find a place to live here in town over the last couple weeks and hadn't had any luck. So, I told her she could crash here till she found something. Jeez!"

"And you didn't even stop to think about how I would feel about that?" he asked loudly, throwing his hands up in the air.

"Well, I didn't think you'd have puppies over it, Jack." Amanda glared at him while Jimmy hunted around for his clothes. He'd obviously recognized that sexy-time was over. Jack stared at him balefully.

"How exactly did you think I'd react? Or did you even get that far?" he continued, training his scowl back on Amanda.

"I'm...uhh...I'm gonna head out, then," Jimmy mumbled. He made a dash to the door wearing just a pair of boxers, his shirt and jeans held over his crotch as he took his leave.

"Thanks a lot, Jack," Amanda said, waving her arm toward the departed man and hitching the sheets up higher on her chest.

"I don't give a shit about Jimmy. I want to know what gives you the right to just invite anyone you please to live with us."

"Oh, relax! It's just for a little while till she finds a place to live."

"You don't even *know* her!" Jack stressed, his voice rising again. "What if she's an axe murderer or a thief?"

"Dramatic much? Come on, Jack." Amanda rolled her eyes and shook her head. "Jimmy did a background check on her; he does with all his employees."

That stopped Jack for a moment. "Really?" he asked curiously. "Even us?"

"Yes, even us."

"Huh," he huffed and then shook his head, getting back on track. "Anyway, I'm still pissed off that you didn't even *ask* me!"

"I'm sorry. I honestly didn't think you'd give a shit."

"I don't want her living here," he hissed between clenched teeth, lowering his voice finally. He realized there was a good chance Vicky was at the bottom of the stairs, listening to the yelling going on in the bedroom.

"What am I supposed to do, Jack?" Amanda answered, also lowering her voice. "Kick her out onto the streets?"

Jack contemplated that for a second before coming back to himself. "Well, can't she stay at a hotel or something?"

"I don't know if she has enough cash to do that. She's just starting a new job, you know. And plus, I *promised.*"

"Mandy..." Jack whined, running his hands through his hair and making it stand on end.

"Come on, Jacky," she whined back. "We have the extra bedroom. It's just temporary."

"Fuck me," he groaned, flopping down on the side of the bed and scowling at his friend.

"Ew," Amanda replied, crinkling her nose at him, and he started laughing despite himself. Amanda grinned and started chuckling as well. They'd been together since they were kids and had passed into the realm of a brother-sister-like relationship a long time ago. Jack had never considered her in *that* way, and he knew she felt the same.

"I really *am* sorry," she said after a few moments. "If I knew you'd be so pissed, I never would have asked her to crash here. I swear."

"I know."

"Do you want me to ask her to leave?"

Jack looked at Amanda to gauge how serious she was. He knew that if he put his foot down, she would ask Vicky to go. She wasn't even pouting or giving him the guilt-trip face. He could tell she felt really bad for not taking his opinion into consideration. That almost made up for her inviting the girl to stay without asking him. But not quite.

"No," Jack sighed, finally, before offering a grudging reply. "I guess she can stay for a bit."

"Are you sure?"

"Yeah. But if anything goes missing or there's any funny business, I'm kicking her out."

"No problem." Amanda nodded solemnly.

"And it's only *tem-po-ra-ry*."

"Swear." Now she crossed her heart with her finger.

Jack rolled his eyes at her and exhaled sharply. They sat in silence for a while longer.

"I guess I'd better find Vicky," Amanda said, reaching down to grab a shirt and pulling it over her head as Jack turned away. "She's probably freaking out or something."

Jack picked up Amanda's shorts and flung them at her as he got off her bed. "I'll let *you* deal with it. I'm going to sleep," he said, heading for the door. As he ran down the stairs, he was pretty sure he saw a girl-sized shadow flee into the living room. He grumbled to himself while he headed down the hallway back to his bedroom.

For the first time in he didn't know how long, he shut and locked his bedroom door.

Linda's morning started off badly. When she walked out of her house, she noticed that her headlights had been left on all night. There was barely any illumination coming from them at all. She cursed to herself as she ducked back inside to grab her keys. Hopefully she could still get the battery to turn over to run the engine long enough to charge it.

When she stuck the key in the ignition and turned it, the car chugged grudgingly and then died. "Come on, come on, come on," Linda whispered under her breath as she tried again. This time, all she heard were the muted clicks of a dead engine. "Damn it!" she yelled, smacking the heel of her hand on the steering wheel.

She headed back into the house and called Tony. He answered on the first ring. "What did you do now?" he asked unceremoniously, making Linda laugh.

"Hi to you, too!"

"Spare me the bullshit, Linda. You never call me in the mornings unless you've done something to your car or you need a ride to the hospital."

"You suck."

"But you love me." He chuckled warmly.

She ducked her head and mumbled in a rush, "I ran down my battery."

"I *knew* it!" Tony crowed triumphantly, and Linda cringed.

"*Tonyyy…*"

"Oh, don't whine at me. Is it an emergency? 'Cause I'm kinda swamped this morning."

"Not an emergency. I don't need it until this afternoon."

"Oh, okay. That works. I'll come jump your car then."

They decided on a time and said good-bye. Sure enough, Tony was on her doorstep about seventeen minutes before she was scheduled to be at her appointment with Jack. He gave her engine a boost and then stood by the car as it ran. "So where are you going?"

"To the gym."

"That's it?" he asked, frowning down at her.

"Yeah, why?"

"Linda, you need to charge the battery. A five-minute drive probably isn't going to be enough. It'll likely be dead again by the time you're done."

"Ah, shit!" she groused, giving her car the evil eye.

"That's okay," Tony said amicably. "Hop in. I'll drive you and then take the beast out to the garage. I'll pick you up when you're done. That way, if it dies, I can start it up again before I get you."

"I love you, Tony," Linda replied, batting her lashes at him in dramatic adoration.

"I know it."

He disconnected the cables, put them away, and then turned off his truck, pocketing the keys as Linda slammed her hood closed and got into the passenger side of her car. Tony mumbled as he tried to push her seat back to fit his massive frame while she giggled at him. They had always gotten along well since they were kids, originally thrown together because their fathers played cards.

They had tried to kiss once as young teens, both of them pulling back and making faces. Something just hadn't been right. That had been the end of that, but they'd still remained close. Linda had met Graham not long after, and Tony had always just played the field, never really finding someone to settle down with and mostly happy to be on his own, working in his shop with his two best friends.

"Hi," Linda said brightly when she saw Jack waiting for her at the gym.

"Hello to you, too," he replied, his pretty green eyes crinkling in amusement. She could have sworn there was also a hint of mischief in them. "Hey, do you mind if we do your private session today instead of Wednesday?"

"Not at all."

Before they could leave, Linda heard her name being called from the front of the club. "Hey, Lin!" She turned to see Tony jogging up to her. "I forgot to ask what time to pick you up."

"Oh," she answered. "Hour and a half or so?"

"See you then!" He waved and ran back out the door. She laughed as he hopped in her car, which he'd left running at the curb, and sped off.

"Who was that?" Jack asked from behind her.

She turned, surprised to see him frowning all of a sudden.

"Oh, that's my friend Tony," she answered waving a hand around. "Car fail."

"But…wasn't *that* your car?"

"Yeah. Battery died. Tony came over to give me a jump start. Now he's going to run it around town for me to recharge it."

"Sounds like a good friend," Jack grumbled at her, and she shot him a perplexed look. He hadn't quite stopped frowning.

"Yeah, he is. So, let's go!"

Jack turned around and headed to the back of the club with Linda following and sighing internally as she watched him walk. He moved so gracefully. His wide shoulders rolled with every stride, his arms swung casually, and his legs flexed and released with his steps. She also had the rare opportunity of checking out his backside, which was quite simply perfect. What she wouldn't do to be able to get her hands on it, just once.

As soon as the door closed behind them, Jack unzipped his jacket and started tearing at it, removing the thing and tossing it on the floor. Linda gaped at him as he revealed what was underneath.

"Thank God," he said in a relieved voice. "I was dying of heat in that thing!"

She just stood there and blinked like a moron as he paced around pulling the tight muscle shirt away from his chest to try to air it out. While most of the T-shirts he wore were relatively form fitting, they weren't anywhere near as tight as this black ribbed one. The fabric clung to every muscle on his torso. She thought for sure if he stood still long enough, she'd be able to count his abs. It also showcased his spectacular arms. Usually she only got a peek at his biceps on occasions when his sleeves slid up, but now they were on full display. His beautifully sculpted triceps popped out enticingly as his arms moved.

And to top it off, Linda noticed for the first time that Jack's entire shoulder was covered in an intricate tattoo. It looked like a coiled dragon, but from this distance, she couldn't tell for sure. She didn't know why that tattoo excited her so much, but for some reason it did. She resisted the urge to go up and run her fingers over it.

"Oh, man," Jack sighed. "That's so much better."

"Why didn't you just take off your jacket before?" Linda asked in confusion.

"Are you kidding?" he asked, goggling at her. "I couldn't walk around out there like this! Mrs. Bellham already tries to stare up my shorts. I'd never get her off me if I wore this getup out there."

Linda started laughing at the visual of Candy Bellham wrapped around Jack like a Koala bear. "Then why did you wear it?"

"I didn't get a chance to do laundry," he admitted sheepishly, turning a bit pink about the cheeks.

Linda laughed harder.

"It's not funny! Some of these chicks are friggin' animals!"

"I'm sorry." Linda chuckled, trying hard to sober up in the face of his indignation. Then she felt a little guilty for ogling him earlier. "Aren't you afraid I'm going to molest you too?"

"Nah," he replied, shrugging slightly. "It's different with you."

Different? Linda wondered what was so different. Was it that he felt comfortable enough around her because they were friends? Or was it that he thought she wouldn't care? Maybe he just figured that she'd be too scared to ever try anything, anyway. And he would be right.

Because she was so distracted by Jack and all the skin he was showing, Linda had neglected to notice something balanced on top of the yoga ball. Frowning, she walked up to it and looked down in disbelief at the newspaper perched on top. But not just any newspaper. It was the Baltimore Daily News. And not just any page. It was flipped specifically to *her* article.

"Why, you curious bugger," she said in a low voice, only to hear laughter ring out behind her.

"I was wondering how long it would take you to notice," Jack said amusedly. "Really, Linda? You're a *gossip columnist?*"

Putting her hands on her hips and huffing, Linda turned toward the chiding voice. She was almost annoyed enough not to become sidetracked once more by his stellar body. Almost.

"Well, someone has to do it!"

Jack reached past her to snatch up the newspaper. "Angie or Jen?" he mocked. "The battle for Brad continues!"

"Say what you will, Jack," she said, feeling slightly rankled, "but people want their gossip, and I actually enjoy my job. So there!"

"Yeah," he said, looking at her and smiling sweetly. "I mean, how many people do you know that do something they love? I'm jealous."

"Have you ever thought about trying to be a musician for a living?"

"That's a pipe dream, Linda." He smiled sadly and turned away.

"Jack, you're really talented," she protested.

"So are a lot of people. I figure right now, I may as well take advantage of the gifts I have while I can," he said, placing a hand on his chest. "Can't do this forever, you know? And when that ends, I'll figure something else out to do. Maybe I'll open my own gym. If a blockhead like Jimmy can do it, I should be able to, right?"

"But—"

"Come on. Let's get started," he replied curtly, effectively shutting the door on that conversation.

Their session started off a little more morosely than Linda would have liked. Especially since both of them had been in such good moods previously. She felt bad for bringing up his music and hearing him doubt he could do it professionally; that was the complete opposite of what she felt. She thought Jack was wildly talented, and it was a shame that he practically kept it to himself.

As they went through the motions, Jack started to unwind a little, and she noticed he seemed less serious. As her worry for his well-being lessened, her focus on his body increased. That shirt was absolutely killing her. The ripple of Jack's muscles underneath the fabric and his bare arms brushing against hers, flexing and releasing as he helped her with the harder positions, was driving her crazy. She was in a constant state of distraction throughout their whole session.

Now she really understood why he'd been wearing the warm-up jacket, and if she wasn't enjoying the sight of his body so much, she'd wish he'd put it back on.

It was because he was turning her on so much that when Jack asked her in the middle of doing crunches if she'd given any thought to what her reward would be, that her true answer went sailing from between her lips before she had a chance to censor it.

"I want to get fucked," she said while on the rise. "Hard."

Jack's eyes nearly popped out of his head at her crude statement. She figured since the cat was out of the bag, she might as well just continue. Her words were punctuated each time she executed a body curl. "I want…one night…of raw…pure…*sex*. All night…Every position." Linda collapsed to the ground, breathing heavily. "*That's* what I want."

It was then that what she'd actually said hit her. Her legs were socked between Jack's, his hands were on her knees to keep her stable, and he was much too close. Linda was completely mortified at her admission, and even though her face was already red due to exertion, she felt it flame even hotter as she stared up at the ceiling in utter humiliation.

"Oh, God," she groaned, throwing both arms over her face. She was too ashamed to even look at Jack. "Just…agh…can you just forget I said all of that?"

"Why?" he asked her in a low voice.

"Just 'cause," she begged, still unable to look at him. "That wasn't supposed to come out. It's just been a…*really* long time. And plus, it's not like it's ever going to happen."

"Why not?" he asked again, his voice still low, curious, almost seductive.

"Because I have no one to *do* it with." Linda thought her level of embarrassment couldn't have gotten any worse. It turned out she was wrong. Having to admit to Jack that no one would fuck her was about as rock bottom as she could get.

And then he said the one thing that made her heart completely stop.

"What if it was me?"

Jack stared down at Linda in stunned disbelief. He couldn't believe that he had just offered her his sexual services. He wasn't sure why, but when she admitted what she wanted her reward to be, unlike before when his visualization of doing more with her had failed, this time, images pounded into his brain of him and Linda in every sexual position imaginable.

Maybe it had something to do with the irrational jealousy he'd felt over that guy Tony. Even though Linda told him they were just friends, how did he know that she wouldn't ask *him* to fuck her senseless? And how did he know that Tony wouldn't just say yes? Something about that huge guy all over Linda had made Jack rage. For some inexplicable reason, he wanted to make sure that if anyone was with Linda, it would be him.

It could also be the fact that when she had said she wanted to be fucked—*hard*—his cock had given an almighty jerk in his pants, practically volunteering for the job. Apparently his mouth was on the same damned wavelength, because before he knew it, he was asking her if she'd let him be the one. In his head, he had added the *to fuck you hard.*

Linda kept her arms over her face for a moment, which was good and bad. Good because he didn't know if he could look her in the eye yet. And bad because now he couldn't help staring at her breasts, which were currently pulled up high and round against her shirt because of her position. This was certainly not helping his resolve, and the unbidden thoughts from just a second ago were circling back through his mind. There was one in particular where he was lifting up her shirt and fastening his mouth to one of her nipples.

His cock jerked again, and for a second, he thanked the Lord that Linda's bent legs blocked from her view the erection that was currently tenting the front of his shorts. Shit. He'd have to figure out a way to hide the damned thing. Jack eyed his jacket tossed in the corner. It seemed a million miles away.

All of these thoughts took less than a minute to process, and Jack realized that in that timeframe, Linda hadn't said a word. He wasn't sure if that was a bad sign.

"'Scuse me?" she finally squeaked out, keeping her arms over her face.

Lie! his brain screamed. *Deny it! It's not too late to take it back and make yourself look like less of an ass!*

His cock and his mouth disagreed. Apparently they had taken the lion's share of the decision-making ability today.

"I…uh…" He cleared his throat. "I said, what if it was with me?"

"Are you shitting me?" she asked, her voice full of disbelief.

"Uhh…no."

Linda finally threw her arms away from her face and sat up partially, resting her weight on her elbows. She squinted up at him with her head cocked to the side. "Look…Jack. I appreciate the great lengths you're going through to get me into shape, but this may just be a little bit *above and beyond.*"

"You're starting to give me a complex," Jack complained. "What's wrong with *me?*"

"What's *wrong* with you?" Linda sputtered, looking at him like he'd grown another head. "What's wrong with *you?*"

"Yeah!"

"What's *wrong* with him, he asks!" Linda laughed, throwing herself backward and cackling, as if she had lost her mind.

Jack was nonplussed. "Linda, what the hell?"

"There is absolutely *nothing* wrong with you, Jack! That's the problem!" Linda was still lying on her back but waving a hand in his general direction. "Jesus, you are as damned close to perfection as a human being can get!" She ran her fingers along her forehead and frowned. "What's *wrong* with you?" she said with a snort, shaking her head.

"I don't get it." Jack was torn between being mollified and utter confusion. By the sounds of it, Linda thought he was attractive, so then why was it so difficult to accept his offer? On the upside, his cock had completely deflated during the course of this conversation.

"You don't get it?" Linda asked, propping herself up on her elbows again.

"No."

"Jack, why would someone who looks like *you* ever in a million years fuck someone who looks like *me?* Besides pity, of course."

"What the hell is wrong with *you?*" he asked, now completely frustrated.

"What's wrong with me?" Linda threw herself down again. "What's wrong with *me,* he asks."

"Are we going to do this again? And why would you automatically assume it was just a pity fuck?"

"Because what else would it be?"

If Linda hadn't sounded so sad right then, he probably would have been really pissed off at her. They stared at one another in silence for a moment. Jack had no idea what to say to make her understand that maybe he just wanted to be with her for her own sake and nothing more. And wasn't that a sobering thought? He wasn't quite sure when it had happened, but in the last couple months of getting to know Linda better, he had started to care for her well beyond what he'd thought possible after their first meeting.

"Linda—"

Before he could get any further, the door to the room swung open. Amanda poked her head in and gave them an odd look, as if she were trying to puzzle something out in her head.

"Oh, there you guys are," she said after a moment. "Hey, Linda, there's this huge hunk of man waiting for you at the front."

"That's Tony." Linda scooted away from Jack, and he felt a distinct sense of loss.

"Good job!" Amanda said, giving her a thumbs-up, to which Linda smiled weakly.

"He's not my boyfriend, Amanda. Just a good friend."

"Oh!"

Jack groaned internally as he saw that telltale twinkle in Amanda's eyes before she disappeared, leaving them alone.

Linda had gotten up and was already at the door. She turned back but wouldn't look him in the eyes. "I'll think of something else…Just forget I said anything, okay?"

As she slipped through the door, leaving Jack alone in the aerobics room, her words echoed in the empty space. He realized then that he didn't want her to think of something else. And he didn't want to forget what she'd said. He wanted to keep his original promise, and he wished Linda did, too.

7
The Hidden Meaning Behind Pinky Wiggles

Linda didn't even bother taking a shower. She just ran out of the aerobic room as if something was chasing her. And something was. Her complete and utter mortification over what had just happened with Jack. No matter how fast she went, she couldn't outrun it.

Stupid! Stupid! Stupid! Linda chanted in her head. What the hell was she thinking blurting out something like that in front of Jack? And poor, sweet boy that he was, he'd offered himself up like some sacrificial lamb to the pathetic sex-starved moron who couldn't get any from anyone else.

It was enough to make her choke on her own idiocy.

She almost expected Jack to come after her and was relieved that he didn't. How could she possibly explain the subsequent conversation to Tony? Knowing him, he'd probably feel obligated to offer up his dick for loan too! Linda groaned at the possibilities. Perhaps the men would sit there and squabble over who had more of a right to be the martyr in that situation. Dueling penises. She snorted at the visual and smiled for the first time since that whole doomed conversation. It was short-lived as she remembered the humiliation of what happened.

Tony was standing at the reception desk, letting Amanda feel one of his flexed biceps. The girl was the epitome of feminine wile: all batting lashes, pouty lips, and flirtation. Her body contorted to show off all her assets. Linda hated her at that moment. Not because Amanda was setting her sights on Tony, but because she was everything Linda wished she could be. Young, thin, sexy, and desirable. Amanda would never have needed to guilt someone into fucking her. She wouldn't even have to *ask*. It was obvious by the way men looked at her that they would be begging to take her home. Did someone like Amanda even fully understand the power she wielded? Did she grasp how much easier life was for someone who looked like her as opposed to someone who looked like Linda?

She hesitated for a second, not wanting to intrude. Then she thought, *Screw it.* Linda just couldn't stay here a moment longer, so she marched up to the couple. "Ready to go?" she asked without preamble.

Tony turned and grinned at her. "Hey, Lin. Yeah, sure." He turned to a now pouting Amanda. "Maybe I'll see you around sometime?"

"Maybe," she said, batting her eyelashes in a "definitely" kind of way.

"I'll just, uh, wait outside," Linda said, snatching her keys from Tony's loose hand.

She walked to the back of the building, got in her car, and stuck the key in the ignition. Linda cringed as she turned it, expecting the car to not start. That would be just her luck, being unable to escape the club and, subsequently, Jack. The engine turned over with no problems at all, and she breathed a sigh of relief. She was also relieved to see Tony jogging to her car.

"Sorry to keep you waiting," he said before facing her with a lazy grin on his face.

"You know she has a boyfriend, right?"

Tony just shrugged in a nonchalant way, indicating that wasn't really his concern, and Linda sighed dramatically. It wasn't her concern either. Amanda and Tony were adults; what they did in their spare time was none of her business. Currently, she was still eyeball-deep in regret and didn't have much mind space for anyone or anything else at the moment. She pulled out of the parking lot and headed home.

It wasn't until after Linda showered that she realized she'd left her knapsack in the aerobics room of the club. She'd been so intent on getting the hell out of there that she had completely forgotten to grab her bag by the door. Linda shoved her forehead in her hands and groaned. If it were only her clothes, she wouldn't have cared so much, but she'd left her wallet in the bag as well. She had to drive down to Baltimore tomorrow to meet with her editor, and she would need her ID, not to mention her bank card so she could fill up her tank.

Looking at the clock, Linda noticed that the gym was closing soon, and she probably wouldn't make it back in time. She wasn't too keen on the idea of seeing Jack again, either. She'd have to wait until the morning and sneak in, hoping her bag would be waiting at the front for her.

She was in the middle of contemplating what to eat for dinner when there was a soft knock at the door. Not thinking much of it, she walked to her foyer and yanked the door open, only to find an embarrassed-looking Jack on her doorstep, holding her knapsack. Linda felt her face turn beet red as soon as she made eye contact with him, their entire conversation from the club shouting in her head.

"You forgot this," he said, breaking the silence. He held out the bag, and she grabbed it awkwardly.

"How did you know where I lived?"

"Your, uh, driver's license had your address." Jack dropped his gaze to the floor and looked uncomfortable for a second.

"Oh, okay…thanks. So I guess I'll see you Wednesday?" *Please say yes. Please say yes…* Linda was terrified that he would now feel too awkward after her crazy sex admission.

"Actually, do you think I could come in for a second?" Jack's eyes flipped back up to hers, and he had such an earnest expression on his face, Linda found herself nodding and stepping back so he could walk in.

This was it. She fully expected Jack to call the whole thing off. He was too polite to make her waste her time by coming to the club, and she guessed he hadn't wanted to do it while standing outside on her porch either. Linda tried not to walk like she was going to the gallows as she led him into her living room and perched on the edge of her couch. Jack hesitated and then joined her, sitting at the complete opposite end. She tried not to cringe, thinking he was probably afraid to be alone with her now and had secretly added her to the ranks of perverted women who threw themselves at him on a daily basis.

Although she hadn't really thrown herself at him. And it was Jack who suggested he be the one she use for her reward.

Linda hadn't given that too much thought. She figured he had only said it to make her feel better but hadn't planned on actually *acting* on it. At least she hadn't humiliated herself further by jumping at the opportunity. That would have been much, much worse.

Jack was leaning forward and had his forearms against his thighs. He remained silent as Linda chewed the hell out of her thumbnail. Since he had invited himself in, she figured it was only fair for him to speak first. And she was in no hurry to get to the part where he thought it was best for her to find a new personal trainer. Oh God, Linda thought in a panic. That left only *Vicky!* Even the thought of having to spend time with that girl a few times a week made her want to hyperventilate. She wouldn't do it. No way. She'd just find someone new in Baltimore and go on the days she headed in to the office. Even though it would break her heart to no longer see Jack, it was better than the alternative.

"Look, Linda," he finally began. "This afternoon shouldn't have happened."

Agreed, she thought.

"And I'm sorry about what I said."

Of course you are.

"And believe me when I say, I didn't mean to make you feel uncomfortable."

Right…wait, what? Linda looked at Jack incredulously. He thought *he'd* made *her* feel uncomfortable? How was that even possible?

"I just didn't want you to feel awkward at our next session. So, I came to apologize."

Linda couldn't believe what she was hearing. She had pretty much guilt-tripped him into offering her his body as a reward for losing weight, and he was apologizing to her over it. Who was this guy?

"Jack," she finally said, "you're not the one who needs to apologize here. I'm the one who should be apologizing to you. I should have never said that out loud. And then to make you feel sorry enough for me to 'offer your services'?" She lifted her hands to make air quotes. "It was inexcusable."

"I wasn't feeling *sorry* for you," Jack said, sounding mildly exasperated.

She merely shook her head and waved her hand back and forth to get him to stop. "Don't worry about it, okay? Let's just forget it ever happened."

Jack exhaled sharply and then eyed her for a few moments before saying grudgingly, "Fine."

"Great." Linda breathed a sigh of relief. She'd been convinced he was going to *un*-hire himself as her personal trainer, but this conversation had gone better than she'd expected.

"Before we drop the subject completely, can I ask you a question?"

Linda's dread returned. She wasn't sure if she wanted to answer any questions, but the look on his face was just so sincere, she knew she wouldn't be able to turn him down. "Well, okay...I guess."

"Why did you pick that for your reward?"

"Ugh." Linda rubbed her face in embarrassment and moved farther back onto the couch. She shoved herself into the corner and pulled her feet up on the cushion. "I knew I should have said no."

Jack chuckled, and he got more comfortable as well, arranging himself until they were facing one another fully.

"Seriously. What makes this different than a greasy pizza? You can have sex whenever you want."

"No...No, I can't," Linda replied, looking down at her knees.

"Why not?"

"Because I can't."

"Why?" Jack asked again, persistent to the very end. "Have you got a disease or something?"

"No!" Linda glared at him, even though she could tell he was joking. She knew she was clean. After all the suspected infidelity, she'd been sure to get tested for everything on the planet.

"Well then, why? If you don't have a disease, why can't you just go out and have sex?"

"Because I'm fat!" she finally cried out. "You think I want any man to see me naked looking like this?" Jack cringed in the face of her outburst. "I mean, with Graham it was different. He got to witness the progression, so I didn't really care — not that he'd laid a hand on me in forever. But someone new? There's no way. Not until I'm skinny again. So, there you have it. That's why I can't just go out and get laid. Happy now?"

"Not really, no," he said in a low voice. "I think you're being too hard on yourself."

"I hate to break it to you, Jack, but most guys? They don't want to fuck a fat chick either. So, even if I *did* get over how I look, it wouldn't be that easy for me to find someone to have sex with."

"You might be surprised," Jack replied, frowning down at his hands, which were in his lap.

"What? Pick myself up a chubby chaser?" Linda barked out a laugh. "No, thanks."

"That's *not* what I meant," he said, looking at her in frustration.

"And anyway, Jack," she continued. "I don't want *just* sex. I want *good* sex. No, I want *fantastic* sex! I want to have sex with a guy who can give me a goddamned orgasm! But not just any orgasm. I want a mind-blowing orgasm!"

Linda knew she was crossing all kinds of professional and even friendship boundaries, but at this point, she had stopped giving a shit. She figured she might as well just get it all out there and be done with it. Jack was goggling at her again, but anything was better than pity.

"You've never had an orgasm?" he asked in a shocked voice.

"Not unless it was one I've given myself."

"So, you've had an orgasm. Just not during sex."

"Nope."

"How is that possible?" Jack asked, looking confused.

Linda held up her pinky and wiggled it at him. It took him a second to get it, but soon he was roaring with laughter. She began to chuckle along with him and was amused when Jack began wiping tears from his eyes from laughing so hard. Well, at least someone found it funny.

"I'm sorry," he said while hiccoughing. "I shouldn't be laughing. That's actually pretty fucking sad. How long were you together?"

"About twenty years," Linda replied, nodding.

"Twenty years of bad sex…Oh, man."

"So, anyway. When I do find the man I want to take to my bed, it better be good!"

"Point taken."

They subsided into a comfortable silence. The air between them had been cleared, and the awkwardness from before was gone. Linda took a deep, cleansing breath. She actually did feel better now that she had gotten everything off her chest. Now they could just move on.

She could think up a new reward for losing the weight, even while still shooting for this one. Who knew? Maybe after she did shed the pounds, she'd have enough courage to see if Jack was interested. At least then, if he said yes, she'd know it wasn't out of pity.

Linda woke up Tuesday morning humming like a livewire. Like most mornings, Jack was on her mind. She'd had an incredibly vivid dream that at first could have been mistaken for a nightmare. They were back in the aerobics room after she had made her embarrassing confession, and like before, she'd flung her arms over her face. And then she heard his voice. Like always, it was as soft as a caress.

"What if it was me?"

And that was when everything changed, because instead of that question hanging between them like an albatross, Jack took it one step further. The hands that had been splayed against her knees began to travel down her thighs. Linda moaned softly at the light sensation. She moved her arms away from her face but kept them above her head. She wanted to see him. He was kneeling upright, bent over her body. His eyes flashed with erotic light, and his hands drifted up her hips and over her stomach.

Linda was spasming and contracting uncontrollably as he continued to feel his way up her body. She didn't know how much of this she could handle, and the apex between her thighs had taken on a needy ache that she hadn't felt in years. Maybe not ever. It was a hot pulse that was begging for attention, and God, she wanted Jack to take care of that need for her.

"Spread your legs, Linda," he said in a low but commanding voice.

"Yes, Master," she breathed as she arched up, and he finally cupped her breasts.

Linda had startled awake just then and almost wanted to cry in frustration. Why now? It was just getting good, damn it! She was still throbbing like crazy and felt as if she'd been on the verge of orgasm right then. She was tempted to roll over and try to get back to that dream but knew it was no use. First, she didn't have that kind of luck. Second, there was no way she was going to be able to fall back to sleep when she was so riled up. There was an emergency that needed to be taken care of, so she closed her eyes, lowered her hand between her thighs, and picked up where her dreams left off.

The rest of the day went by rather quickly; they always did when she had to run into the city. It seemed like time just flew while she was at the office, but she supposed that was a good thing. The only black spot on her day was when she left the building and there was no Jack to greet her. Of course he wouldn't be. He worked during the week. Saturday had been simply a fluke. That didn't stop her from feeling disappointed anyway.

As a counterpoint to that, she hadn't run into Graham either. Which was definitely a relief. It was bad enough she would have to see him during divorce proceedings. Luckily, things shouldn't take too long. They didn't have children and for the most part had purchased items using their own money. The only bone of contention really was the condo. That had been the one item they had both paid into equally, and the mortgage had ended sometime last year.

Linda knew her lawyer wanted her to push for Graham to sell it and give her half the profit, which was only fair, but to be honest, Linda didn't even really feel like fighting him for it. She had her home, she was happy with her career, she even had a little nest egg set aside for rainy days. Did she really need to go after Graham for the money? She supposed people would find her stupid for not doing so. Especially since the condo was worth almost twice as much on the market now as it was when they'd bought it fifteen years ago.

Decisions, decisions. This divorce stuff was for people made of sterner stuff.

When Linda walked into the club the next day, Jack was waiting for her as usual. She grinned at him, and a sweet, slow smile appeared in return. God, she loved it when he smiled at her like that, like only half of his mouth was following orders. It completely took her breath away. Perfect in its imperfection.

If there was any lingering awkwardness from the other day, Jack didn't show it. He simply said hello and tugged Linda's ponytail, as had become custom. At first, she thought he did it to tease her, but now she thought he just liked to do it. Either way, she didn't care because she loved the way he played with her hair. Any excuse to have him near her was always good.

They went through their paces as usual, but close to the end of the session, Jack had Linda try something new with disastrous results.

Well, disastrous for Linda, who ended up on the floor howling in pain as her hip tried to defect from her body. She lay on the floor holding on to her leg for dear life as Jack got down beside her and cursed a blue streak under his breath.

"Come on, let's get you out of here," he said in a low voice over her whimpers. He shoved his arm underneath her shoulder and hoisted her up.

Linda gritted her teeth as she tried to put weight on her leg and it buckled under her.

"Sure, let's walk it off," she said through clenched teeth. "*Great* plan!"

Jack chuckled, and if she weren't in a boatload of pain, she would have gladly kneed him in the nuts. He led her limping and mumbling swear words to the nearest aerobic room and shouldered them in. He lowered her gently to the ground, and she tried not to cry out. Linda watched as Jack ran to the mats, grabbed two of them, and brought them both to her, assembling them quickly.

"On the mat, beautiful," Jack said softly. He helped to move her gently so that she was lying on her back. He got on his knees on the opposite side of the leg that was giving her trouble. Linda barely caught his term of endearment but couldn't think of anything but the pain as he reached across her body, grabbed the offending leg, and pulled it toward him.

Linda yelled out and felt a faint pop as her hip settled back into the proper position. The pain diminished but didn't go away completely. Still, it was enough to wonder why he had brought her here instead of doing this in the other room.

"Is the pain gone?" he asked, using the look on her face as a gauge.

"Not completely."

"Yeah, I figured. On to step two."

"What's step two?" Linda watched as Jack let go of her leg and then shifted over. Her right leg was still horizontal across her body while the left was pointing straight down. Jack straddled her left leg, put his arms on either side of her upper body, and then laid his body directly on top of hers. His pelvis pushed into her hip, the pressure helping to alleviate any leftover discomfort.

"This is step two," he said in a low voice, his face only about six inches above hers.

"Ah," Linda replied, trying to keep her voice from shaking. "Position number fifty-six of the Kama Sutra."

Jack began chuckling, the shaking of his body on top of hers doing curious things to her. "Do you have that book memorized or something?"

"No, I'm just being a smartass."

"Oh, I thought you were brushing up on your reading for the night of your reward."

Linda's heart began to accelerate. This was so not the position she wanted to be in while discussing this particular subject. In a voice much steadier than she expected, she said, "I thought we agreed I was going to think of something else."

Up until this point, Jack had been suspended over her as if he were about to execute a push-up. He lowered his upper body until he was resting on his forearms, his entire body now flush against Linda's, and she was having a hard time controlling her urges. He leaned his head down until his mouth was by her ear. "No, *you* agreed to think of something else. *I* like your original idea." The husky whisper brushed against her skin in a faint caress.

Linda tried not to whimper, although she supposed she could always pass it off as a reaction to the residual pain. Of which there was currently none.

"You really don't need to keep your promise." This time her voice wasn't nearly as steady.

Jack pulled back and stared down at her. Now his face was scant inches from hers. "I know." Silence suspended between them for a very long time. His eyes were burning intensely as he gazed at her. "How's your hip?"

"What hip?" she asked. Jack broke out into a huge grin, and Linda wanted to smack herself in the head. "Oh! My hip. Yeah, it's good."

"Are you sure?" He pushed his own hips inward while looking down the length of his body, and Linda had a very vivid and clear visual of him doing that naked…but her legs were spread and he was sheathed between them. *Oh good fucking Lord!* she cursed to herself. She had to get him off her. *Now.*

"I'm sure," she said, swallowing hard as she kept her hands balled into fists to keep from yanking him back down against her as he started to rise off her body slowly.

Just then, the door swung open. There was a gasp and a shrill voice broke the silence.

"What the hell is going on in here?"

8
Changeroom Confessional

Jack turned toward the door and wasn't surprised at who stood there. "Linda hurt her hip," he replied, much more calmly than he anticipated.

"Well, why haven't you done anything like that with me?" she asked belligerently.

"Because last time I checked, your hips haven't come out of alignment during any of your sessions."

"They could if it meant getting treatment like that." Mrs. Bellham placed her hand on her hip and tried to look inviting.

Jack recoiled in disgust. Sighing, he looked down at Linda, who was still underneath him. "Are you okay now?"

She nodded, and he got up from his position and helped her sit. He was trying very hard to control his rising temper.

"Is there a reason why you're interrupting my session with Ms. Tanner?"

"Ms. Tanner?"

"Yes," Linda replied in a tired voice. "*Ms.* Tanner. Not that it's any of your business, Candy, but Graham and I are separated."

"So, like I was saying," Jack interrupted before the other lady could speak, "why are you barging in here?"

"I wanted to know what you do back here," she sputtered at him. "You always come in here with her, and I wanted to know why. I mean, I pay you the same money and don't get any private sessions."

"You've been *spying* on me?" Jack was now completely pissed off. Not only did this lady treat him like a slab of meat for public consumption, but now she had the nerve to keep tabs on him?

"Well, I wouldn't call it spying…"

"No? What would you call it, then?" he asked incredulously. "Not like I have to explain myself to *you*, but Ms. Tanner has a different regimen than yours. What she and I do together is none of your concern. Got it?"

"Why? Because she's fatter than I am?"

Jack heard Linda suck in a breath from behind him, and he'd never wanted to tell off a woman as badly as he did now. He leveled Candy Bellham with a vicious stare.

"Mrs. Bellham, I believe you are no longer in need of a personal trainer. Our sessions end now."

"You can't do that!"

"I just did. If you think you need more help, I hear Vicky is looking for clients."

"Jack, it's fine…" Linda said softly.

He held a hand up to stop her from saying more.

"You know, I'm sure Jimmy would be really interested in hearing what you've got going on back here," Candy Bellham spat out. "And I don't think he'd be very happy to lose a client either!"

"And I'm sure your husband would love to hear how you've propositioned me in one way or another since you hired me. *Don't* test me, lady," Jack said menacingly.

Mrs. Bellham gasped, and her hand flew to her throat.

"Do we have an understanding?"

"Yes."

"Great." He smiled. "Have a nice day, Mrs. Bellham."

The woman didn't say another word. She merely stumbled out of the room, and Jack watched her go with a marked sense of relief.

"You didn't have to do that, you know."

"Yes, I did," he replied, turning to face Linda. Her eyes were huge, and she was paler than usual.

"She could get you fired."

"Please," Jack scoffed. "She's lucky I don't sue her for sexual harassment."

"Well, still. I don't want you losing clients over our private sessions."

"Don't worry, Linda. There will be plenty of horny housewives lining up to take her place," he said bitterly. "After all, my day isn't complete until someone tries to look up my fucking shorts." He heard Linda gasp slightly as she began turning pink.

"I'm sorry," Jack rushed to say. "That was rude."

"No, you have a right to not be treated like that." Linda frowned and looked down.

Jack exhaled slowly and sat in front of Linda. "You think I mean you, too, don't you?"

"Well, why wouldn't you?"

"Linda, it's different."

"How?"

"Because it is," Jack replied, and then he stopped for a moment to collect his thoughts while she looked at him. "First of all, you've never made me feel like I'm just a body. Secondly, if I remember right, you never propositioned me. I offered. Thirdly, I wouldn't care if you looked up my shorts."

Linda snickered but then started to chuckle, which was Jack's intention all along. He smiled at her amusement, glad the tension between them was gone. He had been really afraid that what Candy Bellham had said would cause a major setback, but Linda seemed to be taking it in stride. Jack wasn't sure if that was a good or bad thing. Either she had just passed it off as a jealous client's rant or she believed what that shrew had said was right. He hoped it was the former. What Linda didn't know was that, even though she wasn't near her goal weight, the fifteen or so pounds she'd lost had already changed her body quite a bit. Jack had begun to notice that her clothes were starting to hang on her, and she would soon need to replace some of them. Yes, she was still on the bigger side, but now her waist was more defined and her hips and thighs were slimmer. He didn't think she should be ashamed of what she had to offer.

"How's the leg?"

"Good." Linda straightened it out in front of her and moved it up and down.

"Do you think you can keep going?"

"Yeah, should be fine."

The interruption with Mrs. Bellham had wasted a chunk of Linda's session, so they didn't have much time left. When Jack offered to extend it, Linda agreed, and they finished up later than usual. When Linda bent over to help him clean up, he stopped her.

"Don't worry about that. I'll take care of it."

"Are you sure?"

"Yeah, I've got you running late. Go on and take a shower."

"Okay," she answered, giving him the sweetest smile. "I'll see you up front to say bye?"

"As always." He winked at her and made her blush. Every time she did that, he wanted to run his thumb down her cheek.

When she turned to walk out the room, Jack watched her leave. She had a little shake to her hips that he'd never noticed before, and he hoped it was because she was feeling more confident these days.

After a while, Jack looked at his watch and realized he'd spent way more time daydreaming than he'd thought. He put the yoga ball away and stacked the mats before leaving the room. Humming a little happy tune, he walked toward the reception desk to wait for Linda. As he passed by the women's change room, Vicky walked out with one of her clients. Jack nodded at them and kept going.

When he stopped at the reception desk, the two ladies passed him by as Vicky walked her client out. They began giggling as they walked by, and the other woman looked at him askance and then grinned and elbowed Vicky, who made a face at her. Jack watched this exchange in confusion before turning away and watching for Linda. He loved the way her freshly scrubbed cheeks glowed. Still slightly shower-damp and warm, she always smelled so good.

Vicky sauntered over, souring his thoughts. He hadn't completely forgiven her when they had first met a month ago. At least the girl had the sense to stay out of his hair as much as possible. He thought it would be a major inconvenience to have her living at the house, but she hadn't been too much of a nuisance. Now he was pretty much used to her. He still didn't completely trust her for some reason, and that kept him somewhat on edge. He also noticed that she didn't seem to be looking too hard to find a new place to live. For something that was supposed to be temporary, it was looking more permanent as every day passed.

"Hey Jack," she said, smiling up at him.

"Vicky."

"You should smile more. You always look so serious."

Only when you're around, he thought. He just shrugged instead and looked back toward the change room. Just then Linda walked out, and he waited for her to look over. She wasn't looking at him, however.

"Oh, you have a little something on your shirt," he heard Vicky say before he felt her hand as it brushed against his chest. He glanced down at her and noticed she stepped even closer to him as she ran her fingers down his stomach.

Jack grabbed her hand before it could go any farther. "What are you doing?" he hissed, leaning in so as not to make a scene.

"Nothing," she said, smiling up at him again. "It's gone now."

Vicky stepped away, winked at him, and then sauntered off, leaving Jack perplexed as to what game she was playing. When he looked back toward Linda, she was merely staring at him with a defeated expression that he couldn't decipher. When he smiled at her, she smiled back, but it didn't touch her eyes. Linda looked down and walked over to him.

"Hey, pretty lady," he said when she was close.

Linda winced, but when she raised her face, it had a carefully blank expression.

"Are you all right?"

"Yup, I'm fine."

Jack then noticed something else. Linda had her hair tied up completely. It was twisted in a messy bun atop her head. He felt a moment of confusion as well as a touch of disappointment. One of his favorite things was running his hand along her hair, and now he felt as if he were being denied. But hell if he knew why.

"So, I've decided that my reward for losing the weight is going to be a trip to Hawaii," Linda said, just loud enough for him to hear. "I've never been there before, and I figure it'd be a great place to debut a new bikini or two. I don't even remember the last time I wore a bikini."

Jack frowned down at her. "What are you talking about?" he whispered. "What about your *other* reward?"

"I changed my mind," she said evenly. "It was stupid. This one is more…realistic."

"Are you doubting my prowess?" he asked jokingly. It fell flat. Linda merely stared at him and smiled sadly.

"Not at all," she replied. "But it's such a long way away; I'd never expect you to still be available."

"Linda—"

"I'm running late," Linda murmured. "See you in a couple days." She turned quickly and left.

Jack cursed under his breath. They were really back at square one. Fucking Mrs. Bellham. And now he had to wait an entire weekend before seeing Linda again.

Linda was preoccupied with Jack's invitation to look up his shorts. She'd never take him up on it, but she got a secret thrill knowing the invitation was there. She stepped into the shower to wash off all the sweat from her session and took her time, soaping herself up while thinking about Jack. She replayed the session over and over in her head. She was starting to think maybe, just maybe, Jack wasn't only being nice. He might actually be feeling something for her. She didn't know what, but at this point, she wasn't going to question it.

She turned the water off and was drying herself in the small seating section in the shower stall when she heard other women walk into the change room. Linda continued what she was doing. Since she had everything in the stall with her, she wasn't overly concerned about anyone seeing her naked. She was shimmying into her bra when the two women started talking, making Linda grit her teeth.

"Thank you so much, Vicky. That was an awesome workout!"

"Not too hard?"

"Well, I'm sure I'll be stiff tomorrow, but that's okay."

The women chatted amicably for a bit, and Linda put on the rest of her clothing. Then she sat down in the stall and pulled up her feet. She really wasn't in the mood to deal with Vicky, and by the sounds of it, she was with Michelle Jones. Another high school blast from the past. Arnold really was too small sometimes.

"So, were you able to find a place to live?" Michelle asked.

Linda bounced her head against the wall, hoping they would move on so she could get the hell out of here and see Jack.

"Actually, I'm living with the two other trainers, Jack and Amanda."

Linda's head shot up. Vicky was living with *Jack?* Why hadn't he said anything to her about it? They talked about so many things; she was certain he would have said *something*.

"Nice. I wouldn't mind living with Jack," Michelle cackled. "How did you manage that?"

"Well, we met and just really hit it off, you know?" Vicky said smugly. "Can you keep a secret?"

"Sure."

"Seriously, you can't tell *anybody.*"

"Okay!"

"Me and Jack are kind of a thing," Vicky said in a conspiratorial whisper. "We've been seeing each other pretty much since I moved in."

Linda's stomach plummeted, and she felt nauseated. How could he? Vicky of all people! She felt as if her heart was going to break. She'd really hoped that Jack was different and he wouldn't have fallen for the innocent charm Vicky exuded. Especially since she was far from innocent.

"Why's it a secret?"

"Jimmy is really against his employees getting together."

"What? But isn't he with the blonde?"

"Yeah," Vicky scoffed. "But he's the boss! He can do whatever the hell he wants. If he finds out me and Jack are together, we'll both lose our jobs."

"Can he do that?"

"I don't know, but I'm not going to chance it. So you have to keep this hush-hush, Michelle. Please?"

"All right…on one condition."

"What?"

"I get all the gory details!" Both ladies burst out laughing, and Linda sat there numb, fighting back tears.

"Deal."

They finally left the change room, leaving Linda alone and shattered. She managed to stumble out of the shower stall, and the first thing she saw was her reflection. Her big, fat, huge reflection. She felt like throwing something to smash the glass. Smash it into a million shards so that it looked like how her heart felt.

How could she have been *so* stupid? How could she have entertained for one *second* the thought that Jack could want her? Why the hell would he choose her when he had women like Amanda and Vicky to choose from?

Linda couldn't cry. She absolutely wouldn't. Not here, anyway, where people could see her. She would just have to wait until she got home and wallow in her sorrow there. For now, she just had to finish getting ready, gather her things, and leave. She grabbed her brush from her bag, pulled out her elastic band, and started yanking through the thick mass of hair. Linda tugged viciously against the knots, the pain momentarily distracting her from the soul-deep ache of Jack and Vicky.

As she was tying it back up, she realized that if she had to let Jack caress her hair, knowing where his hands had been, she would scream. She would scream, and she would beat him against the chest for being such a good fucking liar. She knew that would just cause a scene, and even though she felt betrayed, she couldn't be the cause of Jack losing his job. Especially not over a waste of skin like Vicky. No one was supposed to know about their affair, so Linda would keep the secret to herself, even if it killed her.

Linda twisted the ends of her hair until it coiled up around the band and then tucked the end under a loop of elastic. Packing up her things, she made sure she had everything before she left. She looked at herself in the mirror one last time before finding the courage to leave.

When she walked out, she thought she was prepared to see Jack again. And she might have done all right if she hadn't had to witness Vicky running her hand down Jack's chest like a lover and him grasping her hand tightly and leaning forward to whisper something in her ear. Linda's shoulders slumped as everything became real for her.

It was oh-so-surprising that Jack still had the nerve to smile at her like he did, although he had no idea that she knew his dirty little secret. Of course, he would have to keep up the charade.

Well, what he didn't know was that Linda could act too. As she walked toward him, she prepared for the role of her life. She could pretend everything was perfectly fine. She may not have pulled it off as well as he did—his concern for her felt so damned genuine—but the truth of the situation galvanized her, and she got through it.

She walked out of the club and took a deep shaky breath. It wasn't until she got home with a pint of chocolate chunk ice cream that she allowed the tears to flow freely.

9
Don't Mess with PMS

Linda had had a week from hell. She had spent the weekend after Vicky's revelation in a sugar-induced haze. By Sunday, she was sick to her stomach and sick of herself. All that hard work had probably gone down the drain because, like a weakling, she had resorted back to her habit of using junk food for comfort. But what had it gotten her? Nothing, except maybe a few pounds gained back. It certainly hadn't made the situation between Vicky and Jack go away.

A knife speared her heart, and she realized dimly that this hurt more than when her husband of fifteen years had left her. How that was possible she didn't know. All she knew was that it did.

She had a ton of thinking to do. Despite the bingeing, Linda's plan to lose the weight hadn't been completely derailed. She threw away any remaining junk food — sadly, there was barely anything left to throw out — and went for a long, brisk walk. The damp air cleared her head, and she breathed in huge lungsful of it as she walked.

What would she do now? She really only had two choices. Either she kept quiet about what she'd heard and continued to see Jack in a strictly professional manner, or she quit *Self-sational* and joined a gym in Baltimore. She was positive she could find a new personal trainer easily enough in the larger city, and this time she'd make sure it was a woman.

That's where Linda had gone wrong. She'd let her obvious attraction to Jack change her mind, and now look where it had led: with her being half in love with the guy and him screwing the tramp who had fucked her husband. Had she just stuck to her original plan, none of this would have ever happened. She would have seen Jack around the club and admired him from afar, but that was it.

Truthfully, Linda had no clue if she was strong enough to keep seeing Jack several times a week. How could she go on as if nothing was wrong? How could she be holed up with him alone and continue to keep her distance? It was obvious now that Jack wasn't interested in her at all, not like she had been hoping. Maybe she wasn't just his client anymore — they had certainly become friends — but there was nothing more than that. If she pulled back, she figured Jack would get the hint and stop being overly friendly.

Linda had somehow made it through the week and breathed a sigh of relief when her Friday session was over. She didn't think she could continue like this and had made a decision to go check out a gym close to her work on Saturday. If she could secure a personal trainer, she would consider the switch. The thought made her sad, but she couldn't see any other way. Even those three hours spent with Jack were killing her. His touch, his voice, the way he looked at her, the ever-present concern for her well-being. It was torturing her. And whenever she wanted to relent, she thought about him sharing his bed with Vicky and withdrew within herself.

After meeting with her editors, Linda walked out of the building and stood still. Like that day about a month ago, the sun was shining bright in the sky. She closed her eyes and lifted her face up, fighting back tears as she thought of Jack and saying good-bye to him. She remembered the last time they had met here and how things had been simple and uncomplicated.

"I wonder why the sun always shines whenever I find you here."

Linda gasped and whirled around to find Jack leaning up against the wall. Slightly blinded by the sun, she hadn't noticed him when she had walked out. Not expecting to see him, she was caught off guard and said the first thing that came to mind.

"You must bring it with you when you come."

"I don't think it's me the sun is following," he said, smiling a little sadly. Jack shrugged away from the wall, and before she could think to stop him, he reached forward and ran his fingers down a thick lock of her hair. She was wearing it down today. His eyes were focused on that piece of hair. "How're you doing, pretty lady?"

Linda wanted to weep at the sound of his voice, the hand in her hair, and the sun that bathed him in a glow like an angel. And then she remembered why she couldn't get caught up in his spell once again. "Why are you here, Jack?"

He seemed to think about that for a second, then dropped his hand to his side and looked in her eyes. Linda almost preferred that he hadn't done that since there was so much hurt and sadness there, but for the life of her, she didn't know why. She almost asked. She wanted to reach up and caress his face until he smiled happily again, but it wasn't her place.

"I'm singing at the bar again tonight," he answered, smiling slightly. "We had a lot of fun last time, so I was wondering if you wanted to go again."

"Where's Vicky?" she blurted without thinking. Scrambling, she added, "and Amanda?"

"I don't know," Jack answered with a perplexed look on his face. "Off doing girl stuff?"

"You didn't invite…them?"

"No. I didn't think of it, actually."

This made Linda pause. If Vicky were Jack's girlfriend, why wouldn't he ask her to come see him play? Why would he come to see if Linda wanted to go instead? The only reasons she could think of was that Vicky had turned him down, and he was just playing it off, or maybe they only had a physical relationship. Vicky hadn't said anything about Jack being her boyfriend; she'd just said they had a "thing." Whatever the hell that meant.

Linda didn't know which was worse, Jack wanting to be in a relationship with the tramp or just using her for what was between her legs. On one hand, he was a blind fool, and on the other, he was a player. Thing was, from what Linda knew of Jack, he seemed neither. He'd always come across as a good judge of character, and from what she'd seen at the club, she figured he could have been sleeping with most of the women who patronized it. But he didn't.

"So? Will you come?"

Linda realized she'd never really answered the question, so caught up was she in her contemplations.

"I don't know if that's such a good idea, Jack."

"Come on, Linda," he begged, reaching forward to grasp her hand in his. He threaded his fingers with hers and swung their joined hands between them. "Cici and Rob will be there."

"Really?" she asked, watching their hands moving back and forth, mesmerized by how good it looked to be holding his hand.

"Yeah, Cici was bugging me to get you to come. You don't want to disappoint her, do you?"

"Oh." Suddenly this made more sense. It wasn't so much that Jack wanted her there, but that he was asking on behalf of a friend. "No, I wouldn't want to disappoint Cici." She extracted her hand from his and held up her backpack. "I just have to run this to the car."

"I'll come with you." A cloud passed over his face. "Last time I left you alone here, you got yourself into trouble."

Linda couldn't help but smile a little at the memory of Jack shoving Graham against the wall. "That wasn't my fault."

"Even still, I'm coming with you."

Jack walked by her side, his hand brushing against hers every so often, as if he wanted to link their fingers again, but he didn't quite dare. This was even more confusing to Linda, and she wondered if she was losing her mind. Why did it always seem as if Jack wanted more from her? If that was the case, then why was he sleeping with someone else?

Because you won't let him sleep with you, a voice from deep inside her said.

Linda frowned at the errant thought. It was stupid. Ludicrous, even. It made no sense whatsoever, and she ignored the voice. They had reached her car, and she unlocked the doors. As she leaned in the backseat to drop her bag, Jack got into her passenger seat.

"What are you doing?"

"Waiting for you to get in and drive to the club."

"Jack," Linda laughed in amusement. "We can just walk. I don't have an evil ex lurking in the bushes this time."

"That you know of," he replied, frowning. She knew that look all too well, and since she didn't have the physical strength to pull him out of her car, she sighed dramatically, slammed the back door, and got in the car.

"Happy?"

"Yes." His frown turned into an adorable grin. It was her favorite one, and she melted just a teeny tiny bit. "I miss you," he said suddenly, making her draw breath.

"You just saw me yesterday," she scoffed. The space in the car had shrunk to nothing all of a sudden.

"It's not the same. This whole week has been...*off.*"

"I told you why."

"And I don't believe you," he replied, looking at her closely. "Otherwise we would have had this problem before."

Crap. Busted. Linda had used the PMS excuse out of desperation. She figured if Jack was anything like Graham and Tony, talk of a woman's time of the month would send him scrambling for the hills. It had mostly worked. Leave it to him to be perceptive enough to figure out they'd never dealt with "feminine issues" previously in the last three months.

"I think," he continued, "this has to do with what Mrs. Bellham said. It has to be. She barged in, asked about the private sessions, and now you've been acting really different, and I can't figure out why."

Linda just stared at Jack. She wanted to tell him that she had overheard Vicky telling a client about their relationship. But then what? What would that accomplish, except to showcase how completely crazy Linda was over her personal trainer? It's not as if she could get mad at him; she was nothing to him. Even if she played it off that she was merely concerned about him becoming involved with a little viper like Vicky, it would still make her look petty. What if Jack cared for the girl? As unsavory a thought as that was, if he did have feelings for her, how would he feel about Linda's less-than-stellar opinion of her? Would he think she was jealous? She was, absolutely... just not all that anxious to admit it. Maybe he would pass it off as vindictive ramblings of a scorned, soon-to-be ex-wife.

In any case, Linda didn't want to be any of those things in Jack's eyes. She would just keep everything to herself and hope that Jack saw through Vicky's shiny veneer to the mottled thing beneath.

"There's just a lot of stuff going on in my life right now, Jack," Linda sighed instead.

"You can't talk to me about it?"

"No." *Because it's all about you.* "Maybe soon, okay?"

"All right, Linda."

He was no longer looking at her, but Linda could hear an undertone of sadness and disappointment, and her heart twisted in grief as well. She hated lying to him, but there wasn't much left she could do unless she was ready to reveal to him what she felt. She didn't think she could handle the revulsion and subsequent pulling away if that happened. She would rather walk away on her own terms, retaining her pride.

Linda started her car and drove the few blocks to the bar. She parked beside Jack's car again and waited for him to get his guitar. They walked into the bar together and were immediately accosted by Cici.

"You came!" she said, bouncing on her toes and clapping gleefully. "It's just so much more fun watching the show with a friend."

Cici's high spirits were infectious, and Linda found herself smiling at the small girl. If they could harness the girl's energy, she was sure they could power up all of Arnold…maybe even Baltimore. Linda found herself wondering how it was possible to have so much vigor. Just watching Cici tired her out; she couldn't even imagine *being* Cici.

"I have to head backstage," Jack murmured in her ear. His hand was against the small of her back, and it seemed like such an intimate gesture. She had to stop herself from leaning in closer, so she just nodded her assent.

"You two are so cute together," Cici said, smiling as she watched Jack walk away.

"Oh, we're not together," Linda replied in a surprised voice.

"I know," she murmured, looking at Linda again. "But you would make a great couple."

They went to find a table at the back while the men did their sound checks. Linda enjoyed talking to Cici. When Cici invited them out to dinner with her and Rob again, and this time, Linda felt confident in answering for them both. Silly as it was, it gave her a little thrill to pretend she and Jack were a couple. Even though she had spent the better part of the week denying those feelings, she let them come forth now. Jack was with *her* tonight, not Vicky. What harm would it be to pretend?

Dinner was a happy affair. Once Linda had stopped trying to repress her feelings for Jack, things seemed to click back into place. It was like riding a bike again; their banter came so naturally. This was the happiest she had been since she'd had that bomb dropped on her last week. And surprisingly enough, this was the happiest she'd seen Jack in that time period as well. Linda soaked in his laughter like it was water, and she was desert-parched. She hadn't realized just how badly she'd missed the sound. And his smiles were like sunshine, radiant and warm, especially when he looked at her.

Jack was pressed against her in the booth, even though he was on the outside edge. Every time Linda scooted over, he would follow. He had his arm stretched across the top of the booth so she was practically cradled against him. Every so often, she felt the brush of his fingers against her hair, and it made her want to lean her head back against his hand. This was what joy felt like, she mused to herself.

It was a shame when they had to leave, but Linda was anxious to get to the bar so she could hear Jack sing again. She thought that tonight was even better than the last time and was looking forward to what the rest of the night would hold.

Jack was feeling great, and his plan seemed to be working.

On Friday, he had called down to the bar to see if they could squeeze him in for open mic night and had been pleased to find out they could. With that set up, he called Cici to see if she and Rob would be there. He figured if he couldn't talk Linda into going just for him, maybe some friendly faces at the bar would help convince her.

And now, walking beside her, letting his hand brush against hers, he was as close to ecstatic as he could get. Jack had been worried at first because things hadn't gone very well when he'd first made his presence known. He'd had a hard time controlling his emotions. Seeing Linda in the sunshine brought back memories of the first time they'd run into one another in Baltimore. There was one big difference, however, and it was that she looked sad when she raised her face to the sun. It reminded him of the past week and how, occasionally, he'd catch that look on her face.

Jack had felt a moment of doubt right before he spoke but had known he couldn't leave without at least talking to her. He didn't regret it because that had led to the here and now where he'd been able to keep her close to him. Secure by his side, laughing and happy. And he'd been able to caress her hair, stealing furtive touches and strokes. Of course, he knew that even as secretive as he was trying to be, she must have noticed. The fact that she didn't pull away from his touch, or worse, ask him not to touch her at all, was heartening.

He'd missed her. This Linda. The one who was sassy and smiling. The one who rolled her eyes at his stupid jokes but laughed anyway. The one who looked at him like he was the only man in the room. Jack was so happy when she finally appeared again.

Tonight, his whole set was going to be love songs. Would she know that he was serenading her as he sang? He certainly hoped so. Maybe later, when he walked her to her car, he'd kiss her on the lips instead of the cheek and see how she reacted. Jack knew it was a risk for various reasons, but after having her pull away from him once, he realized that wasn't something he was interested in going through again. He hoped she would kiss him back.

As they neared the bar, he started to get excited. He always felt that way before a show, but this time was different. He was anxious to see how Linda would react to his song choices. Jack had a passing fancy to dedicate them to her from the start, but he didn't want to put her on the spot. He kind of wanted her to get the hint from the words he sang. Perhaps realization would dawn on her face, which was something he definitely wanted to witness.

When they walked in, the bar was only half full because the performances weren't starting for about twenty minutes. Jack was still hopeful that they could find a table near the front so he would have an unobstructed view of Linda. As they wove through the tables, he heard someone call out to them.

"Jack! Hey! Jack!"

Turning, he was surprised to see Amanda standing at a table near the stage waving her hand over her head. At first, he began to smile, happy his friend had managed to make it this time. He didn't know how she had found out; maybe she'd overheard him calling the bar. The smile faded quickly when Amanda moved aside and sitting just behind her was Vicky. Jack groaned internally. While he had been on okay terms with her as of late, he didn't want to spend any more time in her presence than he had to. And judging by the look on Linda's face, she didn't either.

"I thought you said Vicky wasn't coming," she murmured to him when he turned toward her.

"I didn't know," he replied, shrugging in a helpless manner. "I don't even know how they found out."

"I told Amanda," Cici piped up, looking between everyone, a small furrow between her brows. "She dropped by the shop, and I asked if she was coming to the show. I'm sorry…Was I not supposed to?"

Jack didn't know how to answer that question. It really wasn't Cici's fault. She knew that Amanda was his roommate, and of course it would be normal to ask if she would be going. Only he knew what he'd had planned for tonight. He didn't care that Amanda was here, but he knew that Vicky made Linda uncomfortable for whatever reason, and he hated putting her in that position.

"Maybe I should go home?" Linda asked him softly. Her eyes were large and sad-looking.

"No," he answered quickly. "Why?"

She looked at him expectantly for a moment, eyebrows raised. He stared back. "Well," she said when he remained quiet, "your *friends* are here; you don't need me to stay anymore."

Yes, I do. "Come on, Linda. Don't leave. I really want you to stay." He gave his best stranded puppy imitation and could see her starting to relent.

"Yeah, Linda. *Please,*" Cici jumped in, doing her own pathetic lip pouty thing.

Linda closed her eyes and sagged a little in defeat. "Okay."

Jack gave Linda a huge grin as Cici jumped around spastically.

They all walked over to the table Amanda was holding for them. Linda was lagging behind slightly, but she hadn't left, which made him very happy. It was because Jack was in front that he managed to get accosted by the two girls waiting. They clapped and squealed, making him cringe, and then out of nowhere, Vicky threw her arms around his neck and kissed him on the side of the mouth.

"What the hell?" he said in shock before grabbing her hands and unlocking them from around him. Was she drunk or something?

Amanda took hold of his arm and sat him down in a chair before plunking down beside him on his left. Vicky took the seat to his right. Jack looked around to where Linda was standing awkwardly and made a move to get up. She just shook a hand at him and went to the other side of the table, where she sat beside a bemused Cici and Rob. He must have looked just as perplexed by everything that just happened.

Jack considered moving to Linda's side of the table, but his set was coming up soon. He figured once he was done and returned to the table, he could grab a chair and put it beside her. Amanda and Vicky chattered about how Cici had mentioned him playing and neither of them had plans, so they hopped in Vicky's car and came to catch the show. He tried a few times to get Linda's attention so he could roll his eyes about the two girls, but she wasn't looking at him. She was looking down at the table and tearing a napkin into tiny pieces. Every once in a while, she'd glance at Cici when the girl spoke to her, but never at him.

When he started singing, Linda closed her eyes for a moment and smiled. Whether it was at the sound of his voice or because she recognized the song he sang, he wasn't sure. Opening her eyes, she focused on him intently, and for the briefest moment, he saw something flicker in them. Something close to adoration. It didn't last long, because halfway through the song, she was distracted by something and turned her head away toward Vicky.

And then she didn't really look at him again, not truly. She kept her eyes focused on the table and continued to slowly shred another napkin. Occasionally her gaze would flicker to his face, but that was it. He wanted to call out her name to draw her attention but knew it would embarrass her. What had made her turn away?

Jack finished the next two songs in no time and inclined his head woodenly at the applause. He couldn't give two shits about what anyone in that room thought of his performance, save for Linda. He went to put his guitar away for the night until he could come back to get it and then went out to the main room. This time, he refused to get accosted; he was going to sit beside Linda and see why she had looked so sad. That was definitely not the reaction he had wanted. Did he choose a song that reminded her of her ex? Or one that gave her bad memories? He hoped not.

Approaching the table, he noticed two empty seats. The one he had vacated earlier and Linda's. He hoped she just had gone to the ladies room, but his heart sank because he didn't think that was the case.

"Where's Linda?" he asked Cici as soon as he reached her.

"She left, Jack," the girl replied cheerlessly. "I tried to get her to stay, but she said she had to be up early in the morning."

He didn't wait to hear any more and went tearing out after her. If he moved quickly, maybe he could catch her in the parking lot. Unfortunately, her parking space was empty. Jack looked to and fro, but he knew he'd never catch her now. Cursing, he ran his hands through his hair. All his planning had somehow gone to shit, but only God knew why. He glanced back into the bar and frowned.

Moving through the now crowded main room, he stalked up to the table where everyone was sitting. He planted his palms on it and leaned forward, looking at Amanda and Vicky. "Why did Linda leave?" he barked at them.

Amanda's brows went shooting high in obvious confusion, and Vicky looked way too innocent.

"What did you say to her?"

"Nothing!" Vicky answered. "I just asked her if she'd ever had someone sing love songs to her before. That's it!"

Amanda nodded. "Yeah, that's all she said."

"What the fuck?" Jack muttered, standing up. Now he was even more confused than before. Morosely, he sat down in the chair Linda had vacated and ran his fingertips through the scattered pieces of napkin before him. He considered leaving but decided it would be rude to go before Rob had played his set. Luckily, his band was up next.

"Don't give up on her," a quiet voice said by his side. He looked up to find Cici peering at him closely. "She cares more than she lets on."

"I don't know about that," he answered ruefully.

"You don't see the way she looks at you when you aren't watching," she continued in a low voice. "Just don't give up, okay?"

Jack smiled slightly in thanks at the girl seated next to him. "Okay."

Cici turned away and began hollering when her man stepped on stage. It was almost as if Jack had imagined their whole conversation. He shook his head and listened to Rob's band play.

10
It's not Over till the Fat Lady Sings

On the drive home from the bar, Linda had a lot of time to think. Today had been like a rollercoaster ride. Up and down and all around, leaving her with a mishmash of emotions.

Something wasn't adding up.

Jack had gone to such lengths to get her to join him tonight. During dinner, he acted more like they were on a date than anything else. When they saw who was waiting at the bar, he hadn't seemed happy at all. Was it only because he wanted to keep his and Vicky's relationship a secret? If so, she didn't seem to be on board with that plan. Linda had wanted to grab the girl by her long blond hair and rip her off Jack when she wrapped her arms around him and gave him a kiss.

It looked like her fantasy date with Jack was officially over.

Linda should have left. She should have turned tail and headed to her car as soon as she saw Vicky, but she was too weak. When Jack had practically begged her to stay, and then Cici joined in, she couldn't say no. So what happened? She had to witness Vicky manhandle Jack, steal him away, and monopolize his attention. And if that wasn't bad enough, she had to sit there and listen to Jack croon out one love song after another at the little witch.

At first, Linda had been content to just close her eyes and imagine he was singing to her. When she opened them again, she found that Jack was indeed looking at her as he sang before staring back down at his guitar. His voice was so beautiful, clear and angelic. The lyrics washed over her.

"Awww, isn't he sweet?" Vicky said in her little baby voice, completely destroying Linda's vibe. "So, Linda. Have *you* ever had anyone sing you love songs?"

The implication was clear. Vicky was subtly letting her know that Jack was singing to her, not to Linda. She took the hint. It was also a jab at Linda herself, one patently understood. She didn't have the looks or the body to merit that kind of attention. It was duly noted, and from then on, she kept her eyes on the table and tried not to let the last ten minutes of the night affect her too deeply.

Cici had been a lifesaver, talking to her and keeping her sane while Jack finished his set. Linda wanted to wait for him to come back, but she felt that she just wouldn't make it if she had to watch Vicky be oh-so-thankful to Jack for the beautiful songs he'd sung for her tonight. She didn't want to watch them be together in front of her face. Her imagination was bad enough. And it was running wild.

When she reached home, it was with great resolve that Linda strode past her kitchen. There was no longer any junk food in there, but an overabundance of healthy food wasn't much better. Linda had done enough bingeing last weekend. She refused to fall back into that destructive pattern again. If anything, her stubborn nature was a boon this time around.

Wasn't it a kick that her personal trainer, the man who was in charge of whipping her ass into shape, was now the one responsible for throwing her into a gluttonous tailspin? Linda chuckled mirthlessly.

At least now she was aware of what she was doing and how her habitual behavior could be damaging in the long run. Admitting it was half the battle. The other half was stopping herself from running out to find the nearest place that sold large tubs of ice cream. Or chocolate bars. A big bag of Doritos sounded good right about now, too, washed down with a few cream sodas. Or maybe root beer. She hadn't had root beer in a while.

As she walked into her room, Linda started stripping off her clothes. When she was naked, she did something she hadn't done in what felt like forever: she looked at herself in the full-length mirror.

Usually, the only time she used the thing was to check to make sure her outfits looked okay and then turned away quickly. She couldn't even remember the last time she had actually looked at her body. Honestly looked at it.

The first thing Linda noticed was that she was still very well-padded. Her arms were still wobbly, her thighs still thick, her hips still incredibly wide, and her belly still round. Turning to look at her backside, she nearly cried at the dimples of cellulite showcased there.

Over the course of her time working out with Jack, she had lost just over twenty pounds. She was still overweight but no longer considered obese. According to the BMI chart, she was still twenty pounds shy of being within normal weight range. And even when she hit that milestone, she would still be thirty pounds away from her goal weight.

Taking a deep breath, Linda decided to try something different. Instead of focusing on all the negative things, which was so damned easy to do, she was going to try to focus on some positive things. She was most definitely slimmer, and her waist had tucked in quite a bit, giving her what could be considered a flattering hourglass shape. *Maybe a bigger-than-average hourglass...* She snickered angrily at herself for jumping back to the negative so quickly.

Linda concentrated on her body again. Her calves were almost slim now and kind of shapely. Maybe she should buy a pair of high heels? Smiling, she took in her backside again. Yes, it was dimpled, but she had some decent junk in her trunk, and in the right pants, it actually didn't look *too* bad. Linda turned to face herself in the mirror once more.

Currently, her breasts were her claim to fame. They were high and round and perky. Since they hadn't grown during her weight gain, she wasn't too concerned about them shrinking as she lost the extra pounds. She tweaked one nipple and nodded smartly when it rose to the occasion. Everything in proper working order, she was pleased to note.

That, along with her bendiness, might come in handy one day, too.

Blushing, she remembered the day Jack had called her bendy and the position they'd been in when he'd said it. Linda whimpered slightly, her stomach tightening. She closed her eyes and called that image back up. He'd looked so good, so incredibly sexy, perched above her like that. In her mind, he was now bending toward her and fastening his lips to her neck. Linda's breath quickened. Fantasy Jack then grasped the leg that was between them, pushing it to the side and bending it at the knee so that it was up high against his ribs, her calf gripping his lower back. Now he was rocking his hips against hers as he slid his hand down her other thigh and pulled that leg up to wrap around him as well.

Linda was getting all worked up at the images playing out before her. It was definitely time to take a shower. She washed her hair first, almost mourning the loss of Jack's scent, and then spent the next while soaping herself up slowly. She took her time and tried to imagine it was Jack touching her. Linda pushed out any and all other thoughts from her head, concentrating instead on her body and impending release. It had been a while, and the force of it shocked Linda as her body continued to tremble even when her orgasm was over.

The high didn't last long. By the time she had dried off, thrown her hair in a damp, messy knot on top of her head, and gotten dressed for bed, she was depressed again. It was all fine and dandy to pretend that Jack was hers, but the reality of the situation leeched through eventually. Vicky poked her nasty little head into Linda's subconscious, making her gnash her teeth in frustration. She sincerely hated that girl more than she'd hated anyone else, ever. Even more now than before.

Linda went to bed and tried to make her mind go blank. It worked eventually, and her eyes became heavy. She fell into a fitful sleep and had strange dreams that seesawed between nightmares and erotica. It was a very long night.

Linda was looking in the mirror as she tied up her hair. As she began twisting it to wrap into a bun, she stopped. Suddenly, she felt a small streak of vindictiveness. Letting her hair go, the ponytail went free and swinging. For some reason, she knew there was no way Jack wouldn't reach out to give it a tug. It gave Linda a bit of perverse pleasure to think that Vicky would see that. What would she think of her boyfriend stroking another woman's hair? A *fat* woman at that.

Two could play this game.

Maybe Linda wasn't ready to give up her fantasies of having a shot at Jack. Surely a vapid thing like Vicky couldn't keep him interested for long. Generally she would never consider going after Vicky's sloppy seconds, but she'd make an exception for Jack. So, fine, let him play. That would give Linda time to lose the rest of her weight, and when the time was right, if necessary, she'd come out swinging.

When Linda pulled up behind the club, she was a mass of jitters. She was excited to see Jack but dreaded seeing Vicky. With her new mindset, she pushed that aside, stiffened her spine, and headed to the front of the club. She saw Jack waiting for her at the reception desk, and unlike last week when she was in her blue funk, she smiled at him like she used to. He did a double take before grinning at her widely.

"Hey, gorgeous," he said when she was close enough to hear.

Gorgeous? That was a new one, but Linda loved it all the same.

"Hello, handsome."

"You've got your hair down today," he said softly before reaching out to give it a small tug. She just shrugged as he twirled one of her curls around his index finger. "I like it better all the way down, but this works."

"I'll have to remember that," she said in a teasing voice and watched as Jack's eyes blazed for a second.

"You do that," he replied huskily.

Hot damn. She would tackle him down to the pavement and straddle him here and now if he continued using that voice.

"Yes, Master."

It'd been a while since she'd used that term, and it seemed to have a visible effect on Jack. His eyes widened slightly, and his nostrils flared. Then he smirked at her. The one she adored. The lickable one.

"I guess we should get started," Jack said after a moment. He sounded somewhat regretful.

When they got to the mats, Linda started with her stretches like she always did. Jack watched her move, and she was very aware of his stare. She was very aware of *him*. Where he was, how he moved, the way he helped her with the more difficult maneuvers. There always seemed to be some sort of connection between them that Linda couldn't deny.

"So, why did you leave early on Saturday?" Jack asked about halfway through their session.

"I had to wake up early the next day."

"How come?"

How come? Uh-oh…Linda hadn't gotten that far into her reasoning. She figured the excuse would be good enough. Apparently not. "I had to help a friend."

"Do what?"

"This and that," she answered noncommittally.

"Oh," Jack replied, and she felt a little guilty for deceiving him. But what else could she say? "I thought maybe someone said something to upset you."

Linda paused. "Would it matter to you if they did?"

"Absolutely," Jack replied indignantly. He came around to face her, squatting in front of the weight bench she was sitting on. "*You* were my guest." He looked at her closely, and Linda wondered, not for the first time, about the nature of his and Vicky's relationship. "Is that what happened?"

She considered his question and almost admitted the truth. Uncertainty kept her mouth shut. "Why does it matter if I left early?" she blurted out instead.

"Because you didn't say good-bye," Jack replied quietly. He was looking down at his hands when he said it. Linda stopped herself from yanking his head up so she could see what he was hiding.

"I'm sorry," she whispered. "I won't do it again."

"You'd come again?" Jack smiled a little shyly but still wouldn't look at her.

"Absolutely."

"Okay," he replied, his eyes finally coming up to meet hers. "It's a date."

They smiled at one another. Jack placed his hands on Linda's knees, and he squeezed gently. Her stomach did a lazy flip at the contact. He was staring at her mouth in a way that should be illegal, and when his tongue snaked out to lick his lips, she started to clue in on a little something. Even if Jack *was* with Vicky, there was something that drew him to her as well. She was almost sure of it.

Eventually, they got back to Linda's workout. Once it was over, she went to the change room to wash up. When Linda finished with her shower, instead of brushing her hair and putting it back up in a ponytail, she left it down. She knew there was no way Jack would be able to resist, and damn if she wanted him to. Apparently, Vicky must not have touchable hair. Linda smiled to herself in the mirror. Her eyes were bright, her cheeks were flushed, and she bit on her lips to make them extra red. She may have been out of the game for a while, but she still remembered a few tricks.

In one last move, she pulled out a simple necklace from her bag and bounced it up and down in her palm for a second. This was her failsafe.

With a spring in her step and a shimmy she'd forgotten she had, Linda walked out of the change room and focused on Jack, who was waiting in his usual spot for her. Once again, she noticed his eyes widen as he took her in. She was dressed up today, which was also part of her plan, and the look of approval she was getting from Jack made her want to grin until her face broke. She kept her look demure with a lot of effort.

"You look nice today," Jack told her when she got to him.

"Thanks."

"What's the special occasion?"

"Oh, I'm meeting up with someone from work."

Jack frowned. "Who?"

"No one you know," she replied flippantly. Jack didn't need to know it was with her sixty-year-old editor. "You know," she continued before he could ask her anything more, "I was thinking…I'd like to try that one move. You know, the one where I pulled my hip? I figure we should be in private, just in case that happens again."

Jack blinked at her a few times, speechless. She hoped he was thinking about what exactly had happened in the aerobics room that time, and when he swallowed thickly, she thought perhaps he was. "Okay," he agreed and nodded slowly. She was playing dirty, but for once, she simply didn't care. And now for her coup de grâce.

"Hey, Jack, do you think you can help me with this necklace?" she asked, opening her hand and looking up at him guilelessly.

"Sure." He held out his hand for the object.

"Oh, no," Linda replied. "This clasp would probably be too small for you to get. But if you can just hold up my hair for me, I can put it on."

Linda turned around expectantly before he could answer. It didn't take long for him to step closer to her and run his hands along her neck as he gathered her thick hair and swept it up. She took her time threading the thin chain around her neck so she could clasp it in front of her, making sure to miss the catch a few times. As Jack waited patiently, he moved in even closer, and she distinctly felt the expansion of his chest against her back when he inhaled deeply.

Smiling, she turned the chain around until the clasp was at the nape of her neck. She looked over her shoulder and met Jack's eyes. The force of his gaze sucked the breath from her body, and she just barely managed to say, "Thank you."

"Anytime," he replied before releasing her hair. Instead of letting it go and allowing it to cascade down her back, he ran his fingers along its length, making Linda shudder against him.

"I was also thinking...maybe I was a bit hasty about Hawaii, too." Linda watched as Jack's head swung up, comprehension flaring in his eyes right away.

"So, what do you want your reward to be now?" he asked cautiously.

"I think I had it right the first time," she replied coyly.

"I think you did, too." His voice was low, husky.

They stared at one another for a few more seconds until Jack broke out into a grin. Linda had to look away to maintain her composure. When she looked ahead, Linda saw Vicky staring at her and Jack, slack-jawed with a spiteful look on her face. She looked back over her shoulder at Jack once more.

"So," she said, "I guess I'll see you Wednesday?"

"Wednesday it is."

After saying good-bye, she looked directly at Vicky again and smiled sweetly. Linda's look clearly said one thing.

Suck it. Bitch.

11
Hurts So Good

Jack was practically jittering in agitation as he stood waiting for Linda to arrive. He'd kept himself busy the day before so that he didn't crawl out of his skin waiting for this exact hour. Now it was here, and it still wasn't good enough. It wouldn't be good enough until he had Linda in his clutches. Maybe this time he'd just never let her go.

He had plans for Ms. Tanner.

When Linda finally turned the corner, Jack felt his anticipation ratchet up a few notches. He didn't even bother trying to play it cool, merely threw open the door of the club in a bid to get her to him more quickly. Jack could hear the sweet sound of Linda's laughter as she came up the walk toward him. He held the door as she swept in.

"Straight to the back," he instructed, catching the mischievous smile she threw over her shoulder as she passed him by.

"Yes, Master," she replied coyly before turning to face front again and head in the direction of the aerobics room.

Jack really *did* like it when she called him Master.

After he followed her into the aerobics room, he used his heel to kick the door shut while Linda flipped up the light switches. He'd already set up the room for what they needed, and Jack watched her look at the thin yoga mats on the floor. When she turned to ask him what the plan was, he was already unzipping his warm-up jacket.

"Is it just me, or is it hot in here?" he asked, smirking at Linda as he stripped it off, revealing a white-ribbed muscle shirt underneath. Her eyes widened as she took him in, and he flexed his arms slightly, making the muscles ripple. Linda's eyes bounced around, as if she couldn't decide on where to focus, and he reveled in the look of naked lust that was now on her face.

"Aren't you going to ask me what we're doing today?" he asked when the temptation to resist was getting too great.

"Sure."

"Yoga."

That snapped Linda out of whatever daze she was in, and she looked puzzled. "Yoga?"

"Mm-hmm."

"You know yoga?"

"In this business, you have to know a little bit of everything," he said nonchalantly. "I know the basics, and if you like it, we offer a class here a couple nights a week you can join. You have the flexibility for it, and I figured you'd enjoy trying something different."

"Don't you need to have some kind of balance for yoga?" Linda asked doubtfully.

"That's what I'm here for," Jack said, flicking her ponytail back and walking behind her. "I won't let you fall," he said in her ear softly. "And if worse comes to worst, we can focus on the lying-down positions."

He let her absorb this for a moment, but she still seemed hesitant. Knowing there was the potential for this to backfire, Jack stepped closer to Linda until his chest was against her back. He placed his hands on her shoulders lightly before running them down her arms. "Do you trust me?" he asked in a low voice.

"Yes," she whispered in reply.

"Come, then."

Jack reached for one of Linda's hands, turned her around, and began leading her to the thin mats he had on the floor. He toed his shoes off and waited for her to do the same. After she followed his lead, he stepped onto the mat, and she did as well, so that they faced one another.

"We'll start with the big toe pose."

Linda snorted, her nose curling up in a cute way. "Who names these things?"

"Probably a guy who couldn't pronounce the actual names," he replied, trying to remain serious and failing miserably. His lips quirked involuntarily.

"What's the actual name?"

"I don't know." He shrugged, now fully smiling. "I'm one of those guys."

Linda started laughing at him, and he scowled at her good-naturedly.

"Pay attention, Ms. Tanner."

"Sorry, Master," she said with a flash of a smile.

"Okay. Big toe pose. Spread your legs about six inches apart, contract your thigh muscles, exhale, and bend forward from your hips." Jack executed the move. "Hook your fingers around your big toes and point your elbows out."

Jack stood up and watched as Linda moved her feet, exhaled, and then folded forward.

"Like this?"

"Yes, but keep your head hanging down," he answered and walked to her side. This position was killing him. Linda had her ass in the air and her legs spread, and the images flying through his mind right then were downright dirty. Jack reached out and ran his hand along Linda's spine. "Nice, straight back," he said, his voice sounding almost like a growl in his ears. "Now inhale and make like you're going to stand up, keeping your fingers hooked under your toes."

It took most of Jack's willpower to move away from Linda and copy her. They stayed in this position for a minute before he instructed her to stand fully and then move into hands and knees position. Linda flicked a brow at him, and he grinned at her as he lowered himself to his knees. She followed suit, and then both of them were on hands and knees, facing one another, faces barely six inches apart. What Jack wouldn't give for Linda to crawl forward slightly to kiss him.

He waited for a few beats just to see if she would, but Linda stayed where she was, looking at him somewhat expectantly.

"This next position is the downward facing dog."

"Sounds kinky," Linda quipped, making Jack think that it *could* be if she gave him a chance. He kept that thought to himself as he explained what to do next.

Linda struggled with this position because, in order to execute it properly, you needed to balance on feet as well as hands while folded at the waist to form a human triangle. Jack stood beside her, hands on her hips as she maintained the pose. Every time he thought she was steady enough, he'd loosen his grip, but Linda would begin to wobble, so he'd grab hold again. Not that he minded.

From there, they moved into various poses as they continued through the session. During the lunging positions, Jack would straddle Linda's back leg and hold onto her shoulders until she was able to master it. While in one of the high lunges, she had her arms stretched up to the ceiling, hands clasped. After he pressed her palms together, he ran his fingers down her arms and placed his hands just below her underarms to keep her upright. He hadn't done it with much conscious thought, but once Linda was balanced, Jack realized the tips of his fingers were grazing the sides of her breasts. It would take nothing to slide in a little closer and cup them in his hands.

Thinking like that would definitely get him in trouble, so he moved his hands down her rib cage instead. Linda giggled and shifted her body side to side before he took hold of her hips. She tried to get back into the pose, but now she'd caught his attention. His fingers began creeping upward again, and she twitched under him.

"Are you ticklish?" he asked over her shoulder.

"No," she answered, but he could hear the warble in her voice, and she was wiggling more frantically now as his fingers moved over her ribcage.

"I think you are."

"No, Jack...*don't!*" Linda exclaimed in breathy exhalations, which made him laugh. She clamped her arms down over his hands, but the position she was in made her slightly helpless since she was still in a lunge and he was still straddling her back leg.

Linda tried to pull that leg upright and ended up hooking one of his calves, throwing Jack off balance and sending both of them toppling over. This time, there were no soft mats to land on, so he tried to break Linda's fall by throwing an arm down and holding her close to him to absorb the shock. It kind of worked, but they ended up on the floor anyway, laughing.

Jack was on his back, and she was on her side facing away from him.

"Are you okay?" he asked, still laughing.

"Owww…" Linda groaned as she rolled onto her back as well. She was also giggling, so he knew she wasn't really hurt. "Jerk!" she exclaimed, raising the arm closest to him and smacking him on the stomach.

"I tried to catch you!" he protested, seizing her flailing arm and holding it to his chest.

"You missed! And we wouldn't even be here if it wasn't for you and your fiddly fingers."

Entwining their hands, Jack rolled over and propped his head up so he could stare at Linda. Her eyes were bright, cheeks pink, and mouth parted in a gentle smile. He held their clasped hands against his chest over his heart. Once again, he found himself imagining what it would be like to really kiss her. Linda's lips looked so soft, kind of pouty. He'd bet they were even softer than they looked, and he wanted badly to find out if he was right.

Linda reached up, and for a moment, he thought she was going to pull his face down to hers and make his fantasy a reality. Instead, she pushed a lock of hair off his forehead. He closed his eyes as she continued to play with his hair. Jack was just about to turn his head and nuzzle her wrist when she moved her hand away. He opened his eyes and saw that she was focused on his tattoo, her hand hovering over it. The tattoo covered his deltoid, starting above his bicep, and went up across the top of his shoulder toward his neck, not far enough that a T-shirt wouldn't cover it fully. No one could see it unless he was shirtless or wearing a muscle shirt, like now.

"I like this," she said in a husky voice.

"You can touch it if you like," he said, hoping she did. He was craving the feel of her and figured he couldn't get into too much trouble if she was only touching his shoulder.

When Linda's hand moved to his arm and her fingers began tracing the thick lines of his tattoo, he realized just how wrong he was. His skin felt hypersensitive to her touch and having her so close yet unable to do anything about it heightened everything. This felt more like foreplay than it did innocent touching. Jack knew that Linda really had no clue about the effect she was having on him as she continued over the curve of his shoulder toward his collarbone, still following the pattern. If she went anywhere near his neck right now, he'd lose complete control.

Linda must have heard his silent plea, because her hand stopped where his tattoo ended, and then she did a slow circuit toward his back and down his arm again. Jack breathed a sigh of relief. He wondered how much more of this he could take. He wanted to see Linda away from the gym, somewhere they could be more private, so that if this urge to kiss her struck him, he could perhaps act on it.

"What are you doing tomorrow?" he asked on impulse.

"Not much," she answered, taking her eyes away from his tattoo and looking at him. "Usually, I take a morning walk, work on research for my articles, and then run down to Baltimore for a couple hours to check in. Nothing special."

"You take a morning walk?"

"Mm-hmm." She nodded and then made a wry face. "I don't trust myself to run, so I take a long walk instead."

"I didn't know that," he said, surprised that something so simple would fascinate him. Then he clued into the notion that he wanted to know all of Linda's mundane little daily activities. Only, he knew he wouldn't find them mundane at all. "Is it the same time every day?"

"Usually around seven a.m. The mornings are cooler. Not that it ever really gets hot in Arnold." Linda's nose crinkled, making Jack laugh.

"Why do you live here?" he asked. "You work in Baltimore. Why not live there?"

"This is my home," she said simply. "The house I live in belonged to my parents. I grew up and spent my whole life there. Even when Graham and I lived in Baltimore, it never really felt right. He wanted me to sell the house so we could be debt free when we bought our condo, but I just couldn't."

"How come?"

"It's the only thing I have left of them." Her voice was quiet and her eyes sad.

Jack squeezed her hand, which was still held in his, and she gave him a small smile.

"So you'll never leave here?"

"Well, never is a pretty strong word. Maybe, if it feels right."

He didn't know why that made him happy, but it did. It wasn't like he had any big plans of leaving Arnold anytime soon.

"So…I guess the session is over?" she asked. To Jack, she sounded a little regretful, but it might have been wishful thinking on his part.

"Looks like," he replied, looking at his watch. He didn't bother trying to mask his disappointment. "Did you like the yoga? Is it something you'd like to try again?"

"Sure. It was fun."

Jack didn't want to let Linda's hand go but knew he had to. Before he did, he pulled it up to his mouth and kissed the back of it. Linda turned a pretty shade of pink. He really did hope she was getting used to his little shows of affection. Maybe then she'd believe him when he admitted he wanted to be more than just her personal trainer. More than just her friend.

When Linda left the club, Jack had an idea on how he could see her during off time. While he still hated to say good-bye, this time it didn't seem as bad because he knew he'd be seeing her sooner than usual.

12
We Step in Time

Jack waited outside for Linda to join him. He supposed that after spending more than a week of walking with her every morning, he could just go up to her door and ring the doorbell, but something about seeing her face when she walked outside made his morning. It was almost as good as the first time.

He'd been worried the first morning he showed up at her house that she wouldn't be too crazy about the idea of him intruding on her walks, but he was a desperate man. Desperate for more time with her away from all the distractions and prying eyes of the club. Vicky's statement about Linda still being seen as a married woman bothered him, and while he couldn't care less about who saw them together doing what, he cared enough about Linda not to want to tarnish her reputation. Small towns usually harbored small minds and were breeding grounds for gossip. She may have been separated for a few months now, but it seemed like a lot of people didn't know that.

Frowning to himself, Jack tried not to think about it too much.

Linda practically charged out of the house, and he tried to suppress the chuckle at her enthusiasm. Jack remembered the first time he had waited for her, the nervousness and anticipation that had coiled deep in his gut. How he held his breath as he waited for her to finish locking her front door, look up, and finally notice him standing there. She had stopped, looking like a deer in headlights, eyes wide and startled as she took him in. He tried to keep his hands from curling into anxious fists until, finally, her mouth twitched before spreading into the brightest smile he had ever seen. She was happy to find him there, and he was ecstatic.

It had been like that every day since then.

"Hello, beautiful," he said when she was practically on top of him. "Did you have a good night?"

"I did."

Linda smiled at him, and that, combined with the sweetness of her voice, sparked a kernel of heat that spread pleasantly through his body. Jack reached out to tug the ever present ponytail, and as he brought his hand back, he brushed her cheek with his thumb. It was something new he'd started to do, wanting to be able to touch her in any way she'd allow. So many times as they walked along the wooded paths behind her home, he considered what it would feel like to stop Linda and push her up against a tree, trapping her, kissing her, stealing a fleeting touch. Something. Anything.

For all the time it had taken him to get to this point, he was impatient. He was curious. He was horny.

It wasn't all physical, of course. That had never been what their relationship was about, despite that particular development. Jack loved this time they shared because it felt less hurried and a hell of a lot more private than their sessions at the club, including the ones in the aerobic room. He liked the solitude and the hushed conversations they had. The way they could talk about anything and everything. The way she constantly amazed him with her views on life and how in sync they were with his own. So many times he marveled at how they seemed to be the opposite sides of the same coin.

Sometimes, in the quiet of the morning, when all they could hear was the shushing sounds of the leaves overhead and the birds that nested there, he was overcome by the emotions he felt for this woman who walked by his side. Especially since he hadn't so much as kissed her yet. That was one thing that continuously amazed him — that he could feel such a profound connection with someone he had yet to be intimate with. This also scared him on occasion. He wondered just how deeply he'd fall if they did ever pass into the realm of a physical relationship.

Linda's fingers brushed against his hand, bringing him back to the present.

"You're quiet this morning," she said, her hushed voice barely registering.

"Just thinking," he replied, staring down at the path and smiling to himself.

"Of what?"

"The first morning we went walking."

Linda turned a surprised face to him, her brows arched high, but she was smiling. "Why were you thinking about that?"

"I was just thinking of how surprised you looked."

"I *was* surprised." That secretive little smile was still in place before she looked away.

"You didn't have any idea I'd join you? Not even after I asked what time you went walking?"

"None at all."

"Even though I asked if you went the same time *every* morning?"

Linda laughed in a self-deprecating way. "Now you're making me feel particularly slow."

"I like to think maybe you were just too distracted by my body that day."

Now they both laughed, but he didn't fail to notice the tint that rose to her cheeks. Jack enjoyed throwing out lines like this occasionally just to watch her react. Part of him hoped she'd agree with him so he could stop playing these games, take her in his arms, and kiss her silly. Linda had a visible reaction whenever he mentioned anything to do with his body, but still she remained silent. It was simultaneously cute and annoying as hell.

They lapsed into silence, Jack lost in fantasy and Linda musing about whatever it was that went on in her head during moments like these. Her cheeks were still a little on the pink side, and he'd kill to see the tickertape in her mind that was causing the expression on her face now. He imagined it was good and maybe even similar to the things he thought of when they were together. And apart.

Especially when they were apart.

Too soon, Jack found himself back in front of Linda's house, saying good-bye. He hated when their walks were over, especially on the days when he wouldn't be seeing her in the afternoon for their workout sessions. When they got to his car, instead of stopping like she usually did, Linda continued up the path leading to her porch. She looked over her shoulder at him, not hearing his footsteps any longer. He lingered beside his car, unsure of what to do. Linda turned back to him, looking shy all of a sudden before she thumbed over her shoulder toward the house.

"Did you, um, want to come in for a coffee?"

Jack stood there stunned for a second. This was a new development. Usually, he said good-bye and went home to waste time before going to the gym. Or he headed there directly to take his frustrations out on the weights. This slow-and-steady-wins-the-race attitude sometimes took a toll on him.

"Yeah, sure," he answered finally when he noticed Linda start to fidget nervously.

"You don't have to —" she began in a small voice.

"No, I want to." He rushed to smooth over the awkwardness. "You just caught me by surprise."

"Sorry."

Linda looked down at the ground she was currently toeing with her running shoe. Jack couldn't resist stepping up to her and curling a finger under her chin.

"You don't need to be sorry," he said softly. Her eyes fluttered for a second before she tipped them up to his. Jack's stomach clenched almost painfully from want at the look he saw there. It was pure, naked desire, and if not for his fear that he would molest Linda on her doorstep, he'd have crushed his lips to hers right then. Jack contented himself with running a thumb across her chin, the tip of it skimming her bottom lip for a fraction of a second.

"So," he murmured, "coffee?"

Linda squeed internally and tried not to show the magnitude of her excitement that Jack was sitting in her kitchen. And that he looked so incredibly good right here in her home. It had taken her the better part of the week to get up the courage to ask him to stay, and this morning she'd finally done it. Linda had been so prepared for a refusal that his acceptance had caught her completely off guard.

And that moment they'd shared out in her front yard had made her somewhat giddy. They'd had a few moments like that since he'd started joining her on her morning walks. Linda could swear there were times when Jack looked like he wanted to kiss her or do something. It was still mostly hard to believe, but she couldn't quell the feeling.

Every time it would happen, Linda would wait with bated breath and pray that Jack would bend down to kiss her. And every time, she was disappointed when he pulled back. She took it as a sign that she was seeing things where there was nothing. If she had any type of courage at all, she'd make a move herself and see what happened, but she wasn't ready to do that.

First would be the subsequent humiliation if Jack pulled back in horror. Second was, then what?

His relationship with Vicky was still undefined. Jack had yet to even admit the girl lived with him, much less that there was anything else going on between them. And on top of that were her issues with her body. Linda still didn't think she had it in her to get naked, and a man like Jack wouldn't subsist on kissing alone. At least not for long. Not to mention Linda would probably combust in the meantime.

Even though she was down twenty-five pounds, that still wasn't anywhere near her comfort zone. That being said, if given the chance, Linda was relatively certain she wouldn't be able to refuse. And that left her in quite the quandary. Best to just keep things innocent until she was comfortable enough in her own skin or, best-case scenario, Jack professed his undying love and devotion.

Linda snorted at that thought.

"What's so funny?" Jack asked from behind her, and Linda was happy that she had her back turned to him so he couldn't see the expression on her face.

"Nothing."

"It is too something."

Linda turned to face Jack and cocked a brow at him. "Do you want to tell me what *you* were giggling at outside my house?"

"Touché."

"That's what I thought."

When she finished preparing the coffee, she brought the mugs to the table and debated whether to sit beside or across from Jack. She finally decided to sit on the opposite side of him so she could enjoy the view less obtrusively. Gosh, he was pretty. He'd shaved recently, perhaps even this morning, and his face looked baby-skin smooth. He looked particularly youthful freshly shaven; Linda preferred him with a bit of scruff, if only to make herself feel like less of a cougar chasing after a man who was way too young.

She tried to school her face so she didn't look like she was mooning at him as he lifted his mug to take a sip of his coffee. His brows rose in a surprised expression as he swallowed.

"Is everything okay?" she asked.

"Yeah," he said bringing the mug up again and drinking more. "You made my coffee exactly the way I like it."

"Oh." Linda couldn't believe how ridiculously happy that simple statement made her. "I just made it like I do mine."

"It's perfect," he said, smiling down into his cup. It was the same expression he had outside on her front walk, like he'd discovered some great mystery.

"There's that look again! What is it that you keep laughing about?"

Jack glanced up and raised a brow. "Ready to tell me what you were laughing at while getting the coffee ready?"

"Touché," she said back to him and took a sip from her mug.

They continued to drink in silence, sharing the occasional look and grin. The silence would have been deafening if it weren't so comfortable. Linda could get used to this. She was glad she had asked Jack to join her this morning, especially since it was Friday and the weekends always seemed especially long without his presence. Then she remembered that he would most likely be waiting for her outside tomorrow morning, and that thought cheered her up considerably.

Jack glanced down at his watch and frowned slightly. He looked up with an apologetic expression. "I have to get going," he said in what Linda thought was a regretful voice.

"That's okay."

"I don't mean to just drink and run," he replied earnestly, leaning across the table slightly.

"It's fine, Jack." Linda chuckled. "I know you have to get to work. Thank you for joining me."

"Thank you for asking."

Once again, they were staring at one another as if waiting for something important to happen. Linda wished she knew what it was. Or that she had the courage to find out. The thing was, there was more than just her kitchen table standing between them. Remembering this, she dropped her eyes and fiddled with her mug. She could have sworn she heard Jack sigh before he pushed his chair back from the table.

Linda stood as well and walked him to her door. Every morning before saying good-bye, Jack would kiss her on the cheek in farewell. Usually, it was beside his car after their walk, so Linda got a special little thrill for some reason that today, he'd be kissing her good-bye on her doorstep instead.

"I'll see you later at the club?" he murmured, and she nodded her head. "See you then."

She waited a little breathlessly as he bent toward her. The first few times he'd kissed her good-bye, it had been toward the edge of her jaw, but Linda had noticed over the course of the week that his kisses had been steadily nearing her lips each day. Today was no exception, and ever so softly, she felt them brush just at the side of her mouth. Her stomach exploded in crazy butterflies when Jack pulled back slightly, his tongue curled out to lick against his bottom lip, and he stared at her for a moment. It was pregnant with expectation, and Linda wondered what would happen if she leaned forward *just* a little.

Today, she didn't have the guts, but maybe tomorrow? That way if anything mortifying happened, it would be a Saturday and she wouldn't have to see him until the next Monday. Linda stepped back, and Jack straightened up, and for the life of her, she could swear he looked disappointed.

"Bye," she whispered.

"Bye, Linda," he said in return, giving her a small smile before turning and bounding down her steps toward his car. She watched him leave like she always did, waving slightly in case he was looking.

An hour later, Linda was walking into Cici's shop. The diminutive girl rushed over and hugged her.

"I haven't seen you in so long!" she exclaimed, making Linda laugh.

"Cici, it's only been a few weeks."

"I know, but look at you!" she said, stepping away. "You're disappearing before my very eyes."

Linda looked down at herself. That was almost what Eliza had said too. Was she the only one who didn't see the miraculous weight loss? She recognized that she'd lost weight and was beginning to look better, but she still felt very large, and in comparison to her slim friends and the women at the gym, she felt ginormous.

"So, you're here for clothes, I take it?" Cici continued. She gave a smart tug on Linda's loose pant leg, and it slid halfway down her hip.

"Hey!" Linda cried out in surprise and made a frantic grab before her pants ended up on the floor. Maybe she should have dug deep into her closet to see if she could find any clothes from a couple of years back.

Cici laughed before turning away and making her way to the clothes racks. She eyed Linda's frame critically before grabbing different pairs at random and handing them back for Linda to take. Looking at the tags, she shook her head at the size Cici had picked for her.

"Cici, these are way too small. I'll never fit my fat ass into them."

"Just trust me," the younger woman sang back at her and continued to rummage through the clothing. She also started handing pretty shirts to Linda as well.

"And I only need pants."

Cici snickered at her. "No you don't. You can't wear brand new pants with old ratty shirts. We're doing a fashion overhaul!"

"I kind of wanted to wait until I lost more weight before doing an overhaul," Linda muttered, frowning.

Cici turned and faced her, looking aghast. "Why? You should celebrate how good you look now!"

Linda looked down at herself doubtfully. "Why would I want to celebrate *this?*"

Cici took the clothes from Linda's hands and put them on a nearby table. Once she set them down, she grabbed Linda's hand and propelled her to a full-length mirror. Cici rolled a small wire basket toward them and then started gathering Linda's loose clothing and clipping it together at her back. When she was done, she stepped beside Linda and looked at her in the mirror.

"First of all, you have fabulous tits. I have no idea why you don't show them off more often. And see how your waist nips in? Gives you an awesome hourglass shape." Cici turned Linda sideways and traced the outer curve of her backside. "Your butt's quite nice, too. Very smackable."

With that, Cici pulled back her hand and smacked Linda's ass, making her jump and laugh. She reached back and rubbed the spot, eyeing Cici. She had some power for such a small thing. The girl just laughed at her and turned her to face the mirror again.

"We'd have to do some camouflaging here," she continued, making a circular motion over Linda's tummy, which had yet to show much change since she started exercising. Cici gestured to Linda's sides. "And a little bit here…Ruching. That'll fix it! With a little bit of work, you'll look mahvelous, dahling!"

"I feel like I'm on an episode of *What Not to Wear,*" Linda grumbled.

"Just call me Stacy!" Cici quipped in return before beginning to unclip Linda's clothes.

Linda's facial expression must have given away her doubts, so Cici brought out the big guns. "Come on, Linda. Don't you want to look nice for Jack?"

"Why would I want to do that?" Linda asked, looking down at the floor. She was embarrassed that Cici had read her obsession over Jack so clearly after only spending a few hours with them.

"I don't know…You guys looked kind of cozy when we went to dinner before the show."

"Until his *girlfriend* showed up," Linda mumbled, turning away.

"Amanda's not his girlfriend!" Cici giggled.

"I wasn't talking about Amanda."

"Then who? You mean that blond girl who was with her?"

Linda knew she should probably keep her mouth shut since their relationship was supposed to be hush-hush, but she couldn't help herself. "Yeah, Vicky."

Cici made a face and looked incredibly perplexed. "Linda, I don't think Jack is with Vicky. I mean, he didn't even talk to her after you left that night."

"He didn't?"

"No! He was too busy running after you when he found out you left."

"What?"

"Linda, he was really upset that you left without saying good-bye."

"He was?" she replied, feeling a stab of guilt.

"Yeah. He tried to catch you, but I guess you were already gone. He didn't talk to anyone else the rest of the night and left as soon as Rob's band was finished playing."

"I didn't know that," Linda said quietly.

Cici had just given her quite a bit to think about. Once again, she wondered if Vicky had been lying about being with Jack. She'd always been afraid her emotions for Jack would be painfully transparent, and perhaps they would be, but if Vicky had indeed been lying about their relationship, then it would answer a lot of questions.

And maybe it would serve to prove that she shouldn't be afraid of what she felt for Jack. Because maybe he felt the same way too.

Linda's automatic reaction was to think she was crazy. But then she turned back to the mirror. She took her loose-fitting shirt and pulled it closer to her body. Turning her head to the side, she viewed herself critically and decided that she didn't actually look *too* bad.

"Cici?" she called out.

"Yeah?"

"I think you're right. Let's do a makeover."

Linda cringed at the squeal that sounded out somewhere behind her and then began to laugh.

13
Parking Lot Confessional

As she headed to her car, Linda wondered what it would be like to spend time with Jack in a non-exercise way. Not sex, per se—goodness knew she already spent a good chunk of her time fantasizing about that—but more like the open mic nights in Baltimore. Linda remembered dinner with Rob and Cici and how wonderful it had felt to have Jack sit so close to her. His occasional touches, the whispers in her ear, his easy mannerisms, and how safe she felt because his arm was almost wrapped around her. Linda loved that feeling of being in a couple. Not just any couple, however, but one with Jack at her side.

As usual, the trip to the club was short, and she found herself parking behind *Self-sational* sooner than expected. Of course, this didn't bother Linda because that just meant she would see Jack in the flesh instead of just daydreaming about him. She got out of her car and practically skipped her way to the front of the building.

When she saw Jack, the first thing she thought about was the kiss he'd left her with that morning. She could swear the skin was still tingling by the side of her mouth where his lips had left an imprint. Or it may have been the fact that her face was starting to blaze at the memory. As she got closer, Jack gave her a look, tilting his head to the side as she tried to control her smile.

"Why are you blushing like that?" he asked, moving close enough so he could whisper in her ear.

"No reason," she laughed and shook her head.

"Oh, there's a reason," he replied. "Don't make me drag you to one of the back rooms to find out."

Linda squeaked very unbecomingly, making Jack chuckle. She cleared her throat. "We don't have a session in the back today," she managed to get out.

"Yeah? So?"

"Be good," she replied, even though she wanted him to be bad. Very bad. Naughty, even. "And maybe I'll tell you later."

Linda stepped away quickly and watched the dangerous flash of Jack's eyes. The one that clearly said if he could get away with it, he'd be picking her up bodily and bringing her somewhere private. He looked around surreptitiously and obviously decided against it. Linda was almost disappointed, but then she smiled and walked to the public exercise area of the club.

Since it was Friday, Jack had to behave himself, and she hated it. They just had so much more fun together when they had their private sessions. Since the whole Candy Bellham situation, Linda was very aware that people took notice of them, and she didn't want to get Jack into trouble with Jimmy because he was seemingly showing favoritism to one client over his others. Of course, Linda loved that this was the case, and it gave her a secret little thrill.

As she started her stretching exercises, she began to wonder if perhaps Jack's little dalliance with Vicky was over. Maybe it had just been a quick little fling. Linda still wasn't happy about it happening at all, and it made her grind her teeth together in agitation that Vicky might have had her filthy paws on Jack, but she supposed there was nothing she could do about it now. She couldn't wait to finally ask him about it and clear the air once and for all. She'd ask him tomorrow after seeing if he wanted to come in for coffee. Her body warmed up pleasantly as she remembered him sitting at her cozy kitchen table, and she really wanted more mornings like that.

Thinking about tomorrow reminded her to find out if he was going to be in Baltimore this weekend. She opened her mouth several times to ask but then snapped it shut again, losing courage. Linda didn't really have any idea how to bring it up in casual conversation without it sounding absolutely contrived. Jack was standing behind her, helping keep the alignment of her arms in check as she did flies with the hand weights. He sighed after a few minutes and then came around to face her, squatting down so they were on the same level.

"Spit it out."

Linda started to laugh. "What?"

"I don't know. You tell me. You keep taking a breath like you're going to say something, and then you don't." He cocked a brow at her. "So, either you have something to say, or you're having an asthma attack. Which one is it?"

"Asthma?" she answered, and Jack gave her an *Oh, really?* look.

"Linda."

"Okay, I'm not having an asthma attack."

"I didn't think so," he said, smiling. "So what's up?"

"I was just, um, wondering if you were playing in Baltimore tomorrow."

"That's what you wanted to ask me?" Jack didn't seem convinced, and that, of course, made her blush because when he put it like that, it was stupid that she couldn't have simply asked him.

"Yeah," she replied softly.

"You drive me crazy when you blush like that," he murmured quietly. So quietly, in fact, Linda was sure she had misheard him.

"Pardon?"

Jack shook his head at her. "Nothing…silly girl. You know I'd come find you if I was in Baltimore."

"You would?"

"Yes." Jack's hands had been on her knees, and now they were creeping slowly up her thighs. "You still owe me a date." He leaned in closer, and she had the odd impulse to close her eyes, as if waiting for a kiss.

"That's true," she replied softly instead. "So, are you?"

"I hadn't made plans to, but I can always check if they have an open spot," he mused. "Would you like me to?"

Linda nodded and smiled, and the look of joy on Jack's face stunned her for a second. He looked genuinely happy. And, of course, that made Linda inordinately happy as well.

"I'll call tonight and let you know in the morning."

"Okay."

They sat there smiling shyly at one another for a few beats before Linda realized they were getting side-eyed by the other people in the club. She glanced down, cleared her throat, and then looked around her for a second. Jack got the hint and also snapped out of his reverie. He glanced about and then got up, but not before giving her legs a reassuring squeeze.

Linda began doing flies again, and Jack took up a position behind her like before. When no one was paying attention to them anymore, he began to stroke her hair softly, and she almost dropped the weights. God, she adored it when he did that. It was almost habit now, as if he had no clue he was doing it and no control to stop himself. She really hoped he could swing tomorrow night; she missed the sound of Jack's voice as he sang. And she was really looking forward to spending more time with him.

The rest of the session flew by, and next thing Linda knew, she was heading back to the change rooms for a shower and to make herself look pretty before she said good-bye to Jack. It seemed like such a long time until tomorrow morning. She hummed quietly to herself as the shower stall filled up with body wash-scented steam. While in there, she thought about nothing else but Jack.

"Hurry, hurry!" Linda heard as two women walked into the change room. "Come on! I want to show you!"

"Relax, Vicky!" a voice called out before laughing shrilly. She recognized it as Michelle's.

Crap, Linda thought. *Trapped again.*

"What is the big rush?"

"I just thought you might want to take a look at *these.*" Vicky giggled.

"Oh my God! You lucky, lucky bitch!"

"I know, right? He's so adorable when he's sleeping. I couldn't resist taking a few pictures."

"Aww...look at the two of you snuggled in bed. So cute," Michelle gushed, and Linda's stomach plummeted.

Please, she begged. *Please let it be someone else. Someone new.* Not *Jack.*

"I told you," Vicky said, and Linda couldn't help but note the smugness in her voice.

"I know," Michelle conceded. "It's just weird how he doesn't really pay any attention to you at all here at the club."

Linda put her hands up against the side of the shower stall to keep herself upright. Her worst fears were coming true.

"I already told you why," Vicky whined. "Jimmy still has that stupid rule."

"Hmm…I don't think I could handle it if my boyfriend was friendlier with his clients than he was with me."

"Oh, he's just really serious about his job," she continued, her voice grating on Linda's nerves like nails on a chalkboard. "I tell him he's too nice and he might be leading some of his clients on, but he says he's not. Sometimes he goes a bit overboard trying to help. He's just too sweet to say *no*. Know what I mean?"

"Maybe I should have hired Jack, then!" Michelle cackled; it bounced off the walls of the small space, making Linda cringe.

"Shut up!" Vicky replied, laughing.

The noises the ladies had been making receded, and Linda was left alone with her own thoughts. She reached forward and shut off the water, which left both the dripping from the shower and the words Vicky had said echoing throughout the room. Well, at least now she had her answer. Linda tried to fight the rising hysteria threatening to engulf her. She couldn't be so crazy that she was simply imagining what was going on between her and Jack. Sometimes, the tension between them was so thick you could cut it with a knife.

Was it possible that what Vicky said was right? Jack just took his job so seriously that he was willing to do whatever it took to help her reach her goal? That certainly wouldn't include side trips to Baltimore, she was sure of it. But how could he still be sharing his bed with Vicky while seemingly pursuing her as well? None of it made sense. The only reason Linda could come up with was that Jack wasn't attracted to her but still liked her. He was probably waiting to see what she looked like once she was thin again to see if maybe then he could stomach being intimate with her.

Linda dried herself off and put on her underwear. She walked out of the shower stall in bra, panties, and a towel wrapped loosely around her. When she got to the full-length mirror, she opened her towel and stared at herself dispassionately. She tried to see the good things, she honestly did, but all she could see was cellulite and fat rolls. Linda tried not to sob as she thought about Vicky's tight little body pressed up against Jack's hard, cut one.

Maybe his mind and spirit were with Linda, but his body was elsewhere. That would certainly explain why he never tried to touch her inappropriately or kiss her, despite the multiple chances he'd had. It made sense as to why everything was so chaste. Kisses on hands and cheeks, never on lips. His fingers always on outer edges of her body, never slipping to brush or caress anywhere intimate, not even by accident. There may have been something about her that attracted him, but not in *that* way. Not in the way Linda was attracted to him.

Linda finished getting ready, put on her biggest smile, and went out to face Jack. She tried to act like she normally did, and he didn't seem to suspect anything was wrong. She wondered how she would handle tomorrow. Could she go through with their date now that she knew he'd probably be going home to Vicky in his bed? No, most likely not. She would have to think of an adequate excuse to get out of it.

It was all a little too much for her to take, and as Linda stood on the sidewalk outside of the club, her eyes fell on the pastry shop across the street. She'd always thought it was kind of a cruel twist of fate to have Arnold's only pâtisserie almost directly across from their one fitness club. It didn't take long to make up her mind that she needed some sugar therapy. She felt a pang of guilt and knew that this would only prolong the time it took for her to be good enough for Jack, but she felt the pull regardless.

With hesitant steps, she crossed the street and was soon surrounded by the smell of freshly baked desserts. The scent and warmth enveloped her. It felt almost like coming home.

Jack frowned as he watched Linda leave the club. Something had seemed off, but he couldn't put his finger on it. She had come out of the change room, and he hadn't noticed anything strange until she was standing in front of him. There seemed to be a slight distance there, and for a moment, he was terrified they had regressed again. But then she smiled, and things seemed all right. They made plans to meet in the morning and tentative ones for the evening.

He still couldn't believe that Linda had initiated a date between them. Even if it had taken her forever to spit it out. Jack smiled as he remembered how embarrassed she had looked when asking if he'd be in Baltimore this weekend. This would be perfect since he had been trying to figure out a way to spend more alone time with her. This time, he'd make sure there were no interruptions from meddling roommates, and maybe he'd even see if Linda would like to have dinner with him alone instead of with Cici and Rob.

He was so caught up in his plans that he didn't really notice Vicky standing by the window wall. She only caught Jack's eye when he saw her sidling along the glass with her neck craned to one side. What the hell was she doing? Right then, she spun on her heel with a huge smile on her face and launched over to where he stood.

"Hey, Jack. Are you busy?" she asked in a shy, baby voice. Vicky's arms were behind her back, and she rocked back and forth on her heels.

"Why?" he inquired suspiciously.

"I wanted to grab some coffees and pastries for everyone from the shop across the street, but I can't carry everything back by myself."

"Why don't you ask Amanda?"

"She's busy with a client," Vicky replied quickly. "Please?"

"Okay, sure," he sighed. He wasn't all that jazzed about doing anything with Vicky, but since he had nothing else to do, he figured he could help her out. Plus, a chocolate-covered croissant sounded good right about now.

Vicky smiled at him sweetly, and even though most people would have smiled back, Jack had to repress a shudder. It wasn't that she disgusted him, but more that there was something cold and calculating about her expression, and it made him slightly nervous. He shook it off. It's not like the girl could do anything to him.

When he started walking, Vicky tried to link arms with him. Stopping, he looked down at the hand that was curled around his bicep. He scowled at her, and she dropped her arm right away.

"No?" she inquired innocently.

"No."

"I don't get you, Jack," she said once they resumed walking again. "You are the only guy I know who hates attention from hot women. Are you gay or something?"

Jack rolled his eyes and scoffed openly. "Just because I'm not interested in you doesn't make me gay."

"Well, you're not interested in Amanda either," she pointed out.

"Amanda is like my sister," he answered in a scornful voice.

"Seriously, Jack, why are you single?"

Because the woman I want is in denial. "I don't think that's any of your business."

"*Soooorrryyyy.*"

"Look, I came with you to help, not to get grilled on my marital status."

Vicky snickered but remained blessedly quiet as they crossed the street and walked into the pastry shop. Jack saw a familiar fall of hair at the counter in front of them as the clerk was counting pastries in a box.

"Linda?" he asked happily and was alarmed and confused to see her shoulders hunch up at the sound of his voice. They slumped back down as she turned toward him with a guilty look on her face.

"Jack," she said in a tiny voice.

"Long time no see," he joked, trying to figure out why she looked so upset.

"Oh, my God," he heard Vicky say; he had forgotten she was even there. "You have enough food here to feed an army!"

Jack watched as Linda closed her eyes and her lips pressed into a thin line. Everything made so much more sense now. She was embarrassed for buying sweets and that he had caught her here most likely in a moment of weakness.

"Jeez, Linda," Vicky continued. "All that hard work Jack puts into your sessions, and you turn around and stuff your face with carbs?"

Jack's head turned slowly toward Vicky, and he saw something else very clearly. He was struck speechless at the callousness of the girl's voice and also felt Linda's mortification at being called out, not only in front of him but the entire store.

Making a wounded sound, Linda pushed past them and headed for the door. Jack made a grab for her arm, but she moved too quickly. "Linda, wait!" he called out, but it was too late. He was about to run after her, but when he saw the look of unadulterated glee on Vicky's face in the wake of Linda's humiliation, he knew he had something to do first.

"You scheming little bitch," he spit out. "You *planned* this!"

Vicky pretended to look insulted, and the hand that had been trying to hide her smile fell from her face. "How was I supposed to know she'd be here buying her weight in pastries?"

"Because you saw her from the window!"

"Jack, come on —"

"*She's* why I'm single," he said, pointing viciously at the door. "*She's* the one I want. But because of assholes like you and her ex-husband, she doesn't realize that she is one of the most beautiful women I've met."

"Oh, please!" Vicky huffed, rolling her eyes.

"Fuck you," he replied, cutting off whatever was coming next. "And get the fuck out of my house. When I come back, I want you gone."

"*What?*"

"You heard me."

"You're not the only who can make that decision!" Vicky sputtered at him indignantly.

"You think Amanda's going to choose your skanky ass over me? Trust me when I tell you she won't." He turned away, disgusted, and faced the clerk. "How much for this?" he asked, pointing at the box of treats.

"Seventeen dollars," the wide-eyed girl whispered.

Jack tossed twenty dollars on the counter, closed the box, and picked it up before turning back to a stunned Vicky. "You better be moved out before I get back home, or else I'm throwing you out," he said softly before striding out of the store.

"Sir, your change!" the clerk called out from behind him.

"Keep it."

As soon as he was out of the shop, Jack raced toward the club parking lot. He was hoping to catch Linda before she left, but in the off chance he missed her, he had his car and he knew where she lived. Hopefully she would drive straight home, but if he had to park in front of her house and wait for her to get there, he would.

Jack sighed with relief when he rounded the corner and found Linda standing by her car. And then he was struck anew with anger when he realized she was using it as a means of support. Linda's hands were over her face, and she looked as if she was crying. Jack's heart broke. He hated seeing her like this, especially over something as inconsequential as pastries. It was ridiculous that she was beating herself up over this, but he knew that was exactly what she was doing.

Taking his time, he wove between a few cars until he was close to Linda. Instinctively, he knew she would hate for him to see her like this, but there was no way he was going to let her continue crying.

With the declaration of his feelings still fresh on his lips, he decided it was time to let Linda know how he felt about her, and he prayed that she would believe him.

"Linda?"

Like before, Linda felt her shoulders hunch up at the gentle voice behind her. She kicked herself for not just getting in her car and driving away, but the tears had come on fast and furious, and she was afraid that her blurry vision would cause her to get into a car accident.

Then again, it would fit since bad things usually happened in threes.

Linda was embarrassed, humiliated, mortified. Pick your verb. What had happened in the pastry shop just now was probably one of the lowest points of her life, and that was saying a lot.

It was like a nightmare come true. Linda in a moment of supreme weakness. Jack showing up with Vicky in tow and listening as the little witch denigrated her publicly. This was even worse than the day she'd lost her verbal filter and admitted to Jack that she wanted to be fucked. Hard.

She'd been loath to face him then, and she wished she didn't have to face him now. Linda really didn't want to see the disappointment in his eyes, or worse, the total disgust she was sure to see at the monumental number of sweets she had been about to purchase. Maybe she could convince him to leave her alone so she could go home in shame and in peace.

"It's okay, Jack," she finally replied as she scrubbed the wetness from her cheeks. "Crisis averted. No need to set up a suicide sugar watch."

"Linda," he sighed. "Please, turn around."

"What do you want?" Her voice wavered dangerously.

"You forgot this," he answered. She heard him put something on the hood of her car and slide it over. It was the box of pastries. Linda cringed. Was he trying to rub it in? Embarrass her further?

"Jesus, Jack," she replied acerbically. "Do you make it a habit to yell *Jump!* at the guy standing on the ledge, too?"

"You're allowed to have a pastry, Linda," he replied, a note of exasperation in his voice.

"Yeah," she said, turning to face him. "*A pastry, Jack. Not a box of them," she replied disgustedly.

"Okay, you're right," he answered, still using that sweet, calming tone. "So, then, instead of eating them all, you can share."

"With who?" she asked softly, his demeanor breaking down her self-hatred.

"With me, tomorrow morning for breakfast."

"After our walk?"

"That's not quite what I had in mind." Jack moved closer to her, making Linda turn so that her back was against her car. He was staring down at her in a disconcertingly sexy way.

"What did you have in mind?" she asked in confusion.

"What if I told you I don't want to wait?" he asked, brushing his thumb down her cheek.

"Wait for what?" Linda whispered as she got lost in his intense gaze.

"For you to reach your goal."

"What are you saying?"

"Take me home with you, Linda," he replied in a husky voice.

Jack's hand cradled her face, his thumb sliding underneath her chin. Slowly, he turned her face up toward his, and then he closed the distance between them. His head lowered, and his lips brushed against hers, whisper-soft. Linda took a quick breath, filling her lungs with his essence before his mouth descended on hers once more. Her stomach was quaking, her mind was whirling, and her knees were threatening to buckle.

Linda broke the kiss and asked breathlessly, "What about Vicky?"

"Fuck Vicky," Jack growled in her ear and then began kissing her jaw.

"No, thank you," Linda replied and was rewarded with a deep chuckle. "What about your car?"

"Fuck my car," he answered, moving soft lips down the column of her neck.

"I'd rather fuck your car than Vicky," she muttered distractedly.

"I'd rather you fuck *me,"* was his reply, and now Linda's knees did buckle slightly as a tingle shot from the top of her head all the way down her body.

"Oh, God," she moaned as she leaned back against her car.

"Please, Linda, don't make me beg."

Jack leaned his body against hers fully, and a hard, insistent presence pushed against her soft belly. He began kissing her again, harder this time, more desperately, and that broke the spell. Whatever had been holding her back dissipated like a puff of smoke. She pushed the button on her key fob, praying it was the right one, and heard her car unlock. She broke away again and looked at Jack; he was breathing rapidly, and his eyes were excited.

"Get in," she ordered.

"Yes, Master," he replied with a grin.

14
Breaking Down Defenses

Linda stopped in the entryway of her house with Jack. The drive home had sobered her up, and now she was unsure if she had the courage to go through with this. Her body yearned for Jack and more of that punch-drunk feeling he gave her. She craved him like nothing else.

But her mind was at war with the rest of her. It kept trying to override her senses by screaming obscenities at her. It reminded her that she was still pudgy and nowhere near her goal. Every part of her was still round and soft and dimpled, and how would that feel to Jack, who had probably only known perfection in his previous sexual partners?

Jack stared at her as she stood there. His eyes were hooded, his mouth slightly parted, and she remembered the taste of him with aching clarity. The feel of him. Her body was gaining ground in the battle against her mind, but it wasn't quite strong enough to fight all the verbal abuse and self-hatred.

"I don't think I can do this," she said quietly, looking at the floor.

Jack's feet came into view as he neared. Even his feet were perfect, she thought incoherently.

"Just let me kiss you," he said in a tender voice. "I just want to kiss you, Linda. If that's all that happens, I'll be happy."

Linda looked up then, and he was there. So close, so warm, so tempting. She reached up a hand and caressed his cheek. Jack closed his eyes at her touch and then turned his face so he could kiss her palm. She was amazed and awed at his gentle reverence. His lips were so soft, so sweet. He covered her hand with his, pressed it closer to his mouth, and then inhaled deeply, as if he could breathe in her very essence.

"Let me kiss your lips," he said against her hand, and Linda closed her eyes against the gentle entreaty.

She felt him move closer to her, and now their bodies were touching. She swayed into him involuntarily, and his arms were there to catch her and hold her to him. Oh, so gentle as he encircled her waist. Linda couldn't look at him still, so lost was she to his presence. She had dreamed of this so often, it was hard to believe that, perhaps, it was real. One of his hands traced the curves of her face, and Linda felt fingertips ghosting against her temple and drifting over her eyes, supple against the bridge of her nose and down the slope. And then there was the blunter presence of a thumb, which was brushing over her lips. It was still so light and fleeting, and she opened her mouth slightly to encourage him.

"Can I kiss you?" His breath was a velvet caress. So close. He was just so close.

"Yes."

The thumb trailed down her chin, and then he tilted her face up. She waited in breathless anticipation for the feel of his mouth against hers once more. And it was so much better than she remembered. His lips were tender yet firm, yielding against her own. The hand that had been caressing her face moved to the nape of her neck, cupping the back of her head gently.

At the light brush of his tongue against her lips, Linda reacted automatically. Her mouth opened, and she slid her tongue against his. Velvety smooth and so very slow. Sensual. Erotic. He didn't give too much. Just enough to tease with the promise of more to come. But she sensed he would wait. He would wait for her to want more from him. God, she wanted more.

"Touch me, Linda," he whispered.

Up until that point, Linda's clutched hands had been resting against his hips. She was still afraid that if she let go completely, thought of him as hers, she'd be lost forever. And she wanted to be lost. Just then, it felt right to take what she could while she could. He was offering himself to her in the most intimate of ways, and she couldn't resist him. Her hands finally began to creep up his body from his hips. She felt Jack suck in his stomach and shiver at the touch of her fingers. Linda continued, her palms flat against his torso and moving north.

Linda felt the ridges of tight muscles over his abdomen. The sturdy springiness of his ribs. And then she got to his upper chest and stopped as fingers brushed against hardened nipples. She also felt Jack's quick intake of breath against her mouth as she passed over them gently. He pushed himself into her hands, and she ran her thumbs over his pecs. He groaned deeply, and his hips began a slow rotation.

The knowledge that she had this sort of effect on him broke down the last of Linda's reserves. Her hands shot up into Jack's hair, and she pulled herself as close as she could get. Now the tenderness was gone. Jack moaned triumphantly as his strong arms banded around her. His kiss became more urgent, as did hers.

But he had known that would happen. Of course he did.

After so much time without any type of physical affection, how could Linda not be starved for this? For him?

Jack's hands roved all over her. He stroked her back and shoulders. Caressed hips and thighs. And when his hands cupped her backside, she was torn between wanting to pull away and wanting to push her hips into his. Lust won out, and she swiveled against him.

"Take me upstairs," he begged softly.

Linda shook her head slightly, fear coming back.

"Don't think. Let me love you."

She whimpered softly at his words. She wanted that so badly. "Jack…"

"Can't you feel how much I want you?" he asked, pressing her even closer. His lips caressed the shell of her ear. "Let me show you."

Linda's body began tingling. His voice was low and husky. Sexy. Surreal. The tingles started down low and spread upward and outward. Jack was kissing her neck, and she realized they were walking backward toward her staircase. Who was leading who, she couldn't have said. She kept having to tell her brain to shut the hell up as her body decided it was sick of waiting.

It was a slow progression up the stairs, and oh, so torturous. Jack had a tight grip on her, because God knows if left to navigate on her own, they would have both gone tumbling down the stairs. His kisses were mind-blowing. He alternated between softly tender and hard and insistent. Every so often, Jack would stop Linda and push her against the wall, his body covering hers completely as he moved against her. Hands in her hair. Lips moving feverishly. Hips surging and retreating. Then he would grow restless and impatient and hurry her along until that, too, became too much and he needed to touch her again.

When they finally made it into the bedroom, Linda stopped in horror as she realized just how *bright* it was in there. It was still the middle of the day during the summer. Cloudy it might be; dark it was not. Especially not with her curtains flung open to let in whatever meager daylight there was.

Linda pulled away from Jack and backed up slowly. Her hands came up automatically to cover herself, even though she was fully clothed.

No matter how his body called for her and how hers answered the call, this just wasn't going to happen today.

Jack watched Linda draw away from him slowly, and he despaired. He despaired because the distance wasn't only between their bodies but in her eyes as well. They had come so far and to watch her slip away from him again was threatening to do him in.

He knew exactly what the problem was. She still didn't believe that when she bared herself to him, he wouldn't turn away from her in disgust. Jack knew that the daylight flooding the room made her scared and nervous, and Linda didn't have enough faith in his feelings for her to know that nothing could turn him away from her. Absolutely nothing.

Making a quick decision, Jack reached behind him and shut the bedroom door. Not wanting to frighten her or make her feel as if she was being forced to do something she didn't want to do, he kept his distance as he moved across the room to the large bay windows. Taking the heavy brocade in his hands, he pulled the curtains closed. As the room plunged into darkness, he was thankful for the thick material. He waited for his eyes to adjust before walking to where Linda stood.

"I know you don't believe me," he began in a soft voice, "but I want to see you. And feel you."

"Then why did you close the curtains?"

Jack closed his eyes against the pain in her voice before replying, "Because *you* aren't ready."

"You're right. I'm not ready. I'm sorry."

Jack sighed but moved closer anyway until he stood directly behind her. Reaching out, he stroked her silken hair. The tension in her shoulders slackened slightly with each caress. He swept the heavy curtain of it over one of her shoulders so it cascaded down her chest. His fingers brushed the soft skin of her nape, and she sighed at the touch.

"Why are you so afraid?"

"You know why," she answered, barely audible.

"Do you know I've touched you almost everywhere already?" Her breath hitched slightly, and he reached toward her bared neck once more. "I've touched you here." His fingers stroked from her ear to her shoulder. "And here." Now he raised both his hands and placed them on her shoulders. Jack ran his fingers down her arms, took her hands, and then raised them up. Feeling no resistance, he moved in closer, until she was flush against him, and wrapped her arms behind his neck. "I've touched you here." His hands ran down her sides, and he smiled against her neck as she wiggled her body when he hit a ticklish spot. "And here," he said in her ear as his hands slid down rounded hips to her thighs, which he gripped firmly for a moment. "You feel wonderful to me. You feel fucking *fantastic.*"

Linda whimpered slightly, and her head leaned back against his chest. Jack could feel her melting slowly. He moved his hands back up her body, this time sweeping along the front of her legs, past her hips, and up her belly. He stopped just short of her breasts and ran his thumbs along the undersides of them. "But I've never touched you here," he said with another brush. Linda's breathing spiked. "Will you let me touch you, Linda?"

She moaned and nodded her head just slightly.

"Is that a yes?" His thumbs were still passing gently against the swells. "Please, say yes."

"Yes."

Ever so slowly, he moved his hands upward until he was cupping her breasts. They fit perfectly in his palms, round and firm, as if he was made to touch her like this. Linda took a quick breath and exhaled sharply when he circled his thumbs over her nipples like she had done to him earlier. Jack leaned down to kiss her neck and flicked his tongue against it, loving the way her body shuddered against him.

"You feel so perfect."

"You're crazy," Linda huffed out and then moaned.

"Crazy for you."

"And now you're cheesy, too."

"Cheesy for you?" Jack asked, grinning as he kissed her shoulder, which was shaking with laughter.

He lowered one hand, sliding it past the swell of her belly. Then he brushed his fingers along her pubic bone, not daring to go further just yet. Her laughter stopped as she held her breath. "And here," he said in her ear once again. "I've never touched you here. Can I touch you, Linda?"

"Yes," she breathed. This time, there was no wait and no hesitation.

Jack knew she could still become overwhelmed and pull away. He hoped that didn't happen, but he was prepared for it, just in case. Slowly, he slid his hand lower, fingers moving lightly against her until he was cupping her sex. The heat that he felt between her thighs astounded him, and it was with great restraint that he didn't drop to his knees and yank her pants down right then and there. He knew that he had to go slowly with Linda, no matter how urgently his body wanted to claim hers.

Linda's heart felt like it would pound straight out of her chest as Jack's hand moved lower and finally touched where she ached for him. This was even better than when he had caressed her breasts for the first time. The touches were light as feathers, and her legs shook as she began to tremble. Despite the fact that it had been so long since she had been intimate with anyone, she couldn't remember ever feeling this way before. She felt raw, exposed, electric.

Jack had stopped speaking, but he pressed himself even closer to her. His breathing had become heavier, and she could feel it against her neck, hot, insistent. Linda couldn't stop herself from rotating her hips. One movement caused his erection to press into her even more, and the other pushed her sex against his hand. She couldn't decide which feeling she enjoyed more. Then he slid one finger against the top of her cleft, and that made up her mind.

With slow, deliberate movements, that lone finger brushed up and down and then circled a few times. She had to hand it to the makers of yoga pants; the fabric was so thin, she had no trouble at all feeling every single thing Jack was doing to her. And as if that wasn't bad enough, Jack's other hand was still caressing her breasts, alternating between them. Linda didn't know which pleasure to concentrate on. She simply gave up and just let herself go with the sensations he was drawing out in her. Everything seemed so new and exciting. It was as if she was a virgin again.

And from what was pressed against her, she had an inkling she would feel like a virgin again as well.

Linda's hands had been balled into fists behind his neck, but now she clutched at Jack as she rocked her hips even more. There was an incredible heat building up between her thighs as he continued with those long, wonderful fingers of his.

"I want to touch you," Jack whispered in her ear.

"You are touching me." She gasped as he hit a particularly sensitive spot.

"Your skin." He chuckled into her neck. "I want to feel your *skin*, Linda."

The hand that had been teasing her breasts so torturously moved down, and she could feel his fingers slip under her shirt. They moved against her waist before sliding over her belly. "Yes, this is what I'm talking about," he murmured as his hand traveled up once more. He felt along the lace cups of the bra and then tugged one down just enough so that he could slide his fingers against her hardened nipple. It was sensitive to his touch, and she gasped while punching her chest outward to increase the sensation.

Instead of giving her more, however, he stopped everything and moved both hands to the hem of her shirt. He lifted it slightly but stopped at mid-belly, asking a silent question.

"Okay," she said, her voice wavering slightly.

He continued to slide the fabric up; it came over her breasts, and then it was past her head and fluttering to the floor beside them.

Automatically, Linda began to cover herself. Even though she had given him permission to remove her shirt, to be so exposed made her nervous once more. Jack covered her hands with his, but he didn't try to pull them away, just stilled their movement. She stopped, and his arms wrapped around her, making her feel safe, even small. She closed her eyes, willing herself to get lost in the feel of him once more.

"Please don't hide from me, Linda," he said in a tender voice as he caressed her arms. "Your skin is so soft. I want to feel you everywhere."

"Why?" Linda asked in a pained voice. She simply couldn't understand why this was so important to him. Surely he could go out and crook his finger at any woman, and she would undress in a flash and not be plagued by all of these insecurities. Not have a body to *be* so insecure about.

"Because I think you're beautiful."

"Please don't lie," she whispered, her head hanging forward.

"I'm not *lying,*" he replied, sounding just as pained as her now. "Let me make you feel beautiful."

"How are you going to do that?" she barked out. "Do you have a magic wand I don't know about?"

Linda's face flamed as Jack shifted his hips against her backside and began to chuckle. "Well...I don't know if I'd call it *magic...* "

"Oh, my God." Linda covered her face with her hands and tried not to laugh hysterically.

This was so not how she pictured their first time. She was supposed to be skinny and sexy, and her baggage, along with her extra weight, long gone. Instead, she was fighting him almost every step of the way, and she didn't know *why.* The man had proven to her time and time again today that all he wanted was to make her feel good. To give her pleasure. He wanted her; it was apparent in the way he kissed, touched, and spoke to her.

It was also apparent by his physical reaction to her. Men just couldn't fake arousal. They couldn't fight physiology. Either they were into you or they weren't. Linda hadn't even touched Jack, and he was very obviously ready to go. If he hadn't gotten scared by now, there was a good chance nothing would make him turn away. He wanted her, and God knew she wanted him. Had wanted him since almost the moment she clapped eyes on him. It was time to stop fighting it. Linda took a deep, steadying breath and dropped her arms.

Jack didn't wait; his hands were back on her body before she could change her mind again. He didn't go for any of her obvious erogenous zones. He began by kissing her neck and shoulder, as gentle fingers drew mindless circles over her stomach. Linda relaxed into Jack, enjoying the hardness of his body. She reached back and grasped his thighs, the muscles contracting under her fingers through his thin shorts. He hummed his approval, the skin he was kissing vibrating in a delicious way.

Eventually, Jack's hands began sliding up. He was moving so slowly and carefully, Linda was about ready to put his hands back on her breasts for him when he finally enveloped them in his palms. She inhaled a breath through her teeth, which encouraged him, and he began to tease her nipples through the fabric of her bra. Linda was ready to start panting when he removed his hands from her breasts again and trailed them up her arms. *No!* she thought. *Go back!*

He placed his fingers underneath the straps of her bra and slid them down her shoulders. Once they went as far as they could go, Jack flipped the cups of her bra down, exposing her breasts for a second before he cupped them once more. Linda groaned at the feel of him, and he bit the juncture of her neck and shoulder, making her gasp and buck against him.

"No more hiding," he said in a husky whisper as he licked over the bite.

"No more," Linda concurred.

She looked down at her body. With her bra straps hanging down her arms and her breasts exposed over the cups of her bra as Jack played with them, she felt kind of wanton. It was something new for her, and she reveled in it. It might have taken her a while to get to this point, but now that she was here, she was ready to embrace a different side of herself. Linda reached behind her and ran a hand lightly over Jack's erection. He shot his hips forward and groaned into her neck.

She was being towed backward now, toward her bed, and a tidal wave of tingles descended all over her body. When they got there, Jack's hands left her briefly again, and she heard the rustle of fabric as his shirt came off. Oh God, this was it. She was really going to do this, because for sure now it was too late to stop. Not that Linda wanted to.

Slowly, Jack turned her around so that she faced him. He sat down on the bed with his legs spread as she stood between them. This was the first time she'd seen his face since they had walked in here kissing. Even in the semi-darkness, he looked heavenly, with his sultry eyes and his pouting mouth, which she just wanted to devour. He gazed at her in complete adoration, and she felt a little dizzy.

Then he reached up, cupped her face, and brought her mouth down to his. His lips claimed hers in a blaze of fire. Linda knew he was done playing games. He wanted her. No matter the consequences, he'd pay them. Their mouths moved as one, tongues sliding out and doing a sensual dance. Jack's hands moved from her face and down the slopes of her shoulders, over her collarbones, until he touched her breasts again. He rolled the sensitive tips between gentle fingers, and Linda was about to lose her mind.

"I want to taste you," Jack told her, pulling away from her lips.

He didn't even bother waiting for consent, merely wrapped his arms around her waist and pulled her to him. His mouth covered one distended peak, and Linda almost cried out at the sensation of it. As he sucked her nipple into his mouth, his tongue doing insanely naughty things to it, he reached back and unclasped her bra. Linda let it fall to the floor without a care as he moved his mouth to her other breast and did the same thing, while cupping the unattended one. She buried her hands in his hair as he suckled at her.

Linda was in sensory overload, and he had barely done anything yet, so when Jack's hands began exploring again, her stomach exploded in butterflies. She felt gentle brushes back and forth along the waistband of her pants, and then he hooked his fingers inside and tugged slowly. She knew he was giving her an opportunity to say no, but she had no plans to stop him now. What he was doing felt too good, too sinful. She wiggled her hips to let him know she wanted him to continue.

Jack pulled down her pants, sliding his hands along her thighs as he went. His lips moved down along her stomach as the pants descended, finally pooling at Linda's feet. She kicked them off quickly and could feel Jack smile against her belly at her enthusiasm. Linda smiled, too. His hands circled her upper calves and stroked their way slowly up her legs. He nibbled her skin as he went, his teeth causing tremors all over her body. When his hands cupped her buttocks and kneaded them, he stuck his tongue in her belly button and swirled it around, making her gasp.

"Come on top of me," he murmured against her skin, and all Linda could think was: *I'll come on top of you, below you, beside you, wherever the hell you want me to come.* "I want you to straddle me."

"No," she answered, shaking her head. "I'm too heavy."

"You're not too heavy," Jack said in a firm voice. He pulled her closer to him as he moved farther into the middle of the bed. Finally, he coaxed her onto his lap, her knees on either side of his legs. She kept her weight off of him, just in case, but Jack was not having it. He took her by the waist and sat her directly on top of him, groaning and swiveling his hips underneath her, making Linda bite her lip and whimper. "See? You feel so good."

"You make me feel good," she whispered, running her hands down his chest.

"Do I?" he asked with smug satisfaction. "Good...Look down, Linda. See what you do to me?"

Linda looked down their bodies and watched as his erection slid between her spread legs. The slippery fabric of his rayon shorts against the silk of her panties allowed him to slide back and forth without any effort at all. Linda could see the outline of his erection, and she began rocking her hips, getting even more aroused than before. The movement of his hips was teasing her just where she needed it most, and she shivered from excitement and anticipation.

"I want to be in you so bad," he continued in that same sexy voice as he kissed her neck and squeezed her backside tighter. "I want be buried inside of you as deep as I can go."

"Oh, God," Linda moaned. His hot, starved words made her brain explode with vivid images. She grabbed Jack's head and brought it back up as she crushed her lips against his. His tongue shot into her mouth as his arms pulled her tightly to his chest. She rubbed her breasts against him, loving the feel of his warm skin against hers. Jack's hips continued to move back and forth quickly now, and Linda met him stroke for stroke. Both of them were moaning against each other's mouths as they worked up to a frenzy.

Jack broke away roughly and used his strength to get her to stop. "Linda," he panted into her neck. "Baby, you're going to make me come if we keep that up."

"Oops, sorry," she said, grinning and doing a little dance inside that she was able to work him up so much.

"Don't be sorry. Never be sorry," he answered, kissing her neck. "You make me feel like a kid—coming in his pants before anything good happens."

Linda laughed and hugged Jack even closer, one hand buried deep in his soft, curly hair while the other caressed his back. A second later, she heard Jack curse softly.

"What happened?" Linda asked, pulling back and looking at him. Jack had a sheepish look on his face, and she looked down to see if indeed he had come in his shorts. Everything looked fine. More than fine, if she was honest. "What's wrong?"

"Umm…that just reminded me. I was so excited at the thought of getting you home, I forgot to get you to stop and pick up…uh… condoms."

"Oh," she answered. "Well, that's okay. I have some." Now it was her turn to look sheepish.

"Really? Who were you going to use condoms with?" Jack was frowning sternly, and she was struck dumb at the fact he was actually *jealous*.

"They're…um…from before we met."

"Good," he growled, leaning forward to capture her lips in a kiss. He broke away again. "Wait, will they fit?" At this, he held up his pinky and wiggled it around, making Linda laugh.

"Yeah, they were a gift from Eliza to celebrate my separation."

Jack laughed. "He was honestly that small?"

"Close enough."

"Do you think I'm small?" he asked with a mischievous grin.

"Nope," she answered before attacking his mouth again and moving her hips up and down his impressive length.

Jack groaned, wrapped his arms tightly around her, and then stood up, making Linda whoop in surprise. He turned around and lowered both of them onto the bed so that he was on top of her and thrusting between her legs. She was starting to curse all the clothes he was still wearing. She reached around and slipped her hands under Jack's shorts, gripping his naked ass in her hands and pushing up against him. When she started to tug against the fabric, he stopped her.

"Not yet," he breathed. "If I get naked right now, I'm going to fuck you silly."

"You make that sound like a bad thing." Linda pouted, yanking at his clothes again.

"Ah-ah…I'm not done with you yet."

Jack pulled away from her and knelt between her spread legs. This was a familiar sight. Except this time, it wasn't one of their workout sessions, and it wasn't one of Linda's fantasies. She finally had the man in her bed. Jack reached forward and ran his hands down her body in slow, sensuous sweeps. He played close attention to her breasts, making her arch up against him. Continuing to move down, his fingers brushed over her belly, down her hips and thighs. His thumbs brushed just the outer part of her sex, teasing her. He did it again and again, each time his thumbs moving in closer. Linda felt like one huge live wire.

"Won't you let me look at you in the light?" he asked quietly.

"Not yet," she sighed in return.

"Soon?"

She only smiled at the wistful hopefulness in his voice. His hands made another pass, and this time, his thumb brushed where she was throbbing for him. She groaned and moved her hips against the light pressure. Jack hooked his fingers into her panties and began to shimmy them down. Linda lifted off the bed to help him. He shifted back so he could continue to slide the fabric off her legs.

Linda expected Jack to remove his clothes then and ask for a condom, but he didn't. Instead, he ran his hands along her inner thighs from her knees to her sex and began touching her there lightly. "So soft," he murmured as his fingers drifted up and down in maddening light caresses. Linda groaned and moved around restlessly. Finally, one finger slipped inside her, and both of them sighed at the feeling. He stroked her a few times, and her eyes closed at the incredible feel of him touching her like this. It was definitely a million times better than any fantasy she'd ever come up with. Fantasies and her own hands hadn't even come close to what she was feeling now.

When Jack removed his finger, she opened her eyes and watched in fascinated amazement as he put it between his lips and tasted her on him. He hummed with pleasure, and Linda realized what was coming next. Leaning down, Jack placed a chaste kiss where his hand had just been.

Something had changed.

As soon as he leaned down and kissed Linda between her legs, Jack felt her freeze. It was a subtle shift, but he was so in tune with her body at the moment, he noticed it right away. He pulled back reluctantly and looked at her. Linda's eyes were huge, and her hands gripped the duvet, but it seemed more out of anxiety than pleasure. Jack stopped automatically.

"What's wrong?" he asked her gently. "Did you change your mind?"

Linda shook her head, but her wary look didn't go away.

"Something is wrong, Linda. I can feel it. Please tell me."

"Gah," she exclaimed, putting her hands over her face. She mumbled something unintelligible.

"What?" Jack leaned forward, grasped her wrists, and tugged at them slightly. She let her hands come away from her face, and even in the dark he could tell she was beet red.

"No one's ever done that to me before," she said in a hushed rush.

Jack just stared at her and blinked. He was relatively sure he'd heard her right, but he couldn't reconcile the fact that she had been with someone for so long and he had never tried to please her orally. He figured maybe he heard wrong. "Come again?"

Linda sighed and looked away, distinctly embarrassed. "No one has ever done...*that*...to me before." She stressed the words and this time used her hand to wave at her lower region in demonstration.

"You've never had someone go *down* on you?" Jack asked. He was trying to keep the shock out of his voice but didn't do a very good job, because Linda groaned and covered her face with her hands again. She shook her head no while Jack sat there, dumbfounded. Now he wasn't quite sure what to do. He could forget about trying and just get her ready with his fingers; she seemed to enjoy that. But looking down at her, spread and ready, he really wanted to bend his head down and lick and suck her until she came all over his mouth. Just the thought of it made him get even harder. He wanted to take Linda with his mouth, and if he had to beg and plead, he would.

Jack decided to start with some gentle persuasion first before resorting to all-out begging. Reaching forward, he took Linda's hands away from her face. He leaned forward until his body covered hers and kissed her, gently at first until he felt her beginning to respond. He loved that. It gave him a secret little thrill to break down her defenses and bring out the passion she was keeping under wraps. Jack would stop on a dime if he ever felt he was going too far or pushing her too fast, but every time she gave a little more of herself, he wanted to do a fist pump. It was immature of him, but he couldn't help it. He wanted all of her, every little piece, but he wanted her to give it to him willingly.

Today, as Jack watched Linda fight with herself and then finally just let go, he realized just how deeply he cared for her. For her bravery, because he knew he was pushing her boundaries right now. While his cock pounded at the mere thought of being inside her, slick and hot, he wanted her more intimately than that. He wanted to taste her, swallow her whole. He wanted to take her inside of himself like she would do to him before they were through.

Even the thought of it was getting him excited, and he poured it all out in his kisses. Jack was sliding his hands over Linda's body, and she arched under him as he touched her. Jack wanted her mindless and crazed for him. When he was ready to go down on her, he wanted her to not even think about it. He wanted her so hot for his touch that she'd agree to anything without second guessing. Moving back, he placed his hand between her legs and started stroking her again. When Linda jerked her hips against his fingers, he slid one inside her. After a few thrusts, he added another one, making Linda gasp at the feel of him. She was incredibly tight but wet, and her body accepted him after he rocked his hand gently back and forth before beginning to pick up speed.

Linda's breath was coming out in harsh pants. Her hands were buried in his hair as he continued to suck on her breasts. He could feel her legs sawing back and forth against him. Jack could tell Linda was about to lose control, but he was enjoying prolonging her pleasure. He wanted to keep her on the brink. He knew there were a few things he could do to make her scream, but he wanted his face between her legs when she did. He began kissing down her stomach, and when he got to her belly button, he licked around it with his tongue to tease her.

"I want you in my mouth," he said against the flesh of her stomach. "I want to lick you and suck you."

Linda groaned aloud.

"Will you let me?"

"Yes," she answered, her head moving back and forth against the pillow. "Anything. Whatever you want. I don't care."

Bingo.

Jack didn't need any more invitation than that. With a quick move, he removed his fingers and placed his mouth where they had been. He wanted to be gentle. Try to ease Linda into this new sensation. But as her taste exploded on his tongue, all thought of taking it slow flew out the window. He spread her thighs and drew his tongue up in one long lick.

"Oh…my…*God!*"

As he worked her body, he tried not to smile at her obvious enjoyment of what he was doing to her, but it was damned hard. Jack concentrated on Linda, and true to his word, he licked and he sucked. He swirled his tongue against her clit and all but devoured her. Linda's body was in constant motion. Her hands went from gripping the headboard to grabbing at his hair as she swiveled her hips up against his mouth. Jack was loving her response to him and figured that, after twenty years of bad sex, a little oral would do that to a girl.

Bringing his hand back to her entrance, he thrust his fingers deep inside, making her cry out and push against him. Now that he'd had his fill, he concentrated hard on getting her to come. Since she'd told him it had never happened before during sex, it was Jack's personal mission to change that. He placed his mouth around Linda's clit and ran his tongue over it repeatedly as his hand increased its tempo, fingers curling up slightly.

Linda started moaning louder. Her hips were moving in sync with him, and he heard her saying "yes" over and over again. He wanted to encourage her vocally, but his mouth was busy at the moment, so he contented himself by moving his tongue over her flesh even faster and chanting, *Come baby, come baby, come…*in his head.

"Oh! Oh! *Ohhhh…*"

It was music to his ears as he felt the distinctive clamping down against his fingers and a rush of her juices, which he eagerly lapped up with his tongue. Linda was still moaning and thrashing underneath him as she rode the waves of her orgasm. Jack slowed his movements as she slowed hers, removing his fingers and licking up the length of her a few times gently. Her body quaked with aftershocks.

Finally, he pulled away and looked at Linda while trying to fight the huge-ass grin at her appearance. Her hair was in crazy disarray across her pillow, and her limbs were flung out in every direction. Her chest was rising and falling rapidly, and her mouth was slack. Jack crawled up her body, kissing his way there.

"Thank you," he said while nuzzling her neck.

"For what?" she answered, surprise coloring her tone. Her hands came up and stroked his back.

"For letting me do that."

"I think I should be the one thanking *you.*"

Jack started chuckling. He was running his nose against the sensitive flesh behind her ear and breathing in the perfume of her. She smelled like shampoo and soap, and the scent of her arousal saturated the room, making a heady fragrance. He never remembered being so in touch with an experience like this before. Something felt different. Deeper and more profound for some reason.

"Jack?"

"Hmm?"

"Is it horribly selfish of me to still want you?"

"No," he laughed softly. "Why? Did you think that was it?"

"I wasn't sure," Linda admitted, also laughing. The joyous sound made his heart hurt, it touched him so much.

"Does it feel over to you?"

Jack took Linda's hand, slid it down his torso until she was cupping his erection. She grasped it eagerly, and he couldn't help the pleasurable noise that escaped him as he pumped into her hand. When she let go only to slip her fingers under the fabric of his briefs, he almost had a coronary. She felt so soft yet sure against him as she stroked his shaft. Linda used her other hand to tug at his clothes, and this time he let her slide his shorts down his hips. She pushed him back a little so that she could continue taking everything off. When she got to mid-thigh, Jack took over, moving his legs and using his hands to get his clothes off.

As soon as he was free, Linda reached for him again. She sighed in pleasure as her hands moved up and over him. Jack had his eyes closed, drowning in the sensation of her touching him. Her fingers tickled and teased as she explored. When Linda cupped his balls, he groaned loudly, which prompted her to play with him more. He knew he was too far gone to take much more of this.

"Where are the condoms?" he asked, swallowing hard as she squeezed his balls lightly in one hand while drawing the other up and down his shaft.

"Why? Don't you like this?" She stalled slightly, and he rocked his hips forward and back.

"Too much," he groaned. "If you don't stop, I'm going to come all over your hands."

"Is that a bad thing?"

"Yes, because I want to come inside you."

Linda whimpered at his words before answering his original question. "Top drawer."

Jack lunged for the bedside table. He almost yanked the whole drawer clean out in his haste to get at the box of condoms sitting in there. Wasting as little time as possible, he had the box open and was ripping one of the foil packets so he could roll the thing onto his cock. Linda was lying on her side, watching him and smiling at his enthusiasm.

He finally lay down beside her and drew his hand along her body in a sensuous stroke. Linda closed her eyes and rose to meet him. He slipped his fingers between her legs and was pleased to notice she was still wet. Not that he would have minded a repeat performance to get her ready for him. Jack leaned forward and started to kiss her softly. It intensified quickly, and soon she was tugging at him so that he would roll on top of her. He obliged, and the feel of her heat against his shaft was heavenly. He was almost glad for the condom, because he had a feeling if he tried this bareback, he'd come after a couple of strokes.

"You'll have to take it slow," Linda whispered as he positioned himself against her entrance.

"I will," he whispered back, dropping tender kisses all over her face.

Jack pressed against her, and it almost felt as if he were having sex with a virgin. Even having his fingers inside her earlier hadn't seemed to make much difference. He rocked his hips slowly, surging and retreating, going a little deeper each time. It took an extraordinary amount of willpower for Jack not to simply push forward, but he didn't want to hurt Linda. She was moaning each time he advanced, so he took that as a good sign that she was more than fine.

Once Jack was all the way in, he stopped, breathing heavily into her neck while he waited for Linda to adjust. "Are you okay?" he asked in a hoarse voice.

"Yes," she whispered, stroking his back tenderly. She moved her hands down to cup his ass and pulled him closer.

"Do you want me to do this?" Jack smiled, pulled back, and slid into her once more. Linda made a throaty noise that he took as assent.

He kept his movements slow and controlled for two reasons. One, he wanted her to become accustomed to him. And two, he was about to blow his load if he went any faster. He wanted to make this last for her. Show her what it felt like to be treated properly and loved well. The only problem was that the way Linda's body gripped his shaft felt way too good, and he didn't know if he would have a chance to get her to orgasm again. At least he was happy he'd accomplished it once.

He kept up the torture for quite a while. Linda was panting in his ear and clutching his body closer. He rubbed his pelvis against hers with every long, slow stroke.

"Jack…I need…I need…Oh God, please go faster…"

"If I go faster, I'll come," he groaned, fighting the urge to just piston his hips like a jackhammer.

"I think, so will I…Please!"

Jack resisted for one more second and lost the fight. He pulled back and thrust into her hard and fast. Linda moaned in his ear and continued to do so the more quickly he moved his hips. He kept her body close to his by slipping his hands under her ass and leaning into her. There was no way he could keep this up. Jack sang a song to the heavens when Linda started bucking her hips against his and whimpering in his ear.

"Don't stop," she called out.

"Shit, Linda…fuck…I'm coming," he replied desperately, pumping quicker and harder. "Come baby, come…" he chanted, this time aloud, and thanked the Lord when she cried out and clutched at him with all she had.

When Jack finished, he lay there panting for what felt like forever. He was completely spent and felt weak but in the most wonderful of ways. Linda was kissing him wherever she could reach while caressing his back and whispering words of endearment. He felt like he could stay here in her arms forever and be a happy man.

He finally rolled to the side, bringing her with him. He looked down into her blissed-out face and brushed her damp hair back and away. Leaning forward, Jack kissed Linda's lips tenderly.

"Was it good for you?" he asked in a silly voice while waggling his eyebrows.

Linda's laughter rang out in the room, and he joined her. This was the happiest Jack had been in a very long time.

15
The Aftermath

Linda was spent.

Physically. Emotionally. Spiritually. She pretty much had nothing left. Today had been such a crazy day, and she felt like she had gone from extreme highs to extreme lows and back again. She was still not one hundred percent convinced that this wasn't a dream. The only thing that kept her from thinking it wasn't was the fact she'd actually had an orgasm. Well, two, really. Usually, in her dreams, she woke up well before anything that good happened.

Also, her dreams never felt this real. While vivid, they lacked the same type of sensory impact. Visceral things like Jack's heart thumping under her ear, the feel of his chest as it rose up and down while he breathed, the gentle caress of his fingers up and down her arm. She supposed even those could be fabricated by her overactive imagination, but what really hit home for her were the scents in the room. That earthy, musky essence that could only signify one thing.

Sex.

Linda smiled and burrowed in closer to Jack. The feel of his arm tightening around her as he kissed the top of her head made her feel as if her heart was going to burst out of her chest. That's how insanely happy she was right at that moment.

"Bathroom?" Jack murmured after a few more minutes.

"First door on your right."

"I'll be right back," Jack said before giving her a kiss on the forehead and sitting up.

Even though it was still dark in her bedroom, she enjoyed the view of a naked Jack as he rose up and sauntered out of the room. She definitely appreciated the view. Linda also felt a small pang of envy at his easy demeanor in regard to walking around nude. He was obviously so comfortable in his own skin that he felt no need to cover up. She wished she could feel the same, and even now, in her post-coital bliss, she scrambled underneath the covers and burrowed into the bed.

Linda couldn't resist snuggling with the pillow Jack had lain against and inhaling the scent of him that lingered there. She barely restrained herself from the mad urge to giggle and girly-scream while kicking her legs back and forth like a teen having a fangirl fit. When she heard the door to the bathroom open, Linda practically threw the pillow across the bed and sat up quickly. Somehow, she felt strange just lying there naked in bed. She hoped her cheeks weren't so red he could tell she was blushing.

When Jack walked back into the room, Linda admired him all over again. He moved with an unconscious grace, as if he were in his own home and hadn't a care in the world. That made Linda feel good because she suspected he was so comfortable around her that he could act freely. Or it could be that he had done this previously with so many women that it was second nature.

Linda didn't like that thought at all, but it certainly reminded her that she didn't know much about Jack's private life before he'd come to Arnold.

As he neared the bed, he took in her duvet-covered body and gave her a questioning look before sitting down. Linda had pulled back the cover so he slid underneath as well and tried to catch her eye. Now she was feeling bashful.

"Hi," Jack said as he scooted down under the covers. He was lying on his side, head propped on his hand as he gazed up at Linda.

"Hi," she answered, a shy smile tugging at her lips. "Did you need to take a shower?"

"Why? Are you kicking me out?" He laughed as Linda's mouth popped open.

"No! I just thought—isn't that what guys do after sex?" Generally, that was what Graham had always done, and since he had been her only lover, she wasn't quite sure if that was normal male behavior or not.

"Eventually," he answered slowly, as if piecing something together. "I'd rather stay in bed naked with you, though."

"Oh." Linda looked down, grinning.

"Come here," Jack said in that silky smooth voice. He reached up to cup her face and brought it down to his so he could kiss her gently. She barely contained a whimper when his lips parted slightly under hers, unable to understand how she could still want him this badly when they had just been together.

Jack started to recline back, and Linda followed. Soon, she was pressed against his chest, one of her legs entwined between his as the kiss deepened. She reached up to caress his face, her fingers tracing along the curve of his jaw. So many times she'd wondered what it would feel like to touch him, and the thrill it gave her to be able to do so now made Linda slightly breathless. One hand moved up into his hair, that wonderful softness winding through her fingers. Yes, to be able to touch him so freely and without restraint was wonderful.

The kiss wound down slowly until Jack was just placing his lips against hers chastely once more. He pushed Linda's hair away from her face, gathering it in his hands as he looked in her eyes searchingly. She became self-conscious under his intense scrutiny.

"*Was* it good for you, Linda?" he asked softly.

"You couldn't tell?" she inquired in surprise.

Jack sort of shrugged and stared at her chin. "Women fake it all the time."

"Are you looking for an ego boost?" Linda began to laugh, and Jack looked into her eyes once more. He grinned, but there was still some uncertainty in his gaze.

"Maybe?"

"It was wonderful. Astounding. Incredible. You really *do* have a magic wand—"

"Okay! Okay," Jack chuckled. "I get it! Smartass."

Linda laughed as well but then became completely serious. She ran her hands over his forehead, smoothing his hair back. "For real,

Jack," she said softly, "I've never experienced anything like that before...It was beyond words."

Before she could continue speaking, Jack had his mouth pressed against hers and was kissing her with wild abandon. Linda reciprocated happily. He was such an amazing kisser. It was as if he knew when to be soft and when to be insistent. When to take it slow and when to be demanding. Pulling back slightly, he kissed her face and then rolled them both over so it was he who was suspended over her.

"I was afraid I was pushing you too hard," he said in a quiet voice. "I wasn't as gentle as I wanted to be."

Linda was surprised by his confession and not quite sure what to say. She had actually been relieved he hadn't given up on her. She hadn't felt forced to do anything she didn't want to do. In all honesty, it wasn't anything she hadn't imagined hundreds of times before. Maybe she would have felt more confident had she been closer to her weight loss goal, but not once had Jack made her feel undesirable.

"It was perfect," she told him and raised her head to kiss him gently.

When she pulled back, Jack smiled down at her beatifically and exhaled slowly. Then he snuggled down and laid his head on her chest, his ear over her heart. Linda held him tenderly against her and played with his hair. She couldn't remember the last time she'd felt so happy. She wasn't precisely sure what was happening between them, but she didn't want to examine it too closely. Right now, she just wanted to revel in this feeling.

"You know," Jack said after a few minutes of silence, "I was kind of surprised by what you said."

"When?"

"That your ex had never gone down on you."

Linda squirmed uncomfortably, which made Jack turn his head to look at her.

"Isn't there a rule or something about talking about exes when you're naked with someone else?" Linda inquired, trying for a light tone.

Jack chuckled and rubbed his chin against her chest, the scruffiness making her giggle. "I just thought it was odd, that's all."

"Well," Linda said hesitantly, "he did try once when we first started having sex, but he didn't like it. He, um, said it...tasted funny."

` She blushed furiously when she repeated the words, not liking to recall how humiliated she had been when Graham had told her that. Even now, she felt the sting of his words, and it had happened almost two decades ago.

"That's why you were afraid when I tried?" Jack asked gently, and Linda nodded. She had been terrified that he would pull back and make a face or not be able to go through with it. "Well, he's a fucking idiot. I think you're delicious."

Linda's flush was back, only this time it covered her entire body as she remembered what it had felt like when Jack had been using his mouth to give her pleasure. He had definitely not acted like a man doing an unpleasant duty. Actually, he had really seemed to enjoy making her writhe beneath him. As much as she had liked him doing it.

"I don't get why you stayed with him so long." Jack looked at her with a curious expression, and Linda sighed. She had supposed this conversation was going to happen sooner or later. She hadn't expected to do it now, but what was the point of putting it off?

"Graham and I got together really young," she explained. "I was only sixteen and a virgin when we had sex the first time. Most of the girls my age who had tried it said they didn't like it either, so I figured it was kind of normal. Neither of us was experienced, and we kind of just did the same thing all the time. It wasn't until a long time later that I figured out it wasn't something wrong with *me*. But he was my husband, and I was brought up that you're supposed to be faithful to your husband, so I put up with it."

"But why did you stay with him period?"

"I thought I still loved him. Well, I *did* love him when we first got together. And when my parents died, he was there for me. He took care of me, and I became dependent on him. Graham was all I really knew. Do you understand? Things were fine in the beginning for the most part, and by the time they got bad…" Linda shrugged and stopped speaking.

"I've never been in a long-term relationship before," Jack said softly. "I always figured if things were bad, you got out."

"Yeah, well, after so many years with someone, it's hard to be strong sometimes," Linda murmured. "Much easier to make concessions and ignore things. Better the devil you know and all that."

"I'm sorry. I didn't mean —"

"It's okay, Jack," Linda said, smiling at him gently. "You're right. It doesn't make much sense. But it's over now, and hindsight is twenty-twenty."

Jack nodded and smiled a little in return. She figured since she had just been in the hot seat, she could repay the favor.

"So, what about Vicky?" she asked in challenge. "I guess you guys broke up?"

"Why would I break up with Vicky?" Jack asked, frowning.

Oh, shit, Linda thought, and her stomach plummeted once more. She had automatically assumed that when Jack had come after her, and following the events of the afternoon, that he had ended things with the girl. But now she was wondering if she had jumped the gun. Literally.

She managed to scoot out from under Jack and sat up beside him. He rolled away slightly and looked confused by her sudden movement. Linda swallowed heavily, feeling nauseated. She suddenly remembered that she wasn't supposed to know about them and understood why Jack would be evasive about everything.

"Oh...I didn't realize...*wow.*"

"Linda." His frown had deepened. "Why are you asking me about Vicky?"

"No reason at all," she replied and gave him a tight smile. "I didn't even think that maybe you two weren't exclusive."

Linda started looking on the floor for her clothes. She needed out of the bed and dressed because something about making a fool of herself while stark naked just didn't appeal to her. When she made the move to get up, Jack sat up quickly and grasped her wrist, stopping her. She couldn't look at him, so he forced her face up to look in his eyes.

"Linda, answer me."

"Look," she said in as strong as a voice as she could muster. "I know I'm not supposed to know about you and Vicky. Don't worry, I won't tell Jimmy. Okay?"

"What the hell are you talking about?"

"Jack, I know something is going on between you and Vicky," she finally answered in exasperation. "You can stop lying about it."

"You think I'm fucking *Vicky?*"

"Well, aren't you?"

"Linda, I wouldn't fuck Vicky with Jimmy's dick and Amanda pushing," Jack answered indignantly.

Linda almost started laughing until she remembered the pictures that Vicky had shown Michelle of her in bed with Jack.

"What about the pictures?" she asked softly and watched as Jack's face drained of all emotion. She should have felt some kind of triumph at having caught him in a lie, but all she felt was dead inside that he was continuing with the charade.

"What pictures?" he said in a low voice. It had a menacing edge, and Linda was scared for a moment until she realized it wasn't her he was mad at.

"Of you and Vicky in bed together," she whispered. "I overheard Vicky showing them to Michelle on her phone. That's why I was so upset today."

All of a sudden, there was a flurry of bedclothes as Jack got out of bed. He was seemingly quite angry and muttering obscenities as he searched for his things. Linda scrambled out of bed as well and threw on her shirt before hunting for her pants. When Jack found his shorts, he shoved his legs in them and yanked them up viciously. As she was pulling her pants on, Linda watched him pat at his pockets, not finding anything.

"Where's your phone?" he growled.

Jack was absolutely livid as he stalked out of Linda's bedroom, headed for the kitchen. He heard her running after him but didn't feel inclined to slow down. The last thing he wanted was to get angry with her unwittingly. Bad enough his post-sex vibe was ruined by the information Linda had just given him; he didn't want to ruin the day entirely by being a douchebag to her when none of this was her fault.

Pictures!

That psycho bitch had *pictures* of him in bed? When the fuck had she managed that? He vaguely remembered waking up one morning and noticing his door had been open a crack. At the time, he figured he just hadn't shut it all the way the night before. Now he was kicking himself for losing the habit of locking his door. He knew he was a heavy sleeper, which was probably how she had sneaked into his room in the first place. But what fucking nerve to climb into his bed and pose with him. Who did that kind of shit? Psycho bitch roommates, that's who! Damn Amanda. This was all her fault.

Picking up the phone, he punched in Amanda's number and tried to calm down as it started to ring. Linda stood at the edge of the kitchen wringing her hands, and he knew he was scaring her with his anger. He hoped she would understand when all of this was over and done with.

"Hello?"

"Amanda, it's Jack."

"Jack! Where the hell are you? I've been trying to call your phone, but there was no answer."

"I left it in the car—"

"Your car is here!"

"I know that," he answered impatiently.

"And Vicky came here freaking out and saying you were kicking her out of the house—"

"Is Vicky with you now?" he growled.

"No, I calmed her down. She's with her last client now. What is going on?"

"Good," Jack bit out. "I need you to go to her locker and find her phone."

"What? Why?"

"Because she snuck into my fucking room and took pictures of me when I was sleeping!" he roared out, unable to contain his anger any longer. He saw Linda jump, and he turned away and struck himself in the forehead with a closed fist as he tried to rein in his emotions.

"What?" Amanda asked, sounding aghast. "Are you kidding?"

"No, I'm not kidding, and I want you to break into her fucking locker and find those goddamned pictures!"

He could hear her moving now. As Jimmy's fuck buddy, Amanda had access to his office and his keys to the employee lockers. While he waited, he felt Linda's hand as she placed it against his back. He exhaled slowly as she rubbed calming circles against it. Reaching behind, he took her hand and pulled it gently so her arm was around his stomach. She stepped closer and pressed her cheek against him as her arms wrapped around his midsection. Jack could feel himself wind down as she soothed him. He was grateful that he hadn't scared her away. Sometimes his anger got away from him.

"Found it," Amanda muttered into the phone. "Hopefully she doesn't lock this thing."

"She found it," he said over his shoulder to Linda, who nodded against his back.

"Oh...my...God," Amanda breathed, and Jack ground his teeth together. "She has a ton of them!"

"What?"

"And they haven't all been taken on the same day..." she continued. Jack could hear the disgust creeping into her voice. "Holy fuck, Jack, how heavy do you sleep?"

"Very, apparently," he replied dryly. "Get rid of them."

"Deleting now."

"I want her out of the house. *Tonight!*"

"Not a problem." She had a steely tone that Jack was happy to hear. "Where are you now?"

"At Linda's."

"Oh, really?" The insinuation was thick, and Jack smiled. "When are you coming home?"

Loosening Linda's grip, he turned in her arms so he could face her. "I don't think I'm coming home tonight," he replied, giving her an imploring look. She smiled and nodded her head in the affirmative. He leaned down and gave her a quick kiss.

"Okay," Amanda giggled. "I'll make sure Stalkie McStalkerson is out of the house by the time you come back...*If* you come back!"

"Thanks, Mandy," he said softly before reaching behind him and hanging up the phone. He sighed deeply and wrapped his arms around Linda, holding her tight.

"I'm sorry I lost my temper like that," he offered, chagrined.

"It's okay."

"I didn't mean to scare you."

"I think I'd be pretty mad if I found out someone was stalking me, too," she replied, and Jack winced slightly in response. "So, Amanda found the pictures?"

Jack could hear the note of hesitation in her voice. She was most likely afraid of setting him off again, and with good reason, because he could feel the anger threatening to burst to the surface. He took some cleansing breaths and calmed himself down.

"Yeah, she did," he answered after a few tense seconds. "She said there were a lot on there, and they weren't all from the same day."

"Holy crap."

"Jesus Christ…She was in my fucking bed while I was sleeping! That's just…just…" He couldn't even find the words to describe what he was feeling and made a disgusted noise instead.

"I feel so horrible for not warning you about her."

"You knew she'd do that?" he asked, somewhat stunned that Linda hadn't said a word.

"No!" she replied quickly. "No, no…I didn't know she'd do *that*. Just that she never did seem very stable if you ask me."

"Why didn't you say anything?"

"Well, first of all, I thought you were having some secret affair with her." Linda snickered, and Jack felt her arms tighten around him slightly. "Second, I thought if I said anything bad about her, you would get upset with me and think I was just holding a grudge."

"A grudge from what?"

"I'm pretty sure Vicky was fucking Graham when she worked as his intern."

She had said it matter-of-factly, but Jack sucked in a breath anyway. So, that explained the animosity between the two of them. Everything made a lot more sense now. He hated the fact that it had all been compounded by her assumption that something had been going on between him and Vicky. He imagined it must have hurt Linda quite a bit to think he had been sleeping with that psycho. Even though none of this was his fault, Jack felt horrible.

"Please explain to me how you came up with the idea that I was with Vicky?"

"Vicky," Linda answered simply. Then she moved away from Jack, grabbed his hand, and tugged it gently. "Come on. This is a conversation for the living room."

When they got to the couch, Linda sat away from Jack, but he didn't like the distance between them. He leaned across, slung an arm around her, and pulled her toward him. She smiled and then scooted over until she was tucked against his side.

"Okay, go on," he urged softly.

Linda took a deep breath and then launched into the whole story. She explained how the same day that they'd had the confrontation with Mrs. Bellham, she'd also overheard Vicky telling one of her clients that she was involved with Jack. His hand curled into a fist at the sheer balls of what she had said. The crafty little bitch had made it so that Linda essentially had to keep quiet about the affair because she wasn't supposed to know about it, and Linda thought Jack would get upset because of the threat posed to him. Since Jack had been stupid enough to not confide in Linda about his new living arrangements, she thought he had kept it from her on purpose.

It was an ingenious plan, actually, and had worked exactly like Vicky had wanted it to.

Linda went on to explain about what had happened while they were in Baltimore after he had sought her out, how it had looked when Vicky had attempted to kiss him and when he had gone on the stage and started singing love songs. Jack groaned aloud.

"I was singing those songs for *you*," he told Linda, then felt her stiffen slightly in his arms.

"For me?" she squeaked, making Jack chuckle.

"Yes, for you. Why do you think I was so upset when you left?"

"I wasn't sure."

"And why do you think I tracked you down at work and dragged you with me that night in the first place?" he continued.

"I thought it was because Cici asked you to."

"Linda," he moaned in exasperation. "This whole time, I've been trying to get you to understand that I want to be with you."

"I'm starting to see that."

"But why didn't you see it before?"

"Because, besides Vicky's lies, it didn't make any sense for you to want to be with me."

Jack was going to ask why she would say that and then thought better of it. They had wasted so much time already because of misunderstandings, and he knew it would break his heart if he had to listen to Linda list all of the reasons she thought he shouldn't be with her. Instead, he turned her slightly and tipped her face toward his. He kissed her tenderly a few times and then placed his forehead against hers.

"Well, I do," he murmured. "I do want to be with you."

"Why?" she asked in a small voice.

"Are you looking for an ego boost?" he said, echoing her words from before.

She smiled with eyes downcast. "Maybe."

"I don't know why…"

"That's not a very good ego boost," Linda said, looking indignant.

"You didn't let me finish," Jack laughed. "It's lots of things. It's everything. When I'm with you, I feel invincible and things seem right."

"I'm still waiting for the ego boost."

"I love talking to you. And laughing with you. Being with you makes me happier than I've been in a very long time. Maybe happier than I've ever been. I always wanted more time with you. That's why I invited myself on your walks."

"Really?"

He smiled and linked their hands together, liking the way it felt to have her fingers entwined with his own. "Somehow, I think you'd never believe me if I told you that I find you beautiful. And that I can't wait to get you naked again."

Jack looked at her then, raising their joined hands and kissing the tip of her index finger before sliding it between his lips and running his tongue over it. Linda blinked, her own lips parting as her tongue darted out to wet her bottom one.

"Would you believe me if I told you I've been scheming of ways to get you to kiss me?" he continued as he rubbed the wet digit along his own lips. "That your mouth looks so delectable, all I wanted was for it to be on me?"

Linda was watching him with rapt attention; he heard her exhale slowly.

"I could admit that I know fuck-all about yoga and only learned it so I could get closer to you. So I could touch you. Would you believe that?"

Now she shook her head in disbelief.

"It's true. Being with you, spending time with you, wanting so bad to just run my hands all over you was driving me crazy."

"Why didn't you tell me?"

"Because you wouldn't have believed it."

Jack moved his arm down Linda's back, circled her waist, and pulled her closer. He urged her to turn her body and straddle his lap. It took a little coaxing, but he finally had her where he wanted her, with her sex pressed up warm and inviting against him and her luscious breasts pressing on his chest.

"Do you believe me now?" he whispered against her ear before kissing it. He ran his lips along the tender flesh just underneath, and Linda shuddered against him and leaned her head back so he could continue kissing along her throat. "Hmmm?"

"Starting to," Linda gasped as he sucked on the smooth skin of her neck and flicked his tongue against it.

"I want to fuck you right here on this couch," he whispered, making Linda groan. "Have you ever been fucked on the couch before?"

"No," she half moaned out. "Graham only liked sex in the bedroom."

"He's an idiot," Jack answered, moving his hands down and cupping Linda's ripe ass. It filled his hands, and he just wanted to smack it and then knead it in his hands even harder. He rocked her back and forth, his cock starting to get hard again. "I want to do everything he didn't do."

"That's a pretty long list," she huffed out.

"Even better," he growled, taking hold of Linda's face and pulling it to his roughly.

Jack was getting massively turned on now and thrust his tongue into Linda's mouth. He groaned loudly when she sucked on it eagerly, and he had a very vivid image of her sucking on something else. That mouth of hers had been driving him crazy for weeks now, and he was aching to see it wrapped around the head of his cock. Since she'd had such a tame sex life — practically nonexistent by the sounds of it — he wasn't even sure if she did stuff like that. He tried not to think about it, or else he'd break down crying.

"Damn it," he muttered.

"What's wrong?"

"The condoms are upstairs," he grumbled. "I'm going to start carrying a stash around with me." Linda started to giggle, and he scowled at her playfully. "You think I'm joking, don't you?"

"Probably not," she answered, still chuckling at him. "It's time for dinner anyway. We can pick this up when we're done."

"Dinner?" he half groaned, half whined as he threw his head back against the couch.

"Yes," she replied, clambering up off his lap despite his attempts to keep her there by grabbing hold of her ass. "I need to stock up energy for later!"

Laughing, Jack let her up reluctantly. He considered yanking her back down and making her acquiesce to his wishes, but without a condom on hand, he just stood to get even more frustrated than he was now. Better to gear down and then attack Linda later when he could finish the job. He stood and looked down at the couch wistfully. In his head, he made a date with it for another time. Maybe later this weekend.

Jack cursed under his breath when he looked at the front of his shorts. He'd only been thinking of putting something on to cover his ass while he yelled at Amanda. Being in that much of a hurry, he hadn't put his briefs on first and now the shorts were tented comically. It looked like someone had shoved a pylon in there — only maybe not as big. He snickered at himself and tried to arrange his cock so that it didn't look so ridiculous. It wasn't working.

Linda turned back then, and he froze, trying not to look guilty of manhandling himself in public. Her eyes went wide, and her hand flew to her mouth as she covered a smile and stifled her laughter. "It looks like you have a little problem there, Mr. McAllister," she choked out, making Jack glare at her in mock anger.

"This is all your fault, you know," he teased, looking down at his cock as it bobbed around. He put his hands over it to keep from embarrassing himself further. He couldn't even use the waistband of the shorts to hold the damned thing in place because he was shirtless, and the head of his dick would stick up absurdly.

"Do you need a moment?" Linda snorted at him. She was still trying to contain her giggles, and Jack could feel his ears turning red.

"No, it's fine," he answered, shaking his head. "It'll go down on its own…in like…a year or so."

Linda walked back to where he was standing and reached out to stroke the tip of the pyramid currently residing in the front of his shorts. Jack bit back a groan, but it was kind of hard because Linda was petting his dick like it was a good dog, and the thing in his pants wanted to do tricks for her. All thought of keeping quiet flew out of the window when she grasped his shaft and used the slippery fabric to slide her hand up and down his cock.

"Linda," he hissed out through clenched teeth. "Baby? My hard-on is *never* going to go away if you keep it up."

"I beg to differ," she said, moving in closer and giving the head a small squeeze.

"No condoms, remember? Although, I suppose I could just run upstairs and grab one."

"I don't need a condom for this," she replied, looking down. Both of them were watching her hand move up and down his shaft.

Linda put her other hand against Jack's hip and turned him so that he faced the couch. She slipped between and sat down in front of him. Looking in his eyes, she hooked her fingers into the waistband of Jack's shorts and pulled them forward, releasing his erection. She continued to lower them until they were mid-thigh and then reached a hand to stroke him gently. Jack's eyes closed at the soft touch.

"Let me know if I'm doing this right," she murmured, and Jack's eyes flew open.

"Whoa," he said, pulling away. "Is this another one of those things you've never done before?"

Suddenly, he felt as if he were taking advantage of the situation when there really was no need, cockstand notwithstanding. Jack desperately wanted her mouth on him, but if it was her first time, this didn't seem like the best way to go about it. He didn't know *what* the best way was, but this wasn't it.

Linda blushed a dark red, and he started to withdraw even more. She took hold of his leg before he could get far. "I've done it before," she answered in a low voice. "Just not often. And not for a long time."

"Linda, you don't need to do this," he began. "I'll be fine, really. I was just joking about it taking a year for my hard-on to deflate."

"You don't want me to do it?"

For all the world, she looked hurt at the thought that he didn't want her to suck his dick, and Jack was taken aback. How the hell could he answer that question?

"Fuck, yes, I want you to," he said, opting for the truth. "Jesus Christ, I've been imagining your lips around...*ah, shit...*I mean sure, that would be great, but I don't want to make you do something you don't want to do. Know what I mean? I mean, it's just a stiffie…It'll go away, and if it doesn't, we can always, you know, get a condom—"

"Jack," Linda said calmly, effectively cutting off his babbling. "I want to."

"You do?" he asked, swallowing heavily.

"Yes," she answered. "I want to make you feel good like you did for me."

Jack groaned but let Linda draw him closer until he could feel her breath on his incredibly rigid cock. Her movements were slow and careful, but after a few kisses, she gave him a tentative lick. A bolt of pleasure shot all the way down his cock straight to his balls. Her little pink tongue darted out again and brushed up the underside of his erection.

"God, Linda," he whispered softly. He raised his hand and brushed his thumb along the side of her face. She looked up at him then, and he wasn't quite sure if it was his voice, his touch, or what she saw reflected back at her, but she seemed to become bolder. Opening her mouth, she slipped his cock between her lips, and he had to resist pushing his hips forward as she took him a little deeper.

Jack was entranced by what was happening. Linda didn't have mad porn-star skills when it came to giving head. She was a little timid and shy, and she took things slowly, but all of this combined with the warm wetness of her mouth was actually cranking him up more than any other time he could remember. It was because he knew she was doing this to give him pleasure, and she actually cared enough to make him feel good without making it seem like a chore. His pleasure was her pleasure, and he understood that very well because that's exactly how he had felt earlier this afternoon.

Linda circled one hand underneath his cock and began stroking him between his legs like before. She started moving a bit quicker now, taking him a little deeper. When she glanced up at him again, that was really all it took. The adoration he saw reflected back at him made him begin to shudder. His stomach clenched repeatedly in anticipation, and his breath came out in shallow gasps and moans.

"Linda," Jack said between pants. He squeezed her shoulder to warn her that he was close. She continued what she was doing, and next thing he knew, his knees were about to buckle from the force of his orgasm. "*Fuck,*" he managed to bite out before his vision faded slightly and was replaced by pulsing lights as he came.

Somehow, he had managed to throw his hands up against the back of the couch before he lost his balance and landed on top of Linda. She whooped in surprise as he sent her reeling back into the cushions. It was a good thing he'd stopped coming by then or else it could have gotten messy. Linda started to laugh, and when Jack's brain unscrambled, he began a low chuckle as well.

Jack was too weak to do much and was grateful when Linda pulled his shorts back in place gently and then made room for him on the couch. He collapsed beside her in a boneless heap and smiled blissfully when she leaned forward and kissed his cheek before cuddling into him.

"Was that okay?" she asked hesitantly.

"Uh-huh."

"Uh-huh doesn't sound very good."

"Sorry," he replied. "I'm still trying to find the part of my brain that controls complex speech."

Linda laughed delightedly, and a slow smile spread across his face. He finally had the strength to turn his head and look at her. Bringing his hand up, he cupped her cheek softly and brought her in for a tender kiss. Normally, he wouldn't kiss a girl right after she'd gone down on him, but with Linda, it was different. This time, Jack found it strangely erotic. He felt electric and had a confession on his lips that was much too soon to declare, so he whispered it against Linda's mouth, knowing it would be too quiet for her to hear.

16
Dirty Talk: Check!

The next morning, Jack woke up to a sleep-warm Linda tucked against his body, and he couldn't help the lazy grin that spread on his face.

Linda stirred in his arms. Jack had no idea what time it was; the curtains had remained closed, and the room was still shrouded in darkness. Lifting his head, he looked at the clock and saw it wasn't quite seven a.m. Since they'd had a late night, and an energetic one at that, he was hoping Linda would want to forgo her daily walk so he could stay with her in bed longer. He knew that eventually she had to get up so she could go to Baltimore, and he had to go and make sure that Amanda had managed to clear the trash out of their house. But for now, he didn't even want to think about any of that. He just wanted to stay here, warm and happy.

"You're really here," Linda murmured softly before rolling over and cuddling against his chest. He cradled her close and smiled when she snaked one of her legs between his as she got comfortable.

"Mm-hmm."

"I thought maybe this was all just a *really* good dream," she said on a breathy exhale into his neck.

"If it was, I'd have to wonder which one of us was dreaming," he replied, still smiling.

"You're such a cheeseball." Linda shook with laughter against him.

"Hey, I thought chicks dug that kind of stuff."

"How long have you been single?"

Jack snorted. "Not all of us have been in a twenty-year marriage, you know."

"Fifteen," Linda retorted smartly. "So, what's the longest you've been with someone?"

"Umm." He stopped to think about that for a second and wasn't very encouraged by what he found. "I think my longest relationship was six or seven months."

"That's it?"

"Yeah."

"How come you've never really been serious with anyone?"

"I never found anyone I wanted to be serious with," he replied and added *until now* in his head.

"I wonder why that is," Linda mused quietly, almost to herself. Jack wondered if he should answer her rhetorical question.

"Most of the time, it ended up that I didn't have much in common with them, so things never really worked out."

Linda remained quiet for a few moments, and the silence made him uncomfortable. How could he possibly explain that, for the most part, he'd dated women he found fuckable from the get-go, and it wasn't until the lust died out that he figured out there really wasn't much else to hold those relationships together? First of all, that made him sound like an asshole, and second, it would be glaringly obvious that the opposite had happened this time around. This time he'd gotten to know the woman first before finding her physically attractive. *That* made him feel like an asshole, too. And he knew that admitting it would hurt Linda. Jack knew her ego was a fragile thing, having been shattered repeatedly before, and he wasn't ever going to be the guy to do that to her.

"Maybe I just needed a sugar mamma to hold my attention," he joked, tickling Linda to get her to giggle.

"Well, you came to the wrong place, then." She snickered before succumbing to his probing fingers.

"Oh, yeah?" he answered, rolling her onto her back and hovering over her. "You have your own house, a good-paying job, a hot young stud to do your bidding..."

"Think highly of yourself, don't you?" she said with a laugh, wiggling madly as he continued relentlessly.

"I'm the shit." He smirked down at her. "Don't you know?"

"And you're going to be covered in pee in about two seconds if you don't stop!"

"Ah!" he yelled, jumping away from Linda and almost falling off the bed. She watched him trying to recover and subsided in a fit of giggles as he scowled at her. "That wasn't funny."

"Sure it was. You should have seen your expression!"

Jack tossed himself onto his back and threw an arm over his face dramatically. He loved hearing Linda laugh, and he tried not to grin as she continued chortling at him. "My ego is wounded," he said in as pathetic a voice as he could muster.

"Aww, poor baby," she crooned. Jack could feel the sheets rustling as she came closer, and he bit back a rumble of approval as Linda straddled him and began kissing his chin and neck. "I take it back. You looked very manly almost falling out of the bed."

"Manly, huh?" he asked, trying to keep from chuckling.

"And sexy, too."

He took his arm away from his face and beamed up at her. "Okay, you're forgiven."

"Wait a second," Linda said, scowling down at him fiercely. "How the hell did I end up being the one to apologize when you were the one who almost tickled me till I peed?"

She just looked so adorable, perched on top of him, a look of righteous indignation on her face, that Jack couldn't resist pulling her down for a kiss. Morning breath be damned. It took but a second for Linda's fingers to twine through his hair and press closer to him. It didn't take much longer than that for his cock to stiffen. He hadn't been kidding when he'd told Linda she was going to be the death of him. Even after sleeping for seven hours, he was surprised the thing still worked after the workout he'd given it yesterday.

"How do you do that?" Linda murmured against his neck as she sucked on the skin there, driving him more than a little crazy.

"Do what?" he ground out, grabbing her ass and swiveling his hips.

"Make me want you so bad," she gasped out as she rubbed against his cock. He wasn't even inside of her yet and already felt like he was going to lose control. Condom. He needed a condom. Stat.

As if reading his mind, Linda reached over and opened her bedside table. Jack let go of her long enough for her to grab one. As soon as she got it on him, he shifted her body and sheathed himself inside her. The sex was hard and fast. He pulled Linda up slightly so he could thrust upward with his hips. Linda held on to his wrists for dear life, her face contorted in pleasure. She began to cry out and rock her hips to meet his frenzied movements.

"*Fuck*," Jack spit out between clenched teeth as he felt his whole body contract. That second before his release felt as long as a year and then sweet blessed relief.

Linda collapsed on top of his chest and hummed contentedly. He hugged her close and felt secretly triumphant that she no longer worried about crushing him or being too heavy, which was preposterous since he outweighed her by quite a bit and was over half a foot taller. She could no more crush him than she could a car. Although leave it to Linda to think that feat possible. Jack was working hard to chip away at that shroud of continual self-doubt, and it seemed to be working.

"I suppose we should get up and shower or something," Linda sighed.

"Nooo…" Jack whined, tightening his hold. "Let's just stay in bed all morning."

"That sounds nice…"

"But?"

"But I really need to do some research before I have to drive down to Baltimore today."

"It's just gossip," Jack grumbled. "None of it's true. Just make something up!"

"I can't do that," she replied amusedly. "Tell you what…Tomorrow we'll spend all morning in bed."

Jack paused for a moment at her words. "You want me to spend the night again?"

"Oh…well, only if you want."

Linda had stiffened in his arms, so he ran his hands down her back in a soothing gesture and kissed the top of her head. "I want."

They stayed like that for a while longer, pressed together, breathing quietly and gently touching. Jack sincerely didn't want to move and was tempted to hold Linda to him when she stirred and then rolled off his body. She leaned down and kissed him softly before getting out of bed, scooping his T-shirt from the floor and throwing it on. He grinned hugely at the sight and watched as she padded out of the bedroom. He heard the creaking of stairs and figured she'd gone downstairs to take care of something.

After Jack had cleaned up, he threw on his boxers and went to look for Linda. She was waiting for the coffee machine to finish percolating, two mugs on standby. There was a plate in the middle of the table with pastries on it. Jack had almost forgotten about them with everything that had happened. He should feel thankful for those pastries; he doubted he'd be standing half naked in Linda's kitchen had it not been for them. Jack walked up behind her and slipped his arms around her waist before kissing her temple. They stayed like that as Linda prepared the coffee. He only let her go to grab the mugs, and then they sat down at the table together.

Linda pushed the plate of pastries over to him and said, "Help yourself."

He went straight for the chocolate-covered croissant and broke it in half over a napkin. "Want some?" he asked, offering her the other half.

Linda shook her head ruefully. "No pastries for me. I'm over the hump, thanks."

"Linda, you can have a pastry. It's all about moderation."

"No," she replied, shaking her head at him. "It's better if I don't."

"Come on," he said, breaking off a piece and holding it out toward her.

"As my personal trainer, aren't you supposed to be discouraging this type of behavior?" she asked sternly. Her eyes, however, were trained on his fingers.

"I promise to help you work it off later," he said in a low voice, raising an eyebrow. "Let me feed you."

Their eyes met, and she moved toward him, her mouth opening enough so he could slip the piece of pastry between her lips. They closed over his fingers for a moment, the wet warmth turning him on. When she drew back, he brought his thumb to his mouth and licked off the remaining chocolate. He did the same with his other two fingers as he watched Linda chew the pastry slowly, in obvious enjoyment. As she ate, he took a bite. They alternated like that until it was finished.

"More?" he asked, hovering his hand over the plate.

"No," she said, smiling shyly. "I'm good."

"Are you sure?" he teased. "That just means more *exercise* for us tonight."

"Now you're being cruel," Linda replied, swatting at his arm before picking up her coffee and taking a drink.

"Okay." He swiped a cherry cheesecake bite off the plate and popped it in his mouth. "These are really good."

"I know," she sighed, eying the plate. "You should take them home with you. Give them to Amanda; she could stand to gain a pound or ten."

Jack reached over and took Linda's coffee mug from her hand, setting it down on the table.

"What are you —"

"Come here," he said gently, taking her hand and tugging to make her stand. He pushed his chair back and pulled her down onto his lap. Wrapping her arms around his neck, he kissed her softly. Gradually, she lost her tension and kissed him back. She tasted like chocolate and coffee. Delicious.

"I'll take the pastries home if you want me to." Jack waited until she looked at him. "But I don't think it's necessary."

"Trust me, it's necessary."

"Listen to me, because now this is your personal trainer talking." He tipped his head down and raised his eyebrows, giving her an authoritative look. "You can't keep depriving yourself of food like this, because after you lose the weight, you'll balloon up again once you introduce it back into your diet."

"So then I won't introduce it back into my diet."

"That's no way to live, Linda. You can't diet forever," he said, trying to keep his face neutral. "Like I said, it's all about moderation. If you indulge a little, then you do twenty extra reps at the gym the next day to work it off. As long as you're aware of what you are eating and how much activity you need to do to burn the calories, you'll be fine."

Linda nodded with her lip caught between her teeth. He ran his thumb over it, loosening it before kissing her.

"Smile, beautiful," he whispered, and she did slightly before leaning her forehead against his. "So, I'm leaving these here."

"No, take them with you. I'm not ready yet."

"I'll take *half.* The rest we can share."

"Deal," she replied, smiling at him for real this time.

When they finished breakfast, Jack decided he'd better go home. He didn't bother taking a shower, figuring he'd just do that at his house, as he didn't want to waste more of Linda's morning. She had work to do, and he'd be seeing her later anyway. Linda drove Jack back to the club to pick up his car. Luckily, the place was open so he could grab his keys from his locker. After a quick kiss good-bye, he went in, got his things, and left for home.

Jack was happy to see Vicky's car missing from his driveway and was hopeful that meant she was gone. He'd been ready to kick her out on her ass just for that stunt she pulled in the bakery. Now that he knew the extent of her fuckery and just how badly she'd messed with his chances to be with Linda, he was even more irate. She did not want to step foot in this house again or else he'd show her what a crazy-ass fucker looked like.

When he walked into the house, he heard someone blowing their nose loudly and rounded the corner to find Amanda balled up on their couch. Her nose was pink, her eyes red-rimmed, and tissues surrounded her. She was also wearing her "mourning" pajamas, which was never a good sign. Usually, those were saved for when someone broke up with her. Jack neared her with trepidation.

"Oh, Jack!" she wailed when she saw him standing in the entryway to the living room.

"What's wrong?" he asked, walking into the room.

"Me and Jimmy broke up!"

"Why?"

"'Cause of that fucking *bitch* Vicky!" she spat out. "You were so right about her!"

Jack sat down at the edge of the couch, wary of being sucked into the fabric quicksand. He looked at Amanda and asked, "What happened?"

"Well, I confronted Vicky about the pictures, and Jimmy heard us fighting about it, so he came to find out what was going on." Amanda sniffled and rubbed her nose with a Kleenex. "I told him about what I found, and that miserable bitch called me a liar and said I had no proof! Which I didn't, 'cause like an idiot, I erased all those pictures. She said I was trying to frame her 'cause *you* hated her! And then she told him I was kicking her onto the streets, and Jimmy said she could stay with *him!*"

"Idiot."

"So, I told him that if he took her in, we were *over,* and he said he couldn't just let her live on the streets! Can you believe this shit?"

Unfortunately, after what he'd witnessed himself and then heard from Linda, he could believe that shit. All too well. He knew there had been something not right about that psycho. It was too bad Amanda hadn't had any proof, but at this point, he was just relieved those pictures had been deleted. Something about Vicky in possession of pictures of him sleeping creeped him right the hell out.

"I guess this means we have to look for new jobs?" he said flatly.

"*No,*" Amanda bit out scornfully. "Jimmy's not stupid. We're the bread and butter of that gym. Plus, Vicky quit." She waved her hands around dramatically and rolled her eyes. "She told him she was afraid for her life. And that dumbass ate it up with a spoon!"

Jack tried very hard not to laugh at her emphatic expressions; he knew that she was pretty pissed off about the whole situation.

"Are you okay to go back?" he asked carefully.

"Yeah, I'll be fine. He can have her, and every day, he'll have to look at all this—" she gestured to her body "—and regret his decision."

Now he did smile because Amanda sounded more like her usual self. She generally snapped back quickly, and he'd be surprised if she didn't have a new man lined up soon.

"I'm sorry, Amanda," he said contritely.

"No, *I'm* sorry," she said, turning big, leaky eyes to him. "I should have listened to you when you said you didn't trust Vicky. I was just so happy to have a new girlfriend, and I figured you were being kind of a drama queen. Anyway, I never should have invited her to live with us, and I should have been a better friend. I'm s-s-sorry, Jack."

Her lip began to tremble and tears threatened to breach. Not one to play the crying trump card, Jack knew she truly was sorry for everything that had happened. Amanda was more likely to smack him and tell him to fuck off. Ignoring the vortex that was the couch, he sat closer to her and slung an arm over her shoulder to comfort her.

"I know," he sighed.

"Jesus fucking Christ, Jack!" she said disgustedly. "You smell like *pussy!*"

Jack could feel his ears get hot, and then he burst out laughing as Amanda pushed against his chest to escape him. Both of them had become prisoners of the couch, and he was too helpless from the laughter to be of much help. Amanda started to chuckle as well, and soon, both of them were howling as Jack tried to move away. Somehow, he managed to escape the gravitational pull of the cushions and roll onto the floor, where he lay in a heap, still laughing.

"Fuck, I hate that couch." He snorted.

Amanda flopped sideways and hung her head off the side of it. "Leave my couch alone!"

"I only sat on it because you were upset over Jimmy."

"He's a goof."

"Told you." Jack snickered good-naturedly. "You can do better than that loser."

"Yeah," Amanda replied. She paused for a few seconds before asking, "So, you finally got laid, eh?"

"No," he answered, because in truth, what had happened the night before was much more than that. "That's not what it was about. It wasn't just getting laid. It was...*better...*" He let the sentence drift because he didn't even have the proper words to describe it.

"Well, no wonder you smell like pussy." She snorted. "You've gone and grown one of your own."

"Fuck you," Jack replied affectionately.

"I'm glad you're happy," Amanda said softly. "She makes you happy, right, Jack?"

"Yeah," he answered, smiling blissfully.

"Good."

17
A Diabolical Plan

The rest of the weekend passed quickly. Maybe a little too quickly for Linda, who was loath to go back to her regular workweek. Having Jack with her for so much time straight had spoiled her. Now they would be relegated to their morning walks and the three hours she went to the gym to work out until the weekend. But at least now she would have the nights, too. She hoped.

Linda wasn't quite sure how they would handle their new relationship. Did Jack like spending lots of time with the women he was involved with? Would he want his space? Would they spend most of their time at her house or his, and would he even want her to spend the night at his house? She hadn't dated anyone besides Graham, and she was pretty sure things were different for a mature couple dating than it had been when she was a teen. Obviously, one major difference was that this time around, she was allowed to have sleepovers.

Late Saturday afternoon, Jack had met her in Baltimore, much to her amazement. They hadn't really discussed their date because they had been otherwise occupied, so she just expected to see him when she arrived back in Arnold. It had been a sweet and wonderful surprise to find him propped up against the wall outside of the Baltimore Daily News. Out of habit, she now checked whenever she left work on Saturdays, never really expecting him to be there but unable to stop herself nonetheless.

This time, he'd been standing there looking sexier than anyone had a right to be. He was wearing a tight black T-shirt and beat-up dark-wash jeans that hugged him in all the right places. Linda couldn't help ogling him, then blushing, and then breaking out into a huge grin when she realized Jack was *her* man. He was there waiting for *her.*

"Hi," she said happily as he pushed off the wall, and she closed the distance.

"Hi," he returned, wrapping his arms around her and bending to give her a kiss.

Linda's stomach exploded in butterflies when their mouths touched. It didn't take long for her to part her lips against his when she felt the tip of his tongue flick out lightly. Jack's chest rumbled slightly, and he gripped her tighter.

Linda slowed the kisses down before she was tempted to start humping the man's leg. Or drag him off to her car to take advantage of him.

"What are you doing here?" she asked, grinning up at him.

"We had a date, remember?" he answered, reaching up to tuck a strand of hair behind her ear. "And I missed you."

"Oh," Linda said in a squeaky voice. She was amazed she didn't melt into a puddle at his feet. "I wasn't sure if that was still happening. We kind of got…*distracted.*" Jack smirked at her. Then she whispered, "And I missed you, too."

"Hmm…I like these," he said softly, looking over her shoulder as he ran his hands over her backside.

"They're new," Linda answered, speaking of the jeans she had on. "Cici helped me pick out some new outfits."

"She did, did she?"

"Mm-hmm. The top is new, too." Linda pulled back slightly to show off her new shirt, which had a deep V-neck. It wasn't a style she would have chosen herself, but by the way Jack was staring at the fabric clinging to her breasts, she thought maybe it was a flattering look after all.

"How tall are the guys in your office?" he blurted out, still staring.

"Umm, I don't really know…Why?"

"No reason," he answered curtly.

Linda looked down, frowning, and then realized Jack could see down her top and was most likely concerned about other men doing the same. She began to chuckle before saying lightly, "For the record, I generally don't let the men I work with stand this close to me."

Jack looked at her and had the grace to look sheepish, making her grin all the more.

"Mine," he said, running his hands up her sides. His thumbs brushed against the sides of her breasts, making it very clear what he was talking about.

"Good Lord, you've been reduced to single syllables."

"You're lucky I don't club you over the head and drag you to my cave," Jack answered, making her laugh outright. He looked around in amazement, as if someone else could hear. "She thinks I'm kidding."

"Shut up," she replied before cuddling close to him. "You're the only man who pays any attention to me."

"Not if you keep wearing tops like that," he muttered, pulling her into his chest even more.

"Okay, how about you're the only man who has *my* attention?"

This made Jack hum contentedly as he kissed the top of her head. "I like that."

"Good, because it's true."

They had made their way to the bar for Jack's sound check and then went out to dinner on their own. Rob wasn't playing this time, and while Linda missed the other couple, she was also happy to have Jack all to herself. This was their first official date, and she couldn't help but think they had done things sort of backward. Would she have changed it if she could? Nope. Not in the least.

Because his set was almost last this time, they didn't need to rush back after dinner. They held hands as they strolled back, taking their time. Linda loved how affectionate he was. At the bar, Jack sat at a small table with her just to the side of stage, his arm resting along the back of her chair. Like the last time, he stroked her hair and ran his fingers along the side of her face tenderly as they listened to the other musicians playing.

Before Jack had gone up to play, he whispered in her ear, "This time you know I'm singing to you."

Linda was happy that he had chosen different songs. She wanted no reminders of the night Vicky had crashed the party and made her feel worthless and just a little bit crazy. Thinking back, she wished she had said something to Jack sooner. There was nothing she could do to change it, but it would have saved them a lot of time and trouble if she'd just been forthright. Mind you, Jack had been right; she wouldn't have been ready for this at that time.

She wasn't sure she was ready *now.*

Watching all the other women in the bar appraising Jack openly, their hungry eyes passing over her as if she didn't even exist, made her feel insignificant. Even as she sat with Jack while he was being publicly attentive, it seemed as if she was being stared at sideways, open curiosity on everyone's faces. The unspoken but glaring question being, "What is *he* doing with *her?*" The whole thing made her feel short of breath at times.

The only time she didn't feel that way was when Jack was on stage singing. He only had eyes for her, and the sound of his voice washed over Linda like a warm breeze. The songs he sang were full of words of devotion, and the soulful way he sang lent credence to them. She was overwhelmed in the most delicious way and just wanted to take him home.

Then she realized she could. And she did.

Saturday night was one of slow exploration. It was languid and lovely. They got to know each other better and discovered each other's secrets. It was full of soft caresses and low moans of encouragement. Linda still preferred the lights off, and Jack didn't push her. Nonetheless, they loved by touch and by kiss and by taste. All other senses heightened because of the lack of one.

Sunday morning found Linda lazy and sated. Jack was wrapped around her, playing big spoon to her little spoon, and for a while, she actually did feel small. And she felt loved, which was something she hadn't experienced in a very long time. Linda took a deep breath as she tried to get her wavering emotions under control. This was all very new territory for her, and she wasn't quite sure how to handle it. Part of her was scared silly of falling for Jack since he didn't seem like the kind of man to settle down with just one woman for a long period of time, but another part of her was telling her to enjoy it while it lasted and to deal with the aftermath later.

As Jack sighed behind her and hugged her closer reflexively, she decided to follow the second voice's advice. Would she have the chance to experience something like this ever again? Maybe. Maybe not. Why throw it away while it was on her doorstep? She cradled Jack's arm closer to her chest, leaned down, and kissed his hand. Then she closed her eyes and drifted back to sleep.

Linda awoke later to butterfly kisses being placed along her bare shoulder and the side of her neck. She hummed softly in pleasure, and Jack's arms tightened around her.

"Morning," he said in a sleep-roughened voice.

"Morning," she returned, smiling to herself.

"I know you said we'd spend all morning in bed together…"

"But?" she prompted, and Jack sighed behind her.

"That was before Jimmy broke up with Amanda."

"You want to make sure she's okay?"

"Yeah," he answered in resignation. "I don't want to leave—"

"It's okay, Jack," Linda answered before turning in his arms. "She's your friend. She needs you."

While Linda meant the words, she still couldn't help but feel a little pang that he'd be leaving. Then she felt selfish for wanting Jack to herself while his best friend was hurting. She recalled how Tony and Eliza had been there for her when Graham had left, and it had made all the difference in the world.

"Her timing sucks ass, though," he muttered as he snuggled in closer.

Linda loved the feel of his big, warm body against hers. She ran her hands over the planes of his back, feeling the hardness of his muscles under the smooth skin. "It's not really her fault. She kind of got blindsided by Vicky."

Linda felt Jack tense up in her arms at the little witch's name while he muttered choice descriptive phrases about her. She cringed a little. He was still really upset about the whole thing, and she couldn't blame him. They'd managed to discuss everything that had happened, and now she knew how Vicky had ended up living with them. It sounded like Amanda had gotten hoodwinked but good. In a way, Linda felt sorry for Amanda since she hadn't really known Vicky's nature. Now Amanda was left wondering if Vicky had had her paws on Jimmy before they'd broken up, much like Linda wondered about Graham and Vicky. Turned out, she now had more in common with Jack's roommate than she imagined.

"Shower?" Linda suggested, making Jack brighten up immediately. For some reason, he loved taking showers with her. He told her it was something about being hot and wet, and that was always a good thing. Linda just laughed at the glazed look in his eye.

One more thing to cross off the list. Shower sex. On Friday night, they had been too tired to do much of anything, but this morning, it was no holds barred. Jack's soapy hands glided all over her body. He paid special attention to her breasts, washing them reverently and rinsing them off before bending his head to lick the water that streamed from her nipples. While he did that, his hand slipped between her legs, fingers caressing, seeking, and then thrusting inside her. Linda groaned, the noises she made echoing loudly off the tile.

Reaching forward, she grasped his erection and started slowly pumping up and down. Jack moaned against her breast and sucked her nipple into his mouth even harder. She hissed at the sensation that rode the fine line between pleasure and pain. Linda's hand moved faster, and so did Jack's. His thumb came up to caress her clit, and she bucked her hips against his hand as she got closer to the brink.

"Squeeze harder, baby," Jack ground out. "You're gonna make me come."

Linda did as she was told, although it was becoming harder to concentrate with her own orgasm building and ready to crash down on her. Jack called out loudly, and she felt a moment's satisfaction before she was moaning through her own release.

"You really *are* going to kill me," Jack panted out as he leaned against the shower wall for support. "I think I'm going to run out of sperm."

Linda started chuckling and leaned against the tile, giving a small screech at the cold against her back. That got Jack going, and both of them laughed in earnest.

"That's okay," she said, leaning up to kiss him underneath his jaw. "I won't see you till tomorrow. It'll give you a chance to replenish."

Linda tried to keep her tone light, but she didn't think it worked because Jack wrapped his arms around her and held her close for a few moments. The water started to cool, which prompted her to step back and give him a smile. "We better finish before I run out of hot water."

Jack simply nodded, grabbed the body wash again, and they soaped one another up in silence. Once finished, Linda enjoyed helping him to dry off, and his playfulness returned, which made her happy. It ended up with her running out of the bathroom with Jack in hot pursuit and then a tickle match on her bed. The whole thing was utterly ridiculous since they were grown adults and not the teenage counterparts they were currently acting like, but she loved it nonetheless. It was refreshing to be so silly and carefree.

"Why will you let me see you naked in the shower but not in bed?" Jack asked once they had calmed down a bit. He was trying to peek down the towel Linda had managed to keep wrapped around herself.

"Because when I stand still, nothing jiggles," she answered honestly and shrugged in a self-deprecating way.

"What if I *want* to see you jiggling?"

"Ugh," she said, crinkling her nose. "Why would you want to see that?"

"'Cause it means I'm working you hard," Jack answered. His eyebrows flicked up, and his eyes blazed for a second before he attacked her neck with his mouth.

Linda squealed at the stubble tickling her. "We'll see," she answered, and then Jack kissed her, making her forget what they were talking about.

After Jack's departure, Linda called her best friend. Eliza was on her doorstep with a curious expression on her face ten minutes later.

"Girl," she said, "you look like you've been rode hard and put away happy."

Linda stepped back and pointed toward her living room with a huge grin. "This is a convo for the living room."

"Yes!" Eliza said ecstatically. "Those are the best kind!"

Linda laughed and closed the door behind them.

Jack managed to sneak away later that night so he could call Linda and at least hear her voice if he couldn't be with her.

"So, how are things going over there?" she asked him quietly, as if afraid Amanda could hear.

"Oh, God," he answered, knuckling his forehead. "*Horrible!* Absolutely horrible. She's just a fucking mess, which is beyond me because Jimmy is a fucking loser."

"Oh, no," Linda sympathized. "You don't think she'd—you know…"

"No, no," Jack replied. "She always does this. She'd never hurt herself. She just needs some time to get over it. Or get someone under her. Either one works."

Linda laughed, and it warmed his heart. "You know—" she started but was cut off when Jack heard Amanda start wailing in the other room.

"Jesus. She's at it again," he groaned pathetically.

"You better go," she said. "I'll see you tomorrow."

"For our walk?"

"If you're up for it. Sounds like it'll be a long night."

"Yeah."

"I'll just see you at the gym later if you want to sleep in."

"You're so sweet," he said genuinely. "And thank you. Most new girlfriends wouldn't be this…accepting."

"Girlfriend, eh?"

"Yeah," he answered, a lick of nervousness assaulting him. "Is that okay?"

"Yeah," she replied softly. "That's more than okay."

Jack grinned like a fool until he heard another sob come from the living room. "I really do have to go," he said regretfully.

"Okay, go. Miss you."

"I miss you too."

The next morning, he was at Linda's door practically swaying on his feet but not willing to forgo seeing her. When Linda answered the door, her mouth popped open in shock.

"Jack, you look terrible!"

"I missed you too." He grinned wryly, and she shook her head at him in amusement.

"Get in here," she said, grabbing his hand and pulling him into her house. "Shoes. Off."

"Aren't we going for our walk?"

"No."

Once he had his shoes off, she was pulling him toward her staircase. They went into her bedroom, and she gave him a shove so that he sat on her bed.

"Linda, I'd love to, but there's no way—"

"Shut up," she laughed. "I didn't bring you up here for that. You're going to sleep." Linda gave him a gentle push so that he was lying down on her bed. "Sleep, baby. You need rest," she whispered before straightening and turning to leave.

"Wait," he said, grabbing at her hand. "Where are you going?"

"I'll be around doing this and that," she answered, shrugging.

"Stay with me," he asked, giving her hand a small tug. "I sleep better with you."

Linda smiled down at him sweetly and then bent down to crawl onto the bed. Jack made room for her and sighed deeply when she was cradled in his arms. It took barely a minute for him to fall asleep.

Jack woke up from his nap feeling surprisingly refreshed. Linda had made coffee right before waking him, and there was a cup waiting for him on the table made exactly the way he liked. They sat across from one another and chatted amicably before he had to rush off to work.

The morning went by relatively quickly as he tried to play interference between Amanda and Jimmy. The asshole had come in and rushed straight back to his office. Jack had considered taking him out in honor of his friend but stopped himself. They needed these jobs, and he figured shoving that psycho Vicky at him was the best revenge they could have. Let him keep her.

Linda showed up to her session all smiles and brightened up his day considerably. They did their usual workout, and Jack tried to keep his hands to himself since they were out in the public area. When the session was done, Jack waited for Linda at the front desk as always. When she walked toward him, she passed Amanda, and her brows pulled together as she took in his friend's appearance. Bluntly put, Amanda looked like shit today. Her face was still a little puffy around the eyes, she wasn't wearing makeup, and her hair was pulled into a ratty ponytail. She put on a brave face, however.

"Poor Amanda," Linda said quietly. "She looks like she had a hard night."

"Yeah," he agreed and then shook his head a little bit because Amanda was coming toward them.

Linda took his cue and stopped talking.

"Hi, Linda," Amanda said meekly, not at all her usual excitable self.

"How're you doing?" Linda asked sympathetically, and Amanda just shrugged and gave a little smile.

"Oh, hey, Jack," Linda said, looking at him in concern. "You know that funny noise your car was making?"

"My car isn't —" Jack whooshed out a breath as a sharp elbow jabbed him under the ribs. Linda was staring at him with raised brows and an expectant look on her face. "Oh, right, *that* noise," he answered, playing along and making her smile.

"You know, my friend *Tony* is a mechanic," she continued. "You remember Tony, right?"

"Yeah. Big guy?" he answered, nodding, and noticed Amanda's ears perk up.

"Yes, him. You should maybe drop by his shop tonight and see if he can look into that for you." Linda was looking at him with large, grave eyes, and he just wanted to grab her and kiss her silly. "If you come with me to my car, I'll give you his card and directions."

"Good idea. I'll go see him after I drop Amanda off."

"Oh, I can come with you!" Amanda piped up.

"You wouldn't mind?" he asked solicitously. Out of the corner of his eye, he saw Linda bite her lip, most likely trying to keep a Cheshire cat grin from appearing.

"Nope, just let me get changed!" Amanda put a hand against her face while the other ran over her hair. She turned and practically sprinted to the employees' locker room.

Jack started chuckling, and Linda joined in. "I hope you know I'll have to wait for an hour while she gets ready."

"I figured as much. Come on. You'll need Tony's card."

As soon as they were in the parking lot, Jack grabbed Linda and pressed her up against a minivan, effectively blocking them from the view of anyone pulling into the park or leaving the club. He began kissing her right away, his hands creeping up to cup her breasts as he thrust his hips against her body. He heard the thump of her backpack hitting the ground right before her arms came around his waist. Linda moaned into his mouth and moved her body against his eagerly.

"God, I've been wanting to touch you all day," he said in a low voice against her neck. "Not to mention you're a fucking genius."

"Me too, and thank you," she replied, slightly breathless.

"That really is nice that you want to help Amanda feel better."

"It's strictly for selfish reasons. The sooner she gets over Jimmy, the sooner I can steal you away."

"That's kind of evil." Jack chuckled. "I like it."

"Yeah, Tony's a complete manwhore. He'll be perfect for the job."

"Wait. A manwhore?" he said, pulling away slightly and frowning. "I don't know if that's such a good idea."

"She just needs a rebound, right?"

"Well, yeah. But if he ends up hurting her, we'll be right back here again, and I might feel the need to punch him out, and he's your friend…See where I'm going?"

"They're adults, Jack. Tony's pretty good at casual relationships. I'm sure it'll be fine."

"God, I hope so. I don't know how much more of this I can take." Jack pulled Linda to him and started kissing her again. She felt so good against him. His hands traveled down and around until he was grabbing her ass in his hands and grinding into her.

He pulled away for a second. "Is public sex on the list?"

"Jack," Linda laughed. "We are not having sex in the parking lot of your work."

"Is that a no?"

"It's a 'not here in the parking lot,'" she said primly, and he couldn't help grinning down at her.

"Okay, fine," he drawled out. "I better get back inside. Let's get that card."

Linda hung up the phone in complete frustration. She slammed it down a few times for good measure and cursed under her breath.

"Whoa, whoa," she heard from behind her as Jack walked into the kitchen. He came up, slipped his arms around her waist, and kissed her shoulder. "What's wrong, beautiful?"

Feeling him against her body made her calm down slightly but also ignited her anger all over again. It wasn't directed at him, of course. Jack was her angel.

"Graham," she spat out and felt him stiffen. He always had a visceral reaction to her ex's name since he'd met him in Baltimore. "He pushed the mediation back again."

She heard him rumble as his arms held her tighter. "Did they say *why?*"

"Why else? Another 'business trip.'"

"It's okay, baby," Jack said softly as he kissed the top of her head. "It'll get done."

"Not at this rate," she whined, turning in his arms and pressing her forehead against his chest. "I just want it over with."

"Me too." He held her for a few more minutes until she calmed down. "I have to head to work. Will you be okay?"

"Yeah," she answered, her reply muffled by his shirt.

"You're not going to hunt him down while you're in Baltimore, are you?" he said in a joking tone.

"That's not a bad idea," she grumbled.

Jack put his hands against the sides of her face and tipped it up; he was frowning.

"*No.*"

"I won't," she sighed. "Relax."

"I'm serious, Linda. I don't want you near that guy unless you are with your lawyer. I don't trust him."

"I know."

"And if I had it my way, I'd be coming with you to the mediation, too," he said while scowling.

Linda couldn't help but get a little turned on when he went caveman on her. It didn't happen often, as Jack was fairly easygoing, but on occasion, his alpha side would come out to play.

Linda smiled and smoothed down his shirt over his chest. "You know you can't do that. But I wish you could be with me, too."

Leaning down, he gave her a soft kiss. "I'll see you tonight?"

"Yeah," she agreed.

18
Coming Out of the Attic

Jack sat up in bed, gasping for breath. He'd had some crazy dream where he confessed to Linda he liked to exercise naked in his attic and, after tying her to the chin-up bar with some rubber exercise bands, began to spank her ass with a jujitsu belt. It had been the loud crack of the belt against her ass that had startled him to wakefulness. He rubbed his eyes and looked around, realizing he was in bed with Linda and not in some nonexistent attic where he used circuit equipment to perform kinky naked exercise.

Shaking his head, he looked down at Linda who slept by his side. "I gotta get you to stop calling me Master," he mumbled to himself.

"Mmm?" Linda moaned sleepily.

"Nothing, baby," he whispered as he got back under the covers and hugged her close. "Go back to sleep."

"'Kay."

Despite the strange dream, Jack fell back to sleep relatively quickly, but the next day, as he and Linda walked along the path leading to his house, it was still flirting around in his subconscious.

"Are you nervous or something?" Linda asked him, breaking into his private thoughts.

"No, why?"

"You're, uh, squeezing my hand *really* hard," she said, looking down at their clasped hands pointedly.

Jack had a chance to glimpse his white-knuckled grasp before loosening his hold on Linda's hand quickly. "Oh, Jesus!" he exclaimed. "I'm sorry."

"That's okay," she answered amusedly. "Are you sure you're all right?"

"Yeah, I'm fine." Jack shook it off, but flashes of the dream kept returning.

It only got worse when Linda entered the house. Not only did she do exactly what she had done in the dream, but it didn't take long to figure out Amanda wasn't even home. Good thing they didn't have an attic in this house, or he would have been really antsy. Jack scoffed internally for being so idiotic. It was just a dream. And a stupid one at that.

"Would you spank me?" Linda asked, turning away from the mantle and looking at him seriously.

"*What?*" Jack choked out. He felt his ears begin to flame a second before his cheeks joined the party.

"Yesterday," she said, giving him a quizzical look, "you said that if I complained about how heavy I was one more time, you'd take me over your knee. Would you really do that?"

"Oh!" he huffed out, relieved, and then he laughed slightly before walking over to Linda and putting his arms around her. "No," he answered. "Call it the heat of passion."

"Oh, okay." She sighed and burrowed in closer to his chest.

"Why?" he asked hesitantly. "Is it on the list?"

Linda tensed slightly. "Do you want it to be on the list?"

"Not really, no," Jack answered honestly. While the first part of the dream had turned him on slightly, the thought of striking Linda with any type of object had made him feel a little sick. He continued softly, "I don't think I could ever do something that would cause you pain."

"Pfft! What do you call your exercise sessions, then?" She snorted. "There is a reason I call you Master, you know!"

"That's a different kind of pain," he said with a laugh. "But besides a who's-your-daddy smack on the ass, I don't think I could do more."

"What the hell is that?"

"You know," Jack answered, flipping Linda around. He bent her over the back of his chair and pulled her ass against his hips. "Who's yer daddy?" he hollered, smacking her ass with a resounding thwack.

"Ow!" she screeched.

"You're supposed to say '*You!*' Now, who's yer daddy?" he asked again with another smack.

"You!" Linda yelled while squirming around. Both of them were laughing.

"And don't you forget it," Jack said gently, bending his body over hers. He fastened his lips to the back of her neck and sucked softly as his hands slid up her body to cup her breasts.

"Mmm," she moaned, wiggling her ass against his hips.

"I *really* like you bent over this chair," he said in a growl.

"When's Amanda coming back?"

"No clue."

Linda gasped when Jack's searching hand found its way between her legs. He moved his fingers rapidly against the seam of her jeans, using it to push against her clit and make her press her hips back against him desperately. Jack loved Linda's eager response to him. No matter where, how, or when, it took barely anything to get her excited. Usually by this point in a relationship, the lust began to die off a little for him, and it was downhill from there. He didn't worry about that happening this time around because he was even more cranked up over Linda now than when they had first gotten together.

Jack wasn't sure if it was because things still seemed very new with her, or if it was just because of how he felt for her, but he couldn't seem to get enough. It was as if he were doing this for the first time all over again as well. Like he was wound up tight and only she could provide him with the release he needed. There was something about Linda, about them together, that was incendiary.

Just as he was about to pop open the top button of her jeans, Jack heard the front door open.

They jumped away from one another like guilty teens. Linda's face was beet red, and he could feel his ears getting hot. Their casual act didn't fool Amanda, who rounded the corner in the next second. She took in Linda's rumpled shirt and Jack's clasped hands, which were strategically placed over his hard-on, and made a grossed-out face.

"Thank *God* I didn't walk in here five minutes from now," she huffed, rolling her eyes and stalking toward the kitchen.

Linda started giggling, her hand over her mouth to muffle the noise. Jack looked at her and began chuckling. She glanced down at the front of his pants and started to laugh even harder. He shook his head and tried adjusting himself to a more comfortable position before giving up and yanking his shirt down lower.

"You're on your own this time," she choked out before heading after Amanda.

"You're a mean, *mean* woman!" he called out after her, only to be rewarded with more laughter echoing back at him.

Smiling, he sat down and tried to get his mind off bending Linda over his chair and going at her like a crazed man. He couldn't very well follow the girls into the kitchen in this condition. He currently had a divining rod in his pants, and it was looking for its own version of water. With a silly grin on his face, he replayed the last fifteen minutes in his head. It didn't help cure his condition, but it was still fun to reminisce.

Despite her complaints, Jack loved touching Linda. He loved feeling the fullness of her body pressed close to his, the way she filled his hands when he grabbed her. He loved the roundness of her belly, and much to Linda's dismay, he found it cute. Jack was forever kissing and nibbling at it, usually on his way somewhere else. He could never pass up an opportunity to pay it special attention. He also loved her ass to a degree that bordered on obsession. He loved running his hands over it, he loved the way it felt socked against his hips like before, and thanks to today, now he had a newly discovered passion: smacking it.

Personally, if it were up to him, he'd put Linda on a maintenance regimen to help her firm up a few parts of her body she was still unhappy with, but not necessarily for her to lose more weight. He kind of liked her the way she was. Linda always scoffed at him when he suggested this and told him to lose the love goggles, which pissed him off. To keep her happy, they stuck with the harder workout sessions, but he honestly hoped that she would change her mind after she lost a bit more weight. Jack still wasn't convinced it was healthy for her to drop the full seventy pounds.

Worrying about Linda had an unintended but welcome effect. Being concerned about the woman he loved was a definite cock deflator.

After a couple more minutes, he stood and wandered to the kitchen to see if he could help out. Tonight they would all have dinner together like a small family. That made Jack happy. For the first time in a few months, he was actually looking forward to dinner in his home. There was no Vicky to grate on his nerves, and he didn't have to sit and wonder what Linda was up to while pretending to listen to Amanda chatter along. Tonight she'd be with him, and she would stay in his home. He was kicking himself for not having invited her earlier, completely forgetting there was a reason why.

When dinner was over, they kept Amanda company for a couple more hours before heading back to his room. Jack could barely hold in his satisfaction while Linda rifled through his books and made herself at home in his space. He hadn't really given much thought to how nice it would be to have her here where he lived. For some reason, he felt more complete after having merged these two parts of his life.

"I like your room," Linda said a little shyly, turning to face him. "I like being here."

"I like you being here too," he answered. He walked toward her and reached out to run his fingers down the lock of hair that curled against her collarbone.

It didn't take very long for them to pick up where they left off before being interrupted earlier in the day. It was slower and more gentle, but the end result was the same. The two of them wrapped around one another in the dimness of the room and in the warmth of a bed.

Linda lay on her side curled up in bed, staring up at Jack as he strummed his guitar and sang to her. This was so much better than open mic night because he was serenading her *and* he was gloriously naked. The bed sheets were pooled around his hips loosely, but Linda knew there was nothing on underneath, which was good enough for her.

She was seriously considering buying a guitar just so she could have one handy in case Jack decided he needed to sing a song to her while at her house.

Jack was some sort of musical genius. Besides the songs he already had in his repertoire—original as well as covers—he could pretty much play any song by ear if he had heard it before. It had become a sort of game between them they had played over the last hour. Linda would name a song and artist, Jack would hum the tune to make sure he had the right one, and then he'd start to pick it out on the guitar. Once he got the preliminary notes down, it didn't take him long to work out how to play the rest. She had yet to stump him. It was somewhat frustrating, yet amazing all at once.

"Tell me again why you refuse to do this for a living?"

He smiled down at the guitar in his hands and shrugged. "Don't get me wrong. If the opportunity ever came up, I'd jump at the chance, but I don't know if I have the courage to put myself out there. I'm not so hot with rejection." He looked down at her.

"I don't think anyone would ever reject you," Linda said softly.

"Yeah, well, you're my girlfriend. You're supposed to say things like that."

"You know," she said in an annoyed tone, "I really wish you'd stop putting yourself down."

"It's fucking annoying, isn't it?" he shot back, raising an eyebrow.

"That's different! Jack, you are so talented. I'm just—"

"If you say *fat,*" he replied, cutting her off, "I'm taking back my promise not to spank you."

"Fine." Linda exhaled sharply. "But if I can't say I'm fat, then you have to admit you're talented."

"That's not the same thing at all," he answered, frowning.

"Take it or leave it." She raised her brows and shrugged. "I'm going to go get some water. I'll let you think about it."

Linda looked over the side of the bed and fished Jack's T-shirt off the floor. It was always easier to just shrug into one of his large shirts than to dress fully. Plus, she always loved how it felt like being wrapped up in his scent. Jack was grumbling behind her as she scooted out of his room and down the hall to the kitchen. She was still grinning as she turned the corner, and then she let out a screech.

"Hey, Lin!" Tony said. He was half naked and propped up against the counter taking a bite out of a chicken leg. "Lookin' good."

"Tony?" she sputtered, wrapping her arms around herself and realizing she was very naked under Jack's T-shirt.

"The one and only," he said affably.

"I told you we had more privacy at your place," Jack said from behind her. She whirled around to glare at him, but he was too busy taking in Tony's state of undress. "Don't you fucking own a shirt?"

"You're one to talk," Tony replied. Jack was just as naked.

"This is my *house.*"

"Okay, simmer down, you two," Amanda said as she sauntered into the kitchen. She was wearing Tony's shirt, and Linda felt the urge to laugh hysterically. This was like a bad sitcom.

Linda watched as Amanda wrapped her arms around Tony's middle, got up on her toes, and gave him a kiss. "Come back to bed, baby," she said in a sultry voice. "It's cold in there without you."

"Okay, babe. Let me just finish here."

She nodded and turned back, pointing a finger at Jack's chest. "And you, behave!" Amanda winked at Linda as she passed by.

Jack grumbled something under his breath before asking Linda if she was coming.

"I'll be there in a second," she answered, smiling brightly. "I still need to get some water."

"Okay." He glared at Tony for a second before also leaving the room.

As soon as he was gone, Linda turned back to Tony and started beating on his arm with her hand. "What are you *doing* here?" she asked in a panicked falsetto.

"What are *you* doing here?" he asked in return, batting at her hand.

"I'm here fucking my young stud boyfriend!"

"Same," he said, smiling. "Except replace stud boyfriend with bangin' girlfriend."

"*Girlfriend?*" Linda whisper-screamed. "Tony! You were just supposed to be Amanda's rebound guy, not her boyfriend!" She started punching his arm again.

"Ow! Fuck!" he said while wheeling away from her blows. "What is your problem?"

"My *problem* is that your job was to get Amanda out of her funk. Now, if you break her heart, Jack's going to want to punch you, and I'll feel the need to defend your sorry ass. See where I'm going with this?"

"Relax! Jeez."

"I don't want to relax; you could cause problems between me and my young stud boyfriend."

Tony had started laughing at her, and Linda was ready to start punching him again. Suddenly, he stopped and looked at her seriously. "I really like her, Lin."

The tenderness in his voice caught her completely by surprise, and she did stop. He looked guarded but sincere, and Linda felt herself relenting. She lowered her fists, shoulders slumping.

"*Tooooonyyyy,*" she whined at him. "This could end really bad."

He mumbled something unintelligibly while staring down at his feet.

"What?"

"I said I don't want it to end."

Linda stared at him incredulously, and he finally glanced up at her while cringing slightly.

"You've never said that before," she whispered. "Like…ever."

Tony just shrugged his shoulders, and Linda exhaled slowly.

"Don't. *Hurt.* Her," she said and punched him in the shoulder. "Or else Jack isn't going to be the only one coming after you."

She pointed a finger at him severely, and he gave her a lopsided grin before grabbing her finger and kissing the tip. "Okay."

They left the kitchen together, headed in the same direction. Tony was about to head up the stairs but stopped for a moment.

"Oh, hey, Lin?"

"Hmm?"

"Seriously. Looking good." Tony gave Linda a smack on the ass that made her jump and squeal before he winked at her and bounded up the stairs.

Linda was left wondering what the hell it was about her ass today that was begging men to spank it.

When she walked in the room, Jack regarded her warily as she placed her hands on her hips. "When were you planning to tell me about *that?*"

"I tried to warn you."

"Warn me?" she sputtered. "Saying we get more privacy at my house is *not* warning me that I might run into my practically naked best friend in your kitchen!"

Jack started to chuckle. "Trust me, I'm not all that happy that he got an eyeful of *you* half naked either!"

"Oh my God," she answered, bringing her hands up over her blistering cheeks.

Linda felt Jack's hands go around her waist. "And if he wasn't screwing *my* best friend," he said in her ear, "I would have punched him out for the look he *got.*"

"This is horrible," she moaned against his chest.

"Would this be a bad time to remind you that getting them together was your bright idea?"

"Oh, sure, a month ago I was a *genius!*"

"That was before your constantly naked best friend invaded my house!"

Both Linda and Jack subsided into laughter. She clutched him close and tried to keep her guffaws as quiet as possible. Jack didn't even bother trying. Eventually, they made their way back to the bed, collapsing side by side. Linda gazed at the beautiful man beside her; he was lying on his stomach with his head propped up on folded arms. She admired the shape of his back and the sleek lines that comprised his form. Unable to resist, she reached a hand out and ran it through his hair, then caressed the back of his neck and the ridges of muscle along his shoulders.

"Mmm…feels nice," Jack murmured, closing his eyes with a blissful smile.

Linda continued to caress him as she sat up. Moving closer, she straddled him and used both hands to run up along his back and shoulders. He straightened his head, placing it on his forearms. Linda wove her fingers in his hair and gently massaged his scalp, making Jack purr. She smiled at his reaction before returning to his back.

As she passed light fingers over the thick lines of his tattoo, she wondered for the hundredth time what it represented. It was a coiled dragon, perched on his shoulder as if about to strike. The face of the dragon was on the front part of his shoulder just above his collarbone, and the body curved over his shoulder with its back legs looking as if they were digging into his shoulder blade, trying to use it as a launching point. The tail of the beast curled around and came back over his shoulder along the crease where his neck and shoulder met.

The art was impeccable. Not a typical Chinese or Japanese dragon, it seemed to have more of a tribal design feel, with thick lines that tapered to sharp points and edges. The black lines were stark against Jack's skin, making the dragon look almost real, as if it was about to rise straight out of his shoulder and attack.

"When did you get this done?" she asked him softly as she caressed his shoulder.

"About five years ago."

"Does it symbolize anything? Or did you just like the design?"

Jack turned his head so that he was facing the dragon. He seemed to deliberate for a moment, and Linda began caressing his back again. It had suddenly become tense under her fingers. As she massaged it, he became at ease once more.

"It's just a reminder," he said with a sigh after a few minutes.

Linda remained silent despite her curiosity. She got a feeling this was a touchy subject by the way he was acting, and she didn't want to pry.

"After my parents died, I went a little crazy." He smiled wryly. "Got myself into a lot of trouble. I was angry at everything and everyone, and it started to take over my life. One night, I got really drunk and wanted to go out and look for a fight. Amanda tried to stop me, and I didn't take that very well. She ended up locking herself in the bathroom and calling the cops on me."

Jack laughed without humor. Linda tried to picture the man he was describing but couldn't; it was so at odds with the gentle man she knew.

"Anyway, a night in jail sobered me up," he continued softly. "I was so ashamed of myself that I got some help. It took a while to work out my issues and get a grip, but I did it. The counselor who helped me got me into weightlifting and taught me to channel my frustrations in a better way, and then he got me a job as a trainer in the local gym. Then Amanda got into it, too, so she could support me, and here we are."

"And the dragon?"

"He just reminds me that I don't have to give in to the rage."

Linda leaned down and kissed Jack's shoulder right on top of the tattoo. "Thank you for telling me." She brushed his hair back from his face gently until he smiled. It was a little sad, and she knew he did it just for her benefit, but she could handle that.

"Come on," she said while climbing off of him. "I'm tired. Let's go to bed."

She didn't bother taking off Jack's shirt, merely climbed under the duvet and snuggled into his bed. Jack sat up, turned off his bedside lamp, and then got under the covers as well. He gathered her close to him, and she held on to him.

"I would never hurt you, you know," he said softly in the dark.

"I know," she answered with absolute sincerity.

To Linda, it didn't matter what had happened in Jack's past. She knew the man he was now, and she trusted him implicitly. She trusted him with her body, with her emotions, and most of all, with her heart. She didn't need assurances from Jack because he never left any room for doubt.

19
The Green-Eyed Monster

Linda woke up slightly disoriented, and then she realized she was in Jack's bed and smiled. He was moving around the dimly lit room, gathering clothes for after his shower. She remembered him complaining about only having a shower stall in the bathroom on the main floor, so there would be no shared shower hijinks this morning. Then he had grumbled that there was more than one reason he preferred to stay at her house before heading out of the room to wash up.

She had to agree.

While she'd had a good time here, and she enjoyed being in Jack's house, it had more the feel of a co-ed dorm than anything else. And since the chance of running into Amanda, or a naked Tony, was high, Linda figured she was okay if they spent the bulk of their time together in her home from now on. She still did like it here, however, so it would be a nice change to crash at Jack's on occasion.

There was a timid knock on the door, which surprised Linda. Not knowing if Tony was still prowling around, she sat up and made herself decent.

"Come in," she called out, then smiled when Amanda's head poked itself through the opening. "Hey, Amanda. Jack's just in the shower."

"Yeah, I know," she answered shyly. "I actually wanted to talk to you."

"Oh," Linda said, her eyebrows rising. "Sure, come on in."

Amanda bounded into the room and threw herself down on the bed enthusiastically. Linda wondered briefly if she should start taking speed in order to keep up with all the exuberant women she was surrounded by lately. Amanda stretched out her long, willowy frame for a moment and then curled up on the bed and snuggled into it.

"I love Jack's bed." She sighed, smiling to herself.

Linda felt a slight twinge of unease and wondered in what capacity Amanda had shared Jack's bed. He'd always given the impression that their friendship was completely platonic.

"Oh? So, um, did you sleep here often?" Linda purposely used the word *did* because she'd completely lose it if she found out Amanda still slept here.

The younger girl looked up at her with large, shocked eyes, "*Nooo!*" she said, shaking her head vehemently before laughing a little. "Nothing like that. We just hang out in here most times 'cause it's downstairs. I always complain he got the better bed."

Linda smiled and made a mental *phew* noise in her head. "So, you and Jack have never...?"

"Ew. No." Amanda crinkled her nose. "Didn't he already tell you that?"

"Yeah, but..." She shrugged, leaving the sentence hanging.

"Guys lie?" Amanda offered, making Linda duck her head in embarrassment.

"I figured if anything did happen, he might not want me to know. Especially if it was in the past. You know, so I wouldn't feel uncomfortable?"

"Didn't he ever tell you about us?"

"Not in much detail. He just said you've known each other since you were young and grew up together."

"You could say that." Amanda chuckled. "I followed him home from the orphanage when I was four 'cause he had pretty hair. He hid me in his room for a couple days before we got busted."

"What?" Linda asked, laughing along with her.

"I was orphaned when I was two," Amanda explained. "I don't remember my parents at all, but from what I learned, my father took off on my mom, and she didn't take it very well."

"I'm sorry."

"That's okay. It doesn't really mean anything to me now."

"So, how did you end up following Jack home?" Linda prompted to get them past the awkwardness.

"Right," Amanda answered, smiling again. "Well, the orphanage was beside the school, and sometimes we'd see the kids playing in the yard from inside. I don't remember much, but apparently, I somehow got away from the nuns and chased after Jack. He said he didn't notice till he was halfway home, and he didn't know where I came from, so he just brought me home with him."

"Oh my God."

"Yeah, it was kind of crazy." She laughed. "I don't know how he kept me hidden over the weekend, but his mom found me in his closet on Monday when he went back to school. Apparently, the whole town was going nuts over me being missing, and here I was, at the McAllisters' house with no one the wiser."

Her voice had gotten soft with the reminiscing. It was obvious to Linda that Amanda was mostly recounting a story told to her often and not because she remembered it herself.

"Anyway, the police were called, and then Jack came home. He freaked out because they wanted to take his 'sister' away."

"Oh, no…"

"Sarah—that was Jack's mom—she was really kind and soft-hearted, and when she saw how Jack hugged me and wouldn't let me go, she just couldn't let them split us up. She talked Jack's dad into fostering me."

"So…you're Jack's adopted sister?" Linda asked, now slightly confused.

"No, the McAllisters didn't have the money to adopt me—they barely had the money to keep me—but Jack is more like my brother than anything. I wish they could have adopted me because there was always the threat that I could be taken by another family and have to leave them, but as I got older, we didn't worry about it too much. Most people want babies."

Amanda drifted off then; she stared at the ceiling in contemplation for a few moments. Linda wasn't sure if the girl was done with her story or not but didn't want to intrude on her thoughts.

"When they died, I had to go back to the orphanage," she said softly. "Jack had just turned twenty, but I was still sixteen, and since we weren't legally family, I couldn't stay with him. Both of us went a little nuts, especially Jack." Linda saw the tears gathering in Amanda's eyes and felt her own prickling. "As soon as I turned eighteen, I left and moved back in with him." The girl paused in reflection.

"He was *so* different," she whispered. "Losing his parents changed him into someone else completely."

Linda remembered Jack telling her the same thing just the night before. To have Amanda confirm this left her feeling hollow in the chest. She hated thinking of Jack being all alone with no one to love him. Even though it hadn't been for long, the effects must have still been profound.

"Jack told me he went after you one night?"

"He told you about that?" Amanda asked, making Linda nod. "Yeah. That was a pretty fucked-up night. He kept going out and picking fights with guys and coming home all beat up. Someone was going to kill him one day…I couldn't take it anymore. He didn't like it much when I took his keys and locked myself in the washroom." Amanda laughed lightly. "I didn't want to call the cops, but I didn't have a choice. I don't regret it. After that, he started getting better, more like the Jack I grew up with. More like now." Amanda rolled over and stared at her for a minute. "*You* make him really happy, Linda."

"Oh," Linda replied quietly, looking down at her hands clasped in her lap.

"I haven't seen him like this since before his parents died," Amanda continued. "Yeah, he was better and pretty much back to normal, but there always seemed to be something missing. And it's back now."

"I'm glad to hear that," Linda whispered. Looking up, she gave Amanda a tentative smile. "So, you've never been in love with Jack?"

"Of course I was!" Amanda scoffed, and Linda's stomach sank for a moment. What if Amanda still harbored feelings for him? "I was six, and he was nine, but he thought girls had cooties, so that was the end of that," she said, grinning hugely.

Linda's breath huffed out as she began to chuckle.

"What about you and Tony? Did, uh, anything happen between you two?"

"We kissed once," Linda answered honestly and was surprised to see Amanda's face fall. "It was really bad," she was quick to add. "I was fourteen, and Tony was twelve. You wouldn't guess it to look at him now, but he used to be kind of a runt, so I was still taller than him."

"Really?" Amanda asked, her face crinkling in amusement.

"Mm-hmm. We were messing around one day while our dads were playing cards, and I don't remember exactly how it happened, but we made a deal that we'd try kissing each other just to see what it felt like."

"So what happened?" Amanda prompted, staring at Linda with rapt fascination.

"We both had our eyes closed, and we missed." Linda laughed, remembering that day very clearly, despite the fact it was over twenty years ago.

"Missed?"

"Yeah. Tony ended up frenching my nose, while I sucked on his chin. It took us a couple seconds to figure it out."

Amanda started to snicker-snort before beginning to all-out laugh while Linda made a wry face and chuckled along with her.

"Needless to say," Linda sighed dramatically over the laughter, "we just weren't meant to be!"

"I'm kinda glad about that," Amanda said once her laughter subsided. "Although, I do think you were stupid not to snap him up when you had the chance."

"I can say the same about you and Jack," Linda returned, smiling fondly at the pretty blonde beside her. While she still had bouts of envy, she found that Amanda really was just a normal, everyday woman. She had her own flaws and insecurities just like everyone else.

"Good thing I didn't walk in here naked."

Both she and Amanda gasped and turned to find a still wet Jack standing in the doorway. He had a towel around his waist and was rubbing the top of his head with another one. Linda sighed and enjoyed the view, while Amanda made a disgusted face.

"What the hell, Jack? Cover that shit up, would ya?"

"Hey, this is my room!" he shot back, looking at her incredulously.

"I kind of like him naked," Linda piped up, earning her a smug look from Jack and a wounded one from Amanda, as if she had been expecting sisterly solidarity. "Sorry," she mouthed, and the other girl sniffed at her.

"What are you doing in here, anyway?" Jack headed over to the bureau where the clothes he'd collected earlier were piled.

"Oh, I just wanted to say sorry to Linda for what happened last night," Amanda said easily, turning slightly to wink at her. "I should have warned you guys Tony was coming over."

"*Tony.*" Jack snorted as he rolled his eyes.

"You know," Amanda started, "I really wish —"

"You've got three seconds to get out of my room before I'm completely naked." Jack cut her off, tugging at the edge of his towel.

Amanda screamed in horror and scrambled off the bed. She nearly ran into the doorjamb in her haste to get out, leaving a laughing Linda and Jack behind.

"Works every time." He chuckled before crawling onto the bed and nuzzling at her.

"You're still wet!" she complained. Not very effectively because she couldn't keep the grin off her face.

"Oh, darn, look at that, your shirt's all wet now, too. Maybe you should take it off."

"You just took a shower."

"I can take another one," he said huskily, rolling on top of Linda.

Her legs split apart automatically under the weight of his body; it was as if they were trained to respond to him this way. She moaned as she felt the hard length of him against her sex. Linda tried not to feel smugly pleased that his body was trained to react to hers as well.

Jack was kissing her hard. His hips surged and retreated as if of their own accord. His hands were buried in her hair, holding her head in place. She reached down and grabbed a hold of his backside, gripping it tightly and pulling him even closer. She groaned as the pressure against her clit intensified. God, she loved him like this, wound tight, his entire body flexing and releasing, his muscles twitching under her hands. Linda knew that if she pulled back to look at him now, he'd be flushed from arousal, his lips full and red from the force of their kisses, his eyes hooded.

Now Jack was reaching between their bodies, and as soon as the back of his fingers brushed against her, Linda swiveled her hips and moaned loudly. He hooked his fingers into the waistband of her underwear and tugged on them.

"I'm banning panties from my house," he growled at Linda as he lifted off her body so he could remove her clothing. The panties were first, and then Linda sat up and let him lift her shirt straight off while he knelt in front of her.

Linda reached forward and gripped his towel, stripping it off him in a quick jerk. Before Jack could pounce on her again, she took him in her hand and pumped lightly, then leaned forward and pressed her lips to one of his nipples. She loved the low gasp and hiss he made when she ran her tongue over the hard nub. She opened her jaw wider and bit him gently. Jack groaned and thrust his hips back and forth as she tightened the grip on his shaft.

"Feels so good," he whispered as his hands had found their way into her hair again. When she switched to the other nipple, his fingers gripped tight involuntarily, the lick of pain she felt making her feel a surge of power.

By now, Linda had learned what got Jack really going. She'd had time to explore every inch of him, and he'd never discouraged her, halting and amateurish as she was. Instead, he'd encouraged her inept fumbling and taught her the ways of his body and how to touch to please him as well as herself. A patient teacher, not once did he make her feel like she didn't know what she was doing, even when she didn't.

Things had changed over the last few weeks, however, and now she knew just how to stimulate the head of his cock while stroking between his legs. She felt him tremble and listened to his ragged breathing. Wanting to please him further, she then shook her head so he would let her go. As soon as his grip slackened, she leaned down and took him in her mouth.

"*Fuck,*" he ground out, as she slid him in slightly deeper. Linda was still learning the finer details of this particular act, but Jack had told her plenty of times just the feel of her mouth on him was good enough.

She wanted to be better than good enough. Unfortunately, she never got a chance to practice for very long. Jack always lost his patience relatively quickly and stopped her so that he could get inside her. This time was no exception. After only a few minutes, he pulled back swiftly, taking her by the shoulders and pulling her up so he could kiss her. She'd worked him up to a frenzy this time. His tongue plunged into her mouth, and she groaned.

Whenever he let his passion truly go, he always ignited something primal and dark in her. Now she was the one tugging on his hair viciously, making him grunt against her mouth. His hands came around her body, gripping her backside. Seeking fingers ran along the seam of her buttocks until reaching her sex, and then he thrust into her. She pushed against his hand, trying to get him deeper, but it wasn't enough.

"Jack," she panted. "Fuck me. Just fuck me, please…"

"Turn around," he said roughly, hands gripping her body and spinning her.

Jack sat back on his heels and then pulled Linda down onto his lap, his one hand holding his cock up so that she sat directly onto it. Linda cried out. This was something new they'd never tried, and the feel of him deep inside her made her gasp.

"Spread your legs, baby," he whispered in her ear as his hand went between her thighs. "Wider. I want to finger your clit while I fuck you."

Linda moaned and spread her thighs as wide as they could go so that her bent legs were flanking his. Jack had one breast gripped in his hand while his other began running tight circles around her clit. She used her lower body to start moving up and down over the length of him and was incredibly happy she'd spent so many hours doing squats and lunges to work up her thigh muscles. With the way his fingers were moving, it didn't take long for Linda to start feeling that familiar tightening deep in her belly. She bounced up and down quicker, and Jack thrust his hips up to meet her. She began to spasm uncontrollably and clenched her teeth together as she groaned her way through it.

Before she had a chance to come down from her high, Jack wrapped an arm around her waist and hoisted her up as he got up on his knees behind her. He pushed her forward until her face and chest hit the mattress, keeping her ass in the air with him and still buried to the hilt inside her. The shift in sensation had her crying out again. Jack grasped her hips tightly, pulled almost all the way out, and then slammed into her. She shuddered against him.

"That day when you said you wanted to be fucked hard. Is this what you meant?" he asked in a gruff voice. He pulled out and thrust into her deeply again. "Is this what you wanted?"

"Yes!" she cried out as his hips swung toward her again.

"I would have fucked you right then, you know," he continued, still driving into her. "If you'd have let me, I would have taken you right there on the floor."

"Oh God," Linda moaned. The way Jack was moving against her and what he was saying to her was driving her crazy.

"I got so fucking hard when you said that, I could hardly control myself. All I could picture was spreading your legs apart and getting inside of you...just...like...*this,* "he groaned, each word punctuated by a strong surge of his hips. "Was it me you wanted?" he continued. "When you said it, was it me you pictured?"

"Yes," Linda answered automatically. "It's always been you." She began to pant harder now, making breathless exhalations as she geared up to come again. As if sensing this, Jack began driving into her even faster, and she began to chant encouragement until her orgasm barreled down on her, making her clench in long, drawn-out spasms. Her vision became sparks of light, and she shook as every muscle she had vibrated deliciously.

Jack called out her name, his hands digging into the flesh of her hips so hard she was sure he'd have to peel them off. She didn't care. She loved it. The fact that he lost all control when he was inside her like this made her feel smug, and she forgot about all the issues she still had with regard to her body.

Once he stopped trembling, Jack pulled out of her and collapsed onto the bed, dragging Linda with him. Both of them were breathing heavily. There were no other sounds in the room.

"So much for my shower," he murmured against her shoulder after a few minutes.

Linda shook her head and laughed.

A few moments later, Linda turned in Jack's arms and let her gaze wander over his face. He let her stare at him openly with just a small smirk before raising an inquiring brow. Somehow, he always seemed to figure out when she had something to say but was having difficulty spitting it out.

"How come you never told me that you and Amanda lived together growing up?" she said finally.

"No particular reason," he replied, not seeming all that shocked that she'd asked. She wondered if perhaps he'd overheard the last bit of her conversation with Amanda. "It's kind of an odd story. I mean, we lived in a small town, so *everyone* knew what had happened. When we moved here, we figured it wasn't important to tell everyone our situation."

Linda hugged Jack closer to her and mused about the series of events that ended up bringing him to this sleepy little town, where somehow he'd ended up in her arms. While she wished they had both traveled a different path to get to one another, at least they were together now.

"Great job, Mrs. Lewis," Jack said as enthusiastically as possible, plastering on his best smile. "I let you go a bit longer than usual today. How did that feel?"

He pretended to listen attentively as she prattled along, and he walked with her toward the change rooms. They said their good-byes, and he kept going. When he walked into the employees' lounge to grab a bottle of water, Amanda was in there with a great hulking beast pointing out various things.

"Hey, Jack!" she said when she saw him. "You haven't met Matt yet, have you?"

"Nope," he answered, putting out a hand. "Hey, man."

"Nice to meet you," the guy answered, grabbing his hand in a firm grip.

"He's our new personal trainer," Amanda piped in.

"Thank *fucking* God," Jack stated. "The client overload was killing me."

"Our last trainer left in a…hurry," Amanda explained, giving Jack a meaningful look. "We had to take over her clients."

"Oh, I already have clients lined up? Sweet!" Matt said amicably.

"Jack, do you think you can let Matt shadow you for a bit today?"

"Sure." Jack shrugged. "I was just getting some water. I'll show you around the club."

Jack showed Matt around until he noticed that his girl had just turned the corner and was walking toward the door of the club. She was smiling to herself. A little secret smile, and now he was dying to know what caused it. Of course that smile turned into a huge grin when she saw him watching her, and he couldn't help but return it.

"Hey, man," he said to Matt without breaking his stare. "My next client is in. Can we pick this up later?"

"Actually," Matt replied, "do you mind if I watch how you work?"

"Oh," Jack said in surprise. "Um, yeah, sure."

If he turned Matt down, it would look strange. Plus, what did it matter? They'd be out in the public area anyway. It wasn't like Matt couldn't stand there and watch whether Jack wanted him to or not. Linda walked up to them, casting glances Matt's way and most likely wondering who he was.

"Hi," she said shyly and looked at Jack expectantly.

"Linda, this is our new personal trainer, Matt," Jack replied, trying to sound somewhat formal. "Is it okay if he shadows us today?"

Suddenly, Jack wanted her to say no, but he wasn't quite sure why and was disappointed when she shrugged and said, "Sure."

"Hi, Linda," Matt jumped in, putting out his hand. When she put out hers, he engulfed it in his big, meaty paws and then just held it. Jack was three seconds away from biting his hand off. "Linda, Linda. That's a very pretty name," he said in a conspiratorial whisper before giving her a wink.

Jack was nonplussed when Linda's shoulders hunched up as she tittered at Matt. She pressed her lips together when she saw the black look Jack was giving her.

"Wanna see a trick?" Matt continued, completely oblivious to the fact he was about to get sack punched.

"Okay," she answered, giving Jack a quick glance, as if to let him know she was merely an innocent bystander.

"Watch closely."

Jack's jaw dropped as Matt began flexing his enormous pecs and made them dance under his shirt. Linda started laughing, her eyes following the movement in an amused fashion. Jack began to growl.

"That's not a trick," he ground out between clenched teeth. "You're just flexing."

"I know," Matt said, smiling at him wolfishly. "But the girls seem to like it. Am I right?" He turned back to Linda, who was still giggling. "So, Jack, is this one mine?"

"No, she's *mine,*" Jack answered, reaching out and grabbing his girlfriend's arm currently being held hostage by Matt's huge hands and giving it a tug. Matt let Linda go easily enough, and Jack had to resist pulling her into his arms to protect her from the giant oaf. The only thing was, Linda didn't seem to want to be protected. She actually looked like she was enjoying the attention, which made him uncharacteristically pissed off at her.

The next hour was a lesson in restraint as Jack watched Matt flirt shamelessly with Linda. His only saving grace was that she never once flirted back, but she didn't discourage the attention either. Matt's only saving grace was that Jack knew the guy could crush him like a fucking bug. That didn't stop him from scoping out possible weaknesses. Matt was big, but Jack was fast. In the meantime, he kept his death fantasies to himself until the guy crossed the line.

Which he didn't.

Toward the end of the session, Matt excused himself to go to the washroom. As soon as he was out of sight, Jack had Linda's elbow in his hand and was leading her into one of the aerobic rooms. By this point, he was practically seething and didn't quite know how to handle it. He'd never been in a situation where he'd felt this kind of jealous possessiveness, and he felt like he was about to explode. He knew he needed to calm down, but the person who usually reassured him was Linda.

Jack paced around for a few seconds as Linda watched him warily.

"Are you all right?" she asked quietly.

"I don't know," he replied honestly. "What the hell was going on out there?" He looked at Linda, his brow creased in confusion.

"What do you mean?"

"With *Matt*. What the hell was going on with *Matt?*"

"Absolutely nothing," Linda answered, and now her brow was creased. "You were there, Jack."

"That's why I was asking!"

"He was just being friendly. I'm not sure why you're upset."

"You think that was just being friendly?"

"Yes."

"So, you don't think if I wasn't around, he wouldn't have asked for your number?"

"No," she answered slowly. "But even if he did, so what?"

Jack almost choked on his tongue. "*So what?* Are you *trying* to make me jealous, Linda?" he asked, holding his arms out. "Is that what you're trying to do?"

Linda just looked at him incredulously for a second and then her face became sad. "No," she said softly. "I would never want you to feel that way."

Jack stopped, his arms falling to his sides. When she walked up to him and put her hands on his chest, he stiffened and looked away.

"Why would you think I wanted to make you jealous?"

He just shrugged his shoulders.

"I'll admit, another man besides you flirting with me is flattering…" she said, and Jack began to growl again, "but I wouldn't do anything on purpose to make you jealous. I'd never want you to feel like that."

"So, you admit he was flirting with you?"

"I think Matt is just flirty in general," she hedged. "But even still, it shouldn't make you jealous."

"Why not?" he asked, now looking down at her and frowning.

"Jack? How many times do you come home to me, telling me about some woman who threw herself at you that day?"

"Not a lot," he grumbled, not wanting to see her point.

"Try almost every day," she replied curtly.

"But I don't ask for it! And I'd never *do* anything about it!"

"And you think I asked for it?" she inquired softly. "Or that I'd do anything about it?"

"Well…no." Now Jack's hands came up, and he caressed Linda's back. Then he said in a low voice, "But you could."

"I can't believe you just said that! What do you mean?"

"Linda, you're always telling me I'm the only man who's paid attention to you in years," he replied in a resigned voice. "Well, men are going to start paying more attention to you now. How do I know you won't want to explore your options?"

"That's silly."

"Is it? Besides me, you've been with one man practically your whole life."

"Hmm…I suppose you're right," Linda answered, nodding. "I guess I better go sow some wild oats, then."

"*What?*" Jack's stomach fell to his feet, and he wanted to punch himself in the head for giving her stupid ideas.

"Yep. Thanks for the good times, Jack," she said, pushing him away. "Think Matt's free tonight?"

Linda stood in front of him, eyebrows raised, arms folded over her chest.

"I don't know," he said in a steely tone. "Maybe you should go find out."

"Maybe I will," she answered in a matching tone before whirling away and heading for the door.

Jack caught her before her hand could land on the knob and turned her back around. He had his mouth against hers not even a second later. She tried to pull away and hit him against the chest, but he just pushed her against the wall and kissed her harder. Linda whimpered slightly and hit him once more before her arms went around his neck.

"I'm sorry," he whispered. "I'm sorry. I'm being an asshole."

"You are!" she cried out, thumping against his chest weakly. "I don't have to be with a hundred other men to know all I want is *you.*"

"Don't cry, baby," he said, wiping the tears from her face.

"How could you even say that?"

"Because I'm stupid?"

Linda looked up at him in stunned amazement, and then she let out a small, disbelieving laugh. "You're not stupid," she said finally. "But what you *said* was really fucking stupid."

"You know, none of this would have happened if you'd just told Matt to stop flirting with you," Jack grumbled.

"You could have told him to stop, too, you know."

"I thought we were supposed to be on the down low?"

"Well, that's why I didn't say anything!" Linda said in a frustrated tone. "Plus, I still don't think he was *really* flirting."

"Trust me, he was really flirting. And considering it took you two months and *two* sex proposals to finally understand *I* was flirting, I don't think you're the best person to judge."

Linda started to laugh now. "Okay, you win. I'll take your word for it. And I'm sorry, I should have stopped it. And if he does it again, I will. How's that?"

"That's good," he said, breathing a sigh of relief.

"But you know, right?" she asked, her eyes large and imploring. "You know I love you, and I'd never do that, right?"

"Yeah, I know."

"You have to trust me, Jack. You have to trust that even if some guy does ask for my number, he's not getting it."

He didn't bother answering, just lowered his head and kissed her softly and sweetly, hoping she'd understand that she meant the world to him and losing her would decimate him. She sighed against his lips, and that was the answer he needed. Linda's hands were in his hair, gripping gently, and he wrapped his arms around her, pulling her up on her toes so he could hug her close as their tongues slipped against one another.

The door swung open, and Jack and Linda jumped when they heard a muffled, "Oh shit!"

"Fuck," Jack muttered as he pulled away from Linda.

"Hey, dude," Matt said, holding his hands up. "I didn't know."

"No one does." He gave Matt a death glare.

"That's cool," the other man answered before dropping a wink. "I'm good with secrets."

"Thank you," Jack said sincerely before turning to Linda. "See you up front."

"Okay."

Jack watched her leave. She sidled past Matt, gave him a small embarrassed smile, and then beat feet out of there, making both men chuckle.

"Seriously, man," Matt said to him wryly. "I didn't mean to be putting the moves on your lady. She *is* your lady, right?"

"*Yes*. And that's okay," Jack answered, trying not to sound disgruntled. Then he had a marvelous idea. "Hey, Matt, have you met our yoga instructor Denise yet?"

"I don't think so."

"Come on, let me introduce you. She should be here by now." Jack slapped him on the shoulder and propelled him out of the room.

"Is she hot?"

"Fuckhot," Jack answered. "And *flexible.*"

20
A Night of Firsts

Another two weeks passed without much fanfare, and Linda was down forty-two pounds. She was three pounds away from being considered average weight for her height. She also had a date for mediation, and Graham had been given strict orders that if he canceled this appointment, as he had the last three, it would go straight to the courts. He had given his word, in writing, that he would attend, and there was a letter from his employer stating he wouldn't be dispatched on any last-minute business trips. That had been enough to appease Linda and her lawyer.

After a dinner out to celebrate her upcoming divorce, Linda and Jack were walking out the doors of the restaurant when she pulled up short. Jack bumped into her and grabbed her around the waist. "Sorry, baby," he laughed before turning his head and seeing what had stopped her in her tracks. *Vicky.*

"Well, isn't this sweet?" The blonde sneered at them. She was standing on the walk just outside the diner with Jimmy. "You can dress her up as much as you like, Jack, but your girlfriend is still a heifer."

"You fucking little psycho *bitch,*" Jack growled out from behind Linda when he heard her gasp. Vicky's words had hit her like a strike to the gut. He made a move to come around her, and Linda grasped him around the waist.

"Don't," she said softly. "She's not worth it. Come on, babe." Linda tugged at Jack.

They had barely gone a few steps when Vicky's voice called out shrilly. "I fucked your husband, you know!"

Linda's shoulders pulled up, and her lips pressed in a tight line at what Vicky had said. She turned and faced the little witch.

"Well, I'd ask if it was worth it, but having fucked Graham myself, I highly doubt it," she said in a conversational tone. "What is your fucking problem with me, Vicky? What in God's name did I ever *do* to you for you to hate me *so* fucking much?"

"You exist," the girl spat out.

"Whatever," Linda answered, shaking her head. "You're an insignificant little *girl*. A waste of breath and skin. And you're not worth my time."

"He wouldn't leave you!" Vicky screeched as Linda turned her back on the girl. "No matter what I did! He said he could never leave his wife! And then I find out not even months later, you aren't even together anymore!"

"This is about *Graham?*" Linda asked incredulously. "Sweetheart, you could have had him. Pinky dick and all. Anyway, I've moved on to *bigger* and better things." She reached behind her for Jack's hand and found it immediately. "Now, if you don't mind, I'd like to go home and remind myself how much better off I am without Graham."

When they got to Jack's house, he collapsed in his manly chair and coaxed Linda to climb onto his lap. He brushed her hair back from her face and stared into her amazing eyes. She glanced down shyly, and he leaned in to brush his lips softly against hers.

"Thank you for tonight," he said sincerely. "Except for one small thing, it was a wonderful evening."

"You mean the part about your girlfriend being a heifer?" Linda asked wryly. She was avoiding his eyes as she played with the buttons on the front of his shirt.

"You are not a heifer."

Linda opened her mouth as if to reply and then closed it again. She still wouldn't look at him.

"Don't do that," Jack begged softly. "Don't make this night about Vicky and her poison. You are *beautiful.*"

"On the inside, right?"

"Inside *and* out."

"Come on, Jack. If you passed me on the street, you'd have never given me a second glance." Linda smiled sadly. "Certainly not at the size I was when we met and, most likely, not even now."

"How do you know that?" he demanded. "Even when we first met, I thought you had a pretty face and beautiful eyes."

"What about my body, Jack? What did you think about my body?"

"What difference does it make? I fell in love with *you*—all of you."

"Good thing I've got a *great* personality, I guess," she whispered ruefully.

"Why do you make that sound like a bad thing? That I fell in love with your personality?" Jack was beginning to get irritated. "So, what about you, Linda? What if when we met, I didn't have this body? What if I was balding and overweight? Would *you* have still loved me?"

"Of course I would!"

"Are you sure about that?" he stressed, tipping her face up to look in his eyes. "'Cause from what you're saying, you must have only been attracted to me for my body. The only reason you love me is because of the way I look. 'Cause it must be *impossible* to love someone unless they are hot. Is that about right?"

"No! It's not the same at all."

"Why not?" He shrugged. "Admit it. Even if I was an asshole, you'd still have wanted to fuck me. Right? Doesn't matter what I'm like as a *person*. I'm nothing but a hard body and a pretty face."

"Jack, stop it," Linda said in a heartbroken voice. "That's not true at all. Yes, of course I was attracted to you for how you look." She smiled sadly and stroked her hands from his forehead down to his jaw. "But there's so much more to you than that."

"Don't you see?" he pleaded. "You kill me when you say things like that about yourself. When I look at you, all I see is the woman I love. I want you to see her too. She is exquisite."

"I don't know if I can," she replied quietly and then placed her hand over his mouth when he started to protest. "But I'll try."

Linda took her hand away and replaced it with her mouth. She simply brushed her lips against his a few times and then rubbed their noses together, which made him smile a little. Jack was still sad and a little upset, but he pushed that aside. He had meant what he said and didn't want this night to end up being a reminder of Vicky.

"Have I ruined tonight completely?" Linda asked in a small voice.

"No," he sighed, and then he leaned forward to capture her mouth with his. This kiss wasn't soft or gentle. It blazed with the passion he felt for her as he tried to convey what words never could. She had claimed him, body and soul. Regardless of how, he was hers.

Linda reached between them and began tugging his shirt from his pants. He stopped her.

"What's wrong?" she asked. "I thought you wanted it like this."

"Not tonight," he answered. "Not like that tonight."

Jack took Linda's arms and wrapped them around his neck. He moved forward in the chair and held her securely as he stood up.

Linda gasped and held on tightly. "I hate it when you do this," she moaned as he began to carry her toward his bedroom.

"Don't worry. I'll never let you go," he answered softly.

She nuzzled her face into his neck. "I know."

He walked into the dark of the bedroom and lowered her slowly to the floor. Reaching out, he turned on his bedside lamp, forgetting she preferred the dark. "I'm sorry," he murmured and then reached over to shut it again.

"No, leave it on," Linda said.

Jack straightened up slowly and looked at Linda, but her eyes were on the floor. They rose slowly to meet his searching gaze when he cupped her face. "Are you sure?" he inquired gently, his thumb passing along the curve of her cheek.

"Yes."

He looked for uncertainty in her eyes and found none. Something in what he said to her tonight must have resonated. She finally believed him when he said he was in love with her completely, *all* of her. Linda reached up and caressed his face; she brought it down gently to her own and kissed him with tender care. One arm came around her waist, while the hand that had been against her face slipped under her hair at the nape of her neck.

Jack took his time, kissing her slowly. His lips moved against hers, first along the plump curve of her upper lip, his tongue slipping out to taste. And then he sucked her lower lip into his mouth before running his tongue along it, making Linda moan softly. Finally, he covered her entire mouth with his and made a low noise in his throat when Linda's tongue met his. Even though the feel of her against him wound him up, he was determined to take his time and make love to her properly.

His hands moved along her body at a leisurely pace, long sweeps designed to make her feel adored. Revered. He brought a hand up to cup her chin gently before trailing fingers down her neck, along her collarbone, and then tracing between her breasts. When he reached Linda's trembling stomach, he moved his hand along her waist until he reached the tie that fastened her dress. With a sure tug, the knot came loose, and the front of her dress parted, baring one breast covered in a lace bra. He traced a finger along the part that was still fastened until he found where it buttoned along her waist and undid that as well.

Stepping back, he drank her in. Linda's cheeks were flushed, her lips crimson. Her dress was open and draped around her, showing just a sliver of cream-colored flesh. She took his breath away. He wanted this moment preserved forever and had an idea.

"Do you trust me?" he asked softly, and she nodded her head. "Don't move."

Jack went to his desk in the corner and picked up his camera. He'd tried to get Linda to pose for him numerous times, but she always turned him down. He expected as much now, but he hoped, nonetheless, that she would let him try to show her how beautiful she really was. Turning back, he walked toward Linda with the camera held loosely in his hand. He watched her eyes widen and the beginning shake of her head as her arms wrapped around her waist.

"Please," he said simply. "These are just for me and you."

Linda hesitated for a few moments, chewing on her lip before nodding once in assent. "Okay." She lowered her head, her hair swinging forward and obscuring her face.

Not wanting to make her completely uncomfortable, he didn't ask her to pose. Raising the camera, he focused on the fall of hair, the silhouette of her face, which was barely discernable, and snapped the photo. Linda looked up at the sound, and he smiled at her from behind the camera. She smiled shyly in return, and he took another picture, loving the sweetness in her expression. Coming closer, he reached out with his free hand and swept her hair over her shoulder. She glanced down demurely, and he captured that moment as well.

Moving back, he focused on her from the waist up. Her arms were still wrapped around her body, making her dress bunch and gather, the lace of her bra showing as well as the swell of a breast. He took another picture.

"Are you okay?" he asked.

"Yes," she whispered.

"Will you drop your arms for me?"

Slowly, her arms came down, but she gathered her dress to her body, making him smile. Even still, she looked sexy. The fabric was still open in a deep V between her breasts and then split open again at her upper thighs. Linda had her chin dipped down and was looking up at him through her lashes. He nearly groaned at the image of the innocent vixen standing before him. He took another picture instead.

"Turn around, Linda."

Silently, she spun.

"Look at me."

She turned to look at him over her shoulder.

"Yes, like that," he encouraged and waited for her to smile before pressing the button a few times in succession.

"If I asked you to lower your dress a little, would you?"

Linda looked at him for a few seconds, and he was waiting for her to say no. He had no intention of taking any pictures that she might be embarrassed or worried about if they got in the wrong hands. Jack was hoping she truly did trust him. She turned away for a moment and looked down at her body; he saw her part her dress and lower it so that the tops of her shoulders showed.

"Like this?"

"Exactly like that," he said in a low voice and waited for her to look at him before he began taking more pictures. Now he moved around her slowly, giving her time to arrange the dress modestly. She watched him carefully, but she had lost the tension in her body, and he knew she was feeling more comfortable. Even still, he didn't want to push her too far for one night.

"Kiss me," he whispered, and she smiled and lifted up on her toes, pressing her mouth to his. He held the camera out to the side and used his thumb to take more pictures.

"What are you doing?" she laughed, looking toward the camera.

"Trying to get a picture of us kissing." He chuckled. "Now, kiss me."

"Yes, Master."

Jack had no clue if they were even in the frame as the shutter clicked repeatedly, but he didn't care. He figured at least one picture would turn out, and if it didn't, they could keep practicing until one did. He placed the camera on his bedside table before sliding his hands under the fabric of Linda's dress and slipping it farther down her shoulders. He slid it off her arms and then tossed it behind him on his desk chair.

"We're done with the pictures, right?"

"Do you want to be done?"

"Yes."

"Then we're done," he answered softly, kissing her again and pulling her warm body close to his.

Linda sat in the small room, her knee bouncing up and down crazily as they waited for Graham and his lawyer to arrive. She hadn't seen Graham since the altercation on the street that day when she was with Jack. They hadn't even spoken; messages were sent back and forth through official channels only. Knowing she was about to spend hours locked in a room with him in a potentially tense situation was not incredibly soothing. Her own lawyer gave her a look, and she ceased the fidgeting immediately. She smiled at him awkwardly before looking away and glancing at her watch.

The door opened, and the mediator walked in, followed by Graham and another suave-looking gentleman. Linda stiffened and waited for Graham to look at her, expecting him to either sneer or smile that cocky grin that used to make her skin crawl. He did neither. Instead, he kept his eyes straight ahead, and when he sat down, he stared at his folded hands on the table. This was so at odds with what she was expecting that Linda wasn't sure if she should relax or be more wary. She decided to play it by ear as introductions were made around the table.

Graham's lawyer was soft spoken and had a slight accent. He seemed entirely pleasant, but since he was a lawyer, she didn't much trust him. For all she knew, he could be trying to lull them into a false sense of security by acting debonair and had talked Graham into this meek act just to drop the axe on them. She had a bad feeling about all this.

The mediator introduced herself and allowed the lawyers to lay out their terms and conditions. For the most part, they requested the same things. Linda's house was solely in her name, so Graham had no hold there. The vehicles were to stay with their respective owners. Linda had no use for anything in the condo since her house was fully furnished and she had moved out anything of personal importance over the years. It was all just material items that she had no real attachment to, so Graham could keep it all. They had decided to split any joint financial ventures in half. All in all, it was a pretty clean divorce. The last item on the agenda was the condo.

Linda braced herself.

"Mr. Hunter has agreed to Ms. Tanner's terms and conditions in regards to the condo," the lawyer said smoothly. "He will be taking a second mortgage on the property at its current value, and the money will be transferred to her in her name."

"What?" she asked softly, not quite believing what she'd heard. He wasn't going to fight her at all.

"Wonderful," her lawyer replied.

Linda turned to look at Graham. He hadn't said a word this whole time, nor had he been looking at her. He raised his head now, and she finally got a good look at him. Gone was the cocky bastard she knew; he looked completely broken. They stared at one another in silence as the others spoke about inconsequential details. She waited for his old self to emerge, for him to drop this sedate façade, but it didn't happen.

"Linda?" her lawyer said, shaking her arm to get her attention.

She turned toward him.

"We're just going in the next room to start up the preliminary paperwork. Are you all right to stay here for a few minutes?"

She looked back to Graham uneasily, but he was back to staring at the table. "Sure, I guess," she answered, figuring if the old Graham reappeared she could just leave the room.

"We'll be right in there," he said, gesturing to another room.

"Okay."

The mediator and the lawyers stepped into the other room, but the door remained open, which made her feel less anxious. Linda sat there, hands clasped in her lap and looking everywhere except toward her soon-to-be ex-husband. He was watching her now; she could see him in her peripheral vision, and he was facing her. Still, she avoided looking at him.

"You look good, Lin," he said softly.

Linda cringed at his casual use of her pet name. He'd started calling her Lin when they were still in high school.

"Thank you," she answered curtly.

"Lin—"

"Please don't call me that," she whispered and pulled her shoulders up, waiting for the backlash. None came.

"I'm sorry," he replied instead, sounding regretful. "Look, I just wanted to tell you…I'm sorry."

"For what, exactly?" she asked, finally looking at him.

"For everything." He swallowed heavily, his gaze unwavering. "I wasn't a very good husband to you, especially during the last few years."

"Ya think?" She huffed scornfully, folding her arms across her chest and holding on to herself tightly.

"I just…" He took a deep breath before continuing. "I wanted to make this part easy for you, okay? So you can go on with your life and be happy."

Linda blinked at him in confusion. Since when had Graham ever wanted to make something easy on her? Something was very wrong here.

"Are you dying?" she blurted out.

"No," he answered, smiling sadly and shaking his head. "Mom is."

"*What?*" Linda stared at him, aghast at his confession. Mrs. Hunter had been like a second mother to her, especially after her parents had died. She now felt a twinge of guilt that she hadn't remained in contact with the woman after she had separated from Graham. It had just been too difficult, seeing as Graham was her son. Linda didn't feel right letting her know that, despite the woman's best efforts, he'd turned into a monster. "But she was fine just a few months ago!"

"She has cancer, Linda. We didn't know, and they caught it too late."

"I can't believe you didn't let me know."

"I didn't feel right bothering you after you'd moved on," he replied with no acrimony, looking down at his hands again. "She was asking about you. I told her…everything. She was pretty pissed at me and told me that I had to do right by you and give you whatever you wanted. It was the least I could do."

Linda sat there and felt tears well up in her eyes. *How did we get here?* she wondered. Then she decided it didn't matter because there was nothing she could do to change her past. Even if she could, she wouldn't change anything because her life's path had led her to Jack, and now she had a real shot at happiness.

"We'll be done shortly, Ms. Tanner," her lawyer said, poking his head into the room. "You can start getting ready to leave."

"Thank you."

Linda began gathering her things. She had some paperwork with her, which she slipped back into her bag. When she stood to put on her jacket, she saw Graham's eyes pass over her body. While she was still short of her initial goal, she knew that she looked drastically different now than when he'd left her. And even from the last time he saw her in Baltimore. She wanted to feel haughty and victorious, but she didn't. Did it really make a difference now? What had she expected to happen, anyway? For him to drop to his knees and beg for her to come back? She didn't want Graham. She had just wanted to prove something, and now she didn't even know what that something was.

She finished getting ready and stood by her chair waiting.

"So, are you still with the whelp?" she heard Graham ask, a familiar disdainful note creeping back into his voice.

"Yes," she answered, looking at him head on, her chin rising in slight defiance. She didn't bother correcting Graham's notion that she and Jack had been a couple when he'd seen them in Baltimore so long ago. It was pointless now.

He got up from his seat and smirked at her slightly. "Yeah, it's fun to be with someone young, isn't it?"

"You ought to know," Linda replied, unable to help the dripping of venom in her tone.

"But it sucks when the excitement wears off and they realize they can do better," Graham said, looking away.

Linda inhaled sharply at his words.

"Ready to go, Ms. Tanner?" Mr. Goldman asked. He had walked back into the room and was holding the door open for her.

"Bye, Lin," Graham said softly. "Take care of yourself."

"Bye, Graham," she answered, giving him one last look before leaving the room, the uneasy feeling returning.

The next morning, Jack woke Linda by placing kisses along her shoulders and back. She was lying on her stomach with her face toward him; he saw her smile sleepily, but she kept her eyes closed.

"Happy birthday, gorgeous," he said softly. Her smile was replaced by a pout that made him chuckle.

"I thought we agreed I wasn't celebrating my birthday," she whined at him.

"No, I just agreed not to throw you an embarrassing party. Now, wake up. I have a present for you."

"Present?" she asked, cracking open an eye and smiling again.

Jack nodded and reached into the bag at the side of the bed, pulling out a long, flat package. Linda stretched lazily, rolled over, and sat up. He smiled as she rubbed her eyes and got comfy. He placed the present on her lap and waited nervously. Linda looked at him askance and grinned at him before flipping the package over, running her finger under the tape and carefully pulling the edge up. Jack wanted to grab it back and rip all of the paper off, and he was about three seconds from doing that when the paper she'd been trying to be so gentle with tore down the middle.

"Crap," she said and then shrugged. "Oh, well."

Linda ripped the paper off enthusiastically, making him laugh. She gasped when she flipped the frame over and saw the pictures of them together. Her hand came up to her mouth, and he saw the sheen of tears start in her eyes.

"Eliza helped me," he said quietly. Most of the pictures he'd taken of them kissing had been out of focus or he hadn't been able to get both of them in the frame, but a few of them had come out really well. When he'd gone to Rick and Eliza's shop to get them developed, Eliza had taken the pictures and edited them. They were now a rich sepia tone and cropped close, and she had worked on the contrasts and made them look as if a professional had taken them instead of an amateur.

"Oh, Jack…they're beautiful."

"*You're* beautiful," he replied tenderly, tracing the lines of her face in one of the photographs. In it, she had her eyes closed but was smiling as Jack kissed her chin. In another one, their open mouths were barely a fraction of an inch apart. Jack's eyes were closed, but Linda had hers open, watching him. The expression on her face was tender and loving. In the third, she was holding his face and had his lower lip between hers, sucking gently, her eyes closed and her lashes fanning along her cheek. He remembered that kiss vividly. It was right before he'd set his camera down.

"I love it," she said, turning toward him and leaning in for a kiss.

On a scale of one to ten, Linda ranked this birthday an eleven. From Jack's surprise, the incredible sex that followed, and all the calls from her friends wishing her a wonderful day, she thought this was one of the best days she'd had in a very long time.

It got even better when Jack made good on his promise to not go overboard with her celebration. Instead, he banged around in her kitchen, trying to make them some dinner while Linda sat and watched him. Amanda was the one who took care of the meals, and you could definitely tell. Apparently, all Jack could cook was breakfast, but he certainly made a mean omelet and toast.

He lit candles and placed them all around the dining room, making it glow and shimmer, and they sat at her table and shared food with one another. Linda couldn't remember a time in her life when she'd been happier than at that moment. With her divorce almost complete, it just made this day that much sweeter. She felt like a huge weight had been lifted off her shoulders.

When dinner was over, they cleared up the kitchen and then retired to the living room. Linda sat between Jack's legs as they lounged on the couch and spent the next couple of hours talking, laughing, and sharing while music played in the background. Jack had brought the candles into the living room, surrounding them in a muted light.

Linda turned in Jack's arms and reached up to kiss him. His wonderfully strong arms wrapped around her securely as the kiss deepened. Her body was on top of his as she breathed in his breath and tasted his mouth. His hair was silky and soft against her hands, his chest hard and muscled against her breasts. Would she ever stop wanting him? She wondered if the day would ever come when he would stop wanting her, but she killed that thought quickly. It was too painful to even contemplate.

Linda got up and began blowing out candles. When she was done, she held out her hand, and Jack stood and followed her out of the living room. Going up the stairs, he wrapped an arm around her as they ascended. Neither of them said anything. It was if he could read her emotions. All she wanted was to be close to him, to be wrapped around him, to love him. She wanted him in her arms. She wanted to feel him surging against her. She wanted him to hold her and love her while she still had time.

Jack did all that and more. He made her feel desired, wanted, adored, and loved. It was more than she expected, but she drank it all in, soaking it up to store for a time when he might no longer be in her life.

Before they fell asleep that night, he whispered to her, "I love you, Linda."

She closed her eyes against the sting of tears. "I love you, Jack," she whispered in return, afraid of just how much but unwilling to give him any less. And then she fell asleep cradled in his arms.

21
A Scout Goes A'Scoutin'

Linda was fiddling with her pen as they did a round table of all the entertainment journalists working for the paper and what they had planned for the next months' issues of the paper. She was always bored during these meetings because the nature of her articles was last-minute gossip, so it was next to impossible for her to plan anything in advance. Sure, there were always those guaranteed celebs who made the paper continuously, but you couldn't bet on when they'd be pulling their next stunt, and it was difficult to make any hard and fast commitments.

As it was, her editor knew the drill and didn't expect much from her. He still wanted her to sit in on the meetings because she was usually good at making suggestions on other parts of the entertainment pages, even if they weren't directly involved with her work. Lately, though, it was hard to keep her mind from wandering.

Surreptitiously, she glanced at her watch to see how much longer this was going to take. It was Saturday, and Jack was in town, having driven her to Baltimore so that they could spend some time together when she was done. He was playing at the bar tonight, and they were meeting Rob and Cici to grab a leisurely dinner before the boys played their gigs. It had been a while since she'd seen him on stage, and she was strangely excited about it all.

Ryan, who headed up the music section, was moaning about the lack of activity around the city. There wasn't much going on in regard to concerts or anything really exciting now that summer had wound down. Linda perked up for a second, and before she had time to think of it, she was speaking.

"Have you ever thought of doing some stories on the local talent?"

"What do you mean?"

"The local musical talent here in Baltimore."

Ryan frowned slightly, but their boss, Vern, looked speculative. "That might be an idea," he mused.

"How am I supposed to find local talent?"

"Well, you can start at Remy's," Linda suggested, looking at Ryan. "They have an open mic night every Saturday to draw in a different crowd."

She had found out that Remy's bar, which generally catered to an older clientele, had started the open mic nights to lure in the younger set, the ones more apt to drink copiously and spend money. So far it had been a success, with people lining up to play as well as to watch the show. It had become so successful that they now had enough talent to be picky about who they allowed to play. Jack was never turned down.

"Open mic night?" he scoffed. "Come on, Linda. It's probably a bunch of no-talent hacks belting out karaoke."

Linda tried not to bristle; no one here knew that Ryan was indirectly insulting her boyfriend. She didn't want to be upfront with that information either, or else they would all see her agenda clearly. "I've gone a few times," she replied calmly instead. "I think you'd be surprised. Anyway, why don't you pop by tonight and check it out?"

"I like that idea," Vern said, nodding slowly. "A month showcasing local talent. Ryan, make it happen."

"Yes, sir," Ryan mumbled, shooting Linda a sideways glance.

She just shrugged helplessly at him, but inside she was pleased. Jack might not want to aggressively pursue his music, but she wasn't opposed to pimping him out in order to get him some visibility. Maybe if others started to show a real interest in his music, it would build up his confidence.

Linda walked down the stairs of the building, expecting Jack to be waiting for her in his usual spot. She was a little breathless because she'd practically sprinted her way to the exit. They had been together almost three months, but she was just as enthralled with him as she was at the beginning. And what was most surprising was that he seemed to feel the same way. Sure, they had their occasional spats like any other couple, but nothing ever lasted long, and they always seemed to work things out with minimal damage done.

Frankly, she was most surprised by Jack's jealous streak. After their confrontation over Matt, he never made the same mistake of accusing her of trying to make him jealous. Generally, he'd just stare daggers at whoever he deemed was crossing the line. Linda couldn't understand why he'd get that dark look on his face if any other man paid the least bit of attention to her. Even innocent overtures made him clench his jaw and grit his teeth. She tried not to laugh, because often that exacerbated the situation; she would just grab hold of him and kiss him until he lost the tension in his body and began to hum contentedly.

Linda figured the charm would wear off after a while and she would become annoyed, but she didn't. If she was honest, it was actually nice to have a man be possessive of her. Graham had never been like that, not even in the beginning when men actually did pay attention to her. He had been mostly oblivious and didn't even particularly care if another man seemed interested in her. In light of this, Linda was slightly flattered that Jack seemed to find threat wherever they went, especially since so often the opposite was true. Jack attracted way more attention than she ever would.

That was something she battled constantly. While she didn't exhibit the same outward behavior as Jack, it affected her almost as much. Luckily, even though it was internalized, he seemed to know or understand when she needed some extra comfort and maybe a bit of an ego boost. If any woman happened to get out of line in her presence, he made sure to do something to show that Linda wasn't his homely sister, cousin, or friend.

Linda brushed that thought aside as she opened the doors, turned, and smiled before throwing herself at Jack. He was laughing, his strong arms catching her effortlessly.

"Well, aren't you happy today!" He chuckled as she kissed his face everywhere.

"I am now," Linda murmured. She most definitely was in a good mood, and she wondered if she should let Jack know what had happened in her meeting. She decided it might be a better idea to keep it to herself. For all she knew, Ryan might not even show up at the bar.

Monday afternoon was halfway over when Jack got a phone call. It took him a couple of minutes before he deciphered the rapid high-pitched voice as Cici's and calmed her down sufficiently to figure out what she was asking of him.

"The paper! The paper!" she kept repeating.

"Cici," he snapped. "What fucking paper?"

"The Baltimore Daily!" she managed to get out before squawking again. "Section E, page four!"

Jack grabbed one of the newspapers from the front counter and exhaled in annoyance when he realized section E was missing. He hunted around a little and was about to give up the search and ask Cici what the fuck was going on when he spied it on one of the treadmills. Stalking over, he grabbed it and then mumbled to himself as he flipped to page four. It didn't take too long for a caption to catch his eye.

"Did you find it?" Cici exclaimed loudly as his eyes skimmed the article.

It was about the past open mic night that Jack had played in. His eyes jumped around, taking it all in. He let his breath out in a slow gust of air as he saw his name listed, as well as Rob's band and one other performer. Cici was still chattering in his ear, but he'd tuned her out as he began to read the article from the beginning once more.

"Jack? Jaaaaaaaack…"

"Sorry, Cici, I gotta go."

"Did you see the article?"

"Yeah, I saw it," he answered, still in shock. "Talk to you later."

With that, he flipped his phone shut and sat in a waiting area chair. Once he regained his composure, he glanced up at the clock. Almost time for Linda's session. Jack stood and went to one of the aerobics rooms, where he dropped the paper on a stack of mats before going to wait for Linda at the front. It didn't take long for her to turn the corner; she walked up the sidewalk with a spring in her step.

"Hi," she said a little breathlessly.

"Hey, do you mind if we go to the aerobic room for a second?"

"Sure," she answered, smiling at him a little mischievously before heading to the back of the gym.

Jack walked beside her silently. His mind was still working a million miles an hour. "This one," he said, pointing to the first room.

Linda opened the door and stood off to the side, waiting. He walked over to the newspaper on the mats and picked it up while she watched with a quizzical expression on her face. Jack cleared his throat for a second before beginning to read.

"'When a colleague of mine mentioned going to Remy's for their open mic night to scout for local talent, I had to admit I was a little skeptical.'" Jack paused and looked up at Linda. She had gone slightly pale and her eyes widened.

"'As I sat in the bar,'" Jack continued reading aloud, "'listening to what I could only describe as sub-par musical talent, I surmised that I was correct.'" He stopped and looked at Linda again. Her shoulders slumped, and the look on her face could only be described as distressed.

"Oh no," she whispered and began wringing her hands together.

"I suppose you were 'the colleague'?" he asked softly and watched her nod. "And I guess you haven't seen the article yet?"

"No," she replied quietly. "I only told Ryan about it on Saturday. I figured even if he did come to the show that he probably wouldn't write up an article right away."

"Looks like he did."

"Yeah."

"Do you want to hear the rest?"

"Probably not?" she said, cringing slightly.

"Too bad," he answered in a curt voice as he brought the paper back up and picked up where he left off. "'As I sat in the bar, listening to what I could only describe as sub-par musical talent, I surmised that I was correct. That was until Jack McAllister and his acoustic guitar stepped into the spotlight, proving that maybe Baltimore *did* indeed have some local talent.'" He tried not to smirk as Linda gasped a little. He continued to read the flattering description Ryan Christie had written about him and the songs he'd sung. Ryan praised Jack's originality of using his own music as opposed to just singing covers like a lot of the other acts had done. Jack looked up at Linda again during this part and saw her smile somewhat smugly. Ryan praised the songs themselves as well as Jack's singing and the way he played guitar, finishing it off by saying he hadn't seen someone so talented play live in years.

When Jack was done, he dropped his hand and looked at Linda again.

"You jerk!" she said, quickly stepping up and smacking his arm. "You did that on purpose! Making me think the article would be a slam!"

"Teaches you right for meddling," he answered, wheeling away from her and shaking the paper. "Linda, this could have turned out really fucking bad!" This made her stop and look at him shamefacedly. "I mean, what if he really *had* hated my music?"

"I knew he wouldn't," Linda said, speaking quietly once again. "Jack, I never would have done it if I didn't think you were so talented."

"Why didn't you tell me?"

"Because I didn't want you to get nervous. I just wanted you to play like you always do. I figured if he wrote up a piece, I'd have a chance to look at it first, and then I could warn you."

Jack exhaled forcefully, dropped the paper on the mats, and walked into the middle of the room. He couldn't look at Linda. While he was excited and elated about what had been said about him in the paper, it had come as too much of a shock. It was also overshadowed by the fact that he felt as if Linda had gone behind his back and exposed one of his vulnerabilities. While things had turned out well, what if they hadn't? What if he had been lumped in with the other *sub-par musical talent* that had played at the bar Saturday night?

He heard the paper rustle behind him as Linda picked it up. Jack knew she hadn't done it to hurt him, and she'd had his best intentions at heart, but he really did wish she had asked him first and told her as much.

"I knew you'd say no," Linda admitted, shooting him cautious glances.

"Well, if you knew I'd say no, why did you do it?"

"Jack, you know when you tell me that when you look at me, all you see is beautiful? And that you wished I saw the same thing you do?"

"Yeah."

"That's how I feel about you and your music. What I hear is *beautiful*. And it's not just because you're my boyfriend," she said, holding up a hand to stop his protests. "I just wanted a chance to show you that I wasn't the only one who thought so." Linda put the paper down and walked up to him, putting her arms around his waist. "People *love* you. Your music…It's magical."

"Come on…"

"It's true!" she stated emphatically. "And now it's in black and white, right there." She flung her hand back toward the paper. "Ryan is a music critic, Jack. He knows what he's talking about, and he *loved* you."

"What if he'd hated me?"

"But he didn't," she stressed. "Look, I'm not pushing you to do anything with your music if you don't want to, but I'd support you if you did."

Jack nodded and brought his hand up to brush against Linda's face. He was somewhat conflicted. He wanted to be upset, but she was making it really hard. No one had ever shown him so much support as far as his music went. Amanda had bugged him for a while, but after hearing him tell her to fuck off repeatedly, she no longer bothered. Girlfriends had been somewhat impressed, but most of them hadn't been interested in anything more than an occasional serenade. It was strange to have someone go to bat for him and *believe* in him and his talent. It was…nice.

"Are you mad at me?" Linda asked. Her eyes were large and worried, a small pucker between her brows.

He ran a finger over it to smooth it out and shook his head slowly. "No," he replied in a low voice, and then he brushed his lips against hers.

Jack felt the tension leach out of her body as she exhaled in relief. He kissed her again and held her tightly. He'd been honest just now and was no longer upset. It was easy to forget that Linda looked at him in the same way he saw her, and it wasn't fair of him to want to tell her to lose her love goggles if he wasn't prepared to lose his. They were more alike than he wanted to admit at this point. He was now realizing she wanted to show him that he was beautiful to her, not in the traditional sense like how other women saw him but in a more profound way. Not many saw him as more than a hard body and a pretty face. Linda did. And that was one of the reasons he loved her.

As they stood there, he let himself be smugly pleased at what had been said about him in that newspaper article. Maybe he wasn't crazy about the way Linda had gone about it, but if it weren't for her, he wouldn't be feeling this huge sense of pride and accomplishment right now. For that, he was grateful, and he loved her even more than he had before.

22
This One's Serious

It was October, and Linda was staring out her kitchen window at the spattering of color throughout the trees surrounding her house. It was coming on twilight, and the sunset made the colors even more vibrant than usual. The days were crisp and cool now, so her walks with Jack were brisk ones. They always started off moving quickly so they could build up some additional body heat, and then they slowed down to a more casual pace. Linda still loved their little ritual, walking in the fresh air and talking. She loved listening to Jack as he spoke, his soft voice getting swallowed by the trees just after reaching her ears. It was still one of her favorite times of the day.

Jack entered the kitchen, and they sat down for a quick dinner, chatting amicably. When dinner was through, they started cleaning up. Halfway through doing the dishes, the phone rang, and Linda wiped off her hands to grab it. Jack continued without her.

"Hello?" she said happily into the receiver.

"Linda?"

The smile slid slowly off her face as she registered who it was.

"It's me. Graham."

"I know who it is," she answered, perhaps a little sharper than intended, causing Jack to turn and look at her. He lifted his chin slightly in inquiry.

"I wasn't sure you'd recognize my voice."

I've only heard it for the last twenty years of my life, she thought while snickering internally. "What do you want, Graham?" she asked, wanting to cut to the chase and answer Jack's question at the same time.

She watched as his brows cranked down and his lip curled. He had a grip on the glass in his hand so tight that she wondered briefly if he could crush it. She reached out to take it just in case.

"I'm really sorry to bother you…"

"Mm-hmm."

"Look, Mom's taken a turn for the worse," he said in a low voice. "You seemed upset that I didn't tell you she was sick, so I thought maybe you'd want to know she doesn't have much time left."

"Oh," Linda replied, the wind knocked out of her sails. "I'm sorry."

"Yeah, well. We're just getting ready, you know?"

She put a shaking hand to the side of her face as she fought back the tears. This was just horrible. A woman who'd helped take care of her when she was still so young and then orphaned was dying, and there was nothing she could do. A wave of helplessness washed over her. Jack turned off the running water, dried his hands briskly, and reached for her.

"What's wrong?" he mouthed, his face a mask of concern.

Linda just shook her head slightly and closed her eyes for a second.

"Lin? You there?"

"Yeah," she rasped and then cleared her throat. "I'm here."

"Look, I wouldn't have called but…she's asking for you."

"Oh…"

"I, uh, I didn't know whether you wanted to say good-bye."

Linda's chest hitched as a small sob escaped her. Jack was starting to look panicked; he had no idea what was happening and why Graham was making her cry.

"Okay," she answered. "When?"

"Linda, what's going on?" Jack finally whispered fiercely. He looked ready to snatch the phone away from her, and she put a hand on his chest, rubbing it in a soothing circle.

Graham told her which hospital his mother was staying at and gave her the visiting hours. He said they didn't know how long she would last—it could be days, it could be weeks—but it was probably better if she tried to visit sooner rather than later. Linda agreed with him. She'd managed to keep relative control over her voice and wiped the few tears that had fallen from her cheeks. She said good-bye and hung up the phone.

"Linda?" Jack asked again. He had moved even closer during the course of the conversation and had his hands on her waist, staring intently at her face, as if searching for clues to what was wrong.

"Sorry," she said in a shaky voice. "That was Graham."

"Yeah, I *know* that was Graham. What the hell did he want, and why are you crying?"

"His mother's taken a turn for the worse. She's dying."

"Oh," he answered, some of the tension leaving his body. "He just called to tell you that?"

"Well, he wouldn't have called at all, except I was upset he hadn't told me she was sick in the first place, so he thought I'd want to know."

"Do you?"

"Yes, of course," she replied automatically. "She was like a second mother to me. Of course I want to know."

"I'm sorry, Linda." Jack hugged her close and sighed in her hair. "I hate to see you so sad."

"She's evidently been asking for me," she said, her words muffled by his shirt. "I want to go see her to say good-bye."

Jack stiffened again and then gripped her tighter. "Is that what Graham was asking? For you to go see her?"

"Well, he gave me the choice. He just told me she'd been asking for me."

"Huh."

"What do you mean, 'huh'?"

"Nothing," Jack answered quickly.

Linda could feel him shake his head slightly, and she pulled back to look at him. Jack's nostrils were flaring, his eyes were mere slits, and his usual full lips were flattened into a forbidding line. This did not look good.

"What's wrong?" she inquired softly.

"Is *he* going to be there?" Jack asked in a measured tone.

She didn't like how controlled it sounded, as if he were barely reining in his anger.

"I don't know. I never really told him when I was going to go. He might be. His mother is dying, so I'm sure he wants to be with her as much as possible before that happens."

Jack took a deep breath through his nose and exhaled slowly. He did this a couple of times.

"Talk to me, Jack."

"What do you want me to say, Linda?" He pulled away from her and rubbed an agitated hand through his hair. "I don't like the idea of you being alone with that asshole!"

"Even if he was there, which isn't a guarantee, we won't really be alone."

"I don't care!" he said loudly. "I don't care, Linda. He's slime!"

"What do you want me to do?" she asked, matching his tone. "She's dying! You want me to not say good-bye just because you aren't comfortable with the idea that I *might* run into Graham?"

"I. Don't. *Trust.* Him."

"I have to go, Jack. I couldn't forgive myself if I didn't."

"How do you know this isn't all just a trick?" he seethed. "A way to get you back?"

"Yes, Jack. He's given his mother cancer just so he can get me back," she deadpanned. "Be reasonable."

"You don't know men. I *do!*"

"Are you listening to yourself right now?" Linda's eyebrows had risen as high as they could go. Jack was still incredibly pissed off, and now she was too. She tried to accommodate him when he lost it a little, but this was over the top. A woman was about to pass away, and he was accusing Graham of grand plans to steal her from him. It was ludicrous.

"I'm coming with you, then," he commanded, as if that was the end of the conversation.

"Absolutely *not.*"

"What?"

"You heard me. No way."

"Why not?" he demanded, his hands on his hips as he leaned toward her.

"Because you don't even know her!" Linda yelled. "How the hell am I supposed to explain your presence? And to be perfectly honest with you, I'd be afraid to bring you around Graham when you get like this. You're liable to try to knock him out while we're there."

"Only if he stepped out of line," Jack grumbled, and Linda put up a hand as if to say, *You see?*

"And that's why I'm going alone."

"*You're not going alone!*" he roared.

"The hell I'm not!" Linda shouted back. "I'm a thirty-six-year-old woman, Jack, and I'll go wherever the hell I damn well please and with whomever I please. Or *not,* in this case."

Jack grabbed hold of his hair and turned in a semi-circle away from her. He was growling out profanities under his breath. After a few tense seconds, his hands dropped and he nodded, his lips set in a grim line.

"Fuck it," he spit out. "Do what you want."

As he stormed out of the kitchen, Linda followed him in a blind panic. "Where are you going?"

"Home." His voice was low and controlled once more. He forced his feet into his shoes as Linda watched him grab his jacket. He patted his pockets to make sure he had everything and then grabbed the door handle to leave.

"Jack," she said, reaching for his arm.

"Don't," he said curtly. He pulled away from her and yanked the door open. Jack stood on the threshold for a second and then slammed his open palm against the doorframe loudly. He took a deep breath. "I have to go. I'm really pissed off right now, and it's not a good idea for me to stay."

With that, he strode out the door without even a backward glance, shutting the door behind him. She expected him to slam it, so the muted click was more of a shock than the noise would have been. Linda cursed under her breath and leaned her forehead against the door. She wanted to run after him, but she knew that wasn't a good idea.

Fucking Graham.

Even out of her life, he was still wreaking havoc. As soon as the thought popped into her head, she felt guilty. As shitty a husband as he was, he didn't ask for this. Graham had always been a mama's boy; he loved his mother more than anything else in this world, and Linda knew that losing her must be killing him. Even if a small part of her did want him to suffer, not like this. Not at the sake of his mother's life. That woman had always loved Linda and treated her like her own. She was heartsick that Mrs. Hunter was going to pass away.

What the hell was she going to do about Jack now? She didn't like arguing with him, and this had been their worst to date. He'd never stormed off on her before. Never been so mad he felt he had to. They'd always managed to get past any little squabbles and usually ended up laughing at the silliness of it all. Somehow, they managed to compromise so each of them felt good about the resolution. The problem this time was that she couldn't see any compromise.

Linda really didn't think it was a good idea for Jack to accompany her to the hospital, and he didn't feel comfortable with her going on her own. So, where did they go from here?

An hour passed before Linda called Jack. She had paced around her entire house repeatedly and still felt disconsolate at how they'd left things. She still had no idea how to resolve this issue, but she'd rather talk it out with Jack than have this distance between them. Not surprisingly, her call went straight to voice mail.

After another hour of calling at five-minute intervals, she began getting nervous. Against her better judgment but unable to stop herself, Linda found herself in her car and on her way to Jack's house. They were going to talk this through, hopefully rationally. Anything would be better than complete silence. She'd had enough of that during her marriage; she wasn't going to go through it again.

When she pulled up at Jack's house, her shoulders slumped as she realized his car wasn't there. She had no idea what to do now. Maybe he'd had the same idea and had decided to return to her house to talk things over? But wouldn't he have called first if that was the case?

Driven by fear, she exited her car and ran up to the house. There was a light on inside, so Amanda must be home. She'd check with her first before she flew off the handle. Linda stood there shuffling from foot to foot as she waited for someone to answer the door. Finally it opened, and Amanda stared out at her, looking grim.

"He's at the gym," she said without preamble.

"Was it that bad?" Linda asked, wringing her hands.

"I've seen worse," the girl answered with a wry expression.

"Do you think I should go there?"

"Yeah, I do. He needs you right now, even if he is pissed."

"You don't think it'll make things worse?" Linda asked.

"Well, he's been there almost two hours. I'm pretty sure he's weight-lifted himself into oblivion by now. He should be ready to talk."

Linda sighed dejectedly. "I'm sorry."

"Don't apologize to me," Amanda said, shrugging. "Just get it fixed."

"Okay," Linda replied, smiling slightly.

"Here, take these," Amanda said, tossing Linda a set of keys. "Go through the back. The door is probably open, but just in case it's locked."

"Thanks, Amanda."

"I know it," the girl said in dismissal. Linda smiled at the phrase; it was one of Tony's usual sayings. He was obviously rubbing off on her.

With her heart in her throat, Linda drove to the club. She parked at the back beside Jack's car and sat there for a few minutes. Feeling bad about bursting in on Jack unaware, she decided to try his phone one more time. There was still no answer.

Swallowing the lump in her throat, along with her pride, she left her car and walked to the employees' entrance. She tugged on the door and was relieved when it opened. Pocketing the keys, she stepped into the dim hallway. Linda walked past the employees' lounge, washroom, and kitchen area, and then stepped through the entrance to the back of the gym.

Linda heard the clang of weights and harsh, panting breaths interspersed with occasional grunts. Otherwise, the club was eerily silent. She followed the noises to the weights section and felt her heart splinter a little.

Jack was lying on a weight bench. His shirt was off, and his torso was glistening with a fine sheen of sweat. The shorts he wore clung to his body as well. He was completely saturated. She could see him straining as he lifted the weight bar, all of his muscles tense and flexing. In any other situation, the sight of him like this might have turned her on, but today she knew that she was the cause of pain for him, and he was punishing himself to protect her.

Not wanting to distract him at an inopportune time, she waited until Jack had put the weights back on the stand before stepping into the light. Jack was breathing hard. He folded his hands on his chest and grimaced as he flexed and released them a few times. Otherwise, he remained completely still.

"Hi," Linda said softly, unsure if he'd noticed her or not.

"What are you doing here, Linda?" His voice sounded dead to her, and she shied away from it.

"I don't know," she whispered. She hadn't come to apologize, really, because she didn't feel like she'd done anything wrong. By the same token, she didn't feel he'd done anything wrong either. Both of them had just become victim to their own emotions.

Jack continued to stare upward. "You don't know?"

"I didn't like this…this distance between us. We've always been able to talk about anything…" She trailed off uneasily.

"There's nothing to talk about," he answered quietly. "You're going to see your ex's mom at the hospital, and I'm going to be here in Arnold worrying myself sick over it. Done deal."

Linda sighed.

Jack sat up and ran his hands through his hair. It was practically black from the sweat. He grimaced again and then grabbed a towel that had been lying under him on the bench. He used it to wipe his hands and his chest and then ran it over his face and hair.

"I just don't know what you want me to do here, Jack. I don't think it's right to bring my new, young boyfriend to visit my dying soon-to-be-ex-mother-in-law." There was no bitterness or acrimony in her voice, only the helplessness that she felt over this whole situation.

"I know."

"But it's killing me to hurt you." Her voice cracked painfully, and for the first time since she walked in, Jack looked at her. His face was a mask of desperation and pain, and she had an idea that it mirrored her own right now. Without thinking about it, she went over to him and sank down to her knees. She put a hand to his face and whispered, "I don't want to hurt you."

Jack exhaled slowly and turned his face slightly so he could kiss her wrist. "I don't want to hurt you, either."

"We'll figure something out, okay?"

"Okay."

Jack was a wreck. Even with Linda on her knees in front of him, he still wasn't completely eased. This had been the only time he'd felt truly out of control lately, and he'd known he had to do something about it, which is how he'd ended up at the gym. He'd started on the treadmill and tried to outrun his anger. The only problem was, no matter how fast he went, he didn't get anywhere. The same had been true of the emotions that were roiling around in his body. Even after almost an hour, he hadn't been able to outrun a damned thing.

Next, he'd decided to lift weights, and he'd concentrated hard on making sure he didn't crush his chest with the massive load he'd put on the bar. It was stupid to lift this much without someone there to spot for him, but he hadn't been thinking very clearly at the time. All he'd wanted to do was try to replace one type of pain with another. That hadn't worked either. Now, not only did his heart hurt, but his body did too.

As he stared down into Linda's distressed face, he felt acutely just how excruciating it would be if he lost her. They barely ever argued, but this one had been the worst, and he was terrified he would do something to finally drive her away. It was bad enough he was a jealous bastard; now he was forbidding her to see a poor, dying woman just because she had the misfortune of being Graham's mother. He knew it wasn't fair, but he couldn't help the way he felt. He still didn't want Linda in the general vicinity of her ex. Even if it was in a hospital.

Jack truly did hope they could figure something out, because he didn't want to argue anymore. And, judging by the look on Linda's face, neither did she. That relieved him at least. He wasn't completely over their argument, but it was a start.

"Do you want to go home?" he asked softly, rubbing a thumb along her cheek.

Linda nodded.

"Okay, just let me clean up a bit here."

Linda sighed and snuggled into his chest further, her hands gripping his back tightly. From her reactions, he figured the argument had bothered her as much as it had him. They still had the issue to resolve, but at least they'd gotten past the anger. That was the first step. They'd worry about the rest later and deal with it together.

Strange. This was the first time he'd ever wanted to make the effort with anyone before. In his previous relationships, by this time, he was usually looking for excuses to get out, citing silly arguments like this as a reason why he didn't belong with the girl he was with. This time, however, he was praying that Linda wasn't the one wondering why she was sticking around.

If he'd needed more proof that he wanted to be with Linda for the long haul, he had it. No matter what happened between them, he only ever wanted to be closer to her, to make her feel good, to protect her. Jack wanted to be everything for her, anything she needed. He would do that. He would be that for her.

Jack put his shirt on and grabbed his jacket, and they walked out of the club together. He made sure she got to her car safe, and they stood there awkwardly for a second. Linda wasn't looking at him; she was staring down at her hands as she fiddled with her keys. He curled a finger under her chin and lifted it so that she had no choice but to look at him, and then he stared at her expectantly.

"So, um," Linda began, "when you said 'let's go home,' did you mean we go to our *own* homes…?"

"Do you want me to go to my own home?" he asked softly as his eyes searched her face.

"Do you *want* to go to your own home?"

"Linda."

"No, I don't want you to go to your home," she whispered. "I want you to come to *my* home."

"Are you sure?"

"Yes," she answered. Her voice was still soft, but it was certain, and Jack was pleased she still wanted to be around him tonight.

"Okay, I'll follow you there."

The drive to Linda's was quick. Jack parked behind her car, and she waited for him by the back of it. He put his arm around her shoulders, thinking even that ten-minute drive alone was too much. She snuggled against him as they made their way up to the front of the house. When they got inside, they headed upstairs.

"Do you mind if I grab a quick shower?" he asked. He was dry now, but he'd feel better once he was clean as well.

Linda shook her head. Jack pulled his phone out of his pocket; he'd left it in his car while he was working out, not wanting to be tempted to call Linda while still mad. He turned it on and put it on the bedside table before going to clean himself off. While he was showering, he went over everything that had happened. There was still some distance between them that he hoped would dissipate when they got into bed and talked things through.

He didn't take long and was back in the bedroom barely ten minutes later. Linda was already in bed. She was sitting up, wearing a T-shirt, and waiting for him. Since he didn't have any clean clothes with him, he dropped the towel and slipped under the covers. Jack put an arm around her, and then they slid down until they were both lying in the bed. He felt her sink into him as she sighed deeply.

"I love you," he murmured into her hair.

"I love you too."

"I didn't mean to lose my temper like that."

"It's okay. You didn't do anything wrong. We were both pretty pissed."

Just as he was about to ask what happened now, his phone beeped.

"What the hell?"

"Oh, I forgot to tell you. It started beeping about five minutes after you turned it back on."

Jack reached over to his phone and pressed a button. He had fourteen missed calls. All but one of them were from Linda. "You called me thirteen times?" he asked, somewhere between amused at her tenacity and appalled that he had worried her enough that she'd called him repeatedly.

"You weren't answering," she mumbled in explanation, as if he needed one.

"I'm sorry, baby," he said, dropping a kiss on her head.

He also had a voice mail.

"Did you leave me a message?"

"No, I figured you'd call eventually."

"Huh."

Jack called his voice mail and punched in his password. If he didn't check the message, his phone would beep all damned night. He thumbed through the choices and heard a man's voice he didn't recognize.

"Hello, Jack? This is Billy Bishop…"

The message went on for less than a minute, and then a stunned Jack pressed the end button and placed his phone back on the bedside table with an unsteady hand.

"Who was it?" Linda asked, her voice soft from fatigue.

"It was an agent," he said, his voice sounding far away and distant to his ears. "He wants me to send him a demo."

23
The Other Shoe

The following weeks after Billy Bishop contacted Jack were hectic, to say the least. He'd never formally recorded any of his music before, only played it for his own pleasure and more recently in public. When he'd called the talent agent back to let him know he didn't have a demo prepared, the man hadn't been fazed at all. He merely invited Jack to his office in Philadelphia for an impromptu meeting and to hear him play. If he liked what he heard, he'd have a studio rented out to record a handful of songs so he could get it to some labels and see what happened.

When Jack asked how Mr. Bishop had found him, the man told him he'd read the article in the Baltimore Daily. Since Ryan Christie was well known in the industry, and his opinion was respected, he had contacted the bar that hosted the open mic nights for Jack's contact information. It had been as simple as that. Always on the hunt for new talent, he figured he'd give Jack a shot. The whole thing kind of boggled Jack's mind.

Linda had come with him to Philadelphia because she'd told him she worried he'd lose his nerve unless he had a reason to go. She sat quietly on one of the plush sofas in the office as Jack got ready to sing. The only way he managed to get through it was to forget about everyone else in the room and focus solely on Linda. He sang to her, and for her, as she smiled at him sweetly. When he was done, a discreet cough pulled his attention from the woman who had become his sole focus.

"That was great, Jack," Billy said, nodding his head slowly. "Let's book you some studio time."

After a lengthy discussion about his goals, potential career path, and musical interests, that had been pretty much all it took. The company Mr. Bishop worked for had a few well-known artists under their belt, and he was pretty confident he could get some of the recording companies to listen to the demo. At this point in time, Jack wasn't about to be picky. This could be his chance to actually make a career out of his music. It was a humbling thought—and a scary one as well. If it hadn't been for Linda's support, he wasn't sure he would have gone through with it.

Jack booked two weeks of vacation so he could stay in Philadelphia to record some hand-picked songs out of his repertoire. Amanda and Matt were going to pick up his slack while he was gone, and Linda would join him on the weekend. Because of the nature of her job, it was more difficult for her to take time off. He had wanted her to work from his hotel room and submit all of her articles remotely, but she seemed hesitant to do that. Jack didn't want to push. The relationship was still new, and they hadn't really had a chance to get past their first big argument when this whole "being contacted by a talent agent" thing happened.

After Jack had told her about the voice mail, their disagreement had been pretty much pushed aside, eclipsed by this new development. In a way, the timing was perfect because now Jack was going to be so busy, he wouldn't have time to sit around and freak out about Linda seeing her ex's mom in the hospital. He still wasn't happy about it, but they'd made a compromise. Linda agreed to go to the hospital with Eliza keeping her company. It wasn't the best solution, in his mind, but it was better than nothing at all.

He missed Linda terribly the days they weren't together. Busy as he was during the day, she still crossed his mind constantly, especially because one of the songs he was recording had been inspired by her. Each time he sang the words, she would come vividly to mind. Jack tried not getting too distracted or too miserable because he knew that would affect the quality of his music. He just kept reminding himself that he'd be speaking to her soon and seeing her once the weekend arrived. That usually got him through the rough patches.

Linda had switched her schedule around at work so that she went to Baltimore Friday morning instead of Saturday afternoon, and then she was just going to drive straight to Philadelphia from there. Jack had only booked a morning studio session so that way he'd be at the hotel when she arrived. He was twitchy and excited. This had been the longest he'd ever gone without seeing Linda since they had first met. Even though it had only been four days, it felt like an eternity since he'd touched her, especially since they'd spent time together in some capacity almost every single day since they had become a couple nearly five months ago.

Unable to wait in his room, he wandered down to the lobby and paced near the doors, awaiting her arrival. Linda had texted him a half hour previously to let him know she'd made a stop for gas and was just outside the city limits. Since the hotel was in the heart of downtown, close to the studio, he figured she should be arriving soon, even if traffic was a bit heavy. Sure enough, not five minutes later, he saw her coming through the doors of the hotel. Jack had reached Linda in barely five strides and pulled her into a bone-crushing hug.

"I missed you," he said softly into her hair.

"I can see that," she replied in a breathless chuckle. Reluctantly, Jack slackened his hold so Linda could breathe again. When she pulled away, she looked up at him and placed a hand against his cheek. "I missed you, too. So much."

"Take the week off," he asked in as non-whiny a voice as possible. "Stay with me here."

"I can't, Jack," she said with a sigh. "We've been over this already. If everything hadn't been so last minute, I could have gotten some standard articles together—"

"I know," he said in a resigned voice, cutting her off. "I just hate thinking about being without you for another four days while I wrap up here."

"Well, you have me for three days straight before that happens," she replied with a tender smile. "Let's just enjoy them, and you'll be home before you know it."

That first night, they stayed in, ordered room service, and redis-covered one another. Having Linda back in his arms took a lot of the edge off. Jack hadn't realized just how tightly he'd been wound until he felt himself relax in her presence. His sense of balance seemed to be restored again, and he couldn't wait until he was back home with her full-time.

Despite the fact Linda lived less than two hours away from Philadelphia, she hadn't been to the city in ages. Since Jack had moved here only eight months previously, he'd never really had a chance to visit at all. In a way, he was happy Linda wasn't very familiar with the city because that enabled them to tool around and do silly, touristy things and enjoy their time together.

Linda ran the show and told him where to drive. They spent their days walking around in the late autumn air, holding hands and bantering back and forth. The nights were spent at the hotel. While everything seemed the same, Jack couldn't help but feel like there was a sort of undercurrent to their relationship, something that hadn't been there before.

Jack mostly chalked it up to all the sudden changes that had happened between them in such a short time as well as the distance between them while he was in Philadelphia. He debated whether he should bring it up but was hesitant. They only had a short amount of time together, and he didn't want to ruin it. He figured if it was something really important, Linda would tell him about it. Or if worse came to worst and the feeling persisted when he returned to Arnold, he would ask if something was wrong. Sometimes she wasn't the most forthcoming, but Jack knew if he asked and gave her time to gear up, Linda would eventually let him know if something was bothering her.

Sunday came too soon, and before he knew it, he was standing by Linda's car saying good-bye for another four excruciating days. Jack held her tight and resisted begging her once more to stay for the week. She had already made up her mind, and he knew how stubborn she could be. "Yes, Master" only got him so far, and he knew her boundaries by now.

"Call me as soon as you get home," he told her in as strong a voice as he could muster.

"I will."

"I hate that you're driving at night by yourself. Are you sure you don't want to stay tonight and just go straight to Baltimore tomorrow morning?"

Jack was using his most persuasive tone while kissing along Linda's jaw. He was playing dirty, and he knew it, but if he couldn't get her to stay the week with him, at least he could ask for one more night. He was desperate enough to beg and felt victory just around the corner as her hands clutched his waist and her body leaned closer to his.

"Jack…" she sighed.

"Just one more night," he whispered in her ear before nipping the lobe with his lips. "I miss you so much while you're gone. Stay with me."

With a small whimper, she took his face in her hands and kissed him gently. Linda's fingers caressed his cheeks and jaw and then ran along his chin. He was preparing himself for the inevitable no.

"Yes, one more night," she murmured against his lips.

Crushing her to his chest, he kissed her with everything he had, making her smile against his lips when he finally slowed down. Not wanting to wait for her to think about it too hard and change her mind, Jack grabbed her bag, wrapped an arm around her waist, and all but sprinted to the elevators leading back into the hotel from the underground garage.

"Jack!" she laughed shrilly. "I'm going to fall!"

"You won't fall. Promise." When they got into the elevator, he pressed her against the wall with his body. "I told you, I'll never let you fall."

"I know," Linda said before pulling his face to hers. After a gentle kiss, she pushed her face into his chest as she clutched him tightly.

"Linda, what's wrong?"

She merely shook her head quickly and held him even closer, as if she were trying to burrow directly into his body. Jack cradled her to him tightly and ran a hand down the length of her hair. Now she was starting to worry him. He'd thought she was handling this short separation much better than he was, but maybe he was wrong. Maybe it had been harder on her than she'd let on and she had just been trying to be strong.

Jack felt wetness seep through his shirt, and now his panic was about to go nuclear.

"Linda? Baby! Why are you crying?"

She still wouldn't speak, but by then they had reached his floor. Once they were in the room, he led Linda to the armchair in the corner, sat down, and pulled her onto his lap. She hugged him tightly again, her shoulders shaking occasionally while he rubbed her back and made soothing noises.

"Linda?" he asked once she had quieted down. "Please tell me what's wrong."

"I miss you," she whispered. "I'm going to miss you so much."

"I know, baby. I missed you too. But I'm going to be home again before you know it."

Linda took a deep breath and let it out slowly.

"And now that you're staying tonight, it'll go by even faster," Jack said softly. His hand came up to cradle her face, and he used his thumb to wipe away a lingering tear. Then he tipped her face up and smiled lovingly when she looked at him. Her eyes were red-rimmed, and her nose was pink-tipped, but she was still beautiful. Beautiful, but sad. "Linda, is everything okay?"

"I just…We never really got to get over anything," she answered and then frowned. "We had that fight, and then the agent called, and then next thing you know, you're here recording a demo, and things seem to be rushing forward, and…I'm just feeling a little overwhelmed."

"That makes two of us," he mumbled, making her smile tremulously. "I don't know what I'm doing, Linda. None of it. This is exciting and scary, and I expect it to end any second. The only thing that's keeping me going is you."

"Jack…"

"It's true. I need you. Without you, all this means shit."

"I think you'd survive," Linda said softly, reaching up to caress his face. "You'd be fine."

"No way," he answered. "You make me want to be better. I want to be better for you."

"You're perfect just like this."

Leaning forward, she placed her lips against his. The kiss deepened, and her tongue was brushing against his sensuously. Linda's arms went around his neck as she pressed her upper body against his chest. One of her hands found its way into his hair, and she gripped it tightly.

"Love me, Jack," she said against his mouth. "Make love to me."

He nodded before slipping his arm under her knees and standing. They continued to kiss as he made his way to the bed. Even though he suspected Linda was trying to avoid what was really going on, Jack could never refuse her. He allowed her to brush everything under the rug, and it would be one of his greatest regrets.

Linda stayed awake long after Jack had gone to sleep. She knew she was going to be a wreck come morning, but she couldn't shut her brain off. She snuggled closer to Jack, desperate for the feel of his body against hers, wondering how much longer she'd be able to enjoy it.

Because of her, Jack's dreams of becoming a recognized musician were going to come true. She had no doubt that a record label would sign him, and then it was just a matter of time before the rest of the country discovered him. Maybe even the rest of the world. While she'd never regret the part she'd played in this, she had come to the realization that this would most likely end their relationship.

Jack would go off and leave Linda on her own in her sleepy little town as he pursued his career. While he was out there, he was bound to meet women who were more his speed. Younger, thinner, more beautiful. Perhaps even a celebrity to parade on his arm and to keep his bed warm at night. The thought brought back the sting of tears. She'd almost admitted to Jack why she'd been crying before, hoping for some solace. Linda was certain he would give it to her, but she knew, even if he didn't, that it would end up being a lie. Promises made only to be broken.

Really, what did she have to offer Jack? He was already better than she thought she deserved. Now add famous to that list? Her luck just wasn't that good. Maybe she was putting too much stock in this, but she was certain his career would take off, and she didn't want to be the one to hold him back.

Originally, she'd thought maybe if she continued to work on herself, she'd be worthy. Matt had taken her on as a part-time client while Jack recorded his demo, and she thought this would be a way to jumpstart her weight loss plans again. Unfortunately, she seemed to be on a plateau, and she hadn't lost much at all in the last month. Only a few pounds, which was unacceptable. Maybe with Matt as her personal trainer, she could change her usual regimen and finally lose those last twenty-two pounds and reach her goal. Maybe if she hit her goal weight, she'd have a chance of keeping Jack around.

Much to Linda's frustration, Matt had echoed Jack's sentiment that she looked "great" and didn't really need to lose more weight. He had some different ideas on how to tone her problem areas, but he thought the regimen she was on now with Jack seemed fine to him. Linda had almost burst into tears. Seeing this, he had agreed to help her. It was a short-term solution because Jack would be back in two weeks, but she'd worry about that later.

The new workout routine was seemingly working: after the first week, she was now twenty pounds shy of her goal. Since that was the most weight she'd lost in one week for a long time, Linda was ecstatic. Hopefully the second week would net the same results. Even still, it would take her at least three months before she'd hit her goal weight. Would she be in time? Would it be enough? She started to think no, it wouldn't be. And that brought her back full circle.

So, for now, she would just enjoy whatever time she had left with Jack until the realization hit that he could do better.

Eventually, Linda fell asleep. The next morning came too soon, and she put on a brave face. Jack was already suspicious, but she'd managed to buy herself some time. She wasn't quite sure how she'd continue to keep her fears to herself once he came back to Arnold. As they said their good-byes, there was another fleeting moment where she wanted to break down and tell him everything, but once again she stayed quiet. He was still in the middle of recording his demo, and she didn't want him to be distracted. Linda decided to play it by ear. If it killed her to keep this all inside, maybe she'd talk to Jack about it after all.

Leaving Jack was harder than she imagined it would be. Luckily, she was expected at the office that morning; otherwise, she might not have had the strength to leave. Usually, Linda worked Tuesdays, Thursdays, and Saturdays, but she'd had to shift everything around to accommodate her weekend away. When she was done, she headed back to Arnold just in time for her appointment with Matt.

"Hey, Linda!" he said, greeting her warmly.

"Hey, Matt."

"How's Jack doing?" he asked, nodding his head slyly and giving her a knowing look.

"Wonderful, as usual," she sighed. "Maybe a little homesick."

"I'd be homesick too, leaving a fine woman like yourself."

Linda rolled her eyes at his silliness. She'd been right. Matt was a natural-born flirt, but he was like a big playful teddy bear, so you could never get annoyed with him. She enjoyed her sessions with Matt. He was always fun to be around, but she still missed Jack and his way of doing things, even if they weren't quite in line with Linda's goals anymore. Even still, she thought it might be a good idea to switch to Matt full-time. Jack was going to be busy with other things, and she figured it might be better—easier—to find a replacement for him now. She wasn't quite sure how Jack would handle it, but maybe she could make him see this was the best way to go.

The next couple of days went by slowly, but Wednesday night brought some good news. Jack had wrapped up his demo and would be home the next day. He'd stayed in the studio late every night since she'd left so he could get everything finished and make it home early. He'd wanted to get in his car and drive straight to Arnold, but it was already late, and Linda didn't want him falling asleep at the wheel. She'd barely managed to convince him to stay one more night in Philadelphia.

That night, Linda had a hard time sleeping, partly because Jack was coming home and she was excited and partly because she was also nervous. Now they waited to see what would happen with regard to Jack's career. If the executives at the studios liked Jack's demo, they could potentially head into contractual talks, and then it was only a matter of time before Jack was in Philly full-time as he recorded his first album.

They hadn't had a chance to talk about what would happen at that point. Linda had tried to bring it up a few times, but Jack hadn't wanted to talk about it yet. He said they'd cross that bridge if they ever got to it. Linda knew that he was nervous about the whole endeavor and either didn't think it would actually happen or didn't want to jinx himself. He wasn't superstitious by nature, but she knew there were a few things for which he made an exception. His music was one of them.

Linda had called in to the office and made arrangements to go in Thursday morning while Jack was on his way back to Arnold. She would drive straight to his place so they could spend the afternoon and evening together to kick off their weekend. Of course, the time went by insanely slowly while she was in her meeting and while driving home, but eventually, she made it to Jack's house.

He was bounding down the steps as soon as she pulled in, most likely having heard her car when she turned into the driveway. Linda barely had a chance to get out of her seat before Jack had her in his arms, hugging tightly. She closed her eyes and breathed in his scent, getting lost in the sheer size of him wrapped around her. His body was firm and warm, and he smelled like heaven.

After a few moments, Linda came to enough to realize he was standing out in the chill in just a T-shirt and warm-up pants. She wouldn't have been surprised if he was barefoot as well. Looking down, she was relieved to see he was wearing running shoes at least.

"Come on. You must be cold," Linda said, pulling away reluctantly and smiling at Jack. He beamed back at her.

They made their way to the house and straight back to his room. Jack sat down on the bed and pulled Linda onto his lap. He kissed her sweetly and slowly before pulling back and grinning at her again.

"Guess what," he said, his eyes lit with excitement.

"What?"

"Billy already shopped my first two recorded songs to a couple studios, and he says there may be some interest."

"Oh my God. Really?"

"Yeah. They want to wait till they hear the last two songs before making any final decisions, but he said they were really impressed with what they heard so far."

"That is fabulous, Jack." Linda hugged him tightly. "I'm so proud of you," she managed to choke out. And she meant that with all of her heart, even as it was breaking. It looked like her time with him would be shorter than she expected. How much longer? She didn't want to guess.

"We'll see what happens. They might completely hate the two songs I recorded this week," he said, smiling in a self-deprecating manner.

"I sincerely doubt that," she replied and laid a hand against his cheek before chuckling nervously. "Well, I guess that makes this next part easier."

"What?"

"Well, you know I've been working with Matt while you were gone?"

"Yeah."

"I think it might be better if maybe I just keep doing that," she said softly. She had been looking down at her lap when she said it, unable to meet his eyes. Jack stilled immediately but didn't say anything. When she looked up at him, he had a peculiar expression on his face.

"Why would you do that?" he asked after a few seconds of silence. His voice was low and controlled.

"Well, things are going to get busy for you soon, and it would probably just be easier to do this now."

"Busy? Linda, nothing is going to happen right away. Billy's going to want to expose me to as many labels as he can and see if he can start a bidding war. Then if someone wants to sign, he's going to need to go to bat for me to get me the best deal possible. I'm also going to need to find a contract lawyer to make sure I'm not getting ripped off. Anyway, it'll probably be months before I have to make any hard and fast decisions. In the meantime, it's not like I can quit the gym. I'm still going to be there." Jack paused before asking, "What's this really about, Linda?"

"It's about finally reaching my goal," she said, struggling to get off Jack's lap. "I've been stagnant for the last month, and I want to get back on track."

"How many times do I have to tell you? Seventy pounds is too much to lose."

"It's not!" she bristled. "I was at that weight before, and I can get there again."

"When, Linda? In high school? You're not fifteen anymore. It's ridiculous for you to want to look like that again. You're a woman with breasts and hips and curves—"

"According to the BMI, my target weight starts at one-fifteen—"

"The BMI is bullshit!" Jack said angrily. Now he stood as well. "According to the BMI, at six-foot-two and two-twenty, I'm overweight." He gestured to his body. "Do I look overweight to you?"

"Well...no."

"It's just a tool. That's why it's on a sliding scale, because no one carries weight the same way. It doesn't really take muscle mass into consideration. The reason why you haven't lost weight, Linda, is because you're replacing fat with muscle, and muscle mass is *heavier* than fat."

"Does this look like muscle to you?" she asked, grabbing at the roll of fat that made up her belly. "I still need to lose weight!"

"Damn it! Why? So what? You have a little extra around the middle. I love the way you look."

"Because I do!"

"Tell me why!"

"*Because that's when he said I looked my best!*" Linda screamed. Jack's head rocked back as if she'd physically slapped him. Her eyes went wide, and she clapped a hand over her mouth.

"This is about your ex," he said quietly, his face crumpling in defeat. "All the times I've told you how beautiful you are, how incredible you look, how much I love your body, and how much you turn me on…That's still not enough? One thing *he* says overrides everything I've ever told you?"

"Jack—"

"No," he said, putting up a hand and shaking his head. "I can't do this anymore. I thought I was enough, that I could be *enough*. But I'm not. I'm never going to be enough." He walked over to his bed and sat on it heavily, his hands going to his hair.

"What are you saying?" she whispered.

Jack looked up at her. The expression on his face tore her apart. He looked like he was in physical pain. He turned away and pulled out the drawer of his bedside table, reaching inside. Pulling out a flat white rectangle, he held it in his hands for a moment, as if considering something. Finally, he looked up and held his hand out, offering it to her.

"What is this?" Linda asked, reaching for it. It was a business card with a doctor's name and number on it. She looked at him, dread coiling deep in her gut. "What is this, Jack?"

"I think you need help, Linda," he said quietly. "Professional help."

"What?" She barked out a laugh. "Why?"

"Because I think you're one step away from an eating disorder."

"That's insane! It's not like I'm throwing up my dinner."

"Yet." Jack stared at her levelly, and it made her want to scream at him. "How long's it going to be till you are? You need to talk to someone, Linda. You need to talk about what your husband did to you. How he treated you. You need to do this before you start hurting yourself."

"I can't believe this," she said, shaking her head. And then something occurred to her. "Wait a second. Where did you get this card?"

Jack hesitated for a second before speaking. "Your doctor gave it to me. He recommended this doctor in particular. She deals with cases like this all the time."

"You told my doctor about this?" she whispered in mortification.

"I was *worried* about you," he replied, and she could hear the desperation in his voice. "When you started to plateau, I could tell how upset you were about it, and I went to talk to him. I didn't have any choice, Linda."

"You *did* have a choice," she said loudly, tears gathering in her eyes. "You could have come to *me!*"

"I was going to. You have to believe me. But then all this stuff started happening, and I didn't get a chance to."

"How could you go behind my back like that? You're supposed to be on my side!"

"I am on your side. I've only ever been on your side, but I can only help you so much. And it's not working."

They stared at one another, and Linda felt the tears beginning to fall unbridled. This was more than she could take right now. She'd been strung tight for the last few weeks, and she'd reached her breaking point. Jack had, in a way, betrayed her, and she would have never expected something like this from him. She felt as if she was being suffocated and had to leave.

"I'm going to go home," she choked out.

"Linda," Jack said, shooting up from the bed and reaching for her. "Please don't leave. We have to talk about this."

"I can't," she answered, shaking her head. "I can't right now. I just need to be alone for a bit."

She was backing up toward the door, and he was advancing on her.

"Please, baby. Don't leave like this," he begged, reaching out for her wrist. She whipped it away from him.

"I'll call you later," Linda whispered, then turned and ran down the hall.

She thought Jack would come after her, but he didn't. She made it out of the house and into her car with no interference. Linda took a moment to wipe off her cheeks before starting the car and taking off for home. The whole way there, her mind was reeling. Jack thought she had an eating disorder because she wanted to lose weight so she could look good enough to be with him. It was almost laughable.

Too distraught to be paying attention, Linda didn't notice the SUV parked in front of her house. When she walked in the living room of her home, she jumped in surprise, a scream caught in her throat.

"I'm sorry I scared you," Graham said from her sofa. "I still had my key. When you weren't home, I let myself in."

"What are you doing here?" she asked once she'd found her voice again.

He held up a large manila envelope and smiled tightly. "Your copy of the divorce papers came to the condo."

"Oh. I could have picked them up in Baltimore, you know."

"I know," he said quietly. He remained silent for a few moments before speaking again in the same low monotone. "I've been sitting here for almost an hour. Sitting here, remembering. Everything."

"Look, Graham, this isn't—" she began, thinking this was the last thing she wanted to be dealing with right now. The words died as she looked at Graham's face.

"My mom died this morning, Lin."

"Oh my God…"

"And I was sitting here thinking about all the bad shit that happened between us," he continued in that curiously dead voice. "I fucked up so bad, Lin. I shamed her…My mom. I shamed her by the way I treated you. And I shamed you."

"Graham—"

"I have to make it up to you," he said, nodding his head slowly before getting up and walking toward her.

Linda noticed there were tears in his eyes as well as tracks that ran down his cheeks. She'd never seen Graham cry before in all the twenty years they had been together. Before she could think to stop him, he had wrapped his arms around her shoulders tightly. Bending his head, he put it in the crook of her neck and began to sob.

"I'm so sorry, Lin," he said in a choked voice. "I promise I'll make it up to you if you give me a chance."

Graham kept repeating this over and over, but Linda didn't really hear him. She just kept thinking about Jack and the arguments they'd been having lately. Over Graham's begging and pleading, a litany of phrases went through her mind.

I can't do this anymore…I've never been in a long-term relationship before…I always figured if things were bad, you got out…I think my longest relationship was six or seven months…I never really found anyone I wanted to be serious with… Things never really worked out…I can't do this anymore…

As everything Jack ever said to her cycled and picked up speed, one more phrase joined its ranks.

It sucks when the excitement wears off and they realize they can do better…

Linda went numb inside as her arms came up and she embraced Graham.

24
Hitting Rock Bottom

When Linda ran out of his room, Jack was about to rush after her. He wanted to stop her, hold her, make her listen to him. Wanted to tell her that he had only talked to the doctor about her situation because he was scared. Jack had seen the growing desperation in her, and he started recognizing red flags. His intention had been to talk to Linda about everything before springing the whole "you need to see a shrink" convo on her, but her revelation had forced his hand.

Jack had wanted to run after her, but he didn't.

He didn't do it, because he knew what it was like to reach that point where you needed to distance yourself from someone. Even if it was someone you loved. In his case, he could potentially explode into rage of astronomical proportions. He knew Linda probably needed the space for different reasons, but he was going to respect her decision…for a time. If he didn't hear back from her in a couple of hours, he was going to show up at her house and camp out on her front porch until she agreed to talk to him.

In the meantime, he walked a well-worn path around his bedroom, fingers knotted in his hair, staring at the clock as it ticked down the minutes in agonizing slowness. He also berated himself for springing the therapy stuff on Linda with no warning. Jack was a strong believer in seeking help for problems of this nature. Once upon a time, he didn't feel that way, but everything had changed after his parents had died.

Disappeared, actually.

They'd gone on a camping trip just like hundreds of times before. Neither he nor Amanda had been interested in going with them, citing it to be boring. That had been the last time Jack had seen his parents alive. When they didn't return after the long weekend like they were supposed to, he waited another twenty-four hours to file missing persons reports. At first, no one took him seriously, stating his parents were adults and probably had extended their stay, but he knew better. Not only was Jack Sr. a stickler for regimented routine, he would have never stayed away from home longer without letting his kids know.

Finally, after a week of badgering the police, they had conducted a search of the area and found his parents' abandoned campsite. It had been ransacked, and they found what could only be classified as "human remains." Jack wasn't told much more than that. He didn't think he wanted to know much more than that. The case was closed as an animal attack, and his life went swiftly down the shitter.

With his parents gone and Amanda being taken away because they weren't legally considered family, Jack's existence became miserable. He was racked with guilt over not going with his parents, thinking perhaps another person could have saved one or both of them. He was next to despondent over losing his little sister as well. Left with nothing but his self-loathing and anger, he lashed out at anyone and anything.

At the time, he was still young, but tall and much leaner, which translated into getting his ass kicked. A lot. But that was fine with Jack because it was pain that he was in search of, as much pain as he could possibly bear, to try to numb out everything. And what couldn't be accomplished through pain, he had dulled with alcohol. By the time he'd been thrown in jail, he had turned into a complete and utter train wreck.

That was until Adam Cohen had come on the scene. He was the psychologist assigned to Jack's case. The first couple of sessions had been pain of a different variety. He'd been quiet and sullen and very clear about the fact that he thought shrink sessions were for pussies. Adam didn't give a shit. The man was huge, and he had grabbed Jack by the scruff of his neck and shook him around. He didn't take crap from anyone, least of all a punk-ass kid.

He'd been the one to get Jack to the gym and taught him how to channel his energy in a different way. Most of their sessions had been conducted at the local Y, where Jack would lift weights and Adam would listen. It took a while before he started getting into the meat of his issues, but they'd come out eventually. He hadn't realized just how badly the guilt over what happened to his parents had eroded all of his self-worth. And he'd finally come to realize that his anger was misplaced because it wasn't his fault. It had taken a long time for him to come to that realization.

Suffice it to say Jack was now a strong believer in therapy.

Now if only he could get Linda to understand that needing to talk to an impartial person about something that affected your life so profoundly was nothing to be ashamed of. And sometimes you needed a person who had no biases to listen to you and help you work things out. That's all he wanted. He wished he could be that person, but every time she talked about her ex, Jack wanted to find Graham and skin him alive, then pour vinegar over all his exposed nerve endings. Unfortunately, torturing the man wouldn't solve Linda's issues.

Jack looked at the clock. More than an hour had passed with no word from Linda. Remembering how she had chased after him when he'd been the one to take off in the middle of an argument, he decided to wait a little bit longer before tracking her down. He only hoped she hadn't regressed and was sitting at home drowning her sorrows in sweets. Jack wouldn't really mind if she did, but he knew Linda would beat herself up for that moment of weakness, and he didn't want that happening. Before he went over, he figured he should give her a call and maybe see if she was ready to talk.

Linda's phone rang repeatedly until it went to voice mail. He left a short message and then resumed his pacing. Every once in a while he'd redial, but it always dumped into voice mail. Jack wasn't sure if she was avoiding his calls or if her phone was in her purse and she couldn't hear it. He hoped it was the latter.

More time passed, and Jack cursed to himself. Time was up. He was going to find Linda.

Studiously ignoring her buzzing phone, Linda sat on her couch and wondered what the hell she was going to do about her not-quite-ex-husband. They still needed to sign the divorce papers before it was considered final. So, she simply stared at him. Graham seemed like a shell of a man right now. The death of his mother had broken him completely, and even though he didn't deserve it, she felt sympathy for him.

This brought back memories of when she'd lost her own parents and how torn up she'd been about it. Graham had still been a doting boyfriend at the time, and he'd helped her through her own grief and loss. He and his mother had served as her backbone for a while when she was too weak and decimated to be strong herself. And now here was Graham, going through the same sort of heartache and loss. She never really thought they'd come full circle this way.

Her mind shied away from thinking of Jack. To go there hurt too much. Despite her heart's clamoring that in order to be truly happy she must stay with him, her mind sang a different tune. It continued to repeat things Jack had said about previous relationships on a continuous loop. Added to that was the uncertainty of a future with him should his career take off. Even if her heart wanted Jack to remain hers forever, the smarter part of her understood that would be, most likely, impossible.

The smarter part also realized that she would lose her mind if she had to wait for everything to go to pot. All she could see in their future were more bitter arguments, a gradual distance growing between them right before a definitive break. It certainly wouldn't take years for that to happen, like it had with her marriage. Perhaps a few scant months? There was no way she could live like that.

With a heavy heart, Linda knew what she had to do. The only thing she could do, really. She had to let Jack go. He had to have a chance to live his life the way he was supposed to, not being tied down to someone who was too old and too plain and most likely could never give him what he really wanted and needed out of life. Their relationship was a novelty for now, but once that novelty wore off, Linda would be left behind in the dust. Better to be the one to leave, she supposed.

Sometime after, while Graham still sat there in a coma-like state, Linda walked upstairs to her bedroom. In a bit of a trance herself, she walked over to her dresser and picked up the frame with the pictures of her and Jack. Tears tracked down her face as she traced their features and remembered the night he'd taken the photographs. He'd shown her the other pictures he'd taken, and even though he was an amateur, even she could see the artistic detail in the curves of her body and how he'd made sure to catch her most flattering poses and expressions. In those photos, she could almost see why he called her beautiful.

Not bearing to throw the pictures away, she tucked the frame carefully in her underwear drawer. That way, if she ever needed a reminder of happier days, she had one. Linda knew that Graham wouldn't come near this particular drawer to save his life.

Carefully, she sat down on the bed and considered his proposal. He seemed properly chastened and very unlike the man she'd shared her life with over the last few years. Then again, he was in mourning and seemingly in shock. Who knew what man she'd find when that finally wore off? She'd agreed to help him bury his mother but had made no promises other than that.

Linda had also agreed to go back to Baltimore with Graham in order to help him with last-minute arrangements. Until then, she would have to figure out a way to tell Jack she'd be gone for a while. Maybe she'd tell him she just needed some space. Linda really had no clue what she was going to do. All she knew was that it felt as if her world was crumbling down around her.

As she was trying to figure everything out, there was the noise of a car pulling up in the driveway. She scrambled up off the bed, a feeling of dread squeezing at her chest. She took a brief look outside just to confirm her suspicions. One glance at the Honda parked in her driveway had her running out of her room in a panic. She heard the characteristic two knocks before the creak of the door opening. Her steps were thunderous in her ears as she flew around the balustrade and started down the stairs.

"No, no, no…" she moaned quietly to herself as the scene below her unfolded.

Jack was rooted to the spot, staring into the living room at what she presumed was Graham. His lips had peeled back from his teeth in a gruesome expression, a look of pure black hatred marring his usual good looks.

Jack turned toward her, the look of hatred now morphed into one of confusion. "Linda? What the fuck is this asshole doing in your house?" What he didn't say, but was perfectly plain to see on his face, was that the answer had better be good or else there would be bloodshed tonight.

"Didn't she tell you yet?" came Graham's mocking voice from the living room just before he came out into the hallway. "Linda's taking me back."

"Bullshit," Jack spat out, his fingers curling as his hands cranked into fists at his sides.

Linda had finally reached the bottom of the stairs, and she ran between the two men. She placed a hand on Jack's chest; her automatic impulse was to rub soothing circles against it to calm him like she'd always done, but she stopped herself.

"Please go in the kitchen," she asked Graham quietly. When he didn't seem inclined to move, she gave him a stern look. "*Please.*"

Grumbling and shooting Jack a baleful glance over his shoulder, Graham went down the hall into the kitchen. Linda focused on Jack's face as he shot daggers at Graham's back the entire way. Then he turned back to Linda with a thunderous look on his face.

"What is he doing here, Linda?" he said in an ominous undertone.

"He came over to drop off the divorce papers."

"Oh," he replied, his expression relaxing somewhat. "Do you need me to kick him out now?"

"No. Do you mind if we step outside for a minute?"

Jack frowned but nodded his head and went toward the door. Linda put on a pair of shoes and her jacket; her stomach was doing sickening backflips at the impending conversation. While her entire being revolted at the idea of even *saying* she was choosing Graham over Jack, she knew it was her only way of ending things. A declarative break.

Linda didn't want to do it, but she saw no other way. Jack deserved to be free and not saddled with the likes of her. She didn't want him to have to feel guilty or keep her around because he was too nice to hurt her. Better she take the hit for them both. It would hurt him for a little while now, but Jack was young and beautiful and talented, and he would replace her easily. He'd realize that soon enough.

When they were outside with the door closed behind them, Jack stared at her, his face a mask of confusion. Linda crossed her arms over her chest, trying to hold herself together.

"Linda, what the hell is going on? What's that fool talking about?"

"Graham was here when I got home. He still had his key."

"I'll make sure to remedy that once we go back inside," Jack growled. "And tomorrow we're changing your locks in case he's made a spare."

"That's not necessary," Linda replied in a low voice.

"Why not?"

"Jack, Graham and I have been talking." She choked on her next words. "I made a mistake."

"By letting him inside?"

"No."

"Linda, I don't know what you're saying."

"We're going to give it another try."

Jack stood there and blinked for a moment. She could see how he was trying to process her impossible words. Even she didn't believe herself, so how the hell would he?

"Is this some kind of sick joke?" he asked, his brow furrowed.

"No. It's not a joke."

"Linda, we had a stupid fight. That's all. You're telling me you're going to go back to him because of *that?*"

"That's not why," Linda lied, trying to keep her emotions locked down. It was proving to be increasingly more difficult. "You were right; this all had to do with Graham. I didn't realize it until today."

"What? You can't be serious."

Linda felt tears prickling, and she knew if she didn't get away from Jack this instant, she would break down completely and be reduced to nothing.

"I am. I thought I was over him, but I'm not."

"Please," Jack begged quietly. "Don't do this. Don't take him back because you're mad at me."

"That's not what I'm doing," she whispered, knowing full well that was the only honest thing she'd said in the last five minutes.

"Linda." He reached out to touch her, but she stepped away, keeping her balled hands under her armpits. "Look, I'm sorry about the therapist, okay? I take it back. You don't need to see anyone. We'll work through this together."

His last attempt to sway her pierced her heart. This was what pain felt like. Her chest had turned into a cinderblock, and she couldn't breathe. The look on Jack's face was tearing her apart from the inside out. Linda's knees were threatening to buckle from the strain, but she held fast to the idea she was doing the right thing for him. He would see and understand. Maybe not now, but soon.

"I'm sorry, Jack," she replied softly before grasping the handle of her front door, opening it, and slipping inside. She closed the door on his stunned face.

As Linda ran toward the stairs, she heard Graham step out of the kitchen behind her.

"Is he gone?"

"Yes," she answered, trying to keep from sobbing. "He's gone."

"Good."

Without replying, Linda continued up the stairs and shut herself in the bathroom, locking the door behind her. She wrenched the knobs of the shower full throttle and then collapsed to the floor by the tub, trying to keep the noise to a minimum as she cried her heart out.

Jack stood on Linda's porch, unmoving. He was trying very hard to process what had just happened. Did Linda actually say good-bye to him? Was she honestly leaving him to go back to her husband? None of it seemed real. It was like some nightmare. Like every fear he'd ever had rolled into one.

As he stood there, every argument he should have made to try to make Linda see sense ran through his mind like tickertape. All the things he should have said but hadn't. He'd been so completely shocked and disbelieving, he hadn't even thought to try to dissuade her. Jack was still waiting for the punch line. For her to pop out of the door and cry out "April Fools!" even though it was the beginning of December.

Once the shock started to wear off, what Jack wanted to do was storm into Linda's house and beat the ever-living fuck out of her ex. He must have said or done something to turn Linda against him. Damned if Jack knew *what*. All he knew was that slimeball asshole must have had something to do with this.

But when that was done, then what?

Linda seemed to have made up her mind, and murdering her whatever-the-fuck he was would hardly change it. Seeing no other choice, Jack turned around and stumbled off Linda's porch. He wasn't quite sure how he got in his car, much less drove it home, but sure enough, he found himself in his driveway, staring at his house. He sat there for a little while longer. Debated driving back to Linda's and killing Graham again. Almost shoved his keys back in the ignition. Let his hand drop.

Things still felt surreal. Like he'd just imagined the whole thing. No one had ever ended a relationship with him before—not that he'd have been affected all that much if they had—and he was having a hard time coming to grips with how to handle this. Mostly because it was Linda and he was in love with her. He had absolutely no idea what the fuck he was supposed to do now. Ideas flew at him, but he discarded them all.

Seriously, what the fuck was he supposed to do now?

Very much like he had no idea how he'd gotten home, he had no real recollection of how he ended up in his house. No one was home, and the silence was oppressive, closing in on him from all sides. To make things worse, everything Linda had said began clamoring in his head to try to fill the soundless void.

Had she really left him? Had that actually happened?

Slowly, it began to dawn on him that, yes, Linda had told him good-bye. He staggered as a wave of pain assaulted him, and he found it impossible to stay upright. "Oh, God," he moaned to himself as he clutched at the arm of the couch. "This can't be happening."

The world slowly turned an insipid red.

Before he knew what he was doing, Jack had launched to his feet, gripped in a fury like he hadn't experienced in years. He was tearing down artwork from the walls, firing pictures like missiles across the room, kicking at whatever had the misfortune of landing at his feet. He was screaming, bellowing, his voice threatening to go out on him.

Just as he was about to throw the coffee table through the TV, he heard a screech from behind him. He whirled toward the voice, the table whipping out of his hands and crashing into the wall instead.

"What the fuck!" Tony yelled as he pulled Amanda out of the way barely in time.

"Get out!" Jack roared at them before stalking over to Tony and shoving him full force in the chest, driving him backward.

"Oh no. Not again," he heard Amanda moan before he turned toward her, his hands claws, ready to throw them out bodily.

The dragon had been unleashed, and there was no taming it now.

As he made a move in Amanda's direction, he was tackled from behind. "Don't even think of it," hissed Tony in his ear.

Jack managed to slip out of the tight grip and threw himself at the larger man, knocking him slightly off balance. Tony recovered quickly and shoved at him with all his might, obviously not wanting to hurt him. Jack had other plans. He ran at Tony again, trying to force his hand. Looking for pain, seeking it, *wanting* it.

"Amanda!" Tony called out. "What the fuck is wrong with him?"

"I don't know!" she cried out in a panic. "I don't know!"

"Hit me, you motherfucker!" Jack growled, shoving at Tony again before pulling back his fist and slamming it into Tony's gut. He pulled the punch at the last second, wanting Tony to fight back.

"Jesus fucking Christ," Tony huffed out and pushed Jack away from him, still restraining himself, making Jack scream in frustration.

"Amanda!" Tony yelled out once more.

"Hit him," she sobbed, sinking to her knees.

"*What?*"

"Hit me!" Jack hollered in his face and aimed a shot for Tony's head, which he ducked away from deftly.

"Oh, God," Amanda choked out behind him. "If you don't do it, he'll find someone who will."

In a desperate, last-ditch effort at getting what he wanted, Jack feinted a lunge at Amanda, knowing she was the one thing Tony would protect with his life. With his fists. Just like Jack would have done for Linda. He was assaulted with a fresh wave of grief as he thought of her.

Luckily, that heartsick stab of misery was short-lived as he was grabbed from behind and thrown into a wall. There was an inhuman growling in the room, and then he was being struck repeatedly by meaty fists. Jack didn't fight it. He allowed himself to be beaten, letting the pain of the blows replace his anguish.

Just as quickly as it started, it stopped, but it was enough. Jack vaguely heard Tony's labored breath as the room began to flicker and go dark. One of his eyes was swollen shut, the other a mere slit, but he was able to see Amanda crawl over to him, sobbing.

"Jack?" She wept as shaky hands caressed his hair. "What happened?"

"She's gone," he managed to whisper through swollen, split lips. "Linda...She's gone."

And then the world went blessedly black.

25
A Time to Cry

The first four days after Linda had left him, Jack stayed in his room. It was a good thing he wasn't expected back to work until the following Monday, because there was no way he was in any condition to be seen, much less work with clients. His face was a mess. His head was a mess. *He* was a complete and utter mess.

How easily he fell back into old behaviors. Adam would have been disgusted with him.

At least Jack had managed to get it somewhat under control after Tony had waylaid him. He'd woken in his bed the next morning, once again having no clue how he'd gotten there, and hadn't moved much since. Amanda had come in with food, but it mainly remained untouched. Every time he thought of Linda, he felt sick to his stomach. Amanda also tried to talk to him, to cheer him up, to try to distract him. Jack started locking his bedroom door.

He understood that Amanda was worried about him and was holding vigil like he had done numerous times for her, but he wasn't ready for it. So many times he wanted to leave the house and go back to Linda's. Maybe do something to make her take him back, but he had no idea what. She said she wanted to go back to Graham. Even if he had no idea why, how was he supposed to fight that?

How could he possibly be with a woman who didn't want him anymore?

At this thought, he turned on his side on the bed and curled into a ball. He was internalizing the pain and tried to fold himself around it to keep it from spiraling out of control again. It had been like this all weekend. Tomorrow was Monday, and he was expected back at work. He'd already taken all of his vacation time and couldn't afford any additional days. Apparently, life moved on, even after the woman you'd loved with everything you had tore your heart out of your chest and stomped on it but good.

Fuck, he was really sounding like Amanda right now. Who knew having someone break up with you turned you into a pussy? Learn something new every day, he supposed.

His first day back to work was a near disaster. He had no patience with his clients and their incessant questions about what had happened to his face. A few of them tried to comfort him, which was the *wrong* thing to do because he was in no mood to be trifled with. Maybe a lot of people would have tried to fuck themselves senseless with someone new, but Jack couldn't even imagine being with anyone besides Linda. That just wasn't an option.

When it came time for Linda's regularly scheduled session, Jack kept an eye on the front door. He wondered if she would come. It was doubtful she'd expect him to remain her personal trainer, but part of him wondered if maybe she'd just continue to use Matt. She was so overcome with the need to lose those last twenty pounds that it was possible she would want to continue to work out.

What would he do if she did come in? Would he be able to ignore her and go about his business? Maybe he'd just hide out in the back since he no longer had a client filling that spot…yet. Jack laughed at himself bitterly. Who was he kidding? He would probably drag her back into one of the aerobic rooms and make an utter ass of himself as he begged her to take him back.

It turned out he didn't need to worry. Linda didn't show. Not that day, nor the rest of that week.

By Sunday, Jack couldn't stand it anymore, and he found himself driving to Linda's house. He had no idea why. Nor what he would do when he got there. Deciding to be stealthy, he parked up the street and went the rest of the way on foot. The time that had been chosen was purposeful; it was when Linda usually went for her daily walk.

Stupid ideas of following her into the woods and stealing her away were pretty prevalent in his mind. Maybe he could take her somewhere and deprogram her? Even Jack realized the ridiculousness of this plan, but he was starting to get desperate. As he neared the house, he saw that even if he had been planning to act on this bit of insanity, it would have been pointless anyway. Linda's car wasn't in the driveway, and the house had an air of desertion.

Fliers were sticking out of the mailbox, and there was a small pile of newspapers at the front door. Absently, he thought Linda should have had the presence of mind to ask a neighbor to take care of that for her so that it wasn't so obvious that no one was home. He would have taken care of it for her and then remembered she was no longer his concern. She was truly gone.

Jack's shoulders slumped as the feeling of misery took over again. Usually he let the emotion have at him except when he was at work. That was really the only time when he felt slightly normal, and that was because he kept himself too busy to think of anything else. This past week had been sheer and utter hell, and he didn't know if he'd ever be really happy again. With that morbid thought, he turned and went back to his car.

Right after running up to Linda's porch and moving the newspapers so they couldn't be seen.

When he got home, he was met at the door by a stern-looking Amanda. "Where have you been?"

"Nowhere," he mumbled as he toed off his shoes and hung up his jacket. When he tried to creep past Amanda, she stepped in his way.

"You went to Linda's house, didn't you?"

Jack was struck dumb, and before he could think to deny it, he asked, "How did you know?"

"Jack," she sighed. "You have to let this go."

"What difference does it make?" he mumbled. "She wasn't there. I'm starting to wonder if something happened to her. All the newspapers were piled up on her porch, and it's really not like Linda to not have someone take care of that for her. Maybe Graham kidnapped her," he said, the idea making him frown. "Maybe he forced her to go with him. Damn it, I shouldn't have left without checking—"

"Jack," Amanda said, cutting him off. "Stop. Linda wasn't kidnapped, okay? She left for Baltimore on her own."

"How do you know that?" he asked, feeling himself deflate like a balloon.

"Tony told me," she answered softly, taking his arm and leading him to the living room. "He also saw you at Linda's house. That's how I know you were there. He was going to clear the papers off her porch."

"So, Tony's talked to her?"

"No," she answered curtly, a scowl on her face. "She left a message on his machine at home when she *knew* he was at work. Eliza did."

"Eliza went to see her?"

"Yeah. Tony told her what you said, and she went to go check for herself what the hell was going on." Amanda smiled at him sadly. "You might want to know she's Team Jack."

He smiled slightly and looked down at his hands. "Yeah, well. Doesn't matter since Linda doesn't seem to be."

"Oh, *fuck* Linda," she answered with a touch of snarl.

"Been there, done that," Jack said ruefully.

"And now it's time to move on. She made her own fucked-up decision, and she doesn't deserve you."

"Yeah, right."

He spoke the words he knew Amanda wanted to hear but had an idea it would be much more difficult than that. Losing Linda had decimated him, and it was only by sheer force of will that he was able to function. All those times that he'd told Amanda to suck it up whenever a guy had broken her heart were coming back to bite him in the ass hardcore. He was trying to shake it off like he normally did, really he was, but it wasn't working at all. Jack supposed most would argue it had only been a week and he'd need more time, but he knew himself well, and he also knew this wasn't something he'd ever truly heal from.

Jack gave Amanda a small smile, patted her leg, and got up to go to his room. He had a busy day ahead of him, licking his wounds. When he got in there, he lay down on his bed and stared at the ceiling. After a minute or two, he turned his head to look at his guitar. It was on its stand in the corner, gathering dust. He hadn't played since he got back from Philadelphia.

Billy had called a handful of times. Things were looking good as far as his demo went, and it was being seriously considered by a couple of independent labels. There had been a spark of interest with one of the more well-known ones as well. Billy was hoping if the big label didn't pick him up, he could at least get a bidding war going on between the two smaller ones and still get him a good deal. In the back of his mind, Jack knew he should care about all of this, but right now he just couldn't work up the energy to get excited.

Most of it had to do with the timing of Linda's departure, but it also had to do with the fact that none of it seemed real to him. It was like one big dream. Only he'd hoped he would be happier about it. Jack was simply waiting for the call to say that everything had been lip service and no one was interested in his music enough to sign him up for a contract.

"*People love you. Your music…it's magical,*" whispered a soft voice from the recesses of his memory. He closed his eyes against it.

Needing a distraction, Jack got off of the bed and grabbed his guitar. When he sat back down, he couldn't help cringing at how out of tune it sounded when he plucked at the strings. Luckily, guitars were relatively simple instruments, needing little to get them back into regular working order. Just a few twists of the tuning keys, and she sounded just as good as ever. Jack smiled slightly when he was done.

Hand gliding up and down the neck of the guitar, he could feel the frets under the pads of his fingers as they moved along the strings. His other hand rested along the smooth curve of the guitar's binding and then slid down the varnished wood to begin playing. At first he plucked at the strings mindlessly, not playing any song in particular, just going with the flow of notes he was creating. Jack did this sometimes; it was usually how he created his music. Sometimes a series of notes would catch his ear, and he could hear it as an opening for a song or a chorus.

After a few minutes of this, he realized he had picked out the notes of a song he hadn't heard in years. He continued along and then began singing the words quietly, almost under his breath. Jack's voice cracked slightly as he got to the chorus, and he knew this was maybe a bad song to be playing, but he didn't stop. Instead, he started singing louder as his fingers began strumming harder.

With a final cry, he threw his guitar across the room. It crashed in a series of discordant notes as Jack pulled his knees up to his chest and drove the heels of his hands against his eyes.

Jack hadn't cried in years. Not since the death of his parents. But he cried now. There was no way to staunch the tears, no matter how he tried. He wanted to man up and stop being so pathetic, but that wasn't happening.

As he sobbed, he barely heard the sound of footsteps entering his room. He felt the presence on the bed but fought against the hands reaching for him, twisting his face away, embarrassed to be seen in such a state of weakness.

"Shhh, shhh, Jack, baby," Amanda's voice soothed. She managed to tug him so that he was curled in a ball on his bed with his head in her lap. He bawled like a snot-nosed kid as she ran hands through his hair and stroked his back.

Jack thought he heard Amanda crying, too, but he fell into an exhausted stupor before he could think to check.

The next few weeks weren't much better for Jack. He didn't break down again so thoroughly, but he was still mostly listless and not very present. Amanda kept getting on his case about it, and she had started parading other women in and out of the house, hoping that one would catch his eye. Jack had to finally put his foot down and tell her to stop. He was more cruel than usual, pointing out that not everyone could get over their last love by fucking someone new.

That had shut Amanda up, but the crushed look on her face when he'd said it made him feel like a complete and utter asshole.

Jack had tried to apologize, but Amanda had just told him to fuck off and stormed away to her room. Ah, well, at least now he didn't have to worry about being accosted and then forced to make polite conversation with strange women during dinner. The last one had been Tony's plump sister Rachel. It was obvious that Amanda now thought he would prefer larger women since he'd been with Linda. She didn't quite get the concept that he'd fallen in love with Linda regardless of her size, not because of it.

Really, that had been the last straw, and judging by the look on Tony's face, he was just as relieved as Jack that he didn't have to find new women to bring around the house. Least of all his sisters. Apparently, this one had a twin who wasn't particularly happy in her marriage.

All Jack wanted was some peace and quiet to mourn. To try to come to grips with how he was feeling and figure out a way to build a bridge and get the fuck over it. It pained him to think of getting over this—most days he doubted he would—but he was human, and apparently time healed all wounds. Or so he was told. Jack had his doubts.

It was on a particularly bad night when he got up to grab a drink and heard Amanda and Tony arguing upstairs as he passed the stairwell.

"I think we should tell him," Tony said in a stern voice.

"No!" Amanda hissed at him. "Lower your voice."

"Mandy, this is ridiculous. He oughta know!"

"It's none of your fucking business, Tony. Now, keep out of it."

"I just think—"

"I said no!" she answered in exasperation. "He's doing better now. I don't want him suffering any more than he already has been."

"You don't think she's suffering? She's my friend, too, you know."

"I don't give a shit what she's feeling. She deserves it."

"Mandy," Tony begged softly now. "Come on…"

"It's none of our business," Amanda said firmly, and then he heard their bedroom door shut, drowning out the rest of the conversation.

Jack stood where he was for another few minutes straining to hear, but this house was constructed too well—except for the staircase, which creaked like a bitch. He was reminded of that as he debated creeping upstairs to see if he could figure out what the hell the two of them were talking about. Not much of a gambling man, Jack would still bet the contents of his bank account that it had something to do with Linda.

Frowning, he tried to make sense of their brief argument. What did Tony want Jack to know? And what did he mean when he'd said that Linda was suffering? Subconsciously, his hand curled into a fist when he thought of anyone making Linda hurt. Maybe that was it. Maybe her ex was making her life hell again, and Tony wanted him to do something about it. In that case, Amanda was right. It wasn't his business. When Linda had closed the door in his face, she'd made that very clear.

After going to the kitchen and getting his drink, Jack spent the rest of the night tossing and turning, thinking about Linda and worrying about her. Damn it. He wanted to be a hard-ass douchebag, but when it came to Linda, he couldn't be. Just thinking about Graham potentially abusing her again was driving him crazy. He shouldn't care. Maybe he should even be satisfied that she'd made such a horrible choice, but he didn't. There was no vindication for him. Only confusion.

Jack still had no clue why she would ever go back to her ex after some of the stories she'd told him. All Jack had ever been was loving and supportive, and yet that obviously hadn't been good enough. After a lot of introspection, he realized that there was nothing more he could have done to prove to Linda how much he loved her. If that hadn't been enough, then nothing would be. It was a hard realization to come by. It should have given him some peace, possibly some closure, but it hadn't.

The next morning, Jack was dragging ass. He'd barely slept at all and was in a terrible mood again. What little sleep he'd managed to get had been plagued by nightmares. Linda calling for him and Jack stumbling through dark hallways trying to get to her but never quite managing it. Something had always kept them separated. Well, wasn't that a perfect fucking metaphor?

So, when Tony Cross strode into the club later that afternoon and got up in Jack's face, the reception wasn't a welcome one.

"Why didn't you fight for her?" Tony spat at him, his lip curling in contempt.

Jack paused while lifting a hand weight and looked up, somewhat startled at Tony's vehemence. "Fight for who?"

"Don't play dumb. Linda."

"What the fuck are you talking about?" he answered, putting the weight down on the floor with a loud clank.

"When she told you that she was going back to Graham, why didn't you fight for her?"

"How would you know if I didn't?" Jack ground out between clenched teeth.

"Because if you had, she'd never have gone back to him!" Tony had his hands on his hips as he leaned over Jack menacingly.

In a bad mood already, Jack shot to his feet quickly, shoving his shoulder against Tony's chest and sending him stumbling back a step or two. "She'd already made her decision," he growled fiercely.

"And you just let her go," Tony shot back, recovering quickly and closing the gap. "Like a fucking pussy!"

"Back off, Tony," Jack said in a deadly voice. "Last time, I *let* you beat me. That won't happen again."

Jack saw the people in the club stop what they were doing as they tried to figure out what was going on. Suddenly, Matt was there between them. He banded an arm around Jack's chest, separating him and Tony.

"You've got an audience, fellas," he said in a conversational tone. "How 'bout you pick this up another time, eh?"

With that, he proceeded to strongarm Jack away from the weights section and into one of the aerobic rooms. Jack pulled away from Matt as soon as they entered, and he paced around like a horse in a stall. Tony came barreling in right on their heels, and Matt turned toward him, spreading out his arms.

"Dude, this is not a good idea," he told Tony in a low voice.

He didn't listen. "She told me you were smart!" Tony yelled at Jack. "She told me that she hated the fact you think you're no better than a dumb jock because there was so much more to you. Prove her right. 'Cause either you're dumb as a sack of rocks or fucking blind!"

"What are you talking about?" Jack roared, his hands balled into fists at his sides.

"She *loves* you!" Tony yelled in return. "She's still fucking in love with you."

"She made her choice."

"Bullshit, you fucking idiot! She left for your own good."

"*What?*"

"She *never* thought she was good enough for you, and now that you're going to become this famous 'rock star'"—he used air quotes—"she figured that eventually you'd realize that and leave her for someone else. So she did it first. Before *you* could."

All the strength ran out of Jack's legs, and he sat down on the floor in an uncoordinated heap of skin and bones. Tony's words pinged around in his skull, and things started to click. The man was right. Jack was dumb as a sack of rocks to have not figured any of this out, or at least suspected it. The last few weeks, he'd been in a fog, but it had made no sense whatsoever why Linda would have chosen her ex over him, unless she figured she just couldn't do better. Not long-term, anyway.

"How could she even think that?" he asked, mostly to himself. "I would never do that."

"Then prove her wrong," Tony said in a hard voice. "She's back in Arnold, in case you're wondering." He gave Jack one last withering look before turning and striding out of the room.

"He's right, you know," Matt said quietly behind him.

"What would you know about it?" Jack replied, rubbing his eyes. He sounded tired even to his own ears.

"You forget I took over your sessions with Linda while you were gone."

"Trust me, I didn't forget." Jack bristled, beginning to get annoyed again. "You're telling me you know more about Linda than I do? After spending, what? Ten hours with her?"

"Maybe not more. But probably different."

"Jesus Christ. Why can't you all stop talking in fucking riddles?"

Matt sat down beside Jack, pulling his knees up to his chest and resting his forearms on them. He stared across the large room for a moment and took some breaths. Jack figured he was taking a moment to find a way to phrase whatever he was going to say.

"The first session I had with Linda, she was worried that she hadn't dropped much, if any, weight over the last few weeks."

"What else is new?" Jack grumbled. Pain lit off in his chest as he remembered their last argument. The final one before his life ground to a sickening halt.

"No, Jack. This was different. She was, like, in a panic. Desperate. She wanted me to redo her entire regimen. I told her that wasn't necessary because she looked great —" Matt stopped speaking as Jack glared at him. "Come on, bro. It's not a lie. And I wanted to make her feel better. It was completely innocent."

"Yeah, yeah. Go on."

"Anyway, she went crazy. Started talking about not reaching her goal, and she had to hit it before it was too late. It didn't make much sense to me at the time, but after hearing what Tony just said… Well, it kind of does. Anyway, to calm her down, I told her I'd help."

"And you revamped her regimen."

"Yeah," Matt admitted quietly. "I was going to talk to you about it when you got back…"

"But then we split up, and Linda disappeared."

"Yeah."

Jack exhaled sharply before muttering, "Fuck me."

"What are you going to do now?"

"Fuck if I know."

26
Her Splintered Heart

After she'd shut the door on Jack, Linda felt like she was in a haze. She'd made a declarative break for their own good. This time, she wasn't going to wait until her man left her. She wasn't going to wait until the relationship dissolved into nothing. This way, she could always remember the good times. The best times. The times where she was truly happy. Linda could bring it out like a cherished gift to remind herself that once upon a time, she'd known real love.

That's how most fairy tales started, didn't they? With once upon a time. Unfortunately, in this case, there would be no happily ever after. Not for this prince and princess.

That night, she allowed Graham to sleep at her house. She led him up to the spare room and left him to his own devices. When she got into her room, she locked the door behind her and then collapsed into a heap on the bed. Not having the luxury of running water this time, she used her pillow instead to muffle her sobs.

What had she done? She'd taken the heart of someone she loved and crushed it for seemingly no good reason. In the dark of her room, where her sheets still faintly smelled of Jack, she couldn't remember why this seemed like the right thing to do. Instead, she clutched his pillow to her face and inhaled as much of him as she could.

Linda suddenly despised her bed because she knew eventually time would erase the scent of Jack, and then he would truly be gone. But she had no one to blame but herself.

As painful as it was, Linda knew that it would be so much worse for her if she kept investing her heart into a relationship that was eventually doomed.

There was a small voice inside her that kept insisting she should give Jack the chance to prove her wrong, but it was continuously drowned out by the louder, more sure voice that was convinced she was just bypassing the inevitable. It was the same voice that kept reminding her that she was too old and not good enough. That same voice had always overridden Jack's compliments and praise, and if she really thought about it, it sounded suspiciously like Graham.

Another heartbroken sob escaped her, and she just let go and drowned in her own tears.

The next morning, Linda sat at her kitchen table, staring off listlessly. The lack of sleep, coupled with her incessant crying jags, had drained her. Whenever she decided this was too much and that she'd go to Jack's right then to throw herself at his feet, begging for forgiveness, she remembered the look on his face when she'd lied to him. She also remembered that it didn't change anything.

When she heard movement in the doorway, Linda looked up to see her next problem standing there looking just as horrible as she felt. What in God's name was she going to do with Graham? She had made a promise that she would stand by him in this time of need, but nothing more. Linda felt that she at least owed him that much, to try being his support and someone he could lean on. They had too much history and shared grief between them for her to turn her back on him completely right now—no matter how much she wanted to.

In a way, it was almost better that things had ended with Jack, because she knew he wouldn't have stood for any of this, regardless of what she felt her obligations were. There were many people who would think she was insane for even giving Graham the time of day, but she'd loved him once, and even if he did make a bad husband, there was still a bond between them born of spending most of their lives together. It wouldn't just disappear overnight.

"Good morning," he said in a subdued voice, shuffling awkwardly.

"Coffee's on," Linda rasped. Her voice was shot from trying to keep the worst of her crying to herself.

"Thanks."

Graham knew his way around this kitchen since he'd spent enough time here, and Linda was in no mood to be subservient. *He can get his own damned coffee,* she grumbled to herself defiantly. When he was done, Graham joined her at the table. They stared at one another for a second before his eyes slid away from hers to look into his coffee cup. *God, this is awkward* was her next uncharitable thought. Nothing at all like the comfortable mornings with Jack. She closed her eyes briefly at the stab in her chest.

Graham cleared his throat, and she glanced up at him again.

"Thanks. For letting me stay last night, I mean. I'm not sure if I would have made it back to Baltimore."

"Sure."

He cleared his throat again and frowned down into the black depths of the mug. "Look, Lin. I was serious yesterday. About giving me another chance."

"Graham —"

"I know you don't trust me," he said, cutting off her protest. "And you have every right not to," he added quickly. "But all I want is a chance. Can you at least give me a chance?"

"I promised I'd help you bury your mother," Linda replied in a cold voice. "That's all I can commit to right now."

"Okay," he agreed eagerly. "That's great. It's a start, right?"

Bringing her hands up to her head, Linda pushed her fingertips against the persistent ache in her temples.

"Will you stay at the condo? It would probably be easier for you to stay in Baltimore instead of coming back and forth to Arnold."

She opened and closed her mouth a few times in succession, not knowing how to answer.

"No strings attached," Graham clarified hastily. "You can stay in the guest room. I just figured it would be easier…"

He trailed off, fiddling with the handle of his mug as she stared at him dispassionately. She watched him hunch up his shoulders under her steady gaze, and his worried frown deepened. Part of her was waiting for it. Waiting for that tone of voice that struck like the lash of a whip. She waited for the scowl or the sullen expression, but none presented themselves. Again, she couldn't help but think this was not the Graham she had become accustomed to.

"I need you, Lin," he whispered pathetically. "I'm…This is too hard to do by myself. Please…"

"I don't know," she answered, her voice wavering, as she was dangerously close to tears once more. She wasn't sure if her unstable emotions were due to the loss of Jack, the death of Mrs. Hunter, or because of this wretched creature sitting across from her. Or possibly all three. Blinking rapidly, she tried to quell the feeling. She was too emotionally raw to make any final decisions right now. Would Graham be able to sense her vulnerability and take advantage of it? Linda wasn't sure if he was in any frame of mind to do so, but she just didn't know for sure. "Let me think about it, okay?"

"Okay."

As promised, Linda helped Graham bury his mother. Horrible as it was, she was glad to have an excuse to cry in public. Some of the tears were for Mrs. Hunter, but most of them were because she missed Jack with a force she'd never expected. It felt as if someone had carved out her chest and taken her vitals with them. Trying to breathe had become a chore; she never seemed to get enough air anymore. Even her nights were hellish. She was plagued by dreams where she woke on the verge of screaming, gasping, clawing at her chest before collapsing back onto her sweat-soaked pillows in exhaustion.

Too late…she'd moan to herself. *Too late.*

Once his mother was buried, Graham continued with his dogged pursuit of her. He managed to convince her to stay the full week instead of the three days she'd originally agreed on. Linda slept in the guest room, and true to his word, he never tried any funny business. Linda still wasn't convinced. Sure, he seemed different, more caring and considerate, more patient…but she waited for the other shoe to drop. And was surprised when it did.

"What do I need to do to convince you?" he asked one night when the silence had become oppressive. "What can I say to make you see I'm serious?"

"The truth," Linda said after a moment. "I want the truth."

"About what?"

"Everything," she replied, taking in his guarded look and defensive posture. "Anything I want to know."

Graham exhaled and stared at her meditatively for a minute or so. "Fine. The truth."

"But I'm not making any promises," she said sternly.

He gave a curt nod.

"How many were there?" she asked after a moment of deliberation.

"How many what?"

"Cut the shit," Linda snapped. "How many women?"

Graham grimaced and rubbed the back of his neck in agitation.

"You promised," she whispered accusingly. "The truth. You promised."

"Five."

"All interns?"

"Not all."

"Well, I know of Vicky for sure," Linda scoffed. "Did you send her to the club to spy on me?"

"Vicky? God, no! That bitch was fucking crazy," he sputtered. "Like boil-your-fucking-bunny crazy. She about lost her mind when I ended things."

Graham shut his mouth with a snap, obviously realizing he'd shared too much. He looked at Linda uneasily now, seemingly waiting for a reply. She merely nodded her head. The expectation that this information should make some sort of sickening impact plagued her. But it didn't affect her in the least. More or less, it was just a confirmation of what she'd already suspected and known.

"Vicky told me that you refused to leave me for her," she said.

Graham nodded warily.

"So, then, why did you leave?"

"Linda...do we really need to do this?"

"Yes."

Graham leaned his forehead into his hands for a moment and then rubbed his face vigorously. The look of hesitation on his face told Linda what she needed to know. He wouldn't leave her for Vicky because the girl had been batshit crazy, but it was obvious he'd left her for *someone*.

"It was another woman, wasn't it?"

"Yes," he answered and then blew out his breath explosively.

"Do I know her?"

"No."

"Who was she?"

"Come on, Lin…"

"Just *tell* me," she ground out between clenched teeth.

"Her name was Rory. She worked for one of the firms we represented."

"So, what happened to her?"

"What does it matter?" he snapped.

She could see a little bit of the old Graham making an appearance. Linda had thought she'd be prepared for it, but she recoiled slightly all the same.

"I'm sorry," Graham said quickly as he reached a hand toward her. He stopped when she pulled back farther. "She left me. When Mom started to get sick, she said I wasn't *fun* anymore and that cancer was such a buzzkill." He laughed shortly. "So, that's that."

Yes, that's that, Linda thought. She should have been insulted, maybe even a little appalled that he'd left her for someone so callous, a woman who hadn't even any basic consideration for her lover's dying mother. Yes, she could see now why Graham had made that comment about young lovers and how easily they lost interest. It was a testament to the type of women he chose, nothing more. And now Linda couldn't help but think Jack hadn't ever fit that mold. But now it was much too late for realizations.

"What does it matter, anyway?" When she stayed silent, Graham got off the couch and crouched in front of her. "It was a mistake. I should have never left you; I see that now. I just want to make things right between us again, Lin."

"How much of that has to do with the way I look now, Graham?"

He simply stared at her.

"Answer me. If I was the same size as when you'd left me, would you still want to try again? How about even the size I was when we met in Baltimore?" In her mind, she was thinking of Jack and how he'd admitted that even at only fifteen pounds down from her start weight, he'd wanted her.

"Well…uh…yeah, sure."

"So much for honesty," she whispered, pushing his hands off her knees and standing up. "I'm going to bed."

"Fine!" he answered quickly, staring up at her. "I don't know if I'd be as interested if you were still—"

"Fat?" Linda supplied. "Go on, you can say it."

"Yes. Fat."

You're not fat, Jack's voice whispered in her mind. *He's a fool.*

Linda felt a twist in her chest at the sound of his voice. Her breath stopped short.

"Good night," she said, and she walked out of the room.

After the second week, Linda came to grips with the fact that she was hiding. Afraid to go back to Arnold, she instead threw herself into her work, going to the office and staying there as she prepared articles and planned for upcoming social events where there was sure to be a lot of gossip circulating, or if that proved to be boring, she could always fall back on the Best/Worst-Dressed lists.

Mostly, she stayed in her office so as not to be bothered by the lingering looks and expressions of concern. Linda thought she was doing all right, but it was apparent by the way everyone was treating her that she was fooling herself. She passed off her melancholy attitude as being upset over Mrs. Hunter's passing. Finally, she just stayed at the condo and worked from there, taking refuge in the spare bedroom that had become her life.

Graham had been working late, trying to catch up on the things he'd neglected during his mother's illness and death. In the evenings, however, he came home, and they would have ongoing candid discussions about how their marriage had failed and Graham's extracurricular activities.

While he was never pleased to talk about any of it, he did keep his promise, and he answered all of her questions. She knew that he saw this as a potential way to heal the rift between them and start fresh. Linda was just collecting information. She was constantly surprised that the more she heard, the less she cared. All of this would have devastated her six months back, but now? Now it seemed like she was talking about another life, an unknown couple, a different woman.

"I have to go back to Arnold," she told him one evening.

"Why?"

"Because I only brought clothes for around five days, and one outfit was for your mother's funeral."

"Oh," Graham answered thoughtfully. "Well, why don't you just go through the boxes of clothes you had packed away from before? They're still in the bedroom. I never got a chance to give them to Goodwill."

And so Linda found herself going through clothes she'd boxed up to see if anything would fit. She pulled out some pants that looked about her size and tossed them on the bed. Some of the shirts seemed a little large, but she could make do, she supposed. It was when she was trying on the pants that she started to realize exactly how much weight she'd lost. Standing in front of the mirror, she had handfuls of fabric grasped in her fists to keep the pants from falling down.

These used to be her "skinny pants." She'd outgrown them years ago and had kept them in the vain hope of fitting into them once again someday. And now, if she let go of the waist and shimmied her hips a little, they would descend into a puddle at her feet in no time. What was funny was that when Linda had held them up before trying them on, she had scoffed at the idea of trying to squeeze her fat ass in them again.

All of the other pants she'd boxed away were also much too big. In a fit, she began yanking all of the clothes out, looking at the sizes and realizing that *none* of them were small enough. She finally sat down hard on the floor and pulled her knees up. Turning her head, she could see herself in the mirror and took silent inventory. This had been a nasty wake-up call. Instead of feeling happy about the progress she'd made, she felt somewhat sick at the realization that she was much thinner than she'd given herself credit for.

Jack's words came back to haunt her. She thought about the little white card thrown haphazardly onto her bedside table. Maybe she'd needed it more than she'd imagined. Putting her forehead on her knees, she closed her eyes and fought back the tears again.

Once she'd composed herself, Linda got up off the floor, put her pants back on, packed up the boxes, and went to tell Graham she still needed to go home. His offer to drive her came as a surprise, but she declined. Although she wasn't particularly in the mood to drive, she needed to return to Arnold alone.

As he helped her pack her car, he tried to start a conversation a few times, but Linda was non-responsive, and eventually he just stopped. There were too many thoughts going on in Linda's head, so many conflicting emotions that she didn't trust herself to speak. For the millionth time, she asked herself what the hell she was doing. This relationship—she couldn't even, in good conscience, *call* it a relationship—was going nowhere. And she'd known that from the start.

Better the devil you know.

It was an interesting expression. Many people used it in order to pass on trying something different. Whether it was a new job, starting over in a new city, opening your own business, moving to a foreign country…staying with a man much longer than you should have. It always boiled down to the same thing. Better to be comfortably numb than to take a chance and be painfully broken.

As soon as she arrived back at her house, she headed upstairs to her bedroom. When she got there, she sagged against the entrance as images of Jack assaulted her. Like a fool, she went to the bed and picked up his pillow, placing her nose against it, searching in vain for any last scent of him. It was still there, faint but unmistakable.

Linda put the pillow down carefully and smoothed a hand over the fabric covering it. After taking a steadying breath, she got up and went to her dresser drawer. Opening it, she scooped her hand inside to grab some of her underwear and felt something brush against the tips of her fingers. Stopping, her breath came in shallow pants. *Don't do it*, she told herself fiercely. *Don't even think about it!*

Of course, she paid herself no mind, and before she could think it through rationally, she'd dug to the bottom of the drawer and pulled out the picture frame. Linda pressed her lips together to stop the trembling, and her nose began to tingle as the tears gathered once more. Tracing her fingers along the planes of Jack's face, the memories of their time together came back with an aching clarity that was impossible to fight off.

She was a fool.

Placing the pictures back where she'd found them, Linda took care of a few things and left her bedroom. Walking down the stairs, she inhaled deeply and prepared to step into her new life.

27
From Ashes We Rise

After ringing the doorbell, Jack stood outside of Linda's home, trying not to yank on his hair. The curls on his head were in a constant state of upheaval, and trying to tame his hair was no easy feat. He'd gotten it as close to presentable as he could before coming over, not quite knowing why he'd bothered. Linda had never really cared if his hair had been messy or neat. As a matter of fact, he always had the impression that she liked it better when it was its usual crazy disarray so she could run her fingers through it and try to tame the thing.

He had a chance to smile at how he always thought of his hair as some other entity separate from himself. The smile disappeared when he heard shuffling behind the door and then the turn of the knob.

It had taken him two weeks after the confrontation with Tony to show up here. That night when he'd gotten home, he had been severely pissed off. Nothing quite to the same proportions as the night Linda had said good-bye — he liked to think he was able to rein the beast in once more — but it was a near thing. He'd gone straight into his bedroom, slammed the door, and grumbled to himself about fucker not-quite-ex-husbands and *stupid* fucking decisions.

Jack was pissed off at Linda and the fact that she had made a decision for them both which had been fueled by her insecurities. He was pissed because she should have come to him and talked to him about everything instead of tucking tail and running. He was also pissed at Amanda for wanting to keep that information from him and pissed at Tony for telling him about it because now he felt like an idiot for not questioning her more when she'd left him.

He was also pissed at himself because he'd just let her push him away. Jack hadn't even taken into consideration that she'd done it because she thought she didn't deserve to be happy. Or that she didn't have enough faith in their relationship and him to stick it out.

That was what hurt him the most—that lack of faith, even though he'd done nothing to earn her mistrust.

Once the anger had passed, all Jack had left was an emptiness that he couldn't describe. Even now, he still loved Linda to his very core. His anger toward her just couldn't last. A lot of it had to do with the fact that, while he hated what she had done, he also understood it to a certain degree. Her actions weren't so different from his when he was trolling for fights in search of numbing the pain. Self-loathing made you do some dumbass shit.

And Linda choosing to go back to her ex ranked up there.

Now he wanted the truth. And he wanted a chance to let Linda know she didn't have to stay with a man like Graham, even if she did feel unworthy. He wanted her to know that, even though she hadn't given him the chance, he would have fought for her. Linda had hurt him in the worst possible way, but that didn't make the love go away—nor had it diminished his feelings for her. Maybe he was an idiot for trying this, but it was his only hope of reclaiming his life.

Steady as he felt, all of his carefully planned speeches and entreaties flew directly from his mind once that door swung open, and Linda finally stood in front of him, not even an arm's reach away. Her eyes widened, and her lips parted slightly. She seemed to search his face for meaning as to why he was standing on her doorstep. Why now, when it had been almost two months since they'd seen each other last?

Jack tried not to wince as he remembered it was here that she'd ended their relationship. Here where she'd left him wounded and bleeding. And it was a good chance that he'd suffer it all again. This time he thought maybe he'd be better prepared. But as he looked at Linda, his breath came up short. All the emotions he'd been trying so desperately to suppress for the last few weeks rose to the surface in a sickening tidal wave. Right then, he knew he'd be no more prepared for her rejection now than he had been the first time.

"Jack?" she said, her soft voice shattering what was left of him. "What are you doing here?"

That's a very good fucking question, he thought bitterly. *Ask your Neanderthal of a friend.*

"I wanted to see how you are," he answered instead, going for the more diplomatic response.

Linda's brow creased slightly in confusion. "I'm fine."

"Good," he said, bobbing his head like a moron. "Great. So, um, then I guess I'll be going."

Jack turned away, and he had every intention of leaving before he made a colossal ass out of himself. Two things stopped him: Tony's voice echoing in his head that he was a weak-ass pussy who should have fought for Linda; and the small, almost inaudible whimper that came from behind him. That quiet little noise that sounded like a "*no*" could have very well been his imagination, or it could have been Linda wanting to tell him not to leave.

His hands came up to his hair, effectively ruining all his careful handiwork, and he squared his shoulders and turned around. Linda's hand was against her throat, and she looked completely stricken and heartbroken. If she had seemed indifferent, he didn't think he could go through with his plan, but somehow, that look gave him the strength to go on.

"I lied," he said softly. "I came here because I wanted to say what I didn't the last time we saw each other."

Linda continued to look at him mutely, but she shook her head slightly, as if telling him not to continue speaking. He almost lost his nerve, but something made him continue. Jack realized he needed this just as much as she did. If not more. Once she knew the truth, if she still didn't want him, then he could close the door once and for all.

"I should have told you that I loved you more than he ever would. And that I would have spent my whole life just trying to make you happy. That you could have been everything to me."

"That's all past tense," Linda said in a low voice.

"Because that's what I *should* have said," Jack answered. "It's what I would have said if you'd given me a chance. But you'd already made your decision, so I left. I never got a chance to fight for you, Linda."

"It wouldn't have mattered."

"Maybe not then…and maybe it's too late now, but I have to try." He took a deep breath, steadying himself for what he had to say. "I can't get away from you. I can't escape the sound of your voice, the feel of your touch. No matter what I do, I still smell you on my skin. I can still feel you vividly in my hands, against my body. *Taste* you."

Linda began to cry, but he couldn't stop.

"You are still on my mind," he said softly. "In my dreams. You've left a mark on my soul, and no matter how I try, *it won't go away.* So, I'm not trying anymore. I've come to fight. I've come…to fight for you."

"You're too late," she whispered before a small sob escaped her.

"I don't believe you," Jack replied, and quicker than a lightning strike, he stepped toward Linda and wrapped his hand behind her neck. Not a moment later, he pulled her in and had his lips against hers, searching for the truth, once and for all.

Jack liked to think he would have had the strength to pull back had she hesitated at all or shown any type of resistance. But when he felt his mouth against hers, he was taken over by a fierce longing that took root and then exploded in one singular word.

Mine.

He knew that he wouldn't be able to live or to survive unless he managed to make Linda see that she belonged with him. To him. As base and primal as that sounded, he couldn't fight his feelings.

But Linda didn't resist. She didn't hesitate at all. After the first surprised gasp, she melded herself to him, her hands flying into his hair, gripping him as her mouth opened underneath his.

With a noise that was part despair and part triumph, Jack backed Linda into her house. Going completely on instinct, he didn't even try for the stairs. He went for the couch. And as soon as they were in the living room, his hands were at the button of her jeans. He might have slowed or stilled had her hands not been ripping at his belt buckle as well. Somehow, they managed to keep their lips fused together even through the awkward removal of clothing. Once Linda was naked from the waist down, he bent, grabbed her ass, and lifted her up. Then he sat down on the couch so that she was straddling him.

The kiss, frantic to begin with, became even more frenzied as Linda reached between their bodies and pulled his ever-ready cock out of his briefs. His moans were muffled as she ran her hands up and over it.

It felt like forever since she'd touched him like this, and Jack gripped her naked hips tightly in his hands, pulling Linda up onto her knees.

One of his hands slipped between her ass cheeks, following the curve of it until his fingers brushed the moist warmth of her sex. She groaned heavily as his strokes became more demanding, pushing her backside out so he had easier access to the soft flesh between her thighs. His seeking fingers found and circled Linda's clit, making her gasp into his mouth and squeeze his cock almost to the point of pain, but it was so hard right then, everything amounted to sheer pleasure.

Jack wanted to play with Linda more, listen to the panting noises he'd been deprived of so long, but this maddening urge to *take her* overrode everything else. With no more formalities, he moved his hands back to Linda's hips and shifted underneath her. Right away, she understood and positioned him at her entrance. After a few shallow thrusts, Jack's hands came up Linda's back, curled over her shoulders, and he thrust into her as deep as he could go. Linda cried out but threw her head back, signaling he was not to stop. So he didn't. Instead, Jack began kissing and sucking at her neck as he continued to use all his force to drive himself into her. And still she cried out for more.

Grasping the back of her neck in a tight grip, he continued his deep thrusts while his other hand pulled up Linda's shirt. Slipping his fingers into the cup of her bra, he yanked it down. Jack suctioned his mouth to the flesh just above her nipple and sucked hard. At that moment, possible repercussions for Linda due to his actions were the furthest thing from his mind. He needed to mark her. It wasn't good enough that his cock was buried inside her; he couldn't keep it there forever, regardless of how valiant an effort he made. He knew the mark would also wear away, but the angry red of his passion was there now, which made him savagely pleased.

Once he was done, he cupped her breast and sucked her nipple into his mouth, his tongue circling the rigid peak. Linda moaned loudly and gripped his shoulders, her fingers digging into the muscles there. She had lost all of her inhibitions now and was rocking back and forth quickly. Keeping her nipple in his mouth, he moved his hands down her body until he was gripping her ass. He used all his strength to help her in her quest to find release. Jack needed to see her fall over the edge. He needed it more than he needed to breathe. He had to have the validation that even now he could bring her pleasure like no other.

"*Ah, God,*" she cried out, her head falling forward, hair swinging to obscure her face.

Jack had to see it. He swept her hair back, wrapping it around his fist as he pulled her head back. Linda's thrusts had become erratic, and she made high keening noises as she came.

Jack grunted and let himself go as he stared into her eyes. His body began to shudder, and his breath came out in shallow pants. He fought against the natural urge to close his eyes as a flash of heat blasted through his body. The strength eventually leached out of him, and his arms slid down Linda's back, resting against the curve of her waist.

When the force of his orgasm finally faded away, Jack lowered his head in the crook of Linda's neck and fought back tears. "I'm sorry," he whispered against her dampened flesh. "I didn't mean to do that. I didn't come here for that…but God, I miss you so bad. I still want you so fucking bad…I needed you."

"It's okay," she whispered gently, one hand caressing his hair as if he were a child.

"I just came to tell you I still love you. And that I wanted you to choose me."

"Oh, Jack," Linda sighed.

He tensed up, ready for her to tell him despite what just happened, it didn't mean anything.

"When I told you that you were too late, I didn't mean it like that," she continued. "I'm not with Graham. I'm divorced."

Linda stared at herself in the bathroom mirror. She looked a mess. Her hair was snarled and crazy, her face had slashes of red across her cheekbones, and her lips were slightly swollen and scarlet from the force of Jack's kisses. And her eyes…well, they were wide, bright, and excited. That would be remedied soon enough, though.

Remembering why she was in here, she let the blanket that was wrapped around her waist fall to the ground and performed some hasty ablutions before pulling her panties and jeans back on. Then she sat on the toilet seat for a moment to collect herself.

The news of her divorce had come as a shock to Jack. His head had lifted right away, and he stared at her.

"What?" he'd croaked, his brow drawn down in confusion.

"I'm divorced, Jack," she'd repeated, staring sadly at his beautiful face.

"When?"

"Over a month ago."

"But why didn't you call me? Or come to find me?"

The hurt and confusion in his voice had speared her to the core. After his revelations on her porch, she hadn't had the heart to lie to him any longer. "Because he's not why I left you. Graham was just a handy coincidence. He wanted me to give him another chance… but it was just all wrong. So wrong."

"Did you fuck him?" Jack had asked, his eyes downcast. They'd risen to meet hers when she had remained silent.

"No," she'd replied as soon as they'd made eye contact. "I couldn't."

"Yeah, I don't blame you," he'd scoffed, bringing up his pinky and wiggling it at her.

Linda had smiled unhappily, and then it had been her turn to drop her eyes. She'd smoothed Jack's shirt down his chest. "That's not why," she'd finally answered. "It wasn't like that. Even if it was, I wouldn't have because it would have felt like I was betraying you."

"You already did," he'd stated sadly, making Linda want to sob. "Is it true? Did you leave me for my own good?"

"Who told you that?"

"It doesn't matter. Is it true?"

"You know, it's really difficult to have this conversation while you're still inside of me," Linda had replied. While true, she'd also looking for a reason to escape for a minute to clear her head.

Luckily, it had worked. Jack had simply nodded before reaching behind him and pulling down a blanket from the back of the couch. With infinite care, he had wrapped it around Linda's hips, making sure she was covered and allowing her a modicum of decency since her pants and underclothes were strewn haphazardly beside the couch. Not that Jack hadn't seen her naked before, but even still, it would have been embarrassing in this situation to get up and try to cover herself before she left the room.

That small gesture had brought back with aching clarity why she had loved Jack so much. That even then, he had wanted to spare her embarrassment and preserve her dignity. She'd fought off another wave of tears as she'd lifted herself off him slowly, picked up her discarded clothing, and left the room.

And now she was hiding.

Linda thought about the last day she'd seen her ex-husband...

Graham gave Linda a small smile when she walked into the living room of the condo, the boxed clothing packed in her car and the final item, her suitcase, by her side. His smile slowly slid off his face as he noticed she held a large manila envelope in her hand. Placing the envelope on the table carefully, with the papers that had been inside it on top, Linda kept a wary eye on her soon-to-be-ex-husband. For real this time.

"Linda, what is this?"

"It's the divorce papers. I want you to sign them."

"What do you mean? I thought we were going to try to work things out." His voice was more confused than anything, but she could tell anger wasn't far behind.

"Graham, we should have tried to make things work seven years ago," she said in a low voice.

"I know I fucked up, Lin, but it's not too late—"

"No." She stopped him firmly. "It is too late. It's not fair, Graham. It's not fair that you come to me now, after your dying mother tells you what a shitty husband you were and your lover leaves you, to decide and make it up to me. You should have never treated me like that to begin with."

"You're right—"

"I know I'm right. And I don't believe that after a while, you're not going to go back to the way you were. I'm better than that," she continued softly. "And I'm not going to settle for you."

"Settle for me?" he snarled. "Just 'cause you lost some weight, you think you're too good for me? You are nothing special."

"And there it is," Linda said, laughing sadly. "Special or not, I don't want you anymore. I haven't wanted you for years. Fear kept me with you. And you trying to cut me down and make me feel worthless isn't going to change that."

"You realize by now your little boyfriend is probably already fucking someone hotter than you, right?"

"No," she said in a steely tone. "You don't get to do that anymore. Maybe you had that power over me before, but not anymore. Just sign the papers so I can get the fuck out of here."

"Or what, Linda?" he answered, stepping toward her menacingly.

"There is no 'or what,' Graham. This isn't up for debate or negotiation. You don't scare me anymore."

Linda had never stood up to him like this, and she watched the color drain from his face. He glanced down at the papers nervously.

"Sign."

They stared at one another for a few tense moments, he with unbridled anger and she dispassionately.

"You better hurry," she finally said. "I called Tony. He and some friends are already on their way to back me up. I'd recommend you not fight me on this."

"You're going to regret this someday, Lin," he said with a sneer.

"I highly doubt that," she answered flippantly. "I'll wait outside for Tony while you sign the papers."

She wasn't on the porch but a few minutes when she heard the screech of tires turning the corner. Graham darted out the front door and ran to his SUV. Linda wondered if he could hear the ring of her laughter over the engine of the truck barreling toward them.

Graham, having some uncanny instinct for survival, managed to pull out and shoot down the street in the opposite direction. Soon after, Tony's SUV pulled up in front of the condo in a spray of gravel.

"Is he gone?" he yelled at Linda from the open window.

"You just missed him," she called back, smiling.

"Fuck!"

Linda laughed as he confabbed with the guys for a moment, obviously wondering if it was worth the chase. The decision was made quickly, and then Tony got out of the truck and walked toward her.

"Are you okay?"

"Yeah," she answered and then tried to swallow the large lump in her throat. "Thank you for coming all this way."

"No problem," he said, looking down as he toed at the ground for a moment.

"I'm sorry, Tony," she half-sobbed. "I fucked up. Real bad."

"Aw, Jesus," he groaned and then hooked a long arm around her and pulled her close. He patted her back awkwardly as she thoroughly lost it. "It'll be all right."

Linda pulled herself together, took a deep breath, and then stepped away from her friend.

He smiled down at her hugely before saying, "Come on. Let's get you home, Lin."

When Linda went back inside for her suitcase, the divorce papers were sitting where she'd left them, Graham's large, unintelligible scrawl on the line underneath his printed name. Grabbing the papers, she sat down for a moment and breathed a sigh of relief. She was finally free.

As she drove back to Arnold, Linda thought about all the work still ahead of her, but she'd taken the first step to truly breaking the shackles that had bound her. And the feeling was good.

Giving her head a small shake, Linda was transported back to the present. She stared at the bathroom door and thought of the man who waited just beyond it.

This was like her worst nightmare and her wildest dream come true, and she didn't know if she should pinch herself to wake up or let the dream run its course. To have Jack show up unannounced on her doorstep and declare himself had already been too much to hope for. She thought for sure he'd moved on without giving her a second thought. And then what followed…Well, that had always been amazing. But now Jack would expect answers, and she was terrified to give them to him.

It was partly because she didn't want to see the hatred in his eyes when he learned the truth and partly because she didn't know if she was strong enough to watch him walk out of her life again. Even if she truly believed he should. The problem was that none of the reasons she'd left him in the first place had been resolved. She'd heard through the grapevine—namely Cici—that his demo had been circulating and he had a good chance of signing a contract any day now.

And that brought them back to one of the reasons she'd left him in the first place.

With a final sigh, Linda got up, stiffened her spine, and left her small refuge. When she walked back into the living room, Jack was sitting on her sofa, slumped forward with his forearms on his thighs and hands dangling between his knees. He glanced up at her when she entered, sending a mass of butterflies careening throughout her midsection.

She wanted nothing more than to throw herself into his arms, but she restrained herself. Sex—while incredibly fulfilling at the time—hadn't solved a damned thing. Linda had to make Jack see that and understand this didn't mean instant reconciliation, no matter how much she still loved him.

Sitting across from him carefully, Linda shoved her back into the corner of the couch and pulled her legs up, wrapping her arms around her shins. Jack continued to stare at her, his eyes moving over her face and body restlessly, as if looking for answers.

"While you were gone," he said softly, "I realized something."

"What?"

"Since I got here, you've never once told me that you still want me." Jack stared down at his hands now as he picked at his nails. "I spilled my guts, and we fucked...but that means fuck-all, doesn't it?"

Linda felt her chest squeeze painfully at the desolation in his voice. She put her forehead down on her knees as her body was racked with silent sobs. She felt like the biggest piece of shit walking the Earth for hurting him. The fact of the matter was, she'd wanted so many times to show up at his home and grovel at his feet but had stopped herself. Linda felt as if she was toxic and that he shouldn't have to deal with her neuroses. That he was better off not knowing the real reasons why she had left because she couldn't promise she wouldn't get scared and do anything else asinine. Linda had thought that bridge had long since burned, and even though she still loved Jack with a pain that struck her to the heart, she wanted better for him than she could give.

Those were the only things that had stopped her from going to him.

"Jack," she gasped out once she gained control of her voice. "How will that help us? How will it help if you know that I died a little every single day since I said good-bye? That I haven't taken a single full breath in almost two months because of the pain I felt. That it was like you had taken every vital piece of me with you when I sent you away...So many times I wanted to run to you and beg you to take me back, but after what I did, I just couldn't. God, I have been absolutely *miserable* without you! But how does that help?"

"Well, it makes me feel like less of a pathetic idiot, that's for sure," Jack answered quietly. "So, what Tony said was true?"

"Goddamn Tony. What did Amanda bribe him with this time?"

"Nothing," he replied, a strange tone to his voice.

"Yes," she sighed. "What Tony said was true."

Jack laughed disbelievingly in a huff of breath. "Linda…I…*Jesus!*" He turned to face her now, green eyes flashing in anger. "Did you have so little fucking faith in me? What did I *do?* What in God's name did I ever do to make you think I'd up and leave you at the first flash of pussy? *Huh?*"

"Nothing," she answered softly.

"That's right! Fucking *nothing!*" he spat out, jumping to his feet and pacing back and forth, his fingers curled in his hair. "And then to tell me that you're going back to *him!* To that fucking *asshole!* How could you do that to me, Linda? Fuck! You may as well have just slit my goddamned throat and saved me the pain!"

"It was the only way I could think of to make you let me go," she whispered in desperation.

"Well, it worked."

"I can't even begin to tell you how sorry I am, Jack. I never wanted to hurt you."

"Bullshit! That's exactly what you wanted to do. Hurt me so I would shut up and leave you," he yelled. "Do you have any concept at how difficult that was for me to hear? How, after all the shit you told me, you would willingly go back to him? Even if it wasn't true! And Jesus fucking Christ, that's almost worse because you lied to me!" He continued to walk around with short, angry strides. "For my own *good.* What good did it do me? Huh? It didn't do me any good!"

"I'm sorry," Linda repeated. "I didn't know what else to do."

"You should have talked to me. You should have told me what the fuck you were feeling. Why didn't you just *talk* to me?"

"Because then you would have just tried to make promises that you might not be able to keep."

"That's not fair," Jack replied, pointing a finger at her. "You made the decision for us both, and you didn't even give me a fucking chance."

"Come on, Jack!" Linda cried out. "What do you think is going to happen when you get signed and then go off on tour? Huh? What happens when you're traveling and I'm here? Do you think we could survive that? Every day I write about celebrities and their lives. You think that doesn't give me some inkling of how difficult this would be?"

"You're the one who got me discovered!"

"And I don't regret that. You deserve this! To make something of your talent."

"Great, so I get to go after my dream but lose you."

"So what? I'm no one…Completely replaceable."

Jack stared down at her; Linda watched as his anger was wiped away by stunned disbelief. His shoulders dropped, and he lowered himself to the couch once again.

"What happens in a few years, Jack? You'll be famous, and I'll be even older and trying to compete."

"There is no competition."

"What about kids?" she asked reasonably. "You're still young! What if you decide you want children some day?"

"We've never even talked about kids! How do you know I even want any?"

"Do you?"

"I don't know," he answered, shrugging his shoulders. "I don't particularly care either way. I just figured there must be a reason why you didn't have any, but it never bothered me if it wasn't going to happen."

"Graham never wanted any," she said quietly, hating the way Jack cringed at his name.

"Do you?"

"I don't know, either," she answered honestly. "I'd just resigned myself that it would never happen. I'm not sure if I'd want to start a family at this age."

Jack nodded his head.

"What if you changed your mind?" Linda asked in a near whisper.

"Linda, all I want is you. With or without kids, I don't give a shit. We can figure that stuff out as we go along."

"How do you know?" she demanded. "How do you know that you will never stop loving me? Or that you'll never find anyone else that you want to be with more than me?"

"I *don't* know," he answered matter-of-factly. "I don't know any more than you know if you'll get sick of me. That one day you'll up and leave my jealous ass. You don't know, either."

Linda opened and then closed her mouth, and then she frowned.

"See? All I do know is that in twenty-nine years, no one has ever made me feel like you do. I've never loved anyone like I love you. No one has ever broken me like you do."

Linda closed her eyes, and her bottom lip began to tremble. She felt Jack shift toward her, closing the distance between them.

"And I expect," he said softly, his face close to hers, "that I won't find anyone else who'll make me feel that way in the next twenty-nine years."

"What about after that?" she whispered.

"Or the twenty-nine after that."

When he finally reached her, he stopped and gazed at her carefully. "Can I kiss you, Linda? I just want to kiss you."

Her stomach flipped madly for a moment at the sound of his voice. "It's a little late to ask for permission, don't you think?"

His smile turned the flips into a full-body shudder. Carefully, she reached up and placed her shaking hands on his face. Moving in slowly, Linda brushed her lips against his in a soft caress. Tentatively, the tip of his tongue touched against her mouth, and she parted her lips to greet it with her own. The kiss was soft and cautious, very much symbolizing the current state of their relationship.

Jack pulled away slowly and then gathered Linda into his arms. He arranged them so that he was now in the corner of the couch and she was on his lap, tucked against his chest. Sitting there quietly, she inhaled deeply, trying to fill her lungs with his essence as her hand clutched at the front of his shirt.

"I'm scared," she whispered into his neck, and his arms tightened around her.

"So am I," he answered. "But if we just keep talking to one another, we can get through it. Just, please, don't shut down on me again."

"I'll try."

"There is no try, only do."

"Okay, Yoda." Linda snickered and then felt Jack's chest shake with mirth against her. "So, I started seeing a therapist," she said quietly once the laughter died down.

"You did?"

"Yeah…after I left Graham, I made an appointment to see the doctor you'd recommended."

"And how's it going?"

"Good. I mean, it's still new. I've only seen her about four times, but I think it helps." Linda stopped speaking for a moment. "Zoe thinks I was just exchanging one habit for another. Exercising instead of eating. One is healthier than the other, but neither of them helped me deal with my issues."

"Mmm."

"She also thinks I got involved with you too quickly after separating from Graham."

Jack stiffened slightly, and she rubbed his chest in soothing circles like she used to. "She sounds like a quack," he grumbled after a moment.

Linda chuckled at his disgruntled tone and rubbed her nose against his neck. "She's not a quack."

"Do you think she's right?"

"In a way…yeah, I do."

"*Great…*" Jack sighed in defeat. "So, what does this mean? You don't want to be together?"

Linda clutched him to her tightly. Scared as she was, now that she had him so close and knowing there was a possibility he could forgive her, she couldn't bear for Jack to be out of her life again.

"No…but I think she was right. I should have screwed my head on straight before I attempted a new relationship," she murmured. "What Graham put me through makes it hard for me to fundamentally trust. I can *say* I trust you not to cheat on me or leave me, but deep down, I don't think it's true."

"What the—"

"No, listen. I know your instinct is to feel insulted, but you have to realize it's about *me,* not you. *I* don't think I'm good enough to keep you, understand?" She glanced up at him then and was relieved to see the tension leave his jaw.

"But you are," he replied, his voice taking on that desperate tone that made her want to cry.

"Jack…Don't you see? You can tell me that a million times, but I still have to *believe* it. And I don't." Linda caressed his face and sighed. "So, that's why Zoe thinks it was too soon for a relationship."

"No one can love you till you love yourself." He sighed in seeming resignation.

"Something like that. I thought losing the weight would make me love me, but apparently it's not the end all, be all."

"I vaguely remember someone trying to tell you that a long time ago."

Linda smiled at the wryness in his tone. "Yeah, I think I remember that too."

"Linda, I want to tell you that I can wait for you to figure this shit out," Jack started.

She held her breath waiting for the axe to fall.

"And I will…but I don't want to." He hugged her to him tightly. "I want you now, however you are. I don't care. Can't I just be with you and love you while you figure it all out?"

"I'm a mess," she answered, her voice thick with tears.

"Yeah, I know. But I'm kind of a mess too. And I'm more of a mess without you."

"Yeah, me too." Linda burrowed in closer. If she could take residence directly inside of Jack, she thought, even then it wouldn't be close enough.

"Linda?"

"Hmm?"

"What do we do now?"

"I don't know, Jack…but whatever it is, I want to do it together."

28
Back to the Beginning

That night, Jack went home. As stupid as it sounded — especially since the first thing he'd done was have sex with Linda — spending the night seemed too intimate. Too…*together*. And unfortunately, they weren't at that stage yet. Both had expressed their desire to get to that point, but there was still a lot of uncertainty as to how that was going to happen. As Jack drove home, he had a lot on his mind.

When he got home, he found a shirtless Tony in the kitchen digging a fork into the last of the Chinese take-out they'd ordered the night before.

"You're home late," Tony observed, speaking around a mouthful of Shanghai noodles.

"You know, you could have told me Linda wasn't with Graham anymore," Jack answered bitterly, to which Tony gave a wolfish grin.

"Nope," he answered after swallowing his mouthful. "I needed you ready to fight."

"What the hell for? There was no one to fight."

"It was never Graham you needed to fight. It was Linda." Tony stared levelly at Jack. "As long as she was convinced she did the right thing by leaving you, she would have never fixed this, no matter how much she loved you."

"So, you figured getting me righteously pissed off would send me right on over there, huh?"

"Worked, didn't it? But it fucking took you long enough," Tony grumbled, shaking his head.

"Yeah, it worked," Jack conceded.

"Since we're talking about Linda, I know better than to ask if everything is okay now. Just don't give up on her, Jack. I know it's hard to believe now, but she was really happy with you." Tony stopped for a second as he stared down at the floor, and then he squinted up at Jack. "I don't know you all that well, but from what Amanda said, seems like it was the same for you."

Jack let out a small whoosh of breath. "Yeah," he agreed, rubbing a hand along the back of his neck. "It's been a long night. I'm heading to bed."

Tony nodded, picked up his discarded food, and started eating again. Jack wasn't all that crazy about the touchy-feely way they'd left off, so before he left the kitchen, he yelled over his shoulder, "Stop eating all my goddamned food, you animal. And next time, put on a fucking *shirt.*"

"You're welcome," Tony lobbed back. "Asshole."

Jack grinned and kept walking down the hall to his room. Taking a seat on his bed, he thought about what Tony had said. He had to give the guy some credit. He knew Linda, and he also knew what would have spurred Jack into action. That bastard. Had Tony not come to Jack at the gym that day and told him that Linda still loved him, he'd never have shown up at her house looking for answers. He would have just kept on living out his own miserable existence.

After getting undressed, Jack got in bed and then called Linda as promised.

"Hello?" came her sweet voice, and he breathed a sigh of relief. Just knowing he could talk to her again made the hole in his chest shrink just a little.

"I made it home."

"Oh, good…"

They subsided into an awkward silence, which he hated, but he wasn't quite sure what to say. It was much too soon for "I miss you" and "I love you," even if that was what he was feeling. In a way, they were starting from scratch. The only problem with that were all these emotions already attached. It was hard to take things slow when all he wanted was for things to go back to the way they were. That, of course, was impossible.

"Um…I was thinking," Linda finally said, breaking the silence. "Are you busy tomorrow evening?"

"No," he answered quickly and then cringed at his stupid enthusiasm. "I mean, yeah, I'm free."

"I called Zoe after you left. We have an appointment tomorrow and…do you want to come?" she ended in a rushed whisper.

Jack paused for a moment. This was certainly not what he had been expecting or hoping for, but it was a start. "Do you think that's a good idea?"

"I don't know. I've never done this before."

Her little-girl tone made Jack smile despite himself. "Will it be like couples counseling?"

"I think she just wants to meet you and talk about what's going on."

"What *is* going on?"

"Whatever it is, we're figuring it out together," she answered softly. "I promised."

"Right."

"So, do you want to come? I was thinking we could drive into the city early and maybe spend some time together before meeting her."

Now Jack grinned. This was a little more what he'd had in mind. "Sure. What time do you want me to pick you up?"

They made plans, and Jack was excited to see Linda and be able to touch her again, even if it was innocently. About fifteen minutes and a handful of yawns later, Jack decided it might be a good idea to let Linda go.

"I wish you could be here," she said softly.

"I can if you want me to be."

"I thought we agreed it was better to wait."

"Yeah, well…that was before I got home to an empty bed." Jack smiled at Linda's little giggle.

"Soon," she replied in the same quiet voice. "I've missed you."

Closing his eyes, he fought off the urge to break down. "Miss you too."

"I'll see you tomorrow," she said with finality.

"Tomorrow," he echoed. "Bye."

When Jack ended the call, he clutched the phone in his hand and whispered, "I love you," into the night.

The next day, Linda paced back and forth as she waited for Jack. It wasn't as if he was late or anything; she was just nervously excited to see him. Linda had been nervous suggesting seeing Zoe to Jack, but since therapy had been his idea, she thought perhaps he would agree to go.

Her musings were cut off by the sound of a car in the driveway. She froze in place, wondering if she should run out to greet him or if she should wait for him to come to the door. The familiar two knocks sounded, and she waited a second for the creak of the door to open. Then she kicked herself for her assumptions. Jack no longer had that type of familiarity with her. In a way, that was like a small stab to the heart. How she wished she could rewind the last two months and do everything differently.

Hindsight was twenty-twenty they always said, and how true it was. Thinking of the day she'd told Jack it was over made her realize it had brewed like a perfect storm. Her insecurities, already out of control, had been fueled even more when finding out about the potential success of Jack's demo. And then they'd fought about her need for therapy, which had driven a wedge between them. Add a mourning husband to the mix, and it was a recipe for disaster. Certainly now, she could see the error of what she'd done once she'd gained some distance and perspective, but at that moment in time, it had been the only thing she could think of doing.

The sound of the doorbell got her moving, and she pulled open the door to find a bashful-looking Jack. His shoulders were hunched up against the cold, hands deep in his pants pockets and a small grin on his face. And that led to the next awkward thing between them — greetings.

Jack seemed to be at a loss as well, and she saw him hesitate while he tried to figure out if it was okay to kiss her. He'd moved in slightly and then pulled back just before she moved forward to accept the kiss, and then she pulled back also. Both of them gave nervous chuckles, and then Jack moved in slowly again and placed his lips against the side of her jaw tenderly. Linda was reminded of the days when he'd show up at her door and walk with her, leaving her with the same type of kiss. Safe, friendly, but with the hope of more.

"I forgot my wallet at home this morning," Jack said a little sheepishly. "Do you mind if we go there first so I can grab it?"

"We can take my car…"

"No, it's okay." He smiled. "Shouldn't take long at all."

They drove in silence, but at least it wasn't uncomfortable any longer. When they arrived at Jack's house, he jumped out of the car and said he'd be back in a minute. Not wanting to wait, Linda got out and followed him.

"You could have waited in the car," he said, unlocking the door and smiling as the wind blew her hair in crazy swirls.

"It's okay; I'll keep you company."

Jack made a dash to his room after wiping his feet on the welcome mat. Linda wiped hers as well and started down the hall at a slower pace. As she passed the living room, something caught her eye—or rather the lack of something—and she turned toward it, frowning. *Where did all the artwork on the walls go?* Also missing was the coffee table, and the mantle was curiously bare of all the pictures and little knick-knacks that had been there before. When she stepped in, she saw several gouges in the wall and black streaks, as if something had been thrown into them.

"Found it." Jack's breathless voice came from behind her, and she turned to him in confusion.

"Jack, what happened to your living room?"

"Oh," he answered, looking about the room uneasily. "We're redecorating."

Something about his posture and the tone of his voice had Linda frowning even more. "Redecorating…"

"Yeah, come on," he answered, tugging on her elbow. "We should get going."

Before Linda could question him further, the front door blew open, and Tony and Amanda stomped inside. She heard Jack mutter, "Oh shit," just barely over Amanda's exclamations.

"I'm telling you, Tony, *something* is going on with him—" Her next words were abruptly cut off as she spied Jack and Linda standing in the entrance of the living room. Tony's eyes went round in panic, and Amanda's face underwent an alarming series of emotions. "You!" she finally spat out. "What the *fuck* are you doing in my *house!*"

Several things happened all at once. Amanda tried to make a lunge at Linda while Tony grabbed her by the waist and hauled her back. Linda gasped slightly at the complete menace on the girl's face before Jack pushed her behind him and squared off with his best friend.

"What are you doing home?" he asked Amanda in a hard tone.

"My client canceled. What the hell is she doing here, Jack?" Amanda wriggled around, trying to escape, and Jack reached back to wrap a protective arm around Linda.

"I suppose you haven't told her yet?" she whispered in distress.

"No."

"Tony! I swear to God, if you don't let me go right now, you're never getting laid again!"

"Shit," both Jack and Linda said under their breath.

"Not until you calm down," Tony answered, holding her tight against him. "Come on, babe."

"I'll calm down when she's out of my house!"

Linda cringed against Jack's back. She felt his arm tighten against her, and his hand gripped her hip in reflex.

"Shut the fuck up, Amanda," he yelled in return. "This is my house too, and if I want Linda here, then you're just going to have to deal with it!"

"No, don't," Linda said in an undertone against his shoulder. "Please, don't fight."

"I can't believe you! After everything she's done, you're just going to go crawling back?" the girl yelled incredulously.

"You don't know shit!"

Linda felt sick. The fact that she was driving the two of them to fight was too much for her to bear. She had initially been shocked at Amanda's reaction to her, but listening to the girl speak drove home just how much damage she'd done when she left Jack. He hadn't said much about it, but seeing the pain on his best friend's face was enough for her to piece things together.

"Stop!" Linda called out desperately. "Please, stop fighting!"

The room went silent, and she stepped out from behind Jack's shielding body and faced Amanda's glare head-on.

"Tony, let her go." Linda turned to Jack. "Do you mind if Amanda and I borrow your room for a minute?" She was faced with identical looks of horror from the men.

"Lin…" Tony said in warning.

Linda bit down a stab of fear. "It'll be all right," she whispered in return, not sure if she believed it herself. Then she turned and nodded to Tony. Reluctantly, he let Amanda go. She turned and glared at him for a second as she adjusted her clothes. Then, turning that same steely glare toward Linda, she stomped past her toward Jack's room.

"Wish me luck," Linda whispered before heading after her.

She found Amanda pacing angrily. The girl whirled toward her, staring daggers.

"So help me God," she spat out. "If you just came in here to give me excuses, I will *kick* your ass!"

"No excuses," Linda answered carefully. She closed the door behind her and then removed her jacket, figuring this might take a while but knowing she deserved whatever she got.

"As far as I'm concerned, you're not good enough for him."

"You're right."

"Oh. So, you think you can just agree with everything I say and that'll make me happy?" Amanda fumed. "Screw you! Do you have any idea what you did to him? How much you hurt him?"

Linda nodded slightly, even though she knew Jack hadn't told her everything.

"I seriously doubt that," Amanda snapped back quickly. "You know what? I thought you were good for him, special, because he finally loved someone. But you were worse than those other girls he brought home! He was never in love, but at least none of them hurt him. None of them broke him again like you did! I would rather see him with a hundred other women like that than with you, because at least I know they won't damage him…No, don't you cry!" Amanda pointed a finger at Linda, whose eyes had begun to water. "You aren't allowed to cry, because you did this! You did this to him! *You* made *him* cry, and you made him ruin himself again! Do you know what I came home to the day you left? Do you have any idea?"

"No," Linda whispered.

"He was tearing this place apart!"

"Oh, God. The living room."

"Yeah, the living room." Amanda laughed in disgust. "He ripped it apart and then went after Tony, who had to beat him to the ground like a fucking rabid dog."

Linda covered her face with her hands, and the tears she had been trying to hold back began tracking down her face. "I didn't know," she whispered desperately. "I didn't know he would do that. I didn't know…"

"Well, now you know. Happy? Are you happy with what you did?"

"Of course not! I just thought…I thought he'd be okay…"

"What kind of crack are you smoking, lady? In what universe did you ever think telling him you were going back to your ex would be okay? That he would be okay?"

"Because I'm not good enough for him!" Linda cried out. "You said it yourself. I'm not young enough, not good-looking enough, not skinny enough, not special enough. I'm *nothing!* I thought he would figure that out and move on."

"Not smart enough, either, obviously," Amanda supplied spitefully. "I told you that you made him happy! How much more proof did you need?"

Linda sat on the bed and rubbed her face with her hands while Amanda stared at her impassively. Hearing what Jack had gone through was already painful. To know she was the cause made it more so. If she'd had any idea at all the consequences of her actions, Linda would have never ended things the way she did.

"Amanda, I fucked up," she finally said in a hushed tone. "I fucked up, and there is no reason for what I did that will ever make sense to you."

"Why not?"

"Look at you." Linda laughed tearfully, gesturing to the strawberry-blond goddess standing before her. "You're perfect. Just like him. But at least you have Tony, and he's perfect too. No one will ever look at the two of you and wonder what the fuck he sees in you. Or wonder if you're just his ugly sister or chubby cousin." Linda huffed out a laugh. "Or maybe his fucking *aunt*…I've already had one man cheat on me and then leave me for not measuring up. I didn't think I could go through it again."

"Oh, give it a rest," Amanda huffed. "You think because of the way I look, no one has ever cheated on me? Or made me feel shitty about myself? Broke my heart? Maybe it's not hard for me to go out and find someone new to fuck, but most of the time, that's all they want me for. Do you think that's better? One meaningless relationship after another instead of finding *one* guy who will love you forever?"

"But…Tony loves you…"

"And Jack loved you," Amanda retorted.

"I know," Linda replied in a small voice.

"And apparently he still does," Amanda said grudgingly.

"I still love him too," she whispered. "I never stopped."

"You sure do have a funny way of showing it."

"What I did was *wrong.* I know that now. I was foolish, and I underestimated Jack…" Linda said quietly. "All I can say is I'm sorry. I'm sorry to him and to you for having to go through that again." She looked at Amanda imploringly. "If I could change it, I would. But I can't!" Her voice cracked painfully.

"You *hurt* him, Linda," Amanda said in a slow and methodical voice, her eyes taking on the sheen of tears. "And you hurt me, too. Maybe he can trust you again, but I don't know if I can."

With that last remark, the girl turned toward the door and left the room, leaving Linda alone on Jack's bed.

On the drive to Baltimore, Jack kept glancing over at Linda. He didn't like how quiet she was or the forlorn look on her face. It had been a stupid idea to let her talk to Amanda, but he'd been hopeful that maybe they could work out their differences. Really, he should have known better. Amanda had been bitterly against even the remote possibility of a reconciliation, which is why Jack hadn't told her about his confrontation with Tony or his plan to go see Linda again.

Truthfully, he hadn't known what to expect when he'd arrived at Linda's door yesterday and had kept the information to himself, not wanting to rile his friend up needlessly. This would definitely be added to the long list of things that had come back to bite him on the ass. But how the hell was he supposed to know Amanda's last appointment of the day would cancel and she and Tony would show up at the house early?

Jack looked over at Linda again. She was still staring silently out toward the road. It had started to snow again, and since night crept up so quickly during winter, it was almost pitch black on the road. The headlights of the car reflected the large flakes, making them swirl and dance. While it was pretty in a way, Jack didn't think the show was mesmerizing enough to captivate Linda to such a degree.

He knew that the conversation with Amanda was weighing heavily on her mind, but she'd refused to talk about it when he questioned her. She'd simply walked out of the room with her coat on and had given him a small, sad smile before asking if he was ready to go. Jack had a feeling she didn't want him to argue with Amanda over what had been said. What she didn't know was that he'd most likely argue with Amanda anyway, even without knowing the context of the conversation.

"Linda?" he asked when the silence had become too heavy. "Please talk to me."

The careful façade cracked, and he watched in alarm as Linda fell apart beside him. Jack just had a glimpse of her face crumpling before she brought hands up to cover it. From her mouth came the sound of a rending sob that ripped from her chest, almost more a cough than a cry.

"Oh, God," she wept. "What did I do to you?"

"*Fuck,*" Jack muttered as he maneuvered the car to the shoulder of the road. He was out of his seat belt and leaning toward Linda right after throwing it in park. The heartbreaking sounds were still coming from her, even though she tried to muffle them, while babbling incoherently.

"Linda…baby…come on," Jack pleaded softly. Then he ground out between clenched teeth, "Fucking Amanda!"

"No," Linda sobbed. "No, don't blame her. It's me! It's my fault. I br-br-broke you!"

Jack couldn't stand the sound of her sorrow. He reached between them, unlatching her seat belt, and tried to pull Linda into his arms. She struggled feebly, turning her face away and pushing at his chest.

"How can you even forgive me?" she cried out, her voice loud in the confines of the car. "Why don't you hate me right now?"

"Because I don't."

"Why do you have to be so goddamned perfect! You're always so wonderful and so caring! Why aren't you mad at me? Why aren't you making me beg and plead and crawl on my knees to get you back?" she continued, her voice warbling. "Just get mad at me! Yell at me! *Do* something!"

Jack pressed his lips together to stop them from trembling. The desperation in her voice tore at him as he tried to keep it together. He continued to try to draw her near, to hold her, ease her until the demons that were riding her subsided. Finally, she collapsed against his chest, still sobbing.

"Oh, Jack…just do *something,*" she cried in a breathless whisper. "Anything. Make me suffer too."

Linda continued to weep and try to convince him to make her pay for what she'd done to him, but he just couldn't do it. Even if he knew it would ease the burden of her guilt, he didn't have it in him. As far as he was concerned, she had suffered enough, and he wanted nothing more than to just put this all behind them and move forward to happier times. Jack didn't see how making her feel even more horrible about what happened would do either of them any good. All it would do is prolong the agony, and he could do without more angst, thank-you-very-fucking-much.

It wasn't that he'd forgiven Linda for breaking his trust. It would take a while before that happened. But he would rather deal with their issues head-on, and the only way he could do that was if Linda was in his life and a willing participant while they tried to work this out. Making her grovel and beg seemed counterproductive to his plan. And he didn't imagine it would do her non-existent confidence any good either.

"I think we've both suffered enough," he said in a firm voice. "And can you do me a favor?"

"What."

"Get me off this fucking pedestal you have me on."

"What?" she asked, her voice muffled.

"Linda, I'm not perfect," he stressed, shaking his head. "I'm nowhere near perfect, and as long as you keep thinking that I'm perfect and you're not, we'll never get over this."

"How are you not perfect?" she asked, and Jack smiled slightly at the indignant tone of her voice. *Much better than the crying,* he thought with satisfaction.

"Well, first of all, I swear too fucking much." Linda's huff bordered on a laugh and that made his smile grow. "I'm also a jealous and possessive asshole. Plus, I have abandonment and rejection issues." His arms tightened around her imperceptibly, and he went on before she had a chance to dwell on his words. "According to Amanda, I'm a moody emo bitch, and I have a shitty temper. Shall I go on?"

"No," came the sullen reply from the depths of his shirt.

"I'm not perfect," he said softly, caressing her hair gently. "You're not perfect…but maybe we can be perfect together."

"You're such a cheeseball," Linda groaned. "I almost forgot about that."

"Add that to my list of non-perfection." Jack chuckled. "Now, will you stop crying all over my shirt?"

Linda gave a small hiccupping laugh but pulled back to wipe her face and his shirt ineffectually. "I'm sorry," she whispered as her fingers brushed over the wet spots.

"It's just a shirt," he replied, waving off her comment.

"I didn't mean just about the shirt." She looked up at him with grave eyes and a downturned mouth.

Jack placed his hand along the side of her face and swiped a thumb under her eye, catching some moisture still gathered there.

"I know," he answered. "You can spend the rest of your life making it up to me, okay?"

"Okay."

And with that, they sat back and started the journey to Baltimore again. In a way, Jack was a bit disappointed that the time he'd wanted to spend reconnecting with Linda had turned into something much different, but at least they had resolved one small thing, and he wouldn't regret that. It was one step closer to where he wanted to be.

Reaching over, Jack grasped Linda's hand. She threaded her fingers with his and gripped tightly. The hole in his chest shrank a little bit more.

29
Mending Fences

A month had passed since the day Jack had shown up on Linda's porch. While things weren't perfect, the two of them had taken many small steps to repair the damage left behind from their breakup. It was a slow process but one that both were committed to.

Linda continued to see Zoe and had increased her therapy sessions to twice weekly, usually when she was in the city after she'd met with her team at the paper.

Jack couldn't say the road had been completely smooth over the last few weeks. Every so often, Linda would have a panic attack, and that would send him on a trip down anxiety lane, but somehow they managed to talk each other off the ledge and start fresh again.

Zoe had been right; it would take a while. But something felt different now. Linda was actively trying to see herself in a better light, and Jack wasn't always looking for the expression on her face that indicated she wanted to flee. He also noticed that she was more gracious when he gave her a compliment and less critical when she looked in the mirror.

To spare both of them additional stress, Linda had decided to start working with Matt at the gym again. She was no longer dead set on losing that last twenty pounds and had agreed to let Matt put her on a maintenance program. Jack was a little disgruntled that the other man had been able to convince Linda of this while he had failed repeatedly. He was slightly mollified when she brought up the love goggles argument. Matt obviously wasn't wearing a pair, so his opinion was completely professional as opposed to romantic. Damned love goggles…They were always his undoing.

Now, there was only one large bump in the road to their recovery, and she was sitting at the kitchen table munching a bagel.

Amanda had taken the news of Jack and Linda's reconciliation badly. She had become so enraged at Tony for not heeding her wishes that she kicked him out of the house that night and refused to speak to him. After a couple of days of this, Tony had left a scathing message on Linda's voice mail telling her that he'd gone to bat for her relationship and happiness and now it was time for them to repay the favor.

That, of course, sparked a war of epic proportions in Jack's house as he and Amanda went at it over the whole situation. It wasn't pretty. Having known each other all their lives, there was a very large arsenal to choose from in regard to past life mistakes. Jack had gone for the jugular a few times and had it returned in spades.

Nothing had been solved that night.

In the end, it had been left off that Jack was back together with Linda, and Amanda was just going to have to deal with it. He'd stormed off, and things had been awkward between them ever since. Linda refused to come to his house because she didn't want to cause additional grief between the friends. Since he and Linda had decided not to jump straight back into a sexual relationship, that meant he had to come home to a bitchy roommate every night. Sexually frustrated as he was, that made for a bad combination.

It didn't help improve his temper when she and Tony made up and then had a sex marathon to make up for lost time. This was even worse than the first time he'd been craving Linda, because at least then, he didn't know what the fuck he was missing. Jack and his hand had been spending a lot of quality time together; he was surprised he didn't have calluses on his palms.

But today, enough was enough. He missed his best friend, and he was sick of the standoffish attitude they'd taken with one another. Hopefully they could hash everything out and put this behind them.

Jack got a mug from the cupboard and filled it with coffee. After preparing it the way he liked, he took a seat beside Amanda. Her eyes sidled over to where he sat. This was the first time they'd willingly spent more than a few seconds in the same room together. Either they were working or she was with Tony and he was with Linda. The times they were alone in the house, they kept to their own sides, passing each other only in common rooms like the kitchen or living room.

"Hey," he said awkwardly and then cleared his throat a little. He saw Amanda jerk slightly at the sound of his voice, and it made him sad.

"Hi," she returned with a curt head bob.

"So…uh…how're you doing?"

Amanda huffed and then turned to look at him with an expression that screamed "*Really?*"

"Okay, fine," he grumbled. "That sucked. I get it. I'm sick of this, Amanda. This is the longest we've ever gone without talking, and it's bugging me."

"Have you broken up with Linda?"

"No!"

"Then I have nothing to say to you."

"What the fuck, Mandy?" Jack replied, scowling at her. "Why are you being such a bitch about this?"

"How would you have felt if I took Jimmy back?" she asked, complete with raised brows.

"It's not the same."

"No? Why not? He just made a *mistake* by choosing Vicky over me."

"First of all, you weren't in love with Jimmy," Jack pointed out.

"Fine," she answered reasonably. "What if Tony did to me what Linda did and then I took *him* back?"

Jack rubbed his face with his hands and exhaled loudly. If he went with his gut instinct and told her how he'd really feel, then he was shooting himself in the foot. If he lied, Amanda would call him on his bullshit. This was a lose-lose situation if ever he saw one. So, he did the only thing he could. Admit the truth with an exception.

"You're right, okay?" he said evenly. "If Tony had hurt you, I'd want to kick his ass, and if you took him back, I'd think you were a spineless idiot."

"Hah!"

"*But*…if I saw that Tony was *really* trying to make up for what he did and that you guys were happy, I'd let it go," Jack continued. "Maybe I wouldn't completely trust him right away, but I'd try…for *you.*"

"You're an asshole," Amanda said succinctly, and Jack hid a smile in his coffee cup. "And I still think you can do better."

"Yeah, well, you and Linda still have that in common, I see," he retorted sharply.

"How do you know she's not going to do it again?"

"I don't."

"And that doesn't bug you?"

"Sure it does. But we're working on it. I need to make sure Linda knows I'm not going anywhere. Once she realizes that, then it won't happen again."

"See? This is what I mean! Why are you taking responsibility for everything? Why is everything on you? It's not your fault that Linda's self-esteem is shit!"

"It's not her fault, either," Jack said softly as he ran his fingers along the handle of his mug. "She didn't ask to be treated that way by her husband, Amanda."

"Then she should have left him."

"Shoulda, coulda, woulda," he rhymed off with a shrug. "We all make mistakes. Sometimes we don't see the damage being done until it's too late." At this, he lifted his head and stared at Amanda pointedly.

"That's not fair," she whispered. "Your parents *died*. You had a reason to go crazy."

"What's not fair is you making excuses for me but not giving Linda a chance."

"I gave her a chance, and she blew it," Amanda grumbled petulantly.

"Mandy…"

"Jack…"

"I don't want to fight with you anymore," he said quietly. "I love Linda, and she loves me. You don't see it, but I do. We're going to make this work, and it would be a lot easier to do that if you were on my side."

"I'm always on your side," she whispered fiercely. And then she continued in a child's voice, "She hurt you. How can you just expect me to forgive her for that?"

"If I can forgive her, then you can too," he said firmly before turning pleading eyes toward her. "Do it for me?"

"Ugh! I hate it when you do that!"

Jack suppressed a grin.

"You suck!" Amanda continued and then kicked him under the table, her bare foot not doing any damage at all. "Fine," she finally grumbled. "If only to get you and Tony off my ass. But I won't like it!"

Beaming, Jack got up from the table and leaned down to kiss the top of her head. "Thanks, Mandy. Love you."

"Yeah, yeah," she grumbled. "Love you too…Now get the hell out of my face!"

He shot her one last grin before heading out of the kitchen and back to his room. His phone was ringing, so he picked up the pace and caught it just before it dumped into voice mail.

Linda took a deep breath as she stood outside Shutters Photography. Jack had told her of his plans to make amends with Amanda and made her promise that she would reach out to Eliza as well. They hadn't spoken since Linda had left to go back to Baltimore. Even though she had finally divorced Graham, she couldn't bear facing her friend.

After talking it out, Linda stayed in Eliza's shop for a while longer as she finished her tale and then caught up on what her best friend had been up to over the holidays. Eventually, the women parted, and Linda headed home. On her way there, she noticed she was being followed and then smiled when she recognized Jack's Honda. He pulled in behind her, and she waited for him to get out of his car so they could walk to the house together. He seemed keyed-up and anxious, which alerted Linda to the fact something must have happened, but he was also curiously quiet.

Leaving Jack to his own devices, she ran up the stairs to get changed into something more comfortable. Linda knew the news couldn't be good when Jack followed her into her bedroom shortly after, shut the door behind them, and then locked it. They hadn't been in her bedroom since before the breakup. He stood with his back against the door as an additional preventive measure of escape and regarded her warily. Linda was beginning to get nervous; she wrung her hands together and waited for him to speak.

She couldn't help but wonder if things had gone bad at home with Amanda. Or maybe he'd finally gotten sick of dealing with her and all her baggage.

"I'm getting signed," he said quickly in a low voice.

"Oh my God, Jack, that's wonderful!" she said excitedly, relief coursing through her. Then she processed what he'd said, and the relief was replaced by a lick of fear.

"There's that look!" Jack exclaimed, pointing at her face. "Don't you do it. Don't even think about it! You're not breaking up with me because of this!"

"What? I never said anything!" she retorted in a huff.

"You don't have to," he answered sternly. "I've seen that look before, and I swear to God, if you end this, I'm turning down the record deal, and you'll have to live with the guilt that you ruined my career."

Linda gasped and glared at Jack. "That's blackmail!" she sputtered indignantly.

"You should know by now I'm not above blackmail."

"I would never forgive you if you did that! And I wouldn't take you back either!"

"Well, then, I'd just chase you around until you did," he answered with a glint in his eye. He pushed off the door and stalked over to her. "Arnold isn't *that* big."

With a quick lunge, he grabbed Linda by the waist and jumped on the bed, bringing her with him. She whooped in surprise and then started laughing as Jack began peppering her face with kisses. He finally lowered his mouth to Linda's, and she got lost in the kiss, as usual completely forgetting what the hell they were talking about.

"I know this scares you," Jack said once he let her up for air. Propping his head on his hand, he stared down at her tenderly. "And I'm scared too. But I need you to talk to me about this."

"I want to be happy for you," Linda whispered intently. "I *am* happy for you…but how are we going to make this work?"

"Well, first of all, I'm not going anywhere yet," Jack said carefully. "I'll probably have to record in Philly, but that'll give us enough time to figure out how to do this."

"Okay…And then what?"

"I've been thinking about it," he said, still with the tentative voice. "Come with me."

Linda couldn't help but smile a little at the hopefulness in his voice, and then she sighed. "Jack, how are we going to do that? I have a home here and a job—"

"Quit," he answered simply, and Linda stared at him in loving exasperation.

"I can't just quit. What am I supposed to do? Mooch off of you the rest of my life? Plus, I don't know if being your groupie is something I can do as a lifelong vocation."

Jack chuckled and pushed her hair back from her face. "I never said you had to stop working; I just told you to quit the paper."

"Umm…and this is different *how?*"

"Well, you said you wanted to be a journalist. So, here's your chance! You can work freelance and do what you wanted to do. That way you're not tied down to any one spot. You can work while I tour, and we don't need to be apart for long periods of time."

Linda raised her eyebrows at this plan while Jack beamed at his ingeniousness.

"Huh…" she said in surprise.

"And maybe you can cut a deal with Vern," he continued, getting more excited. "You can offer him an exclusive into how things work in the music industry by following my career."

"Hmm," Linda replied. His exuberance was somewhat infectious, and she found herself smiling back at him. "It's kind of crazy, but it might work."

"It's worth a try, right?" he murmured, his hand running along her brow as he continued to caress her hair. His eyes roamed over her face lovingly. "We can make this work if we try."

"Okay," she whispered.

As she stared up at Jack, Linda felt the tingle of tears prick at her eyes. It had been a long while since she'd felt like crying when it came to their relationship, but thinking about how she had almost lost Jack due to fear made her want to break down all over again. It was a constant battle against the dread that gripped her on occasion, but she fought it because the price of losing Jack was too great not to try. She'd lived without him once before and wasn't all that anxious to do it again.

Jack's soft stroking along Linda's hair soothed her. He bent his head close and ran his nose along hers. Linda closed her eyes and sighed. His lips fit against her mouth a second later, and her hand ran up his torso and then along the curve of his neck until she had her fingers twisted in his hair. Jack groaned slightly and leaned his chest against hers as he gathered her closer.

That's when Linda realized that they were in her bedroom, behind a locked door, and on her bed. Horizontal.

They hadn't been sexually intimate since the day he'd shown up at her home, not wanting to confuse their issues by allowing them to get clouded by sex. So, their time had been spent away from bedrooms and beds and locked doors. Sometimes, even being on the couch with Jack was a difficult thing because they'd done some extraordinarily naughty things on it. They managed, however, subsisting on chaste touches and the occasional heated kiss, separating just before it started to get painful.

Right now, though, feeling Jack's hard body pressed against the length of her made Linda throw caution to the wind. She tugged at him until he was between her legs, wrapping them around his hips, digging her heels into his ass, and moaning when the shaft of his erection pressed into the softness of her. Rolling her hips against him made Jack shudder, and he gripped her hair in clenched fists, making a noise of male desperation.

"Linda," he exhaled softly.

"I miss touching you like this," she whispered against his lips. "I miss you touching me."

"I miss it too…but is this too soon?"

"No," she answered, capturing his lips with hers and kissing him again.

"Maybe we should take it slow," he said, pulling away slightly. Linda groaned in frustration, making Jack laugh. "I never said we couldn't have a little fun," he whispered in her ear as his hand drifted down the front of her top.

"What kind of fun?" she sighed, arching her back so that he could cup one of her breasts. He didn't fall for it.

"Well, we never did get a chance to play with one another before we jumped into bed," he said in that low, seductive voice she loved, the one that made Linda feel as if her clothes would incinerate off her body from the sheer heat she was throwing off. "By the time I got you naked, I was so damned horny, I just wanted in your pants."

"So, what's the difference now?" Linda chuckled and ground her hips into his, making Jack inhale sharply.

"Nothing. I still want in your pants…*Jesus!*" He pushed his erection into her and swiveled. "But maybe this time I can be more patient… Or not…*Fuck…*"

Jack's hand pushed up into her hair, and he kissed her forcefully. He snaked his arm under her body until he was gripping one of her buttocks. His hips pumped in a slow and torturous way, so unlike the kiss as to be maddening. Linda gripped him tightly as her body strained into his. If she had the power to wiggle her nose and make their clothes disappear, she'd do it in a heartbeat. Maybe if she got him wound up enough, he'd just agree to get naked.

He didn't fall for *that* trick either. With some sort of unflappable control, Jack lifted himself from the cradle of her body and shifted so that he was lying beside her. His head was propped up on his hand again, and he stared down at Linda with hooded, sexy eyes. Leaning down, he brushed his lips against hers softly as he traced the lines of her face with his fingers.

Linda wanted to drag him down and attack him again, but she was also curious to see what Jack was going to do. When his fingers reached her chin, he slowly tipped it up so her neck was exposed, and then his mouth made its way down her chin and neck. The feathery feel of his lips and occasional touch of his tongue was exquisite. Stopping for a moment, he inhaled deeply when his nose ran along the hollow under her ear. Jack's chest rumbled slightly as he placed an open-mouthed kiss on that spot, making Linda tremble.

Once he finished his explorations of her neck, he kissed down her chest and over the slope of her breast on top of her clothing. Linda inhaled through her teeth when he nuzzled at her and rubbed his lips over her rapidly hardening nipple. She was praying his hand would slip under her shirt, but it didn't. Instead, gentle fingers trailed between her breasts and down her torso, stopping only to drag across the strip of skin where her shirt had ridden up and then circled her belly button.

"Jack?"

"Mmm?" his voice vibrated along her body tantalizingly.

"You're driving me crazy…"

He didn't bother answering, but she saw him smile against the side of her breast as he dragged his face from side to side. Those same fingers had left her exposed belly to trail down her hip and upper thigh. When he got to her knee, he used the back of his fingers to follow her inseam. *Now we're getting somewhere,* she thought as he neared her sex. But still his touch stayed on the fringes. Instead of caressing her at the apex of her thighs, he simply dragged his fingertips down the inseam of her opposite leg, made a circuit around that knee, and then swept along the top of her thigh.

"Now you're being mean," she gasped when he kissed his way down her body and began running the tip of his tongue along the same strip of flesh he'd touched with his fingers.

"You can be mean too," he whispered with a chuckle.

It took a moment for the light bulb to come on, and then she smiled and reached for his body. She was running her hands down the chiseled musculature of his chest when his hand slipped under one of her buttocks and along the back of her thigh, fingers brushing ever so slightly against her sex. Linda groaned and then slid the backs of her fingers over his stomach, the tips of them dipping under the waistband of his pants. Now it was Jack's turn to moan as she caressed the tip of him ever so slightly.

"That's just plain cruel," he ground out between clenched teeth.

"Pay me back," Linda replied and then arched her body as Jack grasped the underside of her knee and pulled it outward, spreading her legs open.

"Oh, I will…"

The fleeting fingers passed up and down her inner thighs and then grazed ever so lightly over where she wanted to be touched. Not enough to offer any sort of relief but enough to cause the throb between her legs to go critical mass. In return, Linda coaxed Jack's top leg up, and she did something similar. When she brushed against the tender flesh between his legs, Jack's hips jerked.

"Not fair," he moaned. "*So* not fair."

His mouth descended on hers again as they became bolder in their movements. Giving up the game, Jack slipped his hand into Linda's yoga pants, and he sighed when it met with the slippery folds of skin. Linda had undone his jeans and was exploring as well. She reveled in the smooth hardness of him, that satiny soft skin that covered the steel core. She stopped only when his fingers slid inside her, setting off tingles all through her body. Linda was so ready just to come. The teasing had brought her as close to the brink as it possibly could without offering the relief she needed.

"So soon?" Jack said in surprise as she started to clamp down after a few quick strokes.

"Yes," she hissed as her stomach jumped and trembled in turns. Shock waves traveled throughout her body, and he kept pumping his fingers even after she'd come the first time.

"More," he whispered in her ear. "I want more."

The way Jack was stroking her, there would definitely be more. Even as she strove toward her second orgasm, Linda had enough presence of mind to start caressing him again. She had rolled to her side to face him and now used both hands, one to grip his shaft and the other to fondle his balls.

"Ah, God. Linda…" Jack moaned softly as she concentrated on the soft skin. "If you keep that up, I'm going to come."

"So soon?" she replied breathlessly, working her hands quickly and loving the harsh panting of his breath, which signaled he was close. Jack had also picked up the pace of his fingers, and she was quickly ascending into her own happy ending.

They went over together. Jack had been holding off, and Linda could feel it in the straining of his body. He let himself go when she cried out and arched her body into his.

Afterward, as Linda came down from her high, she grinned at a breathless Jack on the opposite pillow.

When he looked between their bodies, he grimaced at the mess. "Shit, I forgot why we don't do this more often."

Linda looked down and started to laugh. "Been a while?"

"Not really," he answered wryly. "I had a date with my hand last night. You just seem to suck it all right out of me."

Now Linda's laughter echoed about the room, and after a second, Jack joined her. This was reminiscent of their earlier days together, and Linda felt as if they had broken through the one last barrier that had remained. Not caring about the mess, she lunged at Jack and pressed their bodies together as she kissed him. It was hard and passionate, and in that kiss, she tried to convey to Jack everything she was feeling in that moment. Love, remorse, adoration, relief, but most of all, devotion.

She might have years ahead of her convincing him that she would never leave him again, but she was prepared. More than prepared. Eager, even. She hadn't quite made amends with herself yet, but she knew that would come in time. Until then, she'd be content with herself by showing the man she loved just how much she loved him.

"Stay with me tonight," she asked softly.

Jack smiled and nodded before rolling over so that she was on top of him, her hair creating a shelter for just the two of them.

No time like the present, was her last thought before she drowned herself in Jack.

Epilogue
Silk Scarves and E.T.

Linda left the Baltimore Daily News smiling. Even though she was technically no longer an employee at the paper, she still liked to pop in for a visit whenever she was in town. Unfortunately, that wasn't very often these days, so it was always special to see Vern and her old team, most of whom still worked for the paper.

Jack had joined her this time, which had been a rare treat. He'd left her there to reminisce for a while longer as he went to run a quick errand. They would meet at the instrument shop across the street when she managed to tear herself away. With a tearful good-bye, Linda hugged all of her old coworkers, promised to keep in touch as usual, and took her leave.

Figuring Jack wouldn't be very long, she took her time crossing the street, standing outside of the shop and enjoying the sunshine. Her phone gave a beep, and she was pleased to see a text from Tony. He gave the all-clear for him and Amanda to join them in Baltimore tonight. No mean feat, considering the brood of five children they were leaving behind; the twins were barely a year old. Each time Amanda got pregnant, she always threatened to castrate Tony. It hadn't happened yet.

The news they could make it made Linda smile. That meant everyone would be there tonight. She was excited to see all her friends. Rick, Eliza, Cici, and Rob had confirmed last week, and they'd heard from Matt and Denise last night. It had been a long time since she'd had everyone she cared about all in one spot, and she knew Jack would be thrilled too, once she let him know.

Turning to look inside, she stopped briefly to take in her reflection. Linda never did lose the full seventy pounds. Not that she hadn't tried, but after a while, she came to appreciate her curvier body and wasn't so concerned about the number on the scale as opposed to how she looked and felt. She had even gained a few pounds back when she started integrating regular food back into her diet.

At first this had worried Linda, but with Zoe's help, she was able to start seeing herself in a better light. With Matt's help, she'd maintained a steady weight, and with Jack's help, she realized that what she weighed mattered not at all. If she ever did complain about her body, which wasn't much these days, he'd come to where she was and grab her backside with both hands, squeezing and kneading it while making obscene noises to make her laugh.

"Don't even think about messing with my ass," he'd growl and nip at her ear.

"Your ass, is it?"

"Yes, *mine*. I'm going to get 'Property of Jack McAllister' tattooed over it."

"Fine, I won't mess with the ass," she'd laugh in surrender.

True to his word, he always made her feel loved and revered no matter how she looked, and that was the most healing of all.

Linda smiled into the music shop window as Jack rifled through a jar of guitar picks like a little boy trying to choose a candy. Old habits die hard, and even though he'd finally made one of his dreams come true, he still insisted on buying a new pick for every show. A large shadow loomed behind her in the window, and she was just about to look over her shoulder when a familiar voice made her flesh prickle.

"Linda?" Graham said in surprise, his tone mirroring her expression as she whirled to face him.

It had been many years since she'd clapped eyes on him. Actually, she hadn't seen him since the day he'd made a hasty retreat as he tried to outrun Tony. Linda squeezed her lips together to keep from smirking as she remembered. She kept them like that as she looked Graham over, head to toe. The years hadn't been kind to him at all. Even in just the time that had passed, he'd managed to put on quite a bit of weight and had begun balding. It also looked as if he had been using tanning beds, because his skin was an unhealthy shade of orange.

"Graham," she replied, trying to keep her voice steady as she fought back a giggle.

"What are you doing in Baltimore?"

"Oh, Jack is playing at Remy's tonight for a benefit show," Linda answered, smiling proudly.

Jack's career had taken off, but due to the nature of his music, which was more bluesy and soulful, it didn't lend to the popularity of other artists out there. Instead, he'd culled a loyal fan base, which gave him the pleasure of sharing his music in front of more intimate crowds. It was more his speed, not ever wanting to break into super stardom, and it was more Linda's speed too, because, while he was popular and even relatively famous in certain parts of the world, they were still able to live a peaceful life without too much fanfare. Or too many stalking groupies. Although there had been a handful over the years.

Luckily, he wasn't subjected to too much media press. There were occasional articles in the gossip rags about him having illicit affairs, but Linda knew the drill. She also knew most of the information in those papers was false. She especially loved the one when Jack was caught with a mysterious woman, canoodling and looking oh-so-romantic. The mysterious woman had been Eliza, and they had been meeting privately to plan Linda's fortieth birthday party. Jack had been livid that the surprise had been ruined. El, on the other hand, had blown up the article and doctored pictures into poster-size and hung it up on her shop wall. It was a big joke among the friends.

At the mention of Jack's name, Graham's face changed from curiosity into a mask of hate for a split second before it wiped clear.

"Right, I forgot about that guy. What's he do again?"

"He's a singer," Linda answered, knowing straight off that Graham was lying through his teeth. He knew exactly who Jack was since a big deal was always made whenever he played in Baltimore, where he was discovered. It was kind of hard to miss all the signs and billboards that went up in anticipation of his concerts.

"Must be tough keeping *him* at home, eh?" he jeered. "All that young pussy surrounding him all the time."

"Actually, no," she replied truthfully. "Some men are faithful, Graham. If you can believe it."

The look of indignant outrage on Graham's face was priceless. But Linda wasn't trying to be vindictive; she was merely letting him in on a known fact. Jack adored her, and true to his word, he would never stray. It had taken a long time before Linda had the confidence in herself to believe that one hundred percent, but now there was no shaking that fundamental truth. Jack was her shining star, and no one would tarnish him in her eyes again. Least of all her ex-husband.

"Yeah, well, maybe some ladies are better at keeping their husbands at home," he continued belligerently. "Like my Rory."

"Rory," she repeated. "You mean the girl who dumped you when your mother was dying?"

Graham's jaw clenched tightly, and Linda clamped her teeth together to stop herself from laughing at him. "Yeah," he agreed in a clipped tone. "She came crawling back, of course. I made her pay for that, for sure. She had to beg and plead for *months* before I let her come back."

"Mm-hmm." Linda nodded, losing interest in this show of machismo. All she could think of was how this showcased another big difference between Jack and Graham. A compassionate and caring man who accepted her back with open arms as opposed to a man like Graham, who'd made a woman he supposedly loved grovel for his affections. She shuddered delicately.

"So, it was a good thing I left you after all," he kept yapping. "She's twice the woman you ever were…"

Linda had tuned Graham out because her complete focus was behind his right shoulder, where Jack now stood listening to her ex-husband's nonsensical rant. His green eyes fired off sparks, and his nostrils flared dangerously. He looked like an avenging angel dropped from the heavens. His beauty was completely astounding. Linda felt a slow grin spread along her face at the sight of him.

"Are you even listening to me?" Graham asked, his voice rising petulantly.

"No," she murmured, her grin turning into a smile.

"Now?" Jack begged from behind Graham, who gasped and whirled around.

Linda sighed. "Now," she answered in resignation. It was Jack's turn to smile beatifically as he pulled back his fist and smashed it into Graham's flabby face.

He stood towering over her semi-conscious ex-husband and said in a low, deadly voice, "How many times do I have to tell you? If I see you *ever* talking to my wife again, I'll make you disappear."

Her ex promptly passed out as Linda shook her head in resignation.

"Graham!" came a shrill voice from across the way, and they turned to watch a large woman lumber her way across the street. Linda's mouth dropped open as she took a look at who she supposed was Rory. She and Graham must have had a home-tanning bed, because she was the same sickly orange shade as her husband, and she doubled him in size.

"I guess he was right," Jack said under his breath. "She *is* twice the woman you are. Literally."

Linda elbowed Jack in the ribs. Despite the fact Rory had been sleeping with Linda's ex-husband while they were still married, she held no antagonism. In fact, looking at her, all Linda felt was pity. Judging by the woman's appearance, it was obvious Graham was as bad a husband to Rory as he had been to Linda.

The frantic woman stooped beside Graham and then looked at them. "What happened to him?" she asked in a panic.

"I think he tripped and smashed his face into the wall," Jack answered innocently, making Linda's ribs creak as she tried containing her mirth.

Rory was now squinting at Jack nearsightedly before her eyes popped open. In a dog-whistle scream, she shrieked, "Oh my God! You're Jack McAllister! I love your music!" Graham groaned from behind her, and Rory kicked him to shut up. "Can I get your autograph?"

Jack exchanged a horrified look with Linda. She finally started to laugh when the woman tore at her sleeve, offering her arm to Jack reverently. She was kicking her leg back and forth, trying to knock Graham's desperately gripping hand off her ankle.

"Oh, go on, honey," Linda said magnanimously, rooting through her purse to find a marker. "Give the woman a little something to brighten up her life."

They looked at one another and waved their pinkies in the air as Rory looked on in vapid confusion.

After signing the woman's arm with a large flourish, Jack waved off her gushing, put an arm around Linda, and they got the hell out of there before Graham regained complete consciousness. Turning a corner, they collapsed against a wall, howling with laughter. Jack wrapped his arms around Linda, holding her tight to him.

"Caveman," she murmured against his shirt. Jack never had lost his jealous streak or his absolute hatred for her ex-husband.

"Fucking right," he answered promptly, bending to kiss his adoring wife.

Linda melted into Jack, reveling in his touch. Eons ago, those things Graham had said would have wounded her and sent her into a tailspin. Now? With Jack's love to shelter her, she felt like an impenetrable fortress. He was her strength, her joy, her love. While he said he needed it no longer, every day she continued to pay reparations for the day she'd left him. She was always anxious for him to know how grateful she was for his unconditional love. How lucky she was to have him in her life. And while he let her know she'd repaid her debt with interest, Linda had made a promise to spend the rest of her life making it up to him. It was promise she was bound and determined to keep.

And she did.

acknowledgments

I remember sitting across from my mother and sister, the printed page of my debut novel clutched in my hands to present to them both. When I finally announced I had published my very first novel the looks of wonder and pride reflected back at me was such a joy.

To my sister Anne Marie: thank you. In a moment you went from unknowing to my biggest cheerleader. I won't ever forget that. Love you.

To my mother, who has stood by me during the best and worst times of my life.

I want to also thank my wonderful friend (and lawyer!), Khyaati. Your enthusiasm and help through my publishing journey has been immeasurable. Your friendship means so very much to me.

I also want to acknowledge my awesome team at Omnific for helping me take this beast of a book (over two hundred thousand words when originally penned!) and wrestle it to a more manageable size. For the lovely cover, and of course for stepping in when I was busy with life.

About the Author

Elle Fiore was born and raised in various cities through southern Ontario, Canada. She currently calls Toronto her home with her partner and two sons.

She has always leaned toward the literary and excelled in subjects like English, French, and Drama. She spent a good number of years during her teens and early twenties in the theatre doing makeup, stage management as well as acting in various plays such as *Rebel Without a Cause*, *Annie*, *Rumours,* and *The Apple Tree*. Her active imagination and joie de vivre part of what made her seek out the stage.

During the latter half of her twenties she also enjoyed a variety of other activities such as cycling, martial arts and also took lessons in dance, learning how to Salsa, Merengue, Cha Cha, Bacchata, and Tango.

In 2005 her first son was born changing the course of her life forever. It was during her time on maternity leave with her second son in 2008 that Elle found the time to get back into reading fiction. While in a search for good online stories to read, and not finding what she was looking for, she decided to write a short story herself. One story led to another, and since then she has written four full-length novels, a novella, and several short stories. Her passion for writing grew more as the days passed, until it was all encompassing.

During this time, one of her story ideas grew more epic than she imagined and she knew that it was time to give it voice. *The Sacrificial Lamb* started off as a just a scene from a dream, a scene that wouldn't dissipate. It has since turned into a two book series with a third in conceptualization. It was this series that prompted Elle to finally try to turn her hobby into a career. She sought out Omnific Publishing to help make her dream become a reality.

check out these titles from
OMNIFIC PUBLISHING

⊶→Contemporary Romance←⊶

Keeping the Peace by Linda Cunningham
Stitches and Scars by Elizabeth A. Vincent
Pieces of Us by Hannah Downing
The Way That You Play It by BJ Thornton
The Poughkeepsie Brotherhood series: *Poughkeepsie & Return to Poughkeepsie*
by Debra Anastasia
Recaptured Dreams and *All-American Girl* and *Until Next Time* by Justine Dell
Once Upon a Second Chance by Marian Vere
The Englishman by Nina Lewis
16 Marsden Place by Rachel Brimble
Sleepers, Awake by Eden Barber
The Runaway series: *The Runaway Year* by Shani Struthers
The Hydraulic series: *Hydraulic Level Five & Skygods* by Sarah Latchaw
Fix You and *The Jeweler* by Beck Anderson
Just Once by Julianna Keyes
The WORDS series: *The Weight of Words & Better Deeds Than Words* by Georgina Guthrie
The Brit Out of Water series: *Theatricks & Jazz Hands* by Eleanor Gwyn-Jones
The Sacrificial Lamb and *Let's Get Physical* by Elle Fiore
The Plan by Qwen Salsbury
The Kiss Me series: *Kiss Me Goodnight & Kiss Me By Moonlight* by Michele Zurlo
Saint Kate of the Cupcake: The Dangers of Lust and Baking by LC Fenton
Exposure by Morgan & Jennifer Locklear
Playing All the Angles by Nicole Lane
Redemption by Kathryn Barrett
The Playboy's Princess by Joy Fulcher

⊶→Young Adult Romance←⊶

The Ember series: *Ember & Iridescent* by Carol Oates
Breaking Point by Jess Bowen
Life, Liberty, and Pursuit by Susan Kaye Quinn
The Embrace series: *Embrace & Hold Tight* by Cherie Colyer
Destiny's Fire by Trisha Wolfe

The Reaper series: *Reaping Me Softly* & *UnReap My Heart* by Kate Evangelista
The Legendary Saga: *Legendary* by LH Nicole
The Fatal series: *Fatal* & *Brutal* (novella 1.5) by T.A. Brock
The Prometheus Order series: *Byronic* by Sandi Beth Jones
One Smart Cookie by Kym Brunner
Variables of Love by MK Schiller

New Adult Romance

Three Daves by Nicki Elson
Streamline by Jennifer Lane
The Shades series: *Shades of Atlantis* & *Shades of Avalon* by Carol Oates
The Heart series: *Beside Your Heart, Disclosure of the Heart* & *Forever Your Heart*
by Mary Whitney
Romancing the Bookworm by Kate Evangelista
Flirting with Chaos by Kenya Wright
The Vice, Virtue & Video series: *Revealed, Captured, Desired* & *Devoted*
by Bianca Giovanni
Granton University series: *Loving Lies* by Linda Kage

Paranormal Romance

The Light series: *Seers of Light, Whisper of Light* & *Circle of Light* by Jennifer
DeLucy
The Hanaford Park series: *Eve of Samhain* & *Pleasures Untold* by Lisa Sanchez
Immortal Awakening by KC Randall
The Seraphim series: *Crushed Seraphim* & *Bittersweet Seraphim* by Debra Anastasia
The Guardian's Wild Child by Feather Stone
Grave Refrain by Sarah M. Glover
The Divinity series: *Divinity* & *Entity* by Patricia Leever
The Blood Vine series: *Blood Vine, Blood Entangled* & *Blood Reunited* by Amber
Belldene
Divine Temptation by Nicki Elson
The Dead Rapture series: *Love in the Time of the Dead* & *Love at the End of Days*
by Tera Shanley

Romantic Suspense

Whirlwind by Robin DeJarnett
The CONduct series: *With Good Behavior, Bad Behavior* & *On Best Behavior*
by Jennifer Lane
Indivisible by Jessica McQuinn
Between the Lies by Alison Oburia
Blind Man's Bargain by Tracy Winegar

← —→ Erotic Romance ← —→

The Keyhole series: *Becoming sage* (book 1) by Kasi Alexander
The Keyhole series: *Saving sunni* (book 2) by Kasi & Reggie Alexander
The Winemaker's Dinner: *Appetizers* & *Entrée* by Dr. Ivan Rusilko & Everly Drummond
The Winemaker's Dinner: *Dessert* by Dr. Ivan Rusilko
Client N° 5 by Joy Fulcher

← —→ Historical Romance ← —→

Cat O' Nine Tails by Patricia Leever
Burning Embers by Hannah Fielding
Seven for a Secret by Rumer Haven

← —→ Anthologies ← —→

A Valentine Anthology including short stories by
Alice Clayton ("With a Double Oven"),
Jennifer DeLucy ("Magnus of Pfelt, Conquering Viking Lord"),
Nicki Elson ("I Don't Do Valentine's Day"),
Jessica McQuinn ("Better Than One Dead Rose and a Monkey Card"),
Victoria Michaels ("Home to Jackson"), and
Alison Oburia ("The Bridge")

Taking Liberties including an introduction by Tiffany Reisz and short stories by
Mina Vaughn ("John Hancock-Blocked"),
Linda Cunningham ("A Boston Marriage"),
Joy Fulcher ("Tea for Two"),
KC Holly ("The British Are Coming!"),
Kimberly Jensen & Scott Stark ("E. Pluribus Threesome"), and
Vivian Rider ("M'Lady's Secret Service")

← —→ Sets ← —→

The Heart Series Box Set (*Beside Your Heart, Disclosure of the Heart* &
Forever Your Heart) by Mary Whitney
The CONduct Series Box Set (*With Good Behavior, Bad Behavior* &
On Best Behavior) by Jennifer Lane
The Light Series Box Set (*Seers of Light, Whisper of Light, Circle of Light* &
Glimpse of Light) by Jennifer DeLucy
The Blood Vine Series Box Set (*Blood Vine, Blood Entangled, Blood Reunited* &
Blood Eternal) by Amber Belldene

← —→ Singles, Novellas & Special Editions ← —→

It's Only Kinky the First Time (A Keyhole series single) by Kasi Alexander
Learning the Ropes (A Keyhole series single) by Kasi & Reggie Alexander
The Winemaker's Dinner: RSVP by Dr. Ivan Rusilko
The Winemaker's Dinner: No Reservations by Everly Drummond
Big Guns by Jessica McQuinn
Concessions by Robin DeJarnett
Starstruck by Lisa Sanchez
New Flame by BJ Thornton
Shackled by Debra Anastasia
Swim Recruit by Jennifer Lane
Sway by Nicki Elson
Full Speed Ahead by Susan Kaye Quinn
The Second Sunrise by Hannah Downing
The Summer Prince by Carol Oates
Whatever it Takes by Sarah M. Glover
Clarity (A *Divinity* prequel single) by Patricia Leever
A Christmas Wish (A *Cocktails & Dreams* single) by Autumn Markus
Late Night with Andres by Debra Anastasia
Poughkeepsie (enhanced iPad app collector's edition) by Debra Anastasia
Poughkeepsie (audio book edition) by Debra Anastasia
Blood Eternal (A Blood Vine series single, epilogue to series) by Amber Belldene
Carnaval de Amor (The Winemaker's Dinner, Spanish edition)
by Dr. Ivan Rusilko & Everly Drummond

coming soon from
OMNIFIC PUBLISHING

The WORDS series: *The Truest of Words* (book 3) by Georgina Guthrie
The Poughkeepsie Brotherhood series: *Saving Poughkeepsie* (book 3)
by Debra Anastasia
The Hidden Races series: *Incandescent* (book 1) by M.V. Freeman
The Legendary Saga: *Claiming Excalibur* (book 2) by LH Nicole
The Runaway series: *The Runaway Ex* (book 2) by Shani Struthers
The Forever series: *Forever Autumn* (book 1) by Christopher Scott Wagner
Something Wicked by Carol Oates
Going the Distance by Julianna Keyes